Reviews

by Oscar Wilde

Copyright © 5/18/2015
Jefferson Publication

ISBN-13: 978-1512269390

Printed in the United States of America

Contents

REVIEWS

To Mrs. CAREW

The apparently endless difficulties against which I have contended, and am contending, in the management of Oscar Wilde's literary and dramatic property have brought me many valued friends; but only one friendship which seemed as endless; one friend's kindness which seemed to annul the disappointments of eight years. That is why I venture to place your name on this volume with the assurance of the author himself who bequeathed to me his works and something of his indiscretion.

ROBERT ROSS
May 12th, 1908.

INTRODUCTION

The editor of writings by any author not long deceased is censured sooner or later for his errors of omission or commission. I have decided to err on the side of commission and to include in the uniform edition of Wilde's works everything that could be identified as genuine. Wilde's literary reputation has survived so much that I think it proof against any exhumation of articles which he or his admirers would have preferred to forget. As a matter of fact, I believe this volume will prove of unusual interest; some of the reviews are curiously prophetic; some are, of course, biassed by prejudice hostile or friendly; others are conceived in the author's wittiest and happiest vein; only a few are colourless. And if, according to Lord Beaconsfield, the verdict of a continental nation may be regarded as that of posterity, Wilde is a much greater force in our literature than even friendly contemporaries ever supposed he would become.

It should be remembered, however, that at the time when most of these reviews were written Wilde had published scarcely any of the works by which his name has become famous in Europe, though the protagonist of the æsthetic movement was a well-known figure in Paris and London. Later he was recognised—it would be truer to say he was ignored—as a young man who had never fulfilled the high promise of a distinguished university career although his volume of *Poems* had reached its fifth edition, an unusual event in those days. He had alienated a great many of his Oxford contemporaries by his extravagant manner of dress and his methods of courting publicity. The great men of the previous generation, Wilde's intellectual peers, with whom he was in artistic sympathy, looked on him askance. Ruskin was disappointed with his former pupil, and Pater did not hesitate to express disapprobation to private friends; while he accepted incense from a disciple, he distrusted the thurifer.

From a large private correspondence in my possession I gather that it was, oddly enough, in political and social centres that Wilde's amazing powers were rightly appreciated and where he was welcomed as the most brilliant of living talkers. Before he had published anything except his *Poems*, the literary dovecots regarded him with dislike, and when he began to publish essays and fairy stories, the attitude was not changed; it was merely emphasised in the public press. His first dramatic success at the St. James's Theatre gave Wilde, of course, a different position, and the dislike became qualified with envy. Some of the younger men indeed were dazzled, but with few exceptions their appreciation was expressed in an unfortunate manner. It is a consolation or a misfortune that the wrong kind of people are too often correct in their prognostications of the future; the far-seeing are also the foolish.

From these reviews which illustrate the middle period of Wilde's meteoric career, between the æsthetic period and the production of *Lady Windermere's Fan*, we learn *his* opinion of the contemporaries who thought little enough of him. That he revised many of these opinions, notably those that are harsh, I need scarcely say; and after his release from prison he lost much of his admiration for certain writers. I would draw special attention to those reviews of Mr. Swinburne, Mr. Wilfrid Blunt, Mr. Alfred Austin, the Hon. John Collier, Mr. Brander Matthews and Sir Edwin Arnold, Rossetti, Pater, Henley and Morris; they have more permanent value than the others, and are in accord with the wiser critical judgments of to-day.

For leave to republish the articles from the *Pall Mall Gazette* I am indebted to Mr. William Waldorf Astor, the owner of the copyrights, by arrangement with whom they are here reprinted. I have to thank most cordially Messrs. Cassell and Company for permitting me to reproduce the editorial articles and reviews contributed by Wilde to the *Woman's World*; the editor and proprietor of the *Nation* for leave to include the two articles from the *Speaker*; and the editor of the *Saturday Review* for a similar courtesy. For identifying many of the anonymous articles I am indebted to Mr. Arthur Humphreys, not the least of his kindnesses in assisting the publication of this edition; for the trouble of editing, arrangement, and collecting of material I am under obligations to Mr. Stuart Mason for which this acknowledgment is totally inadequate.

ROBERT ROSS
REFORM CLUB,
May 12*th*, 1908

DINNERS AND DISHES

(*Pall Mall Gazette*, March 7, 1885.)

A man can live for three days without bread, but no man can live for one day without poetry, was an aphorism of Baudelaire. You can live without pictures and music but you cannot live without eating, says the author of *Dinners and Dishes*; and this latter view is, no doubt, the more popular. Who, indeed, in these degenerate days would hesitate between an ode and an omelette, a sonnet and a salmis? Yet the position is not entirely Philistine; cookery is an art; are not its principles the subject of South Kensington lectures, and does not the Royal Academy give a banquet once a year? Besides, as the coming democracy will, no doubt, insist on feeding us all on penny dinners, it is well that the laws of cookery should be explained: for were the national meal burned, or badly seasoned, or served up with the wrong sauce a dreadful revolution might follow.

Under these circumstances we strongly recommend *Dinners and Dishes* to every one: it is brief and concise and makes no attempt at eloquence, which is extremely fortunate. For even on ortolans who could endure oratory? It also has the advantage of not being illustrated. The subject of a work of art has, of course, nothing to do with its beauty, but still there is always something depressing about the coloured lithograph of a leg of mutton.

As regards the author's particular views, we entirely agree with him on the important question of macaroni. 'Never,' he says, 'ask me to back a bill for a man who has given me a macaroni pudding.' Macaroni is essentially a savoury dish and may be served with cheese or tomatoes but never with sugar and milk. There is also a useful description of how to cook risotto—a delightful dish too rarely seen in England; an excellent chapter on the different kinds of salads, which should be carefully studied by those many hostesses whose imaginations never pass beyond lettuce and beetroot; and actually a recipe for making Brussels sprouts eatable. The last is, of course, a masterpiece.

The real difficulty that we all have to face in life is not so much the science of cookery as the stupidity of cooks. And in this little handbook to practical Epicureanism the tyrant of the English kitchen is shown in her proper light. Her entire ignorance of herbs, her passion for extracts and essences, her total inability to make a soup which is anything more than a combination of pepper and gravy, her inveterate habit of sending up bread poultices with pheasants,—all these sins and many others are ruthlessly unmasked by the author. Ruthlessly and rightly. For the British cook is a foolish woman who should be turned for her iniquities into a pillar of salt which she never knows how to use.

But our author is not local merely. He has been in many lands; he has eaten back-hendl at Vienna and kulibatsch at St. Petersburg; he has had the courage to face the buffalo veal of Roumania and to dine with a German family at one o'clock; he has serious views on the right method of cooking those famous white truffles of Turin of which Alexandre Dumas was so fond; and, in the face of the Oriental Club, declares that Bombay curry is better than the curry of Bengal. In fact he seems to have had experience of almost every kind of meal except the 'square meal' of the Americans. This he should study at once; there is a great field for the philosophic epicure in the United States. Boston beans may be dismissed at once as delusions, but soft-shell crabs, terrapin, canvas-back ducks, blue fish and the pompono of New Orleans are all wonderful delicacies, particularly when one gets them at Delmonico's. Indeed, the two most remarkable bits of scenery in the States are undoubtedly Delmonico's and the Yosemité Valley; and the former place has done more to promote a good feeling between England and America than anything else has in this century.

We hope the 'Wanderer' will go there soon and add a chapter to *Dinners and Dishes*, and that his book will have in England the influence it deserves. There are twenty ways of cooking a potato and three hundred and sixty-five ways of cooking an egg, yet the British cook, up to the present moment, knows only three methods of sending up either one or the other.

Dinners and Dishes. By 'Wanderer.' (Simpkin and Marshall.)

A MODERN EPIC

(*Pall Mall Gazette*, March 13, 1885.)

In an age of hurry like ours the appearance of an epic poem more than five thousand lines in length cannot but be regarded as remarkable. Whether such a form of art is the one most suited to our century is a question. Edgar Allan Poe insisted that no poem should take more than an hour to read, the essence of a work of art being its unity of impression and of effect. Still, it would be difficult to accept absolutely a canon of art which would place the *Divine Comedy* on the shelf and deprive us of the *Bothwell* of Mr. Swinburne. A work of art is to be estimated by its beauty not by its size, and in Mr. Wills's *Melchior* there is beauty of a rich and lofty character.

Remembering the various arts which have yielded up their secrets to Mr. Wills, it is interesting to note in his poems, here the picturesque vision of the painter, here the psychology of the novelist, and here the playwright's sense of dramatic situation. Yet these things, which are the elements of his work of art though we arbitrarily separate them in criticism, are in the work itself blended and made one by the true imaginative and informing power. For *Melchior* is not a piece of poetic writing merely; it is that very rare thing, a poem.

It is dedicated to Mr. Robert Browning, not inappropriately, as it deals with that problem of the possible expression of life through music, the value of which as a motive in poetry Mr. Browning was the first to see. The story is this. In one of the little Gothic towns of Northern Germany lives Melchior, a dreamer and a musician. One night he rescues by chance a girl from drowning and lodges her in a convent of holy women. He grows to love her and to see in her the incarnation of that St. Cecily whom, with mystic and almost mediæval passion, he had before adored. But a priest separates them, and Melchior goes mad. An old doctor, who makes a study of insanity, determines to try and cure him, and induces the girl to appear to him, disguised as St. Cecily herself, while he sits brooding at the organ. Thinking her at first to be indeed the Saint he had worshipped, Melchior falls in ecstasy at her feet, but soon discovering the trick kills her in a sudden paroxysm of madness. The horror of the act restores his reason; but, with the return of sanity, the dreams and visions of the artist's nature begin to vanish; the musician sees the world not through a glass but face to face, and he dies just as the world is awakening to his music.

The character of Melchior, who inherits his music from his father, and from his mother his mysticism, is extremely fascinating as a psychological study. Mr. Wills has made a most artistic use of that scientific law of heredity which has already strongly influenced the literature of this century, and to which we owe Dr. Holmes's fantastic *Elsie Venner*, *Daniel Deronda*—that dullest of masterpieces—and the dreadful Rougon-Macquart family with whose misdeeds M. Zola is never weary of troubling us.

Blanca, the girl, is a somewhat slight sketch, but then, like Ophelia, she is merely the occasion of a tragedy and not its heroine. The rest of the characters are most powerfully drawn and create themselves simply and swiftly before us as the story proceeds, the method of the practised dramatist being here of great value.

As regards the style, we notice some accidental assonances of rhyme which in an unrhymed poem are never pleasing; and the unfinished short line of five or six syllables, however legitimate on the stage where the actor himself can make the requisite musical pause, is not a beauty in a blank verse poem, and is employed by Mr. Wills far too frequently. Still, taken as a whole, the style has the distinction of noble melody.

There are many passages which, did space permit us, we would like to quote, but we must content ourselves with saying that in *Melchior* we find not merely pretty gems of rich imagery and delicate fancy, but a fine imaginative treatment of many of the most important modern problems, notably of the relation of life to art. It is a pleasure to herald a poem which combines so many elements of strength and beauty.

Melchior. By W. G. Wills, author of *Charles I.*, *Olivia*, etc., and writer of *Claudian*. (Macmillan and Co.)

SHAKESPEARE ON SCENERY

(*Dramatic Review*, March 14, 1885.)

I have often heard people wonder what Shakespeare would say, could he see Mr. Irving's production of his *Much Ado About Nothing*, or Mr. Wilson Barrett's setting of his *Hamlet*. Would he take pleasure in the glory of the scenery and the marvel of the colour? Would he be interested in the Cathedral of Messina, and the battlements of Elsinore? Or would he be indifferent, and say the play, and the play only, is the thing?

Speculations like these are always pleasurable, and in the present case happen to be profitable also. For it is not difficult to see what Shakespeare's attitude would be; not difficult, that is to say, if one reads Shakespeare himself, instead of reading merely what is written about him.

Speaking, for instance, directly, as the manager of a London theatre, through the lips of the chorus in *Henry V.*, he complains of the smallness of the stage on which he has to produce the pageant of a big historical play, and of the want of scenery which obliges him to cut out many of its most picturesque incidents, apologises for the scanty number of supers who had to play the soldiers, and for the shabbiness of the properties, and, finally, expresses his regret at being unable to bring on real horses.

In the *Midsummer Night's Dream*, again, he gives us a most amusing picture of the straits to which theatrical managers of his day were reduced by the want of proper scenery. In fact, it is impossible to read him without seeing that he is constantly protesting against the two special limitations of the Elizabethan stage—the lack of suitable scenery, and the fashion of men playing women's parts, just as he protests against other difficulties with which managers of theatres have still to contend, such as actors who do not understand their words; actors who miss their cues; actors who overact their parts; actors who mouth; actors who gag; actors who play to the gallery, and amateur actors.

And, indeed, a great dramatist, as he was, could not but have felt very much hampered at being obliged continually to interrupt the progress of a play in order to send on some one to explain to the audience that the scene was to be changed to a particular place on the entrance of a particular character, and after his exit to somewhere else; that the stage was to represent the deck of a ship in a storm, or the interior of a Greek temple, or the streets of a certain town, to all of which inartistic devices Shakespeare is reduced, and for which he always amply apologises. Besides this clumsy method, Shakespeare had two other substitutes for scenery—the hanging out of a placard, and his descriptions. The first of these could hardly have satisfied his passion for picturesqueness and his feeling for beauty, and certainly did not satisfy the dramatic critic of his day. But as regards the description, to those of us who look on Shakespeare not merely as a playwright but as a poet, and who enjoy reading him at home just as much as we enjoy seeing him acted, it may be a matter of congratulation that he had not at his command such skilled machinists as are in use now at the Princess's and at the Lyceum. For had Cleopatra's barge, for instance, been a structure of canvas and Dutch metal, it would probably have been painted over or broken up after the withdrawal of the piece, and, even had it survived to our own day, would, I am afraid, have become extremely shabby by this time. Whereas now the beaten gold of its poop is still bright, and the purple of its sails still beautiful; its silver oars are not tired of keeping time to the music of the flutes they follow, nor the Nereid's flower-soft hands of touching its silken tackle; the mermaid still lies at its helm, and still on its deck stand the boys with their coloured fans. Yet lovely as all Shakespeare's descriptive passages are, a description is in its essence undramatic. Theatrical audiences are far more impressed by what they look at than by what they listen to; and the modern dramatist, in having the surroundings of his play visibly presented to the audience when the curtain rises, enjoys an advantage for which Shakespeare often expresses his desire. It is true that Shakespeare's descriptions are not what descriptions are in modern plays—accounts of what the audience can observe for themselves; they are the imaginative method by which he creates in the mind of the spectators the image of that which he desires them to see. Still, the quality of the drama is action. It is always dangerous to pause for

7

picturesqueness. And the introduction of self-explanatory scenery enables the modern method to be far more direct, while the loveliness of form and colour which it gives us, seems to me often to create an artistic temperament in the audience, and to produce that joy in beauty for beauty's sake, without which the great masterpieces of art can never be understood, to which, and to which only, are they ever revealed.

To talk of the passion of a play being hidden by the paint, and of sentiment being killed by scenery, is mere emptiness and folly of words. A noble play, nobly mounted, gives us double artistic pleasure. The eye as well as the ear is gratified, and the whole nature is made exquisitely receptive of the influence of imaginative work. And as regards a bad play, have we not all seen large audiences lured by the loveliness of scenic effect into listening to rhetoric posing as poetry, and to vulgarity doing duty for realism? Whether this be good or evil for the public I will not here discuss, but it is evident that the playwright, at any rate, never suffers.

Indeed, the artist who really has suffered through the modern mounting of plays is not the dramatist at all, but the scene-painter proper. He is rapidly being displaced by the stage-carpenter. Now and then, at Drury Lane, I have seen beautiful old front cloths let down, as perfect as pictures some of them, and pure painter's work, and there are many which we all remember at other theatres, in front of which some dialogue was reduced to graceful dumb-show through the hammer and tin-tacks behind. But as a rule the stage is overcrowded with enormous properties, which are not merely far more expensive and cumbersome than scene-paintings, but far less beautiful, and far less true. Properties kill perspective. A painted door is more like a real door than a real door is itself, for the proper conditions of light and shade can be given to it; and the excessive use of built up structures always makes the stage too glaring, for as they have to be lit from behind, as well as from the front, the gas-jets become the absolute light of the scene instead of the means merely by which we perceive the conditions of light and shadow which the painter has desired to show us.

So, instead of bemoaning the position of the playwright, it were better for the critics to exert whatever influence they may possess towards restoring the scene-painter to his proper position as an artist, and not allowing him to be built over by the property man, or hammered to death by the carpenter. I have never seen any reason myself why such artists as Mr. Beverley, Mr. Walter Hann, and Mr. Telbin should not be entitled to become Academicians. They have certainly as good a claim as have many of those R.A.'s whose total inability to paint we can see every May for a shilling.

And lastly, let those critics who hold up for our admiration the simplicity of the Elizabethan Stage, remember that they are lauding a condition of things against which Shakespeare himself, in the spirit of a true artist, always strongly protested.

A BEVY OF POETS

(*Pall Mall Gazette*, March 27, 1885.)

This spring the little singers are out before the little sparrows and have already begun chirruping. Here are four volumes already, and who knows how many more will be given to us before the laburnums blossom? The best-bound volume must, of course, have precedence. It is called *Echoes of Memory*, by Atherton Furlong, and is cased in creamy vellum and tied with ribbons of yellow silk. Mr. Furlong's charm is the unsullied sweetness of his simplicity. Indeed, we can strongly recommend to the School-Board the *Lines on the Old Town Pump* as eminently suitable for recitation by children. Such a verse, for instance, as:

I hear the little children say
    (For the tale will never die)
How the old pump flowed both night and day
    When the brooks and the wells ran dry,

has all the ring of Macaulay in it, and is a form of poetry which cannot possibly harm anybody, even if translated into French. Any inaccurate ideas of the laws of nature which the children might get from the passage in question could easily be corrected afterwards by a lecture on Hydrostatics. The poem, however, which gives us most pleasure is the one called *The Dear Old Knocker on the Door*. It is appropriately illustrated by Mr. Tristram Ellis. We quote the concluding verses of the first and last stanzas:

Blithe voices then so dear
    Send up their shouts once more,
Then sounds again on mem'ry's ear
    The dear old knocker on the door.

. . . . .

When mem'ry turns the key
Where time has placed my score,
Encased 'mid treasured thoughts must be
The dear old knocker on the door.

The cynic may mock at the subject of these verses, but we do not. Why not an ode on a knocker? Does not Victor Hugo's tragedy of *Lucrece Borgia* turn on the defacement of a doorplate? Mr. Furlong must not be discouraged. Perhaps he will write poetry some day. If he does we would earnestly appeal to him to give up calling a cock 'proud chanticleer.' Few synonyms are so depressing.

Having been lured by the Circe of a white vellum binding into the region of the pump and doormat, we turn to a modest little volume by Mr. Bowling of St. John's College, Cambridge, entitled *Sagittulæ*. And they are indeed delicate little arrows, for they are winged with the lightness of the lyric and barbed daintily with satire. *Æsthesis and Athletes* is a sweet idyll, and nothing can be more pathetic than the *Tragedy of the XIX. Century*, which tells of a luckless examiner condemned in his public capacity to pluck for her Little-go the girl graduate whom he privately adores. Girton seems to be having an important influence on the Cambridge school of poetry. We are not surprised. The Graces are the Graces always, even when they wear spectacles.

Then comes *Tuberose and Meadowsweet*, by Mr. Mark André Raffalovich. This is really a remarkable little volume, and contains many strange and beautiful poems. To say of these poems that they are unhealthy and bring with them the heavy odours of the hothouse is to point out neither their defect nor their merit, but their quality merely. And though Mr. Raffalovich is not a wonderful poet, still he is a subtle artist in poetry. Indeed, in his way he is a boyish master of curious music and of fantastic rhyme, and can strike on the lute of language so many lovely chords that it seems a pity he does not know how to pronounce the title of his book and the theme of his songs. For he insists on making 'tuberose' a trisyllable always, as if it were a potato blossom and not a flower shaped like a tiny trumpet of ivory. However, for the sake of his meadowsweet and his spring-green binding this must be forgiven him. And though he cannot pronounce 'tuberose' aright, at least he can sing of it exquisitely.

Finally we come to *Sturm und Drang*, the work of an anonymous writer. Opening the volume at hazard we come across these graceful lines:

How sweet to spend in this blue bay
The close of life's disastrous day,
To watch the morn break faintly free
Across the greyness of the sea,
What time Memnonian music fills
The shadows of the dewy hills.

Well, here is the touch of a poet, and we pluck up heart and read on. The book is a curious but not inartistic combination of the mental attitude of Mr. Matthew Arnold with the style of Lord Tennyson. Sometimes, as in *The Sicilian Hermit*, we get merely the metre of *Locksley Hall* without its music, merely its fine madness and not its fine magic. Still, elsewhere there is good work, and *Caliban in East London* has a great deal of power in it, though we do not like the adjective 'knockery' even in a poem on Whitechapel.

On the whole, to those who watch the culture of the age, the most interesting thing in young poets is not so much what they invent as what masters they follow. A few years ago it was all Mr. Swinburne. That era has happily passed away. The mimicry of passion is the most intolerable of all poses. Now, it is all Lord Tennyson, and that is better. For a young writer can gain more from the study of a literary poet than from the study of a lyrist. He may become the pupil of the one, but he can never be anything but the slave of the other. And so we are glad to see in this volume direct and noble praise of him

* * * * *

Who plucked in English meadows flowers fair
As any that in unforgotten stave
Vied with the orient gold of Venus' hair
Or fringed the murmur of the Ægean wave,

which are the fine words in which this anonymous poet pays his tribute to the Laureate.

(1) *Echoes of Memory*. By Atherton Furlong. (Field and Tuer.)

(2) *Sagittulæ*. By E. W. Bowling. (Longmans, Green and Co.)

(3) *Tuberose and Meadowsweet*. By Mark André Raffalovich. (David Bogue.)

(4) *Sturm und Drang*. (Elliot Stock.)

In reply to the review *A Bevy of Poets* the following letter was published in the *Pall Mall Gazette* on March 30, 1885, under the title of
THE ROOT OF THE MATTER

SIR,—I am sorry not to be able to accept the graceful etymology of your reviewer who calls me to task for not knowing how to pronounce the title of my book *Tuberose and Meadowsweet*. I insist, he fancifully says, 'on making "tuberose" a trisyllable always, as if it were a potato blossom and not a flower shaped like a tiny trumpet of ivory.' Alas! tuberose is a trisyllable if properly derived from the Latin *tuberosus*, the lumpy flower, having nothing to do with roses or with trumpets of ivory in name any more than in nature. I am reminded by a great living poet that another correctly wrote:

Or as the moonlight fills the open sky
Struggling with darkness—as a tuberose
Peoples some Indian dell with scents which lie
Like clouds above the flower from which they rose.

In justice to Shelley, whose lines I quote, your readers will admit that I have good authority for making a trisyllable of tuberose.—I am, Sir, your obedient servant,
ANDRÉ RAFFALOVICH.
March 28.

PARNASSUS VERSUS PHILOLOGY

(*Pall Mall Gazette*, April 1, 1885.)

To the Editor of the *Pall Mall Gazette*.

SIR,—I am deeply distressed to hear that tuberose is so called from its being a 'lumpy flower.' It is not at all lumpy, and, even if it were, no poet should be heartless enough to say so. Henceforth, there really must be two derivations for every word, one for the poet and one for the scientist. And in the present case the poet will dwell on the tiny trumpets of ivory into which the white flower breaks, and leave to the man of science horrid allusions to its supposed lumpiness and indiscreet revelations of its private life below ground. In fact, 'tuber' as a derivation is disgraceful. On the roots of verbs Philology may be allowed to speak, but on the roots of flowers she must keep silence. We cannot allow her to dig up Parnassus. And, as regards the word being a trisyllable, I am reminded by a great living poet that another correctly wrote:

And the jessamine faint, and the sweet tuberose,
The sweetest flower for scent that blows;
And all rare blossoms from every clime
Grew in that garden in perfect prime.

In justice to Shelley, whose lines I quote, your readers will admit that I have good authority for making a dissyllable of tuberose.—I am, Sir, your obedient servant,

THE CRITIC,
WHO HAD TO READ FOUR VOLUMES OF MODERN POETRY.
March 30.

HAMLET AT THE LYCEUM

(*Dramatic Review*, May 9, 1885.)

It sometimes happens that at a *première* in London the least enjoyable part of the performance is the play. I have seen many audiences more interesting than the actors, and have often heard better dialogue in the *foyer* than I have on the stage. At the Lyceum, however, this is rarely the case, and when the play is a play of Shakespeare's, and among its exponents are Mr. Irving and Miss Ellen Terry, we turn from the gods in the gallery and from the goddesses in the stalls, to enjoy the charm of the production, and to take delight in the art. The lions are behind the footlights and not in front of them when we have a noble tragedy nobly acted. And I have rarely witnessed such enthusiasm as that which greeted on last Saturday night the two artists I have mentioned. I would like, in fact, to use the word ovation, but a pedantic professor has recently informed us, with the Batavian buoyancy of misapplied learning, that this expression is not to be employed except when a sheep has been sacrificed. At the Lyceum last week I need hardly say nothing so dreadful occurred. The only inartistic incident of the evening was the hurling of a bouquet from a box at Mr. Irving while he was engaged in pourtraying the agony of Hamlet's death, and the pathos of his parting with Horatio. The Dramatic College might take up the education of spectators as well as that of players, and teach people that there is a proper moment for the throwing of flowers as well as a proper method.

As regards Mr. Irving's own performance, it has been already so elaborately criticised and described, from his business with the supposed pictures in the closet scene down to his use of 'peacock' for 'paddock,' that little remains to be said; nor, indeed, does a Lyceum audience require the interposition of the dramatic critic in order to understand or to appreciate the Hamlet of this great actor. I call him a great actor because he brings to the interpretation of a work of art the two qualities which we in this century so much desire, the qualities of personality and of perfection. A few years ago it seemed to many, and perhaps rightly, that the personality overshadowed the art. No such criticism would be fair now. The somewhat harsh angularity of movement and faulty pronunciation have been replaced by exquisite grace of gesture and clear precision of word, where such precision is necessary. For delightful as good elocution is, few things are so depressing as to hear a passionate passage recited instead of being acted. The quality of a fine performance is its life more than its learning, and every word in a play has a musical as well as an intellectual value, and must be made expressive of a certain emotion. So it does not seem to me that in all parts of a play perfect pronunciation is necessarily dramatic. When the words are 'wild and whirling,' the expression of them must be wild and whirling also. Mr. Irving, I think, manages his voice with singular art; it was impossible to discern a false note or wrong intonation in his dialogue or his soliloquies, and his strong dramatic power, his realistic power as an actor, is as effective as ever. A great critic at the beginning of this century said that Hamlet is the most difficult part to personate on the stage, that it is like the attempt to 'embody a shadow.' I cannot say that I agree with this idea. Hamlet seems to me essentially a good acting part, and in Mr. Irving's performance of it there is that combination of poetic grace with absolute reality which is so eternally delightful. Indeed, if the words easy and difficult have any meaning at all in matters of art, I would be inclined to say that Ophelia is the more difficult part. She has, I mean, less material by which to produce her effects. She is the occasion of the tragedy, but she is neither its heroine nor its chief victim. She is swept away by circumstances, and gives the opportunity for situation, of which she is not herself the climax, and which she does not herself command. And of all the parts which Miss Terry has acted in her brilliant career, there is none in which her infinite powers of pathos and her imaginative and creative faculty are more shown than in her Ophelia. Miss Terry is one of those rare artists who needs for her dramatic effect no elaborate dialogue, and for whom the simplest words are sufficient. 'I love you not,' says Hamlet, and all that Ophelia answers is, 'I was the more deceived.' These are not very grand words to read, but as Miss Terry gave them in acting they seemed to be the highest possible expression of Ophelia's character. Beautiful, too, was the quick remorse she conveyed by her face and gesture the moment she had lied to Hamlet and told him her father was at home. This I thought a masterpiece of good acting, and her mad scene was wonderful beyond all description. The secrets of Melpomene are known to Miss Terry as well as the secrets of Thalia. As regards the rest of the company there is always a high standard at the Lyceum, but some particular mention should be made of Mr. Alexander's brilliant performance of Laertes. Mr. Alexander has a most effective presence, a charming voice, and a capacity for wearing lovely costumes with ease and elegance. Indeed, in the latter respect his only rival was Mr. Norman Forbes, who played either Guildenstern or Rosencrantz very gracefully. I believe one of our budding Hazlitts is preparing a volume to be entitled 'Great Guildensterns and Remarkable Rosencrantzes,' but I have never been able myself to discern any difference between these two characters. They are, I think, the only characters Shakespeare has not cared to individualise. Whichever of the two, however, Mr. Forbes acted, he acted it well. Only one point in Mr. Alexander's performance seemed to me open to question, that was his kneeling during the whole of Polonius's speech. For this I see no necessity at all, and it makes the scene look less natural than it should—gives it, I mean, too formal an air. However, the performance was most spirited and gave great pleasure to every one. Mr. Alexander is an artist from whom much will be expected, and I have no doubt he will give us much that is fine and noble. He seems to have all the qualifications for a good actor.

There is just one other character I should like to notice. The First Player seemed to me to act far too well. He should act very badly. The First Player, besides his position in the dramatic evolution of the tragedy, is Shakespeare's caricature of the ranting actor of his day, just as the passage he recites is Shakespeare's own parody on the dull plays of some of his rivals. The whole point of Hamlet's advice to the players seems to me to be lost unless the Player himself has been guilty of the fault which Hamlet reprehends, unless he has sawn the air with his hand, mouthed his lines, torn his passion to tatters, and out-Heroded Herod. The very sensibility which Hamlet notices in the actor, such as his real tears and the like, is not the quality of a good artist. The part should be played after the manner of a provincial tragedian. It is meant to be a satire, and to play it well is to play it badly. The scenery and costumes were excellent with the exception of the King's dress, which was coarse in colour and tawdry in effect. And the Player Queen should have come in boy's attire to Elsinore.

However, last Saturday night was not a night for criticism. The theatre was filled with those who desired to welcome Mr. Irving back to his own theatre, and we were all delighted at his re-appearance among us. I hope that some time will elapse before he and Miss Terry cross again that disappointing Atlantic Ocean.

TWO NEW NOVELS

(*Pall Mall Gazette*, May 15, 1885.)

The clever authoress of *In the Golden Days* has chosen for the scene of her story the England of two centuries ago, as a relief, she tells us in her preface, 'from perpetual nineteenth-centuryism.' Upon the other hand, she makes a pathetic appeal to her readers not to regard her book as an 'historical novel,' on the ground that such a title strikes terror into the public. This seems to us rather a curious position to take up. *Esmond* and *Notre Dame* are historical novels, both of them, and both of them popular successes. *John Inglesant* and *Romola* have gone through many editions, and even *Salammbo* has its enthusiasts. We think that the public is very fond of historical novels, and as for perpetual 'nineteenth-centuryism'—a vile phrase, by the way—we only wish that more of our English novelists studied our age and its society than do so at present. However, *In the Golden Days* must not be judged by its foolish preface. It is really a very charming book, and though Dryden, Betterton, and Wills's Coffee-House are dragged in rather *à propos de bottes*, still the picture of the time is well painted. Joyce, the little Puritan maiden, is an exquisite creation, and Hugo Wharncliffe, her lover, makes a fine hero. The sketch of Algernon Sidney is rather colourless, but Charles II. is well drawn. It seems to be a novel with a high purpose and a noble meaning. Yet it is never dull.

Mrs. Macquoid's *Louisa* is modern and the scene is in Italy. Italy, we fear, has been a good deal overdone in fiction. A little more Piccadilly and a little less Perugia would be a relief. However, the story is interesting. A young English girl marries an Italian nobleman and, after some time, being bored with picturesqueness, falls in love with an Englishman. The story is told with a great deal of power and ends properly and pleasantly. It can safely be recommended to young persons.

(1) *In the Golden Days*. By Edna Lyall, Author of *We Two*, *Donovan*, *etc*. (Hurst and Blackett.)

(2) *Louisa*. By Katherine S. Macquoid. (Bentley and Son.)

HENRY THE FOURTH AT OXFORD

(*Dramatic Review*, May 23, 1885.)

I have been told that the ambition of every Dramatic Club is to act *Henry IV*. I am not surprised. The spirit of comedy is as fervent in this play as is the spirit of chivalry; it is an heroic pageant as well as an heroic poem, and like most of Shakespeare's historical dramas it contains an extraordinary number of thoroughly good acting parts, each of which is absolutely individual in character, and each of which contributes to the evolution of the plot.

Rumour, from time to time, has brought in tidings of a proposed production by the banks of the Cam, but it seems at the last moment *Box and Cox* has always had to be substituted in the bill.

To Oxford belongs the honour of having been the first to present on the stage this noble play, and the production which I saw last week was in every way worthy of that lovely town, that mother of sweetness and of light. For, in spite of the roaring of the young lions at the Union, and the screaming of the rabbits in the home of the vivisector, in spite of Keble College, and the tramways, and the sporting prints, Oxford still remains the most beautiful thing in England, and nowhere else are life and art so exquisitely blended, so perfectly made one. Indeed, in most other towns art has often to present herself in the form of a reaction against the sordid ugliness of ignoble lives, but at Oxford she comes to us as an exquisite flower born of the beauty of life and expressive of life's joy. She finds her home by the Isis as once she did by the Ilissus; the Magdalen walks and the Magdalen cloisters are as dear to her as were ever the silver olives of Colonus and the golden gateway of the house of Pallas: she covers with fanlike tracery the vaulted entrance to Christ Church Hall, and looks out from the windows of Merton; her feet have stirred the Cumnor cowslips, and she gathers fritillaries in the river-fields. To her the clamour of the schools and the dulness of the lecture-room are a weariness and a vexation of spirit; she seeks not to define virtue, and cares little for the categories; she smiles on the swift athlete whose plastic grace has pleased her, and rejoices in the young Barbarians at their games; she watches the rowers from the reedy bank and gives myrtle to her lovers, and laurel to her poets, and rue to those who talk wisely in the street; she makes the earth lovely to all who dream with Keats; she opens high heaven to all who soar with Shelley; and turning away her head from pedant, proctor and Philistine, she has welcomed to her shrine a band of youthful actors, knowing that they have sought with much ardour for the stern secret of Melpomene, and caught with much gladness the sweet laughter of Thalia. And to me this ardour and this gladness were the two most fascinating qualities of the Oxford performance, as indeed they are qualities which are necessary to any fine dramatic production. For without quick and imaginative observation of life the most beautiful play becomes dull in presentation, and what is not conceived in delight by the actor can give no delight at all to others.

I know that there are many who consider that Shakespeare is more for the study than for the stage. With this view I do not for a moment agree. Shakespeare wrote the plays to be acted, and we have no right to alter the form which he himself selected for the full expression of his work. Indeed, many of the beauties of that work can be adequately conveyed to us only through the actor's art. As I sat in the Town Hall of Oxford the other night, the majesty of the mighty lines of the play seemed to me to gain new music from the clear young voices that uttered them, and the ideal grandeur of the heroism to be made more real to the spectators by the chivalrous bearing, the noble gesture and the fine passion of its exponents. Even the dresses had their dramatic value. Their archæological accuracy gave us, immediately on the rise of the curtain, a perfect picture of the time. As the knights and nobles moved across the stage in the flowing robes of peace and in the burnished steel of battle, we needed no dreary chorus to tell us in what age or land the play's action was passing, for the fifteenth century in all the dignity and grace of its apparel was living actually before us, and the delicate harmonies of colour struck from the first a dominant note of beauty which added to the intellectual realism of archæology the sensuous charm of art.

As for individual actors, Mr. Mackinnon's Prince Hal was a most gay and graceful performance, lit here and there with charming touches of princely dignity and of noble feeling. Mr. Coleridge's Falstaff was full of delightful humour, though perhaps at times he did not take us sufficiently into his confidence. An audience looks at a tragedian, but a comedian looks at his audience. However, he gave much pleasure to every one, and Mr. Bourchier's Hotspur was really most remarkable. Mr. Bourchier has a fine stage presence, a beautiful voice, and produces his effects by a method as dramatically impressive as it is artistically right. Once or twice he seemed to me to spoil his last line by walking through it. The part of Harry Percy is one full of climaxes which must not be let slip. But still there was always a freedom and spirit in his style which was very pleasing, and his delivery of the colloquial passages I thought excellent, notably of that in the first act:

What d' ye call the place?
A plague upon't—it is in Gloucestershire;
'Twas where the madcap duke his uncle kept,
His uncle York;

lines by the way in which Kemble made a great effect. Mr. Bourchier has the opportunity of a fine career on the English stage, and I hope he will take advantage of it. Among the minor parts in the play Glendower, Mortimer and Sir Richard Vernon were capitally acted, Worcester was a performance of some subtlety, Mrs. Woods was a charming Lady Percy, and Lady Edward Spencer Churchill, as Mortimer's wife, made us all believe that we understood Welsh. Her dialogue and her song were most pleasing bits of artistic realism which fully accounted for the Celtic chair at Oxford.

But though I have mentioned particular actors, the real value of the whole representation was to be found in its absolute unity, in its delicate sense of proportion, and in that breadth of effect which is to be got only by the most careful elaboration of detail. I have rarely seen a production better stage-managed. Indeed, I hope that the University will take some official notice of this delightful work of art. Why should not degrees be granted for good acting? Are they not given to those who misunderstand Plato and who mistranslate Aristotle? And should the artist be passed over? No. To Prince Hal, Hotspur and Falstaff, D.C.L.'s should be gracefully offered. I feel sure they would be gracefully accepted. To the rest of the company the crimson or the sheep-skin hood might be assigned *honoris causâ* to the eternal confusion of the Philistine, and the rage of the industrious and the dull. Thus would Oxford confer honour on herself, and the artist be placed in his proper position. However, whether or not Convocation recognises the claims of culture, I hope that the Oxford Dramatic Society will produce every summer for us some noble play like *Henry IV.* For, in plays of this kind, plays which deal with bygone times, there is always this peculiar charm, that they combine in one exquisite presentation the passions that are living with the picturesqueness that is dead. And when we have the modern spirit given to us in an antique form, the very remoteness of that form can be made a method of increased realism. This was Shakespeare's own attitude towards the ancient world, this is the attitude we in this century should adopt towards his plays, and with a feeling akin to this it seemed to me that these brilliant young Oxonians were working. If it was so, their aim is the right one. For while we look to the dramatist to give romance to realism, we ask of the actor to give realism to romance.

MODERN GREEK POETRY

(*Pall Mall Gazette*, May 27, 1885.)

Odysseus, not Achilles, is the type of the modern Greek. Merchandise has taken precedence of the Muses and politics are preferred to Parnassus. Yet by the Illissus there are sweet singers; the nightingales are not silent in Colonus; and from the garden of Greek nineteenth-century poetry Miss Edmonds has made a very pleasing anthology; and in pouring the wine from the golden into the silver cup she has still kept much of the beauty of the original. Even when translated into English, modern Greek lyrics are preferable to modern Greek loans.

As regards the quality of this poetry, if the old Greek spirit can be traced at all, it is the spirit of Tyrtæus and of Theocritus. The warlike ballads of Rhigas and Aristotle Valaôritês have a fine ring of music and of passion in them, and the folk-songs of George Drosinês are full of charming pictures of rustic life and delicate idylls of shepherds' courtships. These we acknowledge that we prefer. The flutes of the sheepfold are more delightful than the clarions of battle. Still, poetry played such a noble part in the Greek War of Independence that it is impossible not to look with reverence on the spirited war-songs that meant so much to those who were righting for liberty and mean so much even now to their children.

Other poets besides Drosinês have taken the legends that linger among the peasants and given to them an artistic form. The song of *The Seasons* is full of beauty, and there is a delightful poem on *The Building of St. Sophia*, which tells how the design of that noble building was suggested by the golden honeycomb of a bee which had flown from the king's palace with a crumb of blessed bread that had fallen from the king's hands. The story is still to be found in Thrace.

One of the ballads, also, has a good deal of spirit. It is by Kostês Palamas and was suggested by an interesting incident which occurred some years ago in Athens. In the summer of 1881 there was borne through the streets the remains of an aged woman in the complete costume of a Pallikar, which dress she had worn at the siege of Missolonghi and in it had requested to be buried. The life of this real Greek heroine should be studied by those who are investigating the question of wherein womanliness consists. The view the poet takes of her is, we need hardly say, very different from that which Canon Liddon would entertain. Yet it is none the less fine on this account, and we are glad that this old lady has been given a place in art. The volume is, on the whole, delightful reading, and though not much can be said for lines like these:

There cometh from the West
The timid starry bands,

still, the translations are in many instances most felicitous and their style most pleasing.

Greek Lays, Idylls, Legends, etc. Translated by E. M. Edmonds. (Trübner and Co.)

OLIVIA AT THE LYCEUM

(*Dramatic Review*, May 30, 1885.)

Whether or not it is an advantage for a novel to be produced in a dramatic form is, I think, open to question. The psychological analysis of such work as that of Mr. George Meredith, for instance, would probably lose by being transmuted into the passionate action of the stage, nor does M. Zola's *formule scientifique* gain anything at all by theatrical presentation. With Goldsmith it is somewhat different. In *The Vicar of Wakefield* he seeks simply to please his readers, and desires not to prove a theory; he looks on life rather as a picture to be painted than as a problem to be solved; his aim is to create men and women more than to vivisect them; his dialogue is essentially dramatic, and his novel seems to pass naturally into the dramatic form. And to me there is something very pleasurable in seeing and studying the same subject under different conditions of art. For life remains eternally unchanged; it is art which, by presenting it to us under various forms, enables us to realise its many-sided mysteries, and to catch the quality of its most fiery-coloured moments. The originality, I mean, which we ask from the artist, is originality of treatment, not of subject. It is only the unimaginative who ever invents. The true artist is known by the use he makes of what he annexes, and he annexes everything.

Looking in this light at Mr. Wills's *Olivia*, it seems to me a very exquisite work of art. Indeed, I know no other dramatist who could have re-told this beautiful English tale with such tenderness and such power, neither losing the charm of the old story nor forgetting the conditions of the new form. The sentiment of the poet and the science of the playwright are exquisitely balanced in it. For though in prose it is a poem, and while a poem it is also a play.

But fortunate as Mr. Wills has been in the selection of his subject and in his treatment of it, he is no less fortunate in the actors who interpret his work. To whatever character Miss Terry plays she brings the infinite charm of her beauty, and the marvellous grace of her movements and gestures. It is impossible to escape from the sweet tyranny of her personality. She dominates her audience by the secret of Cleopatra. In her Olivia, however, it is not merely her personality that fascinates us but her power also, her power over pathos, and her command of situation. The scene in which she bade goodbye to her family was touching beyond any scene I remember in any modern play, yet no harsh or violent note was sounded; and when in the succeeding act she struck, in natural and noble indignation, the libertine who had betrayed her, there was, I think, no one in the theatre who did not recognise that in Miss Terry our stage possesses a really great artist, who can thrill an audience without harrowing it, and by means that seem simple and easy can produce the finest dramatic effect. Mr. Irving, as Dr. Primrose, intensified the beautiful and blind idolatry of the old pastor for his daughter till his own tragedy seems almost greater than hers; the scene in the third act, where he breaks down in his attempt to reprove the lamb that has strayed from the fold, was a masterpiece of fine acting; and the whole performance, while carefully elaborate in detail, was full of breadth and dignity. I acknowledge that I liked him least at the close of the second act. It seems to me that here we should be made to feel not merely the passionate rage of the father, but the powerlessness of the old man. The taking down of the pistols, and the attempt to follow the young duellist, are pathetic because they are useless, and I hardly think that Mr. Irving conveyed this idea. As regards the rest of the characters, Mr. Terriss's Squire Thornhill was an admirable picture of a fascinating young rake. Indeed, it was so fascinating that the moral equilibrium of the audience was quite disturbed, and nobody seemed to care very much for the virtuous Mr. Burchell. I was not sorry to see this triumph of the artistic over the ethical sympathy. Perfect heroes are the monsters of melodramas, and have no place in dramatic art. Life possibly contains them, but Parnassus often rejects what Peckham may welcome. I look forward to a reaction in favour of the cultured criminal. Mr. Norman Forbes was a very pleasing Moses, and gave his Latin quotations charmingly, Miss Emery's Sophy was most winning, and, indeed, every part seemed to me well acted except that of the virtuous Mr. Burchell. This fact, however, rather pleased me than otherwise, as it increased the charm of his attractive nephew.

The scenery and costumes were excellent, as indeed they always are at the Lyceum when the piece is produced under Mr. Irving's direction. The first scene was really very beautiful, and quite as good as the famous cherry orchard of the Théâtre Français. A critic who posed as an authority on field sports assured me that no one ever went out hunting when roses were in full bloom. Personally, that is exactly the season I would select for the chase, but then I know more about flowers than I do about foxes, and like them much better. If the critic was right, either the roses must wither or Squire Thornhill must change his coat. A more serious objection may be brought against the division of the last act into three scenes. There, I think, there was a distinct dramatic loss. The room to which Olivia returns should have been exactly the same room she had left. As a picture of the eighteenth century, however, the whole production was admirable, and the details, both of acting and of *mise-en-scène*, wonderfully perfect. I wish Olivia would take off her pretty mittens when her fortune is being told. Cheiromancy is a science which deals almost entirely with the lines on the palm of the hand, and mittens would seriously interfere with its mysticism. Still, when all is said, how easily does this lovely play, this artistic presentation, survive criticisms founded on cheiromancy and cub-hunting! The Lyceum under Mr. Irving's management has become a centre of art. We are all of us in his debt. I

13

trust that we may see some more plays by living dramatists produced at his theatre, for *Olivia* has been exquisitely mounted and exquisitely played.

AS YOU LIKE IT AT COOMBE HOUSE

(*Dramatic Review*, June 6, 1885.)

In Théophile Gautier's first novel, that golden book of spirit and sense, that holy writ of beauty, there is a most fascinating account of an amateur performance of *As You Like It* in the large orangery of a French country house. Yet, lovely as Gautier's description is, the real presentation of the play last week at Coombe seemed to me lovelier still, for not merely were there present in it all those elements of poetry and picturesqueness which *le maître impeccable* so desired, but to them was added also the exquisite charm of the open woodland and the delightful freedom of the open air. Nor indeed could the Pastoral Players have made a more fortunate selection of a play. A tragedy under the same conditions would have been impossible. For tragedy is the exaggeration of the individual, and nature thinks nothing of dwarfing a hero by a holly bush, and reducing a heroine to a mere effect of colour. The subtleties also of facial expression are in the open air almost entirely lost; and while this would be a serious defect in the presentation of a play which deals immediately with psychology, in the case of a comedy, where the situations predominate over the characters, we do not feel it nearly so much; and Shakespeare himself seems to have clearly recognised this difference, for while he had *Hamlet* and *Macbeth* always played by artificial light he acted *As You Like It* and the rest of his comedies *en plein jour.*

The condition then under which this comedy was produced by Lady Archibald Campbell and Mr. Godwin did not place any great limitations on the actor's art, and increased tenfold the value of the play as a picture. Through an alley of white hawthorn and gold laburnum we passed into the green pavilion that served as the theatre, the air sweet with odour of the lilac and with the blackbird's song; and when the curtain fell into its trench of flowers, and the play commenced, we saw before us a real forest, and we knew it to be Arden. For with whoop and shout, up through the rustling fern came the foresters trooping, the banished Duke took his seat beneath the tall elm, and as his lords lay around him on the grass, the rich melody of Shakespeare's blank verse began to reach our ears. And all through the performance this delightful sense of joyous woodland life was sustained, and even when the scene was left empty for the shepherd to drive his flock across the sward, or for Rosalind to school Orlando in love-making, far away we could hear the shrill halloo of the hunter, and catch now and then the faint music of some distant horn. One distinct dramatic advantage was gained by the *mise en scène.*

The abrupt exits and entrances, which are necessitated on the real stage by the inevitable limitations of space, were in many cases done away with, and we saw the characters coming gradually towards us through brake and underwood, or passing away down the slope till they were lost in some deep recess of the forest; the effect of distance thus gained being largely increased by the faint wreaths of blue mist that floated at times across the background. Indeed I never saw an illustration at once so perfect and so practical of the æsthetic value of smoke.

As for the players themselves, the pleasing naturalness of their method harmonised delightfully with their natural surroundings. Those of them who were amateurs were too artistic to be stagey, and those who were actors too experienced to be artificial. The humorous sadness of Jaques, that philosopher in search of sensation, found a perfect exponent in Mr. Hermann Vezin. Touchstone has been so often acted as a low comedy part that Mr. Elliott's rendering of the swift sententious fool was a welcome change, and a more graceful and winning Phebe than Mrs. Plowden, a more tender Celia than Miss Schletter, a more realistic Audrey than Miss Fulton, I have never seen. Rosalind suffered a good deal through the omission of the first act; we saw, I mean, more of the saucy boy than we did of the noble girl; and though the *persiflage* always told, the poetry was often lost; still Miss Calhoun gave much pleasure; and Lady Archibald Campbell's Orlando was a really remarkable performance. Too melancholy some seemed to think it. Yet is not Orlando lovesick? Too dreamy, I heard it said. Yet Orlando is a poet. And even admitting that the vigour of the lad who tripped up the Duke's wrestler was hardly sufficiently emphasised, still in the low music of Lady Archibald Campbell's voice, and in the strange beauty of her movements and gestures, there was a wonderful fascination, and the visible presence of romance quite consoled me for the possible absence of robustness. Among the other characters should be mentioned Mr. Claude Ponsonby's First Lord, Mr. De Cordova's Corin (a bit of excellent acting), and the Silvius of Mr. Webster.

As regards the costumes the colour scheme was very perfect. Brown and green were the dominant notes, and yellow was most artistically used. There were, however, two distinct discords. Touchstone's motley was far too glaring, and the crude white of Rosalind's bridal raiment in the last act was absolutely displeasing. A contrast may be striking but should never be harsh. And lovely in colour as Mrs. Plowden's dress was, a sort of panegyric on a pansy, I am afraid that in Shakespeare's Arden there were no Chelsea China Shepherdesses, and I am sure that the romance of Phebe does not need to be intensified by any reminiscences of porcelain. Still, *As You Like It* has probably never been so well mounted, nor costumes worn with more ease and simplicity. Not the least charming part of the whole production was the music, which was under the direction of the Rev. Arthur Batson. The boys' voices were quite exquisite, and Mr. Walsham sang with much spirit.

On the whole the Pastoral Players are to be warmly congratulated on the success of their representation, and to the artistic sympathies of Lady Archibald Campbell, and the artistic knowledge of Mr. Godwin, I am indebted for a most delightful afternoon. Few things are so pleasurable as to be able by an hour's drive to exchange Piccadilly for Parnassus.

A HANDBOOK TO MARRIAGE

(*Pall Mall Gazette*, November 18, 1885.)

In spite of its somewhat alarming title this book may be highly recommended to every one. As for the authorities the author quotes, they are almost numberless, and range from Socrates down to Artemus Ward. He tells us of the wicked bachelor who spoke of marriage as 'a very harmless amusement' and advised a young friend of his to 'marry early and marry often'; of Dr. Johnson who proposed that marriage should be arranged by the Lord Chancellor, without the parties concerned having any choice in the matter; of the Sussex labourer who asked, 'Why should I give a woman half my victuals for cooking the other half?' and of Lord Verulam who thought that unmarried men did the best public work. And, indeed, marriage is the one subject on which all women agree and all men disagree. Our author, however, is clearly of the same opinion as the Scotch lassie who, on her father warning her what a solemn thing it was to get married, answered, 'I ken that, father, but it's a great deal solemner to be single.' He may be regarded as the champion of the married life. Indeed, he has a most interesting chapter on marriage-made men, and though he dissents, and we think rightly, from the view recently put forward by a lady or two on the Women's Rights platform that Solomon owed all his wisdom to the number of his wives, still he appeals to Bismarck, John Stuart Mill, Mahommed and Lord Beaconsfield, as instances of men whose success can be traced to the influence of the women they married. Archbishop Whately once defined woman as 'a creature that does not reason and pokes the fire from the top,' but since his day the higher education of women has considerably altered their position. Women have always had an emotional sympathy with those they love; Girton and Newnham have rendered intellectual sympathy also possible. In our day it is best for a man to be married, and men must give up the tyranny in married life which was once so dear to them, and which, we are afraid, lingers still, here and there.

'Do you wish to be my wife, Mabel?' said a little boy.

'Yes,' incautiously answered Mabel.

'Then pull off my boots.'

On marriage vows our author has, too, very sensible views and very amusing stories. He tells of a nervous bridegroom who, confusing the baptismal and marriage ceremonies, replied when asked if he consented to take the bride for his wife: 'I renounce them all'; of a Hampshire rustic who, when giving the ring, said solemnly to the bride: 'With my body I thee wash up, and with all my hurdle goods I thee and thou'; of another who, when asked whether he would take his partner to be his wedded wife, replied with shameful indecision: 'Yes, I'm willin'; but I'd a sight rather have her sister'; and of a Scotch lady who, on the occasion of her daughter's wedding, was asked by an old friend whether she might congratulate her on the event, and answered: 'Yes, yes, upon the whole it is very satisfactory; it is true Jeannie hates her gudeman, but then there's always a something!' Indeed, the good stories contained in this book are quite endless and make it very pleasant reading, while the good advice is on all points admirable.

Most young married people nowadays start in life with a dreadful collection of ormolu inkstands covered with sham onyxes, or with a perfect museum of salt-cellars. We strongly recommend this book as one of the best of wedding presents. It is a complete handbook to an earthly Paradise, and its author may be regarded as the Murray of matrimony and the Baedeker of bliss.

How to be Happy though Married: Being a Handbook to Marriage. By a Graduate in the University of Matrimony. (T. Fisher Unwin.)

HALF-HOURS WITH THE WORST AUTHORS

(*Pall Mall Gazette*, January 15, 1886.)

I am very much pleased to see that you are beginning to call attention to the extremely slipshod and careless style of our ordinary magazine-writers. Will you allow me to refer your readers to an article on Borrow, in the current number of *Macmillan*, which exemplifies very clearly the truth of your remarks? The author of the article is Mr. George Saintsbury, a gentleman who has recently written a book on Prose Style, and here are some specimens of the prose of the future according to the *système Saintsbury*:

1. He saw the rise, and, *in some instances, the death, of Tennyson*, Thackeray, Macaulay, Carlyle, Dickens.

2. *See a place* which Kingsley, *or Mr. Ruskin, or* some other master of our decorative school, *have* described—*much more* one which has fallen into the hands of the small fry of their imitators—and you are almost sure to find that *it has been overdone.*

3. The great mass of his translations, published and unpublished, and the smaller mass of his early hackwork, no doubt *deserves* judicious excerption.

4. 'The Romany Rye' *did not appear* for six years, *that is to say, in* 1857.

5. The elaborate apparatus which most prose tellers of fantastic tales *use*, and generally *fail in using.*

6. The great writers, whether they try to be like other people or try not to be like them (*and sometimes in the first case most of all*), succeed *only* in being themselves.

7. If he had a slight *overdose* of Celtic blood and Celtic-peculiarity, it was *more than made up* by the readiness of literary expression which it gave him. He, if any one, bore an English heart, though, *as there often has been*, there was something perhaps more than English as well as less than it in his fashion of expression.

8. His flashes of ethical reflection, which, though like *all* ethical reflections *often* one-sided.

9. He certainly was an *unfriend* to Whiggery.

10. *That it contains* a great deal of quaint and piquant writing *is only to say* that its writer wrote it.

11. 'Wild Wales,' too, because of *its* easy and direct *opportunity* of comparing its description with the originals.

12. The capital *and* full-length portraits.

13. Whose attraction is *one* neither mainly nor in any very great degree one of pure form.

14. *Constantly right in general.*

These are merely a few examples of the style of Mr. Saintsbury, a writer who seems quite ignorant of the commonest laws both of grammar and of literary expression, who has apparently no idea of the difference between the pronouns 'this' and 'that,' and has as little hesitation in ending the clause of a sentence with a preposition, as he has in inserting a parenthesis between a preposition and its object, a mistake of which the most ordinary schoolboy would be ashamed. And why can not our magazine-writers use plain, simple English? *Unfriend*, quoted above, is a quite unnecessary archaism, and so is such a phrase as *With this Borrow could not away*, in the sense of 'this Borrow could not endure.' 'Borrow's *abstraction* from general society' may, I suppose, pass muster. Pope talks somewhere of a hermit's 'abstraction,' but what is the meaning of saying that the author of Lavengro *quartered* Castile and Leon 'in the most interesting manner, riding everywhere with his servant'? And what defence can be made for such an expression as 'Scott, and other *black beasts* of Borrow's'? Black beast for *bête noire* is really abominable.

The object of my letter, however, is not to point out the deficiencies of Mr. Saintsbury's style, but to express my surprise that his article should have been admitted into the pages of a magazine like *Macmillan's*. Surely it does not require much experience to know that such an article is a disgrace even to magazine literature.

George Borrow. By George Saintsbury. (*Macmillan's Magazine*, January 1886.)

ONE OF MR. CONWAY'S REMAINDERS

(*Pall Mall Gazette*, February 1, 1886.)

Most people know that in the concoction of a modern novel crime is a more important ingredient than culture. Mr. Hugh Conway certainly knew it, and though for cleverness of invention and ingenuity of construction he cannot be compared to M. Gaboriau, that master of murder and its mysteries, still he fully recognised the artistic value of villainy. His last novel, *A Cardinal Sin*, opens very well. Mr. Philip Bourchier, M.P. for Westshire and owner of Redhills, is travelling home from London in a first-class railway carriage when, suddenly, through the window enters a rough-looking middle-aged man brandishing a long-lost marriage certificate, the effect of which is to deprive the right honourable member of his property and estate. However, Mr. Bourchier, M.P., is quite equal to the emergency. On the arrival of the train at its destination, he invites the unwelcome intruder to drive home with him and, reaching a lonely road, shoots him through the head and gives information to the nearest magistrate that he has rid society of a dangerous highwayman.

Mr. Bourchier is brought to trial and triumphantly acquitted. So far, everything goes well with him. Unfortunately, however, the murdered man, with that superhuman strength which on the stage and in novels always accompanies the agony of death, had managed in falling from the dog-cart to throw the marriage certificate up a fir tree! There it is found by a worthy farmer who talks that conventional rustic dialect which, though unknown in the provinces, is such a popular element in every Adelphi melodrama; and it ultimately falls into the hands of an unscrupulous young man who succeeds in blackmailing Mr. Bourchier and in marrying his daughter. Mr. Bourchier suffers tortures from excess of chloral and of remorse; and there is psychology of a weird and wonderful kind, that kind which Mr. Conway may justly be said to have invented and the result of which is not to be underrated. For, if to raise a goose skin on the reader be the aim of art, Mr. Conway must be regarded as a real artist. So harrowing is his psychology that the ordinary methods of punctuation are quite inadequate to convey it. Agony and asterisks follow each other on every page and, as the murderer's conscience sinks deeper into chaos, the chaos of commas increases.

Finally, Mr. Bourchier dies, *splendide mendax* to the end. A confession, he rightly argued, would break up the harmony of the family circle, particularly as his eldest son had married the daughter of his luckless victim. Few criminals are so thoughtful for others as Mr. Bourchier is, and we are not without admiration for the unselfishness of one who can give up the luxury of a death-bed repentance.

A Cardinal Sin, then, on the whole, may be regarded as a crude novel of a common melodramatic type. What is painful about it is its style, which is slipshod and careless. To describe a honeymoon as a *rare occurrence in any one person's life* is rather amusing. There is an American story of a young couple who had to be married by telephone, as the bridegroom lived in Nebraska and the bride in New York, and they had to go on separate honeymoons; though, perhaps, this is not what Mr. Conway meant. But what can be said for a sentence like this?—'The established favourites in the musical world are never quite sure but the *new comer* may not be *one among the many they have seen fail*'; or this?—'As it is the fate of such a very small number of men to marry a prima donna, I shall be doing little harm, *or be likely to change plans of life*, by enumerating some of the disadvantages.' The nineteenth century may be a prosaic age, but we fear that, if we are to judge by the general run of novels, it is not an age of prose.

A Cardinal Sin. By Hugh Conway. (Remington and Co.)

TO READ OR NOT TO READ

(*Pall Mall Gazette*, February 8, 1886.)

Books, I fancy, may be conveniently divided into three classes:—

1. Books to read, such as Cicero's *Letters*, Suetonius, Vasari's *Lives of the Painters*, the *Autobiography of Benvenuto Cellini*, Sir John Mandeville, Marco Polo, St. Simon's *Memoirs*, Mommsen, and (till we get a better one) Grote's *History of Greece*.

2. Books to re-read, such as Plato and Keats: in the sphere of poetry, the masters not the minstrels; in the sphere of philosophy, the seers not the *savants*.

3. Books not to read at all, such as Thomson's *Seasons*, Rogers's *Italy*, Paley's *Evidences*, all the Fathers except St. Augustine, all John Stuart Mill except the essay on *Liberty*, all Voltaire's plays without any exception, Butler's *Analogy*, Grant's *Aristotle*, Hume's *England*, Lewes's *History of Philosophy*, all argumentative books and all books that try to prove anything.

The third class is by far the most important. To tell people what to read is, as a rule, either useless or harmful; for, the appreciation of literature is a question of temperament not of teaching; to Parnassus there is no primer and nothing that one can learn is ever worth learning. But to tell people what not to read is a very different matter, and I venture to recommend it as a mission to the University Extension Scheme.

Indeed, it is one that is eminently needed in this age of ours, an age that reads so much, that it has no time to admire, and writes so much, that it has no time to think. Whoever will select out of the chaos of our modern curricula 'The Worst Hundred Books,' and publish a list of them, will confer on the rising generation a real and lasting benefit.

After expressing these views I suppose I should not offer any suggestions at all with regard to 'The Best Hundred Books,' but I hope you will allow me the pleasure of being inconsistent, as I am anxious to put in a claim for a book that has been strangely omitted by most of the excellent judges who have contributed to your columns. I mean the *Greek Anthology*. The beautiful poems contained in this collection seem to me to hold the same position with regard to Greek dramatic literature as do the delicate little figurines of Tanagra to the Phidian marbles, and to be quite as necessary for the complete understanding of the Greek spirit.

I am also amazed to find that Edgar Allan Poe has been passed over. Surely this marvellous lord of rhythmic expression deserves a place? If, in order to make room for him, it be necessary to elbow out some one else, I should elbow out Southey, and I think that Baudelaire might be most advantageously substituted for Keble.

No doubt, both in the *Curse of Kehama* and in the *Christian Year* there are poetic qualities of a certain kind, but absolute catholicity of taste is not without its dangers. It is only an auctioneer who should admire all schools of art.

TWELFTH NIGHT AT OXFORD

(*Dramatic Review*, February 20, 1886.)

On Saturday last the new theatre at Oxford was opened by the University Dramatic Society. The play selected was Shakespeare's delightful comedy of *Twelfth Night*, a play eminently suitable for performance by a club, as it contains so many good acting parts. Shakespeare's tragedies may be made for a single star, but his comedies are made for a galaxy of constellations. In the first he deals with the pathos of the individual, in the second he gives us a picture of life. The Oxford undergraduates, then, are to be congratulated on the selection of the play, and the result fully justified their choice. Mr. Bourchier as Festa the clown was easy, graceful and joyous, as fanciful as his dress and as funny as his bauble. The beautiful songs which Shakespeare has assigned to this character were rendered by him as charmingly as they were dramatically. To act singing is quite as great an art as to sing. Mr. Letchmere Stuart was a delightful Sir Andrew, and gave much pleasure to the audience. One may hate the villains of Shakespeare, but one cannot help loving his fools. Mr. Macpherson was, perhaps, hardly equal to such an immortal part as that of Sir Toby Belch, though there was much that was clever in his performance. Mr. Lindsay threw new and unexpected light on the character of Fabian, and Mr. Clark's Malvolio was a most remarkable piece of acting. What a difficult part Malvolio is! Shakespeare undoubtedly meant us to laugh all through at the pompous steward, and to join in the practical joke upon him, and yet how impossible not to feel a good deal of sympathy with him! Perhaps in this century we are too altruistic to be really artistic. Hazlitt says somewhere that poetical justice is done him in the uneasiness which Olivia suffers on account of her mistaken attachment to Orsino, as her insensibility to the violence of the Duke's passion is atoned for by the discovery of Viola's concealed love for him; but it is difficult not to feel Malvolio's treatment is unnecessarily harsh. Mr. Clark, however, gave a very clever rendering, full of subtle touches. If I ventured on a bit of advice, which I feel most reluctant to do, it would be to the effect that while one should always study the method of a great artist, one should never imitate his manner. The manner of an artist is essentially individual, the method of an artist is absolutely universal. The first is personality, which no one should copy; the second is perfection, which all should aim at. Miss Arnold was a most sprightly Maria, and Miss Farmer a dignified Olivia; but as Viola Mrs. Bewicke was hardly successful. Her manner was too boisterous and her method too modern. Where there is violence there is no Viola, where there is no illusion there is no Illyria, and where there is no style there is no Shakespeare. Mr. Higgins looked the part of Sebastian to perfection, and some of the minor characters were excellently played by Mr. Adderley, Mr. King-Harman, Mr. Coningsby Disraeli and Lord Albert Osborne. On the whole, the performance reflected much credit on the Dramatic Society; indeed, its excellence was such that I am led to hope that the University will some day have a theatre of its own, and that proficiency in scene-painting will be regarded as a necessary qualification for the Slade Professorship. On the stage, literature returns to life and archæology becomes art. A fine theatre is a temple where all the muses may meet, a second Parnassus, and the dramatic spirit, though she has long tarried at Cambridge, seems now to be migrating to Oxford.

Thebes did her green unknowing youth engage;
She chooses Athens in her riper age.

THE LETTERS OF A GREAT WOMAN

(*Pall Mall Gazette*, March 6, 1886.)

Of the many collections of letters that have appeared in this century few, if any, can rival for fascination of style and variety of incident the letters of George Sand which have recently been translated into English by M. Ledos de Beaufort. They extend over a space of more than sixty years, from 1812 to 1876, in fact, and comprise the first letters of Aurore Dupin, a child of eight years old, as well as the last letters of George Sand, a woman of seventy-two. The very early letters, those of the child and of the young married woman, possess, of course, merely a psychological interest; but from 1831, the date of Madame Dudevant's separation from her husband and her first entry into Paris life, the interest becomes universal, and the literary and political history of France is mirrored in every page.

For George Sand was an indefatigable correspondent; she longs in one of her letters, it is true, for 'a planet where reading and writing are absolutely unknown,' but still she had a real pleasure in letter-writing. Her greatest delight was the communication of ideas, and she is always in the heart of the battle. She discusses pauperism with Louis Napoleon in his prison at Ham, and liberty with Armand Barbes in his dungeon at Vincennes; she writes to Lamennais on philosophy, to Mazzini on socialism, to Lamartine on democracy, and to Ledru-Rollin on justice. Her letters reveal to us not merely the life of a great novelist but the soul of a great woman, of a woman who was one with all the noblest movements of her day and whose sympathy with humanity was boundless absolutely. For the aristocracy of intellect she had always the deepest veneration, but the democracy of suffering touched her more. She preached the regeneration of mankind, not with the noisy ardour of the paid advocate, but with the enthusiasm of the true evangelist. Of all the artists of this century she was the most altruistic; she felt every one's misfortunes except her own. Her faith never left her; to the end of her life, as she tells us, she was able to believe without illusions. But the people disappointed her a little. She saw that they followed persons not principles, and for 'the great man theory' George Sand had no respect. 'Proper names are the enemies of principles' is one of her aphorisms.

So from 1850 her letters are more distinctly literary. She discusses modern realism with Flaubert, and play-writing with Dumas *fils*; and protests with passionate vehemence against the doctrine of *L'art pour l'art*. 'Art for the sake of itself is an idle sentence,' she writes; 'art for the sake of truth, for the sake of what is beautiful and good, that is the creed I seek.' And in a delightful letter to M. Charles Poncy she repeats the same idea very charmingly. 'People say that birds sing for the sake of singing, but I doubt it. They sing their loves and happiness, and in that they are in keeping with nature. But man must do something more, and poets only sing in order to move people and to make them think.' She wanted M. Poncy to be the poet of the people and, if good advice were all that had been needed, he would certainly have been the Burns of the workshop. She drew out a delightful scheme for a volume to be called *Songs of all Trades* and saw the possibilities of making handicrafts poetic. Perhaps she valued good intentions in art a little too much, and she hardly understood that art for art's sake is not meant to express the final cause of art but is merely a formula of creation; but, as she herself had scaled Parnassus, we must not quarrel at her bringing Proletarianism with her. For George Sand must be ranked among our poetic geniuses. She regarded the novel as still within the domain of poetry. Her heroes are not dead photographs; they are great possibilities. Modern novels are dissections; hers are dreams. 'I make popular types,' she writes, 'such as I do no longer see, but such as they should and might be.' For realism, in M. Zola's acceptation of the word, she had no admiration. Art to her was a mirror that transfigured truths but did not represent realities. Hence she could not understand art without personality. 'I am aware,' she writes to Flaubert, 'that you are opposed to the exposition of personal doctrine in literature. Are you right? Does not your opposition proceed rather from a want of conviction than from a principle of æsthetics? If we have any philosophy in our brain it must needs break forth in our writings. But you, as soon as you handle literature, you seem anxious, I know not why, to be another man, the one who must disappear, who annihilates himself and is no more. What a singular mania! What a deficient taste! The worth of our productions depends entirely on our own. Besides, if we withhold our own opinions respecting the personages we create, we naturally leave the reader in uncertainty as to the opinion he should himself form of them. That amounts to wishing not to be understood, and the result of this is that the reader gets weary of us and leaves us.'

She herself, however, may be said to have suffered from too dominant a personality, and this was the reason of the failure of most of her plays.

Of the drama in the sense of disinterested presentation she had no idea, and what is the strength and life-blood of her novels is the weakness of her dramatic works. But in the main she was right. Art without personality is impossible. And yet the aim of art is not to reveal personality, but to please. This she hardly recognised in her æsthetics, though she realised it in her work. On literary style she has some excellent remarks. She dislikes the extravagances of the romantic school and sees the beauty of simplicity. 'Simplicity,' she writes, 'is the most difficult thing to secure in this world: it is the last limit of experience and the last effort of genius.' She hated the slang and *argot* of Paris life, and loved the words used by the peasants in the provinces. 'The provinces,' she remarks, 'preserve the tradition of the original tongue and create but few new words. I feel much respect for the language of the peasantry; in my estimation it is the more correct.'

She thought Flaubert too much preoccupied with the sense of form, and makes these excellent observations to him—perhaps her best piece of literary criticism. 'You consider the form as the aim, whereas it is but the effect. Happy expressions are only the outcome of emotion and emotion itself proceeds from a conviction. We are only moved by that which we ardently believe in.' Literary schools she distrusted. Individualism was to her the keystone of art as well as of life. 'Do not belong to any school: do not imitate any model,' is her advice. Yet she never encouraged eccentricity. 'Be correct,' she writes to Eugene Pelletan, 'that is rarer than being eccentric, as the time goes. It is much more common to please by bad taste than to receive the cross of honour.'

On the whole, her literary advice is sound and healthy. She never shrieks and she never sneers. She is the incarnation of good sense. And the whole collection of her letters is a perfect treasure-house of suggestions both on art and on politics. The manner of the translation is often rather clumsy, but the matter is always so intensely interesting that we can afford to be charitable.

Letters of George Sand. Translated and edited by Raphael Ledos de Beaufort. (Ward and Downey.)

NEWS FROM PARNASSUS

(*Pall Mall Gazette*, April 12, 1886.)

That most delightful of all French critics, M. Edmond Scherer, has recently stated in an article on Wordsworth that the English read far more poetry than any other European nation. We sincerely hope this may be true, not merely for the sake of the public but for the sake of the poets also. It would be sad indeed if the many volumes of poems that are every year published in London found no readers but the authors themselves and the authors' relations; and the real philanthropist should recognise it as part of his duties to buy every new book of verse that appears. Sometimes, we acknowledge, he will be disappointed, often he will be bored; still now and then he will be amply rewarded for his reckless benevolence.

Mr. George Francis Armstrong's *Stories of Wicklow*, for instance, is most pleasant reading. Mr. Armstrong is already well known as the author of *Ugone*, *King Saul* and other dramas, and his latest volume shows that the power and passion of his early work has not deserted him. Most modern Irish poetry is purely political and deals with the wickedness of the landlords and the Tories; but Mr. Armstrong sings of the picturesqueness of Erin, not of its politics. He tells us very charmingly of the magic of its mists and the melody of its colour, and draws a most captivating picture of the peasants of the county Wicklow, whom he describes as

A kindly folk in vale and moor,
  Unvexed with rancours, frank and free
In mood and manners—rich with poor
  Attuned in happiest amity:
Where still the cottage door is wide,
  The stranger welcomed at the hearth,
And pleased the humbler hearts confide
  Still in the friend of gentler birth.

The most ambitious poem in the volume is *De Verdun of Darragh*. It is at once lyrical and dramatic, and though its manner reminds us of Browning and its method of *Maud*, still all through it there is a personal and individual note. Mr. Armstrong also carefully observes the rules of decorum, and, as he promises his readers in a preface, keeps quite clear of 'the seas of sensual art.' In fact, an elderly maiden lady could read this volume without a blush, a thrill, or even an emotion.

Dr. Goodchild does not possess Mr. Armstrong's literary touch, but his *Somnia Medici* is distinguished by a remarkable quality of forcible and direct expression. The poem that opens his volume, *Myrrha, or A Dialogue on Creeds*, is quite as readable as a metrical dialogue on creeds could possibly be; and *The Organ Builder* is a most romantic story charmingly told. Dr. Goodchild seems to be an ardent disciple of Mr. Browning, and though he may not be able to reproduce the virtues of his master, at least he can echo his defects very cleverly. Such a verse as—

'Tis the subtle essayal
  Of the Jews and Judas,
Such lying lisp
Might hail a will-o'-the-wisp,
  A thin somebody—Theudas—

is an excellent example of low comedy in poetry. One of the best poems in the book is *The Ballad of Three Kingdoms*. Indeed, if the form were equal to the conception, it would be a delightful work of art; but Dr. Goodchild, though he may be a master of metres, is not a master of music yet. His verse is often harsh and rugged. On the whole, however, his volume is clever and interesting.

Mr. Keene has not, we believe, a great reputation in England as yet, but in India he seems to be well known. From a collection of criticisms appended to his volume it appears that the *Overland Mail* has christened him the Laureate of Hindostan and that the *Allahabad Pioneer* once compared him to Keats. He is a pleasant rhymer, as rhymers go, and, though we strongly object to his putting the Song of Solomon into bad blank verse, still we are quite ready to admire his translations of the *Pervigilium Veneris* and of Omar Khayyam. We wish he would not write sonnets with fifteen lines. A fifteen-line sonnet is as bad a monstrosity as a sonnet in dialogue. The volume has the merit of being very small, and contains many stanzas quite suitable for valentines.

Finally we come to *Procris and Other Poems*, by Mr. W. G. Hole. Mr. Hole is apparently a very young writer. His work, at least, is full of crudities, his syntax is defective, and his grammar is questionable. And yet, when all is said, in the one poem of *Procris* it is easy to recognise the true poetic ring. Elsewhere the volume is amateurish and weak. *The Spanish Main* was suggested by a leader in the *Daily Telegraph*, and bears all the traces of its lurid origin. *Sir Jocellyn's Trust* is a sort of pseudo-Tennysonian idyll in which the damozel says to her gallant rescuer, 'Come, come, Sir Knight, I catch my death of cold,' and recompenses him with

  What noble minds
Regard the first reward,—an orphan's thanks.

Nunc Dimittis is dull and *The Wandering Jew* dreadful; but *Procris* is a beautiful poem. The richness and variety of its metaphors, the music of its lines, the fine opulence of its imagery, all seem to point to a new poet. Faults, it is true, there are in abundance; but they are faults that come from want of trouble, not from want of taste. Mr. Hole shows often a rare and exquisite sense of beauty and a marvellous power of poetic vision, and if he will cultivate the technique of his craft a little more we have no doubt but that he will some day give us work worthy to endure. It is true that there is more promise than perfection in his verse at present, yet it is a promise that seems likely to be fulfilled.

(1) *Stories of Wicklow*. By George Francis Armstrong, M.A. (Longmans, Green and Co.)

(2) *Somnia Medici*. By John A. Goodchild. Second Series. (Kegan Paul.)

(3) *Verses: Translated and Original*. By H. E. Keene. (W. H. Allen and Co.)

(4) *Procris and Other Poems*. By W. G. Hole. (Kegan Paul.)

SOME NOVELS

(*Pall Mall Gazette*, April 14, 1886.)

After a careful perusal of '*Twixt Love and Duty*, by Mr. Tighe Hopkins, we confess ourselves unable to inform anxious inquirers who it is that is thus sandwiched, and how he (or she) got into so unpleasant a predicament. The curious reader with a taste for enigmas may be advised to find out for himself—if he can. Even if he be unsuccessful, his trouble will be repaid by the pleasant writing and clever character drawing of Mr. Hopkins's tale. The plot is less praiseworthy. The whole Madeira episode seems to lead up to this dilemma, and after all it comes to nothing. We brace up our nerves for a tragedy and are treated instead to the mildest of marivaudage—which is disappointing. In conclusion, one word of advice to Mr. Hopkins: let him refrain from apostrophising his characters after this fashion: 'Oh, Gilbert Reade, what are you about that you dally with this golden chance?' and so forth. This is one of the worst mannerisms of a bygone generation of story tellers.

Mr. Gallenga has written, as he says, 'a tale without a murder,' but having put a pistol-ball through his hero's chest and left him alive and hearty notwithstanding, he cannot be said to have produced a tale without a miracle. His heroine, too, if we may judge by his descriptions of her, is 'all a wonder and a wild desire.' At the age of seventeen she 'was one of the Great Maker's masterpieces . . . a living likeness of the Dresden Madonna.' One rather shudders to think of what she may become at forty, but this is an impertinent prying into futurity. She hails from 'Maryland, my Maryland!' and has 'received a careful, if not a superior, education.' Need we add that she marries the heir to an earldom who, as aforesaid, has had himself perforated by a pistol-bullet on her behalf? Mr. Gallenga's division of this book into acts and scenes is not justified by anything specially dramatic either in its structure or its method. The dialogue, in truth, is somewhat stilted. Nevertheless, its first-hand sketches of Roman society are not without interest, and one or two characters seem to be drawn from nature.

The *Life's Mistake* which forms the theme of Mrs. Lovett Cameron's two volumes is not a mistake after all, but results in unmixed felicity; and as it is brought about by fraud on the part of the hero, this conclusion is not as moral as it might be. For the rest, the tale is a very familiar one. Its personages are the embarrassed squire with his charming daughter, the wealthy and amorous mortgagee, and the sailor lover who is either supposed to be drowned or falsely represented to be fickle—in Mrs. Cameron's tale he is both in succession. When we add that there is a stanza from Byron on the title-page and a poetical quotation at the beginning of each chapter, we have possessed the discerning reader of all necessary information both as to the matter and the manner of Mrs. Cameron's performance.

Mr. E. O. Pleydell-Bouverie has endowed the novel-writing fraternity with a new formula for the composition of titles. After *J. S.; or, Trivialities* there is no reason why we should not have *A. B.; or, Platitudes*, *M.N.; or, Sentimentalisms*, *Y.Z.; or, Inanities*. There are many books which these simple titles would characterise much more aptly than any high-flown phrases—as aptly, in fact, as Mr. Bouverie's title characterises the volume before us. It sets forth the uninteresting fortunes of an insignificant person, one John Stiles, a briefless barrister. The said John falls in love with a young lady, inherits a competence, omits to tell his love, and is killed by the bursting of a fowling-piece—that is all. The only point of interest presented by the book is the problem as to how it ever came to be written. We can scarcely find the solution in Mr. Bouverie's elaborately smart style which cannot be said to transmute his 'trivialities' into 'flies in amber.'

Mr. Swinburne once proposed that it should be a penal offence against literature for any writer to affix a proverb, a phrase or a quotation to a novel, by way of tag or title. We wonder what he would say to the title of 'Pen Oliver's' last book! Probably he would empty on it the bitter vial of his scorn and satire. *All But* is certainly an intolerable name to give to any literary production. The story, however, is quite an interesting one. At Laxenford Hall live Lord and Lady Arthur Winstanley. Lady Arthur has two children by her first marriage, the elder of whom, Walter Hope-Kennedy by name, is heir to the broad acres. Walter is a pleasant English boy, fonder of cricket than of culture, healthy, happy and susceptible. He falls in love with Fanny Taylor, a pretty village girl; is thrown out of his dog-cart one night through the machinations of a jealous rival, breaks one of his ribs and gets a violent fever. His stepfather tries to murder him by subcutaneous injections of morphia but is detected by the local doctor, and Walter recovers. However, he does not marry Fanny after all, and the story ends ineffectually. To say of a dress that 'it was rather under than over adorned' is not very pleasing English, and such a phrase as 'almost always, but by no means invariably,' is quite detestable. Still we must not expect the master of the scalpel to be the master of the stilus as well. *All But* is a very charming tale, and the sketches of village life are quite admirable. We recommend it to all who are tired of the productions of Mr. Hugh Conway's dreadful disciples.

(1) *'Twixt Love and Duty*: *A Novel*. By Tighe Hopkins. (Chatto and Windus.)

(2) *Jenny Jennet*: *A Tale Without a Murder*. By A. Gallenga. (Chapman and Hall.)

(3) *A Life's Mistake*: *A Novel*. By Mrs. H. Lovett Cameron. (Ward and Downey.)

(4) *J. S.; or, Trivialities*: *A Novel*. By Edward Oliver Pleydell-Bouverie. (Griffith, Farren and Co.)

(5) *All But*: *A Chronicle of Laxenford Life*. By Pen Oliver, F.R.C.S. (Kegan Paul.)

A LITERARY PILGRIM

(*Pall Mall Gazette*, April 17, 1886.)

Antiquarian books, as a rule, are extremely dull reading. They give us facts without form, science without style, and learning without life. An exception, however, must be made for M. Gaston Boissier's *Promenades Archéologiques*. M. Boissier is a most pleasant and picturesque writer, and is really able to give his readers useful information without ever boring them, an accomplishment which is entirely unknown in Germany, and in England is extremely rare.

The first essay in his book is on the probable site of Horace's country-house, a subject that has interested many scholars from the Renaissance down to our own day. M. Boissier, following the investigations of Signor Rosa, places it on a little hill over-looking the Licenza, and his theory has a great deal to recommend it. The plough still turns up on the spot the bricks and tiles of an old Roman villa; a spring of clear water, like that of which the poet so often sang, 'breaks babbling from the hollow rock,' and is still called by the peasants

Fonte dell' Oratini, some faint echo possibly of the singer's name; the view from the hill is just what is described in the epistles, 'Continui montes nisi dissocientur opaca valle'; hard by is the site of the ruined temple of Vacuna, where Horace tells us he wrote one of his poems, and the local rustics still go to Varia (Vicovaro) on market days as they used to do when the graceful Roman lyrist sauntered through his vines and played at being a country gentleman.

M. Boissier, however, is not content merely with identifying the poet's house; he also warmly defends him from the charge that has been brought against him of servility in accepting it. He points out that it was only after the invention of printing that literature became a money-making profession, and that, as there was no copyright law at Rome to prevent books being pirated, patrons had to take the place that publishers hold, or should hold, nowadays. The Roman patron, in fact, kept the Roman poet alive, and we fancy that many of our modern bards rather regret the old system. Better, surely, the humiliation of the *sportula* than the indignity of a bill for printing! Better to accept a country-house as a gift than to be in debt to one's landlady! On the whole, the patron was an excellent institution, if not for poetry at least for the poets; and though he had to be propitiated by panegyrics, still are we not told by our most shining lights that the subject is of no importance in a work of art? M. Boissier need not apologise for Horace: every poet longs for a Mæcenas.

An essay on the Etruscan tombs at Corneto follows, and the remainder of the volume is taken up by a most fascinating article called *Le Pays de l'Enéide*. M. Boissier claims for Virgil's descriptions of scenery an absolute fidelity of detail. 'Les poètes anciens,' he says, 'ont le goût de la précision et de la fidélité: ils n'imaginent guère de paysages en l'air,' and with this view he visited every place in Italy and Sicily that Virgil has mentioned. Sometimes, it is true, modern civilisation, or modern barbarism, has completely altered the aspect of the scene; the 'desolate shore of Drepanum,' for instance ('Drepani illætabilis ora') is now covered with thriving manufactories and stucco villas, and the 'bird-haunted forest' through which the Tiber flowed into the sea has long ago disappeared. Still, on the whole, the general character of the Italian landscape is unchanged, and M. Boissier's researches show very clearly how personal and how vivid were Virgil's impressions of nature. The subject is, of course, a most interesting one, and those who love to make pilgrimages without stirring from home cannot do better than spend three shillings on the French Academician's *Promenades Archéologiques*.

Nouvelles Promenades Archéologiques, Horace et Virgile. By Gaston Boissier. (Hachette.)

BÉRANGER IN ENGLAND

(*Pall Mall Gazette*, April 21, 1886.)

A philosophic politician once remarked that the best possible form of government is an absolute monarchy tempered by street ballads. Without at all agreeing with this aphorism we still cannot but regret that the new democracy does not use poetry as a means for the expression of political opinion. The Socialists, it is true, have been heard singing the later poems of Mr. William Morris, but the street ballad is really dead in England. The fact is that most modern poetry is so artificial in its form, so individual in its essence and so literary in its style, that the people as a body are little moved by it, and when they have grievances against the capitalist or the aristocrat they prefer strikes to sonnets and rioting to rondels.

Possibly, Mr. William Toynbee's pleasant little volume of translations from Béranger may be the herald of a new school. Béranger had all the qualifications for a popular poet. He wrote to be sung more than to be read; he preferred the Pont Neuf to Parnassus; he was patriotic as well as romantic, and humorous as well as humane. Translations of poetry as a rule are merely misrepresentations, but the muse of Béranger is so simple and naïve that she can wear our English dress with ease and grace, and Mr. Toynbee has kept much of the mirth and music of the original. Here and there, undoubtedly, the translation could be improved upon; 'rapiers' for instance is an abominable rhyme to 'forefathers'; 'the hated arms of Albion' in the same poem is a very feeble rendering of 'le léopard de l'Anglais,' and such a verse as

'Mid France's miracles of art,
Rare trophies won from art's own land,
I've lived to see with burning heart
The fog-bred poor triumphant stand,

reproduces very inadequately the charm of the original:

Dans nos palais, où, près de la victoire,
Brillaient les arts, doux fruits des beaux climats,
J'ai vu du Nord les peuplades sans gloire,
De leurs manteaux secouer les frîmas.

On the whole, however, Mr. Toynbee's work is good; *Les Champs*, for example, is very well translated, and so are the two delightful poems *Rosette* and *Ma République*; and there is a good deal of spirit in *Le Marquis de Carabas*:

Whom have we here in conqueror's rôle?
Our grand old Marquis, bless his soul!
Whose grand old charger (mark his bone!)
Has borne him back to claim his own.
Note, if you please, the grand old style
In which he nears his grand old pile;
With what an air of grand old state
He waves that blade immaculate!
Hats off, hats off, for my lord to pass,
The grand old Marquis of Carabas!—

though 'that blade immaculate' has hardly got the sting of 'un sabre innocent'; and in the fourth verse of the same poem, 'Marquise, you'll have the bed-chamber' does not very clearly convey the sense of the line 'La Marquise a le tabouret.' The best translation in the book is *The Court Suit* (L'Habit de Cour), and if Mr. Toynbee will give us some more work as clever as this we shall be glad to see a second volume from his pen. Béranger is not nearly well enough known in England, and though it is always better to read a poet in the original, still translations have their value as echoes have their music.

A Selection from the Songs of De Béranger in English Verse. By William Toynbee. (Kegan Paul.)

THE POETRY OF THE PEOPLE

(*Pall Mall Gazette*, May 13, 1886.)

The Countess Martinengo deserves well of all poets, peasants and publishers. Folklore is so often treated nowadays merely from the point of view of the comparative mythologist, that it is really delightful to come across a book that deals with the subject simply as literature. For the Folk-tale is the father of all fiction as the Folk-song is the mother of all poetry; and in the games, the tales and the ballads of primitive people it is easy to see the germs of such perfected forms of art as the drama, the novel and the epic. It is, of course, true that the highest expression of life is to be found not in the popular songs, however poetical, of any nation, but in the great masterpieces of self-conscious Art; yet it is pleasant sometimes to leave the summit of Parnassus to look at the wild-flowers in the valley, and to turn from the lyre of Apollo to listen to the reed of Pan. We can still listen to it. To this day, the vineyard dressers of Calabria will mock the passer-by with satirical verses as they used to do in the old pagan days, and the peasants of the olive woods of Provence answer each other in amœbæan strains. The Sicilian shepherd has not yet thrown his pipe aside, and the children of modern Greece sing the swallow-song through the villages in spring-time, though Theognis is more than two thousand years dead. Nor is this popular poetry merely the rhythmic expression of joy and sorrow; it is in the highest degree imaginative; and taking its inspiration directly from nature it abounds in realistic metaphor and in picturesque and fantastic imagery. It must, of course, be admitted that there is a conventionality of nature as there is a conventionality of art, and that certain forms of utterance are apt to become stereotyped by too constant use; yet, on the whole, it is impossible not to recognise in the Folk-songs that the Countess Martinengo has brought together one strong dominant note of fervent and flawless sincerity. Indeed, it is only in the more terrible dramas of the Elizabethan age that we can find any parallel to the Corsican *voceri* with their shrill intensity of passion, their awful frenzies of grief and hate. And yet, ardent as the feeling is, the form is nearly always beautiful. Now and then, in the poems of the extreme South one meets with a curious crudity of realism, but, as a rule, the sense of beauty prevails.

Some of the Folk-poems in this book have all the lightness and loveliness of lyrics, all of them have that sweet simplicity of pure song by which mirth finds its own melody and mourning its own music, and even where there are conceits of thought and expression they are conceits born of fancy not of affectation. Herrick himself might have envied that wonderful love-song of Provence:

If thou wilt be the falling dew
  And fall on me alway,
Then I will be the white, white rose
  On yonder thorny spray.
If thou wilt be the white, white rose
  On yonder thorny spray,
Then I will be the honey-bee
  And kiss thee all the day.
  If thou wilt be the honey-bee
  And kiss me all the day,
Then I will be in yonder heaven
  The star of brightest ray.
If thou wilt be in yonder heaven
  The star of brightest ray,
Then I will be the dawn, and we
  Shall meet at break of day.

How charming also is this lullaby by which the Corsican mother sings her babe to sleep!

Gold and pearls my vessel lade,
  Silk and cloth the cargo be,
All the sails are of brocade
  Coming from beyond the sea;
And the helm of finest gold,
Made a wonder to behold.
  Fast awhile in slumber lie;
  Sleep, my child, and hushaby.
  After you were born full soon,
  You were christened all aright;
Godmother she was the moon,
  Godfather the sun so bright.
All the stars in heaven told

Wore their necklaces of gold.
  Fast awhile in slumber lie;
  Sleep, my child, and hushaby.

  Or this from Roumania:

  Sleep, my daughter, sleep an hour;
Mother's darling gilliflower.
Mother rocks thee, standing near,
She will wash thee in the clear
Waters that from fountains run,
To protect thee from the sun.

  Sleep, my darling, sleep an hour,
Grow thou as the gilliflower.
As a tear-drop be thou white,
As a willow tall and slight;
Gentle as the ring-doves are,
And be lovely as a star!

We hardly know what poems are sung to English babies, but we hope they are as beautiful as these two. Blake might have written them.

The Countess Martinengo has certainly given us a most fascinating book. In a volume of moderate dimensions, not too long to be tiresome nor too brief to be disappointing, she has collected together the best examples of modern Folk-songs, and with her as a guide the lazy reader lounging in his armchair may wander from the melancholy pine-forests of the North to Sicily's orange-groves and the pomegranate gardens of Armenia, and listen to the singing of those to whom poetry is a passion, not a profession, and whose art, coming from inspiration and not from schools, if it has the limitations, at least has also the loveliness of its origin, and is one with blowing grasses and the flowers of the field.

Essays in the Study of Folk-Songs. By the Countess Evelyn Martinengo Césaresco. (Redway.)

THE CENCI

(*Dramatic Review*, May 15, 1886.)

The production of *The Cenci* last week at the Grand Theatre, Islington, may be said to have been an era in the literary history of this century, and the Shelley Society deserves the highest praise and warmest thanks of all for having given us an opportunity of seeing Shelley's play under the conditions he himself desired for it. For *The Cenci* was written absolutely with a view to theatric presentation, and had Shelley's own wishes been carried out it would have been produced during his lifetime at Covent Garden, with Edmund Kean and Miss O'Neill in the principal parts. In working out his conception, Shelley had studied very carefully the æsthetics of dramatic art. He saw that the essence of the drama is disinterested presentation, and that the characters must not be merely mouthpieces for splendid poetry but must be living subjects for terror and for pity. 'I have endeavoured,' he says, 'as nearly as possible to represent the characters as they probably were, and have sought to avoid the error of making them actuated by my own conception of right or wrong, false or true: thus under a thin veil converting names and actions of the sixteenth century into cold impersonations of my own mind. . . .

'I have avoided with great care the introduction of what is commonly called mere poetry, and I imagine there will scarcely be found a detached simile or a single isolated description, unless Beatrice's description of the chasm appointed for her father's murder should be judged to be of that nature.'

He recognised that a dramatist must be allowed far greater freedom of expression than what is conceded to a poet. 'In a dramatic composition,' to use his own words, 'the imagery and the passion should interpenetrate one another, the former being reserved simply for the full development and illustration of the latter. Imagination is as the immortal God which should assume flesh for the redemption of mortal passion. It is thus that the most remote and the most familiar imagery may alike be fit for dramatic purposes when employed in the illustration of strong feeling, which raises what is low, and levels to the apprehension that which is lofty, casting over all the shadow of its own greatness. In other respects I have written more carelessly, that is, without an over-fastidious and learned choice of words. In this respect I entirely agree with those modern critics who assert that in order to move men to true sympathy we must use the familiar language of men.'

He knew that if the dramatist is to teach at all it must be by example, not by precept.

'The highest moral purpose,' he remarks, 'aimed at in the highest species of the drama, is the teaching the human heart, through its sympathies and antipathies, the knowledge of itself; in proportion to the possession of which knowledge every human being is wise, just, sincere, tolerant and kind. If dogmas can do more it is well: but a drama is no fit place for the enforcement of them.' He fully realises that it is by a conflict between our artistic sympathies and our moral judgment that the greatest dramatic effects are produced. 'It is in the restless and anatomising casuistry with which men seek the justification of Beatrice, yet feel that she has done what needs justification; it is in the superstitious horror with which they contemplate alike her wrongs and their revenge, that the dramatic character of what she did and suffered consists.'

In fact no one has more clearly understood than Shelley the mission of the dramatist and the meaning of the drama.

And yet I hardly think that the production of *The Cenci*, its absolute presentation on the stage, can be said to have added anything to its beauty, its pathos, or even its realism. Not that the principal actors were at all unworthy of the work of art they interpreted; Mr. Hermann Vezin's Cenci was a noble and magnificent performance; Miss Alma Murray stands now in the very first rank of our English actresses as a mistress of power and pathos; and Mr. Leonard Outram's Orsino was most subtle and artistic; but that *The Cenci* needs for the production of its perfect effect no interpretation at all. It is, as we read it, a complete work of art—capable, indeed, of being acted, but not dependent on theatric presentation; and the impression produced by its exhibition on the stage seemed to me to be merely one of pleasure at the gratification of an intellectual curiosity of seeing how far Melpomene could survive the wagon of Thespis.

In producing the play, however, the members of the Shelley Society were merely carrying out the poet's own wishes, and they are to be congratulated on the success of their experiment—a success due not to any gorgeous scenery or splendid pageant, but to the excellence of the actors who aided them.

HELENA IN TROAS

(*Dramatic Review*, May 22, 1880.)

One might have thought that to have produced *As You Like It* in an English forest would have satisfied the most ambitious spirit; but Mr. Godwin has not contented himself with his sylvan triumphs. From Shakespeare he has passed to Sophocles, and has given us the most perfect exhibition of a Greek dramatic performance that has as yet been seen in this country. For, beautiful as were the productions of the *Agamemnon* at Oxford and the *Eumenides* at Cambridge, their effects were marred in no small or unimportant degree by the want of a proper orchestra for the chorus with its dance and song, a want that was fully supplied in Mr. Godwin's presentation by the use of the arena of a circus.

In the centre of this circle, which was paved with the semblance of tesselated marble, stood the altar of Dionysios, and beyond it rose the long, shallow stage, faced with casts from the temple of Bassæ; and bearing the huge portal of the house of Paris and the gleaming battlements of Troy. Over the portal hung a great curtain, painted with crimson lions, which, when drawn aside, disclosed two massive gates of bronze; in front of the house was placed a golden image of Aphrodite, and across the ramparts on either hand could be seen a stretch of blue waters and faint purple hills. The scene was lovely, not merely in the harmony of its colour but in the exquisite delicacy of its architectural proportions. No nation has ever felt the pure beauty of mere construction so strongly as the Greeks, and in this respect Mr. Godwin has fully caught the Greek feeling.

The play opened by the entrance of the chorus, white vestured and gold filleted, under the leadership of Miss Kinnaird, whose fine gestures and rhythmic movements were quite admirable. In answer to their appeal the stage curtains slowly divided, and from the house of Paris came forth Helen herself, in a robe woven with all the wonders of war, and broidered with the pageant of battle. With her were her two handmaidens—one in white and yellow and one in green; Hecuba followed in sombre grey of mourning, and Priam in kingly garb of gold and purple, and Paris in Phrygian cap and light archer's dress; and when at sunset the lover of Helen was borne back wounded from the field, down from the oaks of Ida stole Œnone in the flowing drapery of the daughter of a river-god, every fold of her garments rippling like dim water as she moved.

As regards the acting, the two things the Greeks valued most in actors were grace of gesture and music of voice. Indeed, to gain these virtues their actors used to subject themselves to a regular course of gymnastics and a particular regime of diet, health being to the Greeks not merely a quality of art, but a condition of its production. Whether or not our English actors hold the same view may be doubted; but Mr. Vezin certainly has always recognised the importance of a physical as well as of an intellectual training for the stage, and his performance of King Priam was distinguished by stately dignity and most musical enunciation. With Mr. Vezin, grace of gesture is an unconscious result—not a conscious effort. It has become nature, because it was once art. Mr. Beerbohm Tree also is deserving of very high praise for his Paris. Ease and elegance characterised every movement he made, and his voice was extremely effective. Mr. Tree is the perfect Proteus of actors. He can wear the dress of any century and the appearance of any age, and has a marvellous capacity of absorbing his personality into the character he is creating. To have method without mannerism is given only to a few, but among the few is Mr. Tree. Miss Alma Murray does not possess the physique requisite for our conception of Helen, but the beauty of her movements and the extremely sympathetic quality of her voice gave an indefinable charm to her performance. Mrs. Jopling looked like a poem from the Pantheon, and indeed the *personæ mutæ* were not the least effective figures in the play. Hecuba was hardly a success. In acting, the impression of sincerity is conveyed by tone, not by mere volume of voice, and whatever influence emotion has on utterance it is certainly not in the direction of false emphasis. Mrs. Beerbohm Tree's Œnone was much better, and had some fine moments of passion; but the harsh realistic shriek with which the nymph flung herself from the battlements, however effective it might have been in a comedy of Sardou, or in one of Mr. Burnand's farces, was quite out of place in the representation of a Greek tragedy. The classical drama is an imaginative, poetic art, which requires the grand style for its interpretation, and produces its effects by the most ideal means. It is in the operas of Wagner, not in popular melodrama, that any approximation to the Greek method can be found. Better to wear mask and buskin than to mar by any modernity of expression the calm majesty of Melpomene.

As an artistic whole, however, the performance was undoubtedly a great success. It has been much praised for its archæology, but Mr. Godwin is something more than a mere antiquarian. He takes the facts of archæology, but he converts them into artistic and dramatic effects, and the historical accuracy that underlies the visible shapes of beauty that he presents to us, is not by any means the distinguishing quality of the complete work of art. This quality is the absolute unity and harmony of the entire presentation, the presence of one mind controlling the most minute details, and revealing itself only in that true perfection which hides personality. On more than one occasion it seemed to me that the stage was kept a little too dark, and that a purely picturesque effect of light and shade was substituted for the plastic clearness of outline that the Greeks so desired; some objection, too, might be made to the late character of the statue of Aphrodite, which was decidedly post-Periclean; these, however, are unimportant points. The performance was not intended to be an absolute reproduction of the Greek stage in the fifth century before Christ: it was simply the presentation in Greek form of a poem conceived in the Greek spirit; and the secret of its beauty was the perfect correspondence of form and matter, the delicate equilibrium of spirit and sense.

As for the play, it had, of course, to throw away many sweet superfluous graces of expression before it could adapt itself to the conditions of theatrical presentation, but much that is good was retained; and the choruses, which really possess some pure notes of lyric loveliness, were sung in their entirety. Here and there, it is true, occur such lines as—

What wilt thou do? What can the handful still left?—

lines that owe their blank verse character more to the courtesy of the printer than to the genius of the poet, for without rhythm and melody there is no verse at all; and the attempt to fit Greek forms of construction to our English language often gives the work the air of an awkward translation; however, there is a great deal that is pleasing in *Helena in Troas* and, on the whole, the play was worthy of its pageant and the poem deserved the peplums.

It is much to be regretted that Mr. Godwin's beautiful theatre cannot be made a permanent institution. Even looked at from the low standpoint of educational value, such a performance as that given last Monday might be of the greatest service to modern culture; and who knows but a series of these productions might civilise South Kensington and give tone to Brompton?

Still it is something to have shown our artists 'a dream of form in days of thought,' and to have allowed the Philistines to peer into Paradise. And this is what Mr. Godwin has done.

PLEASING AND PRATTLING

(*Pall Mall Gazette*, August 4, 1880.)

Sixty years ago, when Sir Walter Scott was inaugurating an era of historical romance, *The Wolfe of Badenoch* was a very popular book. To us its interest is more archæological than artistic, and its characters seem merely puppets parading in fourteenth-century costume. It is true our grandfathers thought differently. They liked novels in which the heroine exclaims, 'Peace with thine impudence, sir knave. Dost thou dare to speak thus in presence of the Lady Eleanore de Selby? . . . A greybeard's ire shall never—,' while the hero remarks that 'the welkin reddenes i' the west.' In fact, they considered that language like this is exceedingly picturesque and gives the necessary historical perspective. Nowadays, however, few people have the time to read a novel that requires a glossary to explain it, and we fear that without a glossary the general reader will hardly appreciate the value of such expressions as 'gnoffe,' 'bowke,' 'herborow,' 'papelarde,' 'couepe,' 'rethes,' 'pankers,' 'agroted lorel,' and 'horrow tallow-catch,' all of which occur in the first few pages of *The Wolfe of Badenoch*. In a novel we want life, not learning; and, unfortunately, Sir Thomas Lauder lays himself open to the criticism Jonson made on Spenser, that 'in affecting the ancients he writ no language.' Still, there is a healthy spirit of adventure in the book, and no doubt many people will be interested to see the kind of novel the public liked in 1825.

Keep My Secret, by Miss G. M. Robins, is very different. It is quite modern both in manner and in matter. The heroine, Miss Olga Damien, when she is a little girl tries to murder Mr. Victor Burnside. Mr. Burnside, who is tall, blue-eyed and amber-haired, makes her promise never to mention the subject to any one; this, in fact, is the secret that gives the title to the book. The result is that Miss Damien is blackmailed by a fascinating and unscrupulous uncle and is nearly burnt to death in the secret chamber of an old castle. The novel at the end gets too melodramatic in character and the plot becomes a chaos of incoherent incidents, but the writing is clever and bright. It is just the book, in fact, for a summer holiday, as it is never dull and yet makes no demands at all upon the intellect.

Mrs. Chetwynd gives us a new type of widow. As a rule, in fiction widows are delightful, designing and deceitful; but Mrs. Dorriman is not by any means a Cleopatra in crape. She is a weak, retiring woman, very feeble and very feminine, and with the simplicity that is characteristic of such sweet and shallow natures she allows her brother to defraud her of all her property. The widow is rather a bore and the brother is quite a bear, but Margaret Rivers who, to save her sister from poverty, marries a man she does not love, is a cleverly conceived character, and Lady Lyons is an admirable old dowager. The book can be read without any trouble and was probably written without any trouble also. The style is prattling and pleasing.

The plot of *Delamere* is not very new. On the death of her husband, Mrs. De Ruthven discovers that the estates belong by right not to her son Raymond but to her niece Fleurette. As she keeps her knowledge to herself, a series of complications follows, but the cousins are ultimately united in marriage and the story ends happily. Mr. Curzon writes in a clever style, and though its construction is rather clumsy the novel is a thoroughly interesting one.

A Daughter of Fife tells us of the love of a young artist for a Scotch fisher-girl. The character sketches are exceptionally good, especially that of David Promoter, a fisherman who leaves his nets to preach the gospel, and the heroine is quite charming till she becomes civilised. The book is a most artistic combination of romantic feeling with realistic form, and it is pleasant to read descriptions of Scotch scenery that do not represent the land of mist and mountain as a sort of chromolithograph from the Brompton Road.

In Mr. Speight's novel, *A Barren Title*, we have an impoverished earl who receives an allowance from his relations on condition of his remaining single, being all the time secretly married and the father of a grown-up son. The story is improbable and amusing.

On the whole, there is a great deal to be said for our ordinary English novelists. They have all some story to tell, and most of them tell it in an interesting manner. Where they fail is in concentration of style. Their characters are far too eloquent and talk themselves to tatters. What we want is a little more reality and a little less rhetoric. We are most grateful to them that they have not as yet accepted any frigid formula, nor stereotyped themselves into a school, but we wish that they would talk less and think more. They lead us through a barren desert of verbiage to a mirage that they call life: we wander aimlessly through a very wilderness of words in search of one touch of nature. However, one should not be too severe on English novels: they are the only relaxation of the intellectually unemployed.

(1) *The Wolfe of Badenoch: A Historical Romance of the Fourteenth Century*. By Sir Thomas Lauder. (Hamilton, Adams and Co.)

(2) *Keep My Secret*. By G. M. Robins. (Bentley and Son.)

(3) *Mrs. Dorriman*. By the Hon. Mrs. Henry Chetwynd. (Chapman and Hall.)

(4) *Delamere*. By G. Curzon. (Sampson Low, Marston and Co.)

(5) *A Daughter of Fife*. By Amelia Barr. (James Clarke and Co.)

(6) *A Barren Title*. By T. W. Speight. (Chatto and Windus.)

BALZAC IN ENGLISH

(*Pall Mall Gazette*, September 13, 1886.)

Many years ago, in a number of *All the Year Round*, Charles Dickens complained that Balzac was very little read in England, and although since then the public has become more familiar with the great masterpieces of French fiction, still it may be doubted whether the *Comédie Humaine* is at all appreciated or understood by the general run of novel readers. It is really the greatest monument that literature has produced in our century, and M. Taine hardly exaggerates when he says that, after Shakespeare, Balzac is our most important magazine of documents on human nature. Balzac's aim, in fact, was to do for humanity what Buffon had done for the animal creation. As the naturalist studied lions and tigers, so the novelist studied men and women. Yet he was no mere reporter. Photography and *procès-verbal* were not the essentials of his method. Observation gave him the facts of life, but his genius converted facts into truths, and truths into truth. He was, in a word, a marvellous combination of the artistic temperament with the scientific spirit. The latter he bequeathed to his disciples; the former was entirely his own. The distinction between such a book as M. Zola's *L'Assommoir* and such a book as Balzac's *Illusions Perdues* is the distinction between unimaginative realism and imaginative reality. 'All Balzac's characters,' said Baudelaire, 'are gifted with the same ardour of life that animated himself. All his fictions are as deeply coloured as dreams. Every mind is a weapon loaded to the muzzle with will. The very scullions have genius.' He was, of course, accused of being immoral. Few writers who deal directly with life escape that charge. His answer to the accusation was characteristic and conclusive. 'Whoever contributes his stone to the edifice of ideas,' he wrote, 'whoever proclaims an abuse, whoever sets his mark upon an evil to be abolished, always passes for immoral. If you are true in your portraits, if, by dint of daily and nightly toil, you succeed in writing the most difficult language in the world, the word immoral is thrown in your face.' The morals of the personages of the *Comédie Humaine* are simply the morals of the world around us. They are part of the artist's subject-matter; they are not part of his method. If there be any need of censure it is to life, not to literature, that it should be given. Balzac, besides, is essentially universal. He sees life from every point of view. He has no preferences and no prejudices. He does not try to prove anything. He feels that the spectacle of life contains its own secret. 'Il crée un monde et se tait.'

And what a world it is! What a panorama of passions! What a pell-mell of men and women! It was said of Trollope that he increased the number of our acquaintances without adding to our visiting list; but after the *Comédie Humaine* one begins to believe that the only real people are the people who have never existed. Lucien de Rubempré, le Père Goriot, Ursule Mirouët, Marguerite Claës, the Baron Hulot, Madame Marneffe, le Cousin Pons, De Marsay—all bring with them a kind of contagious illusion of life. They have a fierce vitality about them: their existence is fervent and fiery-coloured; we not merely feel for them but we see them—they dominate our fancy and defy scepticism. A steady course of Balzac reduces our living friends to shadows, and our acquaintances to the shadows of shades. Who would care to go out to an evening party to meet Tomkins, the friend of one's boyhood, when one can sit at home with Lucien de Rubempré? It is pleasanter to have the entrée to Balzac's society than to receive cards from all the duchesses in May fair.

In spite of this, there are many people who have declared the *Comédie Humaine* to be indigestible. Perhaps it is: but then what about truffles? Balzac's publisher refused to be disturbed by any such criticism as that. 'Indigestible, is it?' he exclaimed with what, for a publisher, was rare good sense. 'Well, I should hope so; who ever thinks of a dinner that isn't?' And our English publisher, Mr. Routledge, clearly agrees with M. Poulet-Malassis, as he is occupied in producing a complete translation of the *Comédie Humaine*. The two volumes that at present lie before us contain *César Birotteau*, that terrible tragedy of finance, and *L'Illustre Gaudissart*, the apotheosis of the commercial traveller, the *Duchesse de Langeais*, most marvellous of modern love stories, *Le Chef d'Œuvre Inconnu*, from which Mr. Henry James took his *Madonna of the Future*, and that extraordinary romance *Une Passion dans le Désert*. The choice of stories is quite excellent, but the translations are very unequal, and some of them are positively bad. *L'Illustre Gaudissart*, for instance, is full of the most grotesque mistakes, mistakes that would disgrace a schoolboy. 'Bon conseil vaut un œil dans la main' is translated 'Good advice is an egg in the hand'! 'Écus rebelles' is rendered 'rebellious lucre,' and such common expressions as 'faire la barbe,' 'attendre la vente,' 'n'entendre rien,' pâlir sur une affaire,' are all mistranslated. 'Des bois de quoi se faire un cure-dent' is not 'a few trees to slice into toothpicks,' but 'as much timber as would make a toothpick'; 'son horloge enfermée dans une grande armoire oblongue' is not 'a clock which he kept shut up in a large oblong closet' but simply a clock in a tall clock-case; 'journal viager' is not 'an annuity,' 'garce' is not the same as 'farce,' and 'dessins des Indes' are not 'drawings of the Indies.' On the whole, nothing can be worse than this translation, and if Mr. Routledge wishes the public to read his version of the *Comédie Humaine*, he should engage translators who have some slight knowledge of French.

César Birotteau is better, though it is not by any means free from mistakes. 'To suffer under the Maximum' is an absurd rendering of 'subir le maximum'; 'perse' is 'chintz,' not 'Persian chintz'; 'rendre le pain bénit' is not 'to take the wafer'; 'rivière' is hardly a '*fillet* of diamonds'; and to translate 'son cœur avait un calus à l'endroit du loyer' by 'his heart was a callus in the direction of a lease' is an insult to two languages. On the whole, the best version is that of the *Duchesse de Langeais*, though even this leaves much to be desired. Such a sentence as 'to imitate the rough logician who marched before the Pyrrhonians *while denying his own movement*' entirely misses the point of Balzac's 'imiter le rude logicien qui marchait devant les pyrrhoniens, qui niaient le mouvement.'

We fear Mr. Routledge's edition will not do. It is well printed and nicely bound; but his translators do not understand French. It is a great pity, for *La Comédie Humaine* is one of the masterpieces of the age.

Balzac's Novels in English. *The Duchesse de Langeais and Other Stories*; *César Birotteau*. (Routledge and Sons.)

TWO NEW NOVELS

(*Pall Mall Gazette*, September 16, 1880.)

Most modern novels are more remarkable for their crime than for their culture, and Mr. G. Manville Fenn's last venture is no exception to the general rule. *The Master of the Ceremonies* is turbid, terrifying and thrilling. It contains, besides many 'moving accidents by flood and field,' an elopement, an abduction, a bigamous marriage, an attempted assassination, a duel, a suicide, and a murder. The murder, we must acknowledge, is a masterpiece. It would do credit to Gaboriau, and should make Miss Braddon jealous. The *Newgate Calendar* itself contains nothing more fascinating, and what higher praise than this can be given to a sensational novel? Not that Lady Teigne, the hapless victim, is killed in any very new or subtle manner. She is merely strangled in bed, like Desdemona; but the circumstances of the murder are so peculiar that Claire Denville, in common with the reader, suspects her own father of being guilty, while the father is convinced that the real criminal is his eldest son. Stuart Denville himself, the Master of the Ceremonies, is most powerfully drawn. He is a penniless, padded dandy who, by a careful study of the 'grand style' in deportment, has succeeded in making himself the Brummel of the promenade and the autocrat of the Assembly Rooms. A light comedian by profession, he is suddenly compelled to play the principal part in a tragedy. His shallow, trivial nature is forced into the loftiest heroism, the noblest self-sacrifice. He becomes a hero against his will. The butterfly goes to martyrdom, the fop has to become fine. Round this character centres, or rather should centre, the psychological interest of the book, but unfortunately Mr. Fenn has insisted on crowding his story with unnecessary incident. He might have made of his novel 'A Soul's Tragedy,' but he has produced merely a melodrama in three volumes. *The Master of the Ceremonies* is a melancholy example of the fatal influence of Drury Lane on literature. Still, it should be read, for though Mr. Fenn has offered up his genius as a holocaust to Mr. Harris, he is never dull, and his style is on the whole very good. We wish, however, that he would not try to give articulate form to inarticulate exclamations. Such a passage as this is quite dreadful and fails, besides, in producing the effect it aims at:

'He—he—he, hi—hi—hi, hec—hec—hec, ha—ha—ha! ho—ho! Bless my—hey—ha! hey—ha! hugh—hugh—hugh! Oh dear me! Oh—why don't you—heck—heck—heck—heck—heck! shut the—ho—ho—ho—ho—hugh—hugh—window before I—ho—ho—ho—ho!'

This horrible jargon is supposed to convey the impression of a lady coughing. It is, of course, a mere meaningless monstrosity on a par with spelling a sneeze. We hope that Mr. Fenn will not again try these theatrical tricks with language, for he possesses a rare art—the art of telling a story well.

A Statesman's Love, the author tells us in a rather mystical preface, was written 'to show that the alchemist-like transfiguration supposed to be wrought in our whole nature by that passion has no existence in fact,' but it cannot be said to prove this remarkable doctrine.

It is an exaggerated psychological study of a modern woman, a sort of picture by limelight, full of coarse colours and violent contrasts, not by any means devoid of cleverness but essentially false and over-emphasised. The heroine, Helen Rohan by name, tells her own story and, as she takes three volumes to do it in, we weary of the one point of view. Life to be intelligible should be approached from many sides, and valuable though the permanent *ego* may be in philosophy, the permanent *ego* in fiction soon becomes a bore. There are, however, some interesting scenes in the novel, and a good portrait of the Young Pretender, for though the heroine is absolutely a creation of the nineteenth century, the background of the story is historical and deals with the Rebellion of '45. As for the style, it is often original and picturesque; here and there are strong individual touches and brilliant passages; but there is also a good deal of pretence and a good deal of carelessness.

What can be said, for instance, about such expressions as these, taken at random from the second volume,—'evanishing,' 'solitary loneness,' 'in my *then* mood,' 'the bees *might advantage* by to-day,' 'I would not listen reverently as *did the other some* who went,' 'entangling myself in the net of this *retiari*,' and why should Bassanio's beautiful speech in the trial scene be deliberately attributed to Shylock? On the whole, *A Statesman's Love* cannot be said to be an artistic success; but still it shows promise and, some day, the author who, to judge by the style, is probably a woman, may do good work. This, however, will require pruning, prudence and patience. We shall see.

(1) *The Master of the Ceremonies*. By G. Manville Fenn. (Ward and Downey.)

(2) *A Statesman's Love*. By Emile Bauche. (Blackwood and Co.)

BEN JONSON

(*Pall Mall Gazette*, September 20, 1886.)

In selecting Mr. John Addington Symonds to write the life of Ben Jonson for his series of 'English Worthies,' Mr. Lang, no doubt, exercised a wise judgment. Mr. Symonds, like the author of *Volpone*, is a scholar and a man of letters; his book on *Shakspeare's Predecessors* showed a marvellous knowledge of the Elizabethan period, and he is a recognised authority on the Italian Renaissance. The last is not the least of his qualifications. Without a full appreciation of the meaning of the Humanistic movement it is impossible to understand the great struggle between the Classical form and the Romantic spirit which is the chief critical characteristic of the golden age of the English drama, an age when Shakespeare found his chief adversary, not among his contemporaries, but in Seneca, and when Jonson armed himself with Aristotle to win the suffrages of a London audience. Mr. Symonds' book, consequently, will be opened with interest. It does not, of course, contain much that is new about Jonson's life. But the facts of Jonson's life are already well known, and in books of this kind what is true is of more importance than what is new, appreciation more valuable than discovery. Scotchmen, however, will, no doubt, be interested to find that Mr. Symonds has succeeded in identifying Jonson's crest with that of the Johnstones of Annandale, and the story of the way the literary Titan escaped from hanging, by proving that he could read, is graphically told.

On the whole, we have a vivid picture of the man as he lived. Where picturesqueness is required, Mr. Symonds is always good. The usual comparison with Dr. Johnson is, of course, brought out. Few of 'Rare Ben's' biographers spare us that, and the point is possibly a natural one to make. But when Mr. Symonds calls upon us to notice that both men made a journey to Scotland, and that 'each found in a Scotchman his biographer,' the parallel loses all value. There is an M in Monmouth and an M in Macedon, and Drummond of Hawthornden and Boswell of Auchinleck were both born the other side of the Tweed; but from such analogies nothing is to be learned. There is no surer way of destroying a similarity than to strain it.

As for Mr. Symonds' estimate of Jonson's genius, it is in many points quite excellent. He ranks him with the giants rather than with the gods, with those who compel our admiration by their untiring energy and huge strength of intellectual muscle, not with those 'who share the divine gifts of creative imagination and inevitable instinct.' Here he is right. Pelion more than Parnassus was Jonson's home. His art has too much effort about it, too much definite intention. His style lacks the charm of chance. Mr. Symonds is right also in the stress he lays on the extraordinary combination in Jonson's work of the most concentrated realism with encyclopædic erudition. In Jonson's comedies London slang and learned scholarship go hand in hand. Literature was as living a thing to him as life itself. He used his classical lore not merely to give form to his verse, but to give flesh and blood to the persons of his plays. He could build up a breathing creature out of quotations. He made the poets of Greece and Rome terribly modern, and introduced them to the oddest company. His very culture is an element in his coarseness. There are moments when one is tempted to liken him to a beast that has fed off books.

We cannot, however, agree with Mr. Symonds when he says that Jonson 'rarely touched more than the outside of character,' that his men and women are 'the incarnations of abstract properties rather than living human beings,' that they are in fact mere 'masqueraders and mechanical puppets.' Eloquence is a beautiful thing but rhetoric ruins many a critic, and Mr. Symonds is essentially rhetorical. When, for instance, he tells us that 'Jonson made masks,' while 'Dekker and Heywood created souls,' we feel that he is asking us to accept a crude judgment for the sake of a smart antithesis. It is, of course, true that we do not find in Jonson the same growth of character that we find in Shakespeare, and we may admit that most of the characters in Jonson's plays are, so to speak, ready-made. But a ready-made character is not necessarily either mechanical or wooden, two epithets Mr. Symonds uses constantly in his criticism.

We cannot tell, and Shakespeare himself does not tell us, why Iago is evil, why Regan and Goneril have hard hearts, or why Sir Andrew Aguecheek is a fool. It is sufficient that they are what they are, and that nature gives warrant for their existence. If a character in a play is lifelike, if we recognise it as true to nature, we have no right to insist on the author explaining its genesis to us. We must accept it as it is: and in the hands of a good dramatist mere presentation can take the place of analysis, and indeed is often a more dramatic method, because a more direct one. And Jonson's characters are true to nature. They are in no sense abstractions; they are types. Captain Bobadil and Captain Tucca, Sir John Daw and Sir Amorous La Foole, Volpone and Mosca, Subtle and Sir Epicure Mammon, Mrs. Purecraft and the Rabbi Busy are all creatures of flesh and blood, none the less lifelike because they are labelled. In this point Mr. Symonds seems to us unjust towards Jonson.

We think, also, that a special chapter might have been devoted to Jonson as a literary critic. The creative activity of the English Renaissance is so great that its achievements in the sphere of criticism are often overlooked by the student. Then, for the first time, was language treated as an art. The laws of expression and composition were investigated and formularised. The importance of words was recognised. Romanticism, Realism and Classicism fought their first battles. The dramatists are full of literary and art criticisms, and amused the public with slashing articles on one another in the form of plays.

Mr. Symonds, of course, deals with Jonson in his capacity as a critic, and always with just appreciation, but the whole subject is one that deserves fuller and more special treatment.

Some small inaccuracies, too, should be corrected in the second edition. Dryden, for instance, was not 'Jonson's successor on the laureate's throne,' as Mr. Symonds eloquently puts it, for Sir William Davenant came between them, and when one remembers the predominance of rhyme in Shakespeare's early plays, it is too much to say that 'after the production of the first part of *Tamburlaine* blank verse became the regular dramatic metre of the public stage.' Shakespeare did not accept blank verse at once as a gift from Marlowe's hand, but himself arrived at it after a long course of experiments in rhyme. Indeed, some of Mr. Symonds' remarks on Marlowe are very curious. To say of his *Edward II.*, for instance, that it 'is not at all inferior to the work of Shakespeare's younger age,' is very niggardly and inadequate praise, and comes strangely from one who has elsewhere written with such appreciation of Marlowe's great genius; while to call Marlowe Jonson's 'master' is to make for him an impossible claim. In comedy Marlowe has nothing whatever to teach Jonson; in tragedy Jonson sought for the classical not the romantic form.

As for Mr. Symonds' style, it is, as usual, very fluent, very picturesque and very full of colour. Here and there, however, it is really irritating. Such a sentence as 'the tavern had the defects of its quality' is an awkward Gallicism; and when Mr. Symonds, after genially comparing Jonson's blank verse to the front of Whitehall (a comparison, by the way, that would have enraged the poet beyond measure) proceeds to play a fantastic aria on the same string, and tells us that 'Massinger reminds us of the intricacies of Sansovino, Shakespeare of Gothic aisles or heaven's cathedral . . . Ford of glittering Corinthian colonnades, Webster of vaulted crypts, . . . Marlowe of masoned clouds, and Marston, in his better moments, of the fragmentary vigour of a Roman ruin,' one begins to regret that any one ever thought of the unity of the arts. Similes such as these obscure; they do not illumine. To say that Ford is like a glittering Corinthian colonnade adds nothing to our knowledge of either Ford or Greek architecture. Mr. Symonds has written some charming poetry, but his prose, unfortunately, is always poetical prose, never the prose of a poet. Still, the volume is worth reading, though decidedly Mr. Symonds, to use one of his own phrases, has 'the defects of his quality.'

'English Worthies.' Edited by Andrew Lang. *Ben Jonson.* By John Addington Symonds. (Longmans, Green and Co.)

THE POETS' CORNER—I

(*Pall Mall Gazette*, September 27, 1886.)

Among the social problems of the nineteenth century the tramp has always held an important position, but his appearance among the nineteenth-century poets is extremely remarkable. Not that a tramp's mode of life is at all unsuited to the development of the poetic faculty. Far from it! He, if any one, should possess that freedom of mood which is so essential to the artist, for he has no taxes to pay and no relations to worry him. The man who possesses a permanent address, and whose name is to be found in the Directory, is necessarily limited and localised. Only the tramp has absolute liberty of living. Was not Homer himself a vagrant, and did not Thespis go about in a caravan? It is then with feelings of intense expectation that we open the little volume that lies before us. It is entitled *Low Down*, by Two Tramps, and is marvellous even to look at. It is clear that art has at last reached the criminal classes. The cover is of brown paper like the covers of Mr. Whistler's brochures. The printing exhibits every fantastic variation of type, and the pages range in colour from blue to brown, from grey to sage green and from rose pink to chrome yellow. The Philistines may sneer at this chromatic chaos, but we do not. As the painters are always pilfering from the poets, why should not the poet annex the domain of the painter and use colour for the expression of his moods and music: blue for sentiment, and red for passion, grey for cultured melancholy, and green for descriptions? The book, then, is a kind of miniature rainbow, and with all its varied sheets is as lovely as an advertisement hoarding. As for the peripatetics—alas! they are not nightingales. Their note is harsh and rugged, Mr. G. R. Sims is the god of their idolatry, their style is the style of the Surrey Theatre, and we are sorry to see that that disregard of the rights of property which always characterises the able-bodied vagrant is extended by our tramps from the defensible pilfering from hen-roosts to the indefensible pilfering from poets. When we read such lines as:

And builded him a pyramid, four square,
Open to all the sky and every wind,

we feel that bad as poultry-snatching is, plagiarism is worse. *Facilis descensus Averno*! From highway robbery and crimes of violence one sinks gradually to literary petty larceny. However, there are coarsely effective poems in the volume, such as *A Super's Philosophy*, *Dick Hewlett*, a ballad of the Californian school, and *Gentleman Bill*; and there is one rather pretty poem called *The Return of Spring*:

When robins hop on naked boughs,
   And swell their throats with song,
When lab'rers trudge behind their ploughs,
   And blithely whistle their teams along;

   When glints of summer sunshine chase
Park shadows on the distant hills,
And scented tufts of pansies grace
   Moist grots that 'scape rude Borean chills.

The last line is very disappointing. No poet, nowadays, should write of 'rude Boreas'; he might just as well call the dawn 'Aurora,' or say that 'Flora decks the enamelled meads.' But there are some nice touches in the poem, and it is pleasant to find that tramps have their harmless moments. On the whole, the volume, if it is not quite worth reading, is at least worth looking at. The fool's motley in which it is arrayed is extremely curious and extremely characteristic.

Mr. Irwin's muse comes to us more simply clad, and more gracefully. She gains her colour-effect from the poet, not from the publisher. No cockneyism or colloquialism mars the sweetness of her speech. She finds music for every mood, and form for every feeling. In art as in life the law of heredity holds good. *On est toujours fits de quelqu'un*. And so it is easy to see that Mr. Irwin is a fervent admirer of Mr. Matthew Arnold. But he is in no sense a plagiarist. He has succeeded in studying a fine poet without stealing from him—a very difficult thing to do—and though many of the reeds through which he blows have been touched by other lips, yet he is able to draw new music from them. Like most of our younger poets, Mr. Irwin is at his best in his sonnets, and those entitled *The Seeker after God* and *The Pillar of the Empire* are really remarkable. All through this volume, however, one comes across good work, and the descriptions of Indian scenery are excellent. India, in fact, is the picturesque background to these poems, and her monstrous beasts, strange flowers and fantastic birds are used with much subtlety for the production of artistic effect. Perhaps there is a little too much about the pipal-tree, but when we have a proper sense of Imperial unity, no doubt the pipal-tree will be as dear and as familiar to us as the oaks and elms of our own woodlands.

(1) *Low Down*: *Wayside Thoughts in Ballad and Other Verse*. By Two Tramps. (Redway.)

(2) *Rhymes and Renderings*. By H. C. Irwin. (David Stott.)

A RIDE THROUGH MOROCCO

(*Pall Mall Gazette*, October 8, 1886.)

Morocco is a sort of paradox among countries, for though it lies westward of Piccadilly yet it is purely Oriental in character, and though it is but three hours' sail from Europe yet it makes you feel (to use the forcible expression of an American writer) as if you had been 'taken up by the scruff of the neck and set down in the Old Testament.' Mr. Hugh Stutfield has ridden twelve hundred miles through it, penetrated to Fez and Wazan, seen the lovely gate at Mequinez and the Hassen Tower by Rabat, feasted with sheikhs and fought with robbers, lived in an atmosphere of Moors, mosques and mirages, visited the city of the lepers and the slave-market of Sus, and played loo under the shadow of the Atlas Mountains. He is not an Herodotus nor a Sir John Mandeville, but he tells his stories very pleasantly. His book, on the whole, is delightful reading, for though Morocco is picturesque he does not weary us with word-painting; though it is poor he does not bore us with platitudes. Now and then he indulges in a traveller's licence and thrills the simple reader with statements as amazing as they are amusing. The Moorish coinage, he tells us, is so cumbersome that if a man gives you change for half-a-crown you have to hire a donkey to carry it away; the Moorish language is so guttural that no one can ever hope to pronounce it aright who has not been brought up within hearing of the grunting of camels, a steady course of sneezing being, consequently, the only way by which a European can acquire anything like the proper accent; the Sultan does not know how much he is married, but he unquestionably is so to a very large extent: on the principle that you cannot have too much of a good thing a woman is valued in proportion to her stoutness, and so far from there being any reduction made in the marriage-market for taking a quantity, you must pay so much per pound; the Arabs believe the Shereef of Wazan to be such a holy man that, if he is guilty of taking champagne, the forbidden wine is turned into milk as he quaffs it, and if he gets extremely drunk he is merely in a mystical trance.

Mr. Stutfield, however, has his serious moments, and his account of the commerce, government and social life of the Moors is extremely interesting. It must be confessed that the picture he draws is in many respects a very tragic one. The Moors are the masters of a beautiful country and of many beautiful arts, but they are paralysed by their fatalism and pillaged by their rulers. Few races, indeed, have had a more terrible fall than these Moors. Of the great intellectual civilisation of the Arabs no trace remains. The names of Averroes and Almaimon, of Al Abbas and Ben Husa are quite unknown. Fez, once the Athens of Africa, the cradle of the sciences, is now a mere commercial caravansary. Its universities have vanished, its library is almost empty. Freedom of thought has been killed by the Koran, freedom of living by bad government. But Mr. Stutfield is not without hopes for the future. So far from agreeing with Lord Salisbury that 'Morocco may go her own way,' he strongly supports Captain Warren's proposition that we should give up Gibraltar to Spain in exchange for Ceuta, and thereby prevent the Mediterranean from becoming a French lake, and give England a new granary for corn. The Moorish Empire, he warns us, is rapidly breaking up, and if in the 'general scramble for Africa' that has already begun, the French gain possession of Morocco, he points out that our supremacy over the Straits will be lost. Whatever may be thought of Mr. Stutfield's political views, and his suggestions for 'multiple control' and 'collective European action,' there is no doubt that in Morocco England has interests to defend and a mission to pursue, and this part of the book should be carefully studied. As for the general reader who, we fear, is not as a rule interested in the question of 'multiple control,' if he is a sportsman, he will find in *El Magreb* a capital account of pig-sticking; if he is artistic, he will be delighted to know that the importation of magenta into Morocco is strictly prohibited; if criminal jurisprudence has any charms for him, he can examine a code that punishes slander by rubbing cayenne pepper into the lips of the offender; and if he is merely lazy, he can take a pleasant ride of twelve hundred miles in Mr. Stutfield's company without stirring out of his armchair.

El Magreb: *Twelve Hundred Miles' Ride through Morocco*. By Hugh Stutfield. (Sampson Low, Marston and Co.)

THE CHILDREN OF THE POETS

(*Pall Mall Gazette*, October 14, 1886.)

The idea of this book is exceedingly charming. As children themselves are the perfect flowers of life, so a collection of the best poems written on children should be the most perfect of all anthologies. Yet, the book itself is not by any means a success. Many of the loveliest child-poems in our literature are excluded and not a few feeble and trivial poems are inserted. The editor's work is characterised by sins of omission and of commission, and the collection, consequently, is very incomplete and very unsatisfactory. Andrew Marvell's exquisite poem *The Picture of Little T. C.*, for instance, does not appear in Mr. Robertson's volume, nor the *Young Love* of the same author, nor the beautiful elegy Ben Jonson wrote on the death of Salathiel Pavy, the little boy-actor of his plays. Waller's verses also, *To My Young Lady Lucy Sidney*, deserve a place in an anthology of this kind, and so do Mr. Matthew Arnold's lines *To a Gipsy Child*, and Edgar Allan Poe's *Annabel Lee*, a little lyric full of strange music and strange romance. There is possibly much to be said in favour of such a poem as that which ends with

And I thank my God with falling tears
For the things in the bottom drawer:

but how different it is from

I was a child, and she was a child,
In this kingdom by the sea;
But we loved with a love that was more than love—
I and my Annabel Lee;
With a love that the wingèd Seraphs of Heaven
Coveted her and me

The selection from Blake, again, is very incomplete, many of the loveliest poems being excluded, such as those on *The Little Girl Lost* and *The Little Girl Found*, the *Cradle Song*, *Infant Joy*, and others; nor can we find Sir Henry Wotton's *Hymn upon the Birth of Prince Charles*, Sir William Jones's dainty four-line epigram on *The Babe*, or the delightful lines *To T. L. H., A Child*, by Charles Lamb.

The gravest omission, however, is certainly that of Herrick. Not a single poem of his appears in Mr. Robertson's collection. And yet no English poet has written of children with more love and grace and delicacy. His *Ode on the Birth of Our Saviour*, his poem *To His Saviour, A Child: A Present by a Child*, his *Graces for Children*, and his many lovely epitaphs on children are all of them exquisite works of art, simple, sweet and sincere.

An English anthology of child-poems that excludes Herrick is as an English garden without its roses and an English woodland without its singing birds; and for one verse of Herrick we would gladly give in exchange even those long poems by Mr. Ashby-Sterry, Miss Menella Smedley, and Mr. Lewis Morris (of Penrhyn), to which Mr. Robertson has assigned a place in his collection. Mr. Robertson, also, should take care when he publishes a poem to publish it correctly. Mr. Bret Harte's *Dickens in Camp*, for instance, is completely spoiled by two ridiculous misprints. In the first line 'dimpling' is substituted for 'drifting' to the entire ruin of rhyme and reason, and in the ninth verse 'the *pensive glory* that fills the Kentish hills' appears as 'the *Persian* glory . . . ' with a large capital P! Mistakes such as these are quite unpardonable, and make one feel that, perhaps, after all it was fortunate for Herrick that he was left out. A poet can survive everything but a misprint.

As for Mr. Robertson's preface, like most of the prefaces in the Canterbury Series, it is very carelessly written. Such a sentence as 'I . . . believe that Mrs. Piatt's poems, in particular, will come to many readers, fresh, as well as delightful contributions from across the ocean,' is painful to read. Nor is the matter much better than the manner. It is fantastic to say that Raphael's pictures of the Madonna and Child dealt a deadly blow to the monastic life, and to say, with reference to Greek art, that 'Cupid by the side of Venus enables us to forget that most of her sighs are wanton' is a very crude bit of art criticism indeed. Wordsworth, again, should hardly be spoken of as one who 'was not, in the general, a man from whom human sympathies welled profusely,' but this criticism is as nothing compared to the passage where Mr. Robertson tells us that the scene between Arthur and Hubert in *King John* is not true to nature because the child's pleadings for his life are playful as well as piteous. Indeed, Mr. Robertson, forgetting Mamillius as completely as he misunderstands Arthur, states very clearly that Shakespeare has not given us any deep readings of child nature. Paradoxes are always charming, but judgments such as these are not paradoxical; they are merely provincial.

On the whole, Mr. Robertson's book will not do. It is, we fully admit, an industrious compilation, but it is not an anthology, it is not a selection of the best, for it lacks the discrimination and good taste which is the essence of selection, and for the want of which no amount of industry can atone. The child-poems of our literature have still to be edited.

The Children of the Poets: *An Anthology from English and American Writers of Three Generations*. Edited, with an Introduction, by Eric S. Robertson. (Walter Scott.)

NEW NOVELS

(*Pall Mall Gazette*, October 28, 1886.)

Astray: A Tale of a Country Town, is a very serious volume. It has taken four people to write it, and even to read it requires assistance. Its dulness is premeditated and deliberate and comes from a laudable desire to rescue fiction from flippancy. It is, in fact, tedious from the noblest motives and wearisome through its good intentions. Yet the story itself is not an uninteresting one. Quite the contrary. It deals with the attempt of a young doctor to build up a noble manhood on the ruins of a wasted youth. Burton King, while little more than a reckless lad, forges the name of a dying man, is arrested and sent to penal servitude for seven years. On his discharge he comes to live with his sisters in a little country town and finds that his real punishment begins when he is free, for prison has made him a pariah. Still, through the nobility and self-sacrifice of his life, he gradually wins himself a position, and ultimately marries the prettiest girl in the book. His character is, on the whole, well drawn, and the authors have almost succeeded in making him good without making him priggish. The method, however, by which the story is told is extremely tiresome. It consists of an interminable series of long letters by different people and of extracts from various diaries. The book consequently is piecemeal and unsatisfactory. It fails in producing any unity of effect. It contains the rough material for a story, but is not a completed work of art. It is, in fact, more of a notebook than a novel. We fear that too many collaborators are like too many cooks and spoil the dinner. Still, in this tale of a country town there are certain solid qualities, and it is a book that one can with perfect safety recommend to other people.

Miss Rhoda Broughton belongs to a very different school. No one can ever say of her that she has tried to separate flippancy from fiction, and whatever harsh criticisms may be passed on the construction of her sentences, she at least possesses that one touch of vulgarity that makes the whole world kin. We are sorry, however, to see from a perusal of *Betty's Visions* that Miss Broughton has been attending the meetings of the Psychical Society in search of copy. Mysticism is not her mission, and telepathy should be left to Messrs. Myers and Gurney. In Philistia lies Miss Broughton's true sphere, and to Philistia she should return. She knows more about the vanities of this world than about this world's visions, and a possible garrison town is better than an impossible ghost-land.

That Other Person, who gives Mrs. Alfred Hunt the title for her three-volume novel, is a young girl, by name Hester Langdale, who for the sake of Mr. Godfrey Daylesford sacrifices everything a woman can sacrifice, and, on his marrying some one else, becomes a hospital nurse. The hospital nurse idea is perhaps used by novelists a little too often in cases of this kind; still, it has an artistic as well as an ethical value. The interest of the story centres, however, in Mr. Daylesford, who marries not for love but for ambition, and is rather severely punished for doing so. Mrs. Daylesford has a sister called Polly who develops, according to the approved psychological method, from a hobbledehoy girl into a tender sweet woman. Polly is delightfully drawn, but the most attractive character in the book, strangely enough, is Mr. Godfrey Daylesford. He is very weak, but he is very charming. So charming indeed is he, that it is only when one closes the book that one thinks of censuring him. While we are in direct contact with him we are fascinated. Such a character has at any rate the morality of truth about it. Here literature has faithfully followed life. Mrs. Hunt writes a very pleasing style, bright and free from affectation. Indeed, everything in her work is clever except the title.

A Child of the Revolution is by the accomplished authoress of the *Atelier du Lys*. The scene opens in France in 1793, and the plot is extremely ingenious. The wife of Jacques Vaudes, a Lyons deputy, loses by illness her baby girl while her husband is absent in Paris where he has gone to see Danton. At the instigation of an old priest she adopts a child of the same age, a little orphan of noble birth, whose parents have died in the Reign of Terror, and passes it off as her own. Her husband, a stern and ardent Republican, worships the child with a passion like that of Jean Valjean for Cosette, nor is it till she has grown to perfect womanhood that he discovers that he has given his love to the daughter of his enemy. This is a noble story, but the workmanship, though good of its kind, is hardly adequate to the idea. The style lacks grace, movement and variety. It is correct but monotonous. Seriousness, like property, has its duties as well as its rights, and the first duty of a novel is to please. *A Child of the Revolution* hardly does that. Still it has merits.

Aphrodite is a romance of ancient Hellas. The supposed date, as given in the first line of Miss Safford's admirable translation, is 551 B.C. This, however, is probably a misprint. At least, we cannot believe that so careful an archæologist as Ernst Eckstein would talk of a famous school of sculpture existing at Athens in the sixth century, and the whole character of the civilisation is of a much later date. The book may be described as a new setting of the tale of Acontius and Cydippe, and though Eckstein is a sort of literary Tadema and cares more for his backgrounds than he does for his figures, still he can tell a story very well, and his hero is made of flesh and blood. As regards the style, the Germans have not the same feeling as we have about technicalities in literature. To our ears such words as 'phoreion,' 'secos,' 'oionistes,' 'Thyrides' and the like sound harshly in a novel and give an air of pedantry, not of picturesqueness. Yet in its tone *Aphrodite* reminds us of the late Greek novels. Indeed, it might be one of the lost tales of Miletus. It deserves to have many readers and a better binding.

(1) *Astray: A Tale of a Country Town*. By Charlotte M. Yonge, Mary Bramston, Christabel Coleridge and Esmé Stuart. (Hatchards.)

(2) *Betty's Visions*. By Rhoda Broughton. (Routledge and Sons.)

(3) *That Other Person*. By Mrs. Alfred Hunt. (Chatto and Windus.)

(4) *A Child of the Revolution*. By the Author of *Mademoiselle Mori*. (Hatchards.)

(5) *Aphrodite*. Translated from the German of Ernst Eckstein by Mary J. Safford. (New York: Williams and Gottsberger; London: Trübner and Co.)

A POLITICIAN'S POETRY

(*Pall Mall Gazette*, November 3, 1886.)

Although it is against etiquette to quote Greek in Parliament, Homer has always been a great favourite with our statesmen and, indeed, may be said to be almost a factor in our political life. For as the cross-benches form a refuge for those who have no minds to make up, so those who cannot make up their minds always take to Homeric studies. Many of our leaders have sulked in their tents with Achilles after some violent political crisis and, enraged at the fickleness of fortune, more than one has given up to poetry what was obviously meant for party. It would be unjust, however, to regard Lord Carnarvon's translation of the *Odyssey* as being in any sense a political manifesto. Between Calypso and the colonies there is no connection, and the search for Penelope has nothing to do with the search for a policy. The love of literature alone has produced this version of the marvellous Greek epic, and to the love of literature alone it appeals. As Lord Carnarvon says very truly in his preface, each generation in turn delights to tell the story of Odysseus in its own language, for the story is one that never grows old.

Of the labours of his predecessors in translation Lord Carnarvon makes ample recognition, though we acknowledge that we do not consider Pope's *Homer* 'the work of a great poet,' and we must protest that there is more in Chapman than 'quaint Elizabethan conceits.' The metre he has selected is blank verse, which he regards as the best compromise between 'the inevitable redundancy of rhyme and the stricter accuracy of prose.' This choice is, on the whole, a sensible one. Blank verse undoubtedly gives the possibility of a clear and simple rendering of the original. Upon the other hand, though we may get Homer's meaning, we often miss his music. The ten-syllabled line brings but a faint echo of the long roll of the Homeric hexameter, its rapid movement and continuous harmony. Besides, except in the hands of a great master of song, blank verse is apt to be tedious, and Lord Carnarvon's use of the weak ending, his habit of closing the line with an unimportant word, is hardly consistent with the stateliness of an epic, however valuable it might be in dramatic verse. Now and then, also, Lord Carnarvon exaggerates the value of the Homeric adjective, and for one word in the Greek gives us a whole line in the English. The simple εσπεριος, for instance, is converted into 'And when the shades of evening fall around,' in the second book, and elsewhere purely decorative epithets are expanded into elaborate descriptions. However, there are many pleasing qualities in Lord Carnarvon's verse, and though it may not contain much subtlety of melody, still it has often a charm and sweetness of its own.

The description of Calypso's garden, for example, is excellent:

Around the grotto grew a goodly grove,
Alder, and poplar, and the cypress sweet;
And the deep-winged sea-birds found their haunt,
And owls and hawks, and long-tongued cormorants,
Who joy to live upon the briny flood.
And o'er the face of the deep cave a vine
Wove its wild tangles and clustering grapes.
Four fountains too, each from the other turned,
Poured their white waters, whilst the grassy meads
Bloomed with the parsley and the violet's flower.

The story of the Cyclops is not very well told. The grotesque humour of the Giant's promise hardly appears in

Thee then, Noman, last of all
Will I devour, and this thy gift shall be,

and the bitter play on words Odysseus makes, the pun on μητις, in fact, is not noticed. The idyll of Nausicaa, however, is very gracefully translated, and there is a great deal that is delightful in the Circe episode. For simplicity of diction this is also very good:

So to Olympus through the woody isle
Hermes departed, and I went my way
To Circe's halls, sore troubled in my mind.
But by the fair-tressed Goddess' gate I stood,
And called upon her, and she heard my voice,
And forth she came and oped the shining doors
And bade me in; and sad at heart I went.
Then did she set me on a stately chair,
Studded with silver nails of cunning work,

32

With footstool for my feet, and mixed a draught
Of her foul witcheries in golden cup,
For evil was her purpose. From her hand
I took the cup and drained it to the dregs,
Nor felt the magic charm; but with her rod
She smote me, and she said, 'Go, get thee hence
And herd thee with thy fellows in the stye.'
So spake she, and straightway I drew my sword
Upon the witch, and threatened her with death.

Lord Carnarvon, on the whole, has given us a very pleasing version of the first half of the *Odyssey*. His translation is done in a scholarly and careful manner and deserves much praise. It is not quite Homer, of course, but no translation can hope to be that, for no work of art can afford to lose its style or to give up the manner that is essential to it. Still, those who cannot read Greek will find much beauty in it, and those who can will often gain a charming reminiscence.

The Odyssey of Homer. Books I.-XII. Translated into English Verse by the Earl of Carnarvon. (Macmillan and Co.)

MR. SYMONDS' HISTORY OF THE RENAISSANCE

(*Pall Mall Gazette*, November 10, 1886.)

Mr. Symonds has at last finished his history of the Italian Renaissance. The two volumes just published deal with the intellectual and moral conditions in Italy during the seventy years of the sixteenth century which followed the coronation of Charles the Fifth at Bologna, an era to which Mr. Symonds gives the name of the Catholic Reaction, and they contain a most interesting and valuable account of the position of Spain in the Italian peninsula, the conduct of the Tridentine Council, the specific organisation of the Holy Office and the Company of Jesus, and the state of society upon which those forces were brought to bear. In his previous volumes Mr. Symonds had regarded the past rather as a picture to be painted than as a problem to be solved. In these two last volumes, however, he shows a clearer appreciation of the office of history. The art of the picturesque chronicler is completed by something like the science of the true historian, the critical spirit begins to manifest itself, and life is not treated as a mere spectacle, but the laws of its evolution and progress are investigated also. We admit that the desire to represent life at all costs under dramatic conditions still accompanies Mr. Symonds, and that he hardly realises that what seems romance to us was harsh reality to those who were engaged in it. Like most dramatists, also, he is more interested in the psychological exceptions than in the general rule. He has something of Shakespeare's sovereign contempt of the masses. The people stir him very little, but he is fascinated by great personalities. Yet it is only fair to remember that the age itself was one of exaggerated individualism and that literature had not yet become a mouthpiece for the utterances of humanity. Men appreciated the aristocracy of intellect, but with the democracy of suffering they had no sympathy. The cry from the brickfields had still to be heard. Mr. Symonds' style, too, has much improved. Here and there, it is true, we come across traces of the old manner, as in the apocalyptic vision of the seven devils that entered Italy with the Spaniard, and the description of the Inquisition as a Belial-Moloch, a 'hideous idol whose face was blackened with soot from burning human flesh.' Such a sentence, also, as 'over the Dead Sea of social putrefaction floated the sickening oil of Jesuitical hypocrisy,' reminds us that rhetoric has not yet lost its charms for Mr. Symonds. Still, on the whole, the style shows far more reserve, balance and sobriety, than can be found in the earlier volumes where violent antithesis forms the predominant characteristic, and accuracy is often sacrificed to an adjective.

Amongst the most interesting chapters of the book are those on the Inquisition, on Sarpi, the great champion of the severance of Church from State, and on Giordano Bruno. Indeed the story of Bruno's life, from his visit to London and Oxford, his sojourn in Paris and wanderings through Germany, down to his betrayal at Venice and martyrdom at Rome, is most powerfully told, and the estimate of the value of his philosophy and the relation he holds to modern science, is at once just and appreciative. The account also of Ignatius Loyola and the rise of the Society of Jesus is extremely interesting, though we cannot think that Mr. Symonds is very happy in his comparison of the Jesuits to 'fanatics laying stones upon a railway' or 'dynamiters blowing up an emperor or a corner of Westminster Hall.' Such a judgment is harsh and crude in expression and more suitable to the clamour of the Protestant Union than to the dignity of the true historian. Mr. Symonds, however, is rarely deliberately unfair, and there is no doubt but that his work on the Catholic Reaction is a most valuable contribution to modern history—so valuable, indeed, that in the account he gives of the Inquisition in Venice it would be well worth his while to bring the picturesque fiction of the text into some harmony with the plain facts of the footnote.

On the poetry of the sixteenth century Mr. Symonds has, of course, a great deal to say, and on such subjects he always writes with ease, grace, and delicacy of perception. We admit that we weary sometimes of the continual application to literature of epithets appropriate to plastic and pictorial art. The conception of the unity of the arts is certainly of great value, but in the present condition of criticism it seems to us that it would be more useful to emphasise the fact that each art has its separate method of expression. The essay on Tasso, however, is delightful reading, and the position the poet holds towards modern music and modern sentiment is analysed with much subtlety. The essay on Marino also is full of interest. We have often wondered whether those who talk so glibly of Euphuism and Marinism in literature have ever read either *Euphues* or the *Adone*. To the latter they can have no better guide than Mr. Symonds, whose description of the poem is most fascinating. Marino, like many greater men, has suffered much from his disciples, but he himself was a master of graceful fancy and of exquisite felicity of phrase; not, of course, a great poet but certainly an artist in poetry and one to whom language is indebted. Even those conceits that Mr. Symonds feels bound to censure have something charming about them. The continual use of periphrases is undoubtedly a grave fault in style, yet who but a pedant would really quarrel with such periphrases as *sirena de' boschi* for the nightingale, or *il novella Edimione* for Galileo?

From the poets Mr. Symonds passes to the painters: not those great artists of Florence and Venice of whom he has already written, but the Eclectics of Bologna, the Naturalists of Naples and Rome. This chapter is too polemical to be pleasant. The one on music is much better, and Mr. Symonds gives us a most interesting description of the gradual steps by which the Italian genius passed from poetry and painting to melody and song, till the whole of Europe thrilled with the marvel and mystery of this new language of the soul. Some small details should perhaps be noticed. It is hardly accurate, for instance, to say that Monteverde's *Orfeo* was the first form of the recitative-Opera, as Peri's *Dafne* and *Euridice* and Cavaliere's *Rappresentazione* preceded it by some years, and it is somewhat exaggerated to say that 'under the régime of the Commonwealth the national growth of English music received a check from which it never afterwards recovered,' as it was with Cromwell's auspices that the first English Opera was produced, thirteen years before any Opera was regularly established in Paris. The fact that England did not make such development in music as Italy and Germany did, must be ascribed to other causes than 'the prevalence of Puritan opinion.'

These, however, are minor points. Mr. Symonds is to be warmly congratulated on the completion of his history of the Renaissance in Italy. It is a most wonderful monument of literary labour, and its value to the student of Humanism cannot be doubted. We have often had occasion to differ from Mr. Symonds on questions of detail, and we have more than once felt it our duty to protest against the rhetoric and over-emphasis of his style, but we fully recognise the importance of his work and the impetus he has given to the study of one of the vital periods of the world's history. Mr. Symonds' learning has not made him a pedant; his culture has widened not narrowed his sympathies, and though he can hardly be called a great historian, yet he will always occupy a place in English literature as one of the remarkable men of letters in the nineteenth century.

Renaissance in Italy: The Catholic Reaction. In Two Parts. By John Addington Symonds. (Smith, Elder and Co.)

A 'JOLLY' ART CRITIC

(*Pall Mall Gazette*, November 18, 1886.)

There is a healthy bank-holiday atmosphere about this book which is extremely pleasant. Mr. Quilter is entirely free from affectation of any kind. He rollicks through art with the recklessness of the tourist and describes its beauties with the enthusiasm of the auctioneer. To many, no doubt, he will seem to be somewhat blatant and bumptious, but we prefer to regard him as being simply British. Mr. Quilter is the apostle of the middle classes, and we are glad to welcome his gospel. After listening so long to the Don Quixote of art, to listen once to Sancho Panza is both salutary and refreshing.

As for his *Sententiæ*, they differ very widely in character and subject. Some of them are ethical, such as 'Humility may be carried too far'; some literary, as 'For one Froude there are a thousand Mrs. Markhams'; and some scientific, as 'Objects which are near display more detail than those which are further off.' Some, again, breathe a fine spirit of optimism, as 'Picturesqueness is the birthright of the bargee'; others are jubilant, as 'Paint firm and be jolly'; and many are purely autobiographical, such as No. 97, 'Few of us understand what it is that we mean by Art.' Nor is Mr. Quilter's manner less interesting than his matter. He tells us that at this festive season of the year, with Christmas and roast beef looming before us, 'Similes drawn from eating and its results occur most readily to the mind.' So he announces that 'Subject is the diet of painting,' that 'Perspective is the bread of art,' and that 'Beauty is in some way like jam'; drawings, he points out, 'are not made by recipe like puddings,' nor is art composed of 'suet, raisins, and candied peel,' though Mr. Cecil Lawson's landscapes do 'smack of indigestion.' Occasionally, it is true, he makes daring excursions into other realms of fancy, as when he says that 'in the best Reynolds landscapes, one seems *to smell the sawdust*,' or that 'advance in art is of a *kangaroo* character'; but, on the whole, he is happiest in his eating similes, and the secret of his style is evidently 'La métaphore vient en mangeant.'

About artists and their work Mr. Quilter has, of course, a great deal to say. Sculpture he regards as 'Painting's poor relation'; so, with the exception of a jaunty allusion to the 'rough modelling' of Tanagra figurines he hardly refers at all to the plastic arts; but on painters he writes with much vigour and joviality. Holbein's wonderful Court portraits naturally do not give him much pleasure; in fact, he compares them as works of art to the sham series of Scottish kings at Holyrood; but Doré, he tells us, had a wider imaginative range in all subjects where the gloomy and the terrible played leading parts than probably any artist who ever lived, and may be called 'the Carlyle of artists.' In Gainsborough he sees 'a plainness almost amounting to brutality,' while 'vulgarity and snobbishness' are the chief qualities he finds in Sir Joshua Reynolds. He has grave doubts whether Sir Frederick Leighton's work is really 'Greek, after all,' and can discover in it but little of 'rocky Ithaca.' Mr. Poynter, however, is a cart-horse compared to the President, and Frederick Walker was 'a dull Greek' because he had no 'sympathy with poetry.' Linnell's pictures, are 'a sort of "Up, Guards, and at 'em" paintings,' and Mason's exquisite idylls are 'as national as a Jingo poem'! Mr. Birket Foster's landscapes 'smile at one much in the same way that Mr. Carker used to "flash his teeth,"' and Mr. John Collier gives his sitter 'a cheerful slap on the back, before he says, like a shampooer in a Turkish bath, "Next man!"' Mr. Herkomer's art is, 'if not a catch-penny art, at all events a catch-many-pounds art,' and Mr. W. B. Richmond is a 'clever trifler,' who 'might do really good work' 'if he would employ his time in learning to paint.' It is obviously unnecessary for us to point out how luminous these criticisms are, how delicate in expression. The remarks on Sir Joshua Reynolds alone exemplify the truth of *Sententia* No. 19, 'From a picture we gain but little more than we bring.' On the general principles of art Mr. Quilter writes with equal lucidity. That there is a difference between colour and colours, that an artist, be he portrait-painter or dramatist, always reveals himself in his manner, are ideas that can hardly be said to occur to him; but Mr. Quilter really does his best and bravely faces every difficulty in modern art, with the exception of Mr. Whistler. Painting, he tells us, is 'of a different quality to mathematics,' and finish in art is 'adding more fact'! Portrait painting is a bad pursuit for an emotional artist as it destroys his personality and his sympathy; however, even for the emotional artist there is hope, as a portrait can be converted into a picture 'by adding to the likeness of the sitter some dramatic interest or some picturesque adjunct'! As for etchings, they are of two kinds—British and foreign. The latter fail in 'propriety.' Yet, 'really fine etching is as free and easy as is the chat between old chums at midnight over a smoking-room fire.' Consonant with these rollicking views of art is Mr. Quilter's healthy admiration for 'the three primary colours: red, blue, and yellow.' Any one, he points out, 'can paint in good tone who paints only in black and white,' and 'the great sign of a good decorator' is 'his capability of doing without neutral tints.' Indeed, on decoration Mr. Quilter is almost eloquent. He laments most bitterly the divorce that has been made between decorative art and 'what we usually call "pictures,"' makes the customary appeal to the *Last Judgment*, and reminds us that in the great days of art Michael Angelo was the 'furnishing upholsterer.' With the present tendencies of decorative art in England Mr. Quilter, consequently, has but little sympathy, and he makes a gallant appeal to the British householder to stand no more nonsense. Let the honest fellow, he says, on his return from his counting-house tear down the Persian hangings, put a chop on the Anatolian plate, mix some toddy in the Venetian glass, and carry his wife off to the National Gallery to look at 'our own Mulready'! And then the picture he draws of the ideal home, where everything, though ugly, is hallowed by domestic memories, and where beauty appeals not to the heartless eye but the family affections; 'baby's chair there, and the mother's work-basket . . . near the fire, and the ornaments Fred brought home from India on the mantel-board'! It is really impossible not to be touched by so charming a description. How valuable, also, in connection with house decoration is *Sententia* No. 351, 'There is nothing furnishes a room like a bookcase, *and plenty of books in it.*' How cultivated the mind that thus raises literature to the position of upholstery and puts thought on a level with the antimacassar!

And, finally, for the young workers in art Mr. Quilter has loud words of encouragement. With a sympathy that is absolutely reckless of grammar, he knows from experience 'what an amount of study and mental strain *are* involved in painting a bad picture honestly'; he exhorts them (*Sententia* No. 267) to 'go on quite bravely and sincerely making mess after mess from Nature,' and while sternly warning them that there is something wrong if they do not 'feel *washed out* after each drawing,' he still urges them to 'put a new piece of goods in the window' every morning. In fact, he is quite severe on Mr. Ruskin for not recognising that 'a picture should denote the frailty of man,' and remarks with pleasing courtesy and felicitous grace that 'many phases of feeling . . . are as much a dead letter to this great art teacher, as Sanskrit to *an Islington cabman.*' Nor is Mr. Quilter one of those who fails to practice what he preaches. Far from it. He goes on quite bravely and sincerely making mess after mess from literature, and misquotes Shakespeare, Wordsworth, Alfred de Musset, Mr. Matthew Arnold, Mr. Swinburne, and Mr. Fitzgerald's *Rubaiyat*, in strict accordance with *Sententia* No. 251, which tells us that 'Work must be abominable if it is ever going to be good.' Only, unfortunately, his own work never does get good. Not content with his misquotations, he misspells the names of such well-known painters as Madox-Brown, Bastien Lepage and Meissonier, hesitates between Ingrès and Ingres, talks of *Mr.* Millais and *Mr.* Linton, alludes to Mr. Frank Holl simply as 'Hall,' speaks with easy familiarity of Mr. Burne-Jones as 'Jones,' and writes of the artist whom he calls 'old Chrome' with an affection that reminds us of Mr. Tulliver's love for Jeremy Taylor. On the whole, the book will not do. We fully admit that it is extremely amusing and, no doubt, Mr. Quilter is quite earnest in his endeavours to elevate art to the dignity of manual labour, but the extraordinary vulgarity of the style alone will always be sufficient to prevent these *Sententiæ Artis* from being anything more than curiosities of literature. Mr. Quilter has missed his chance; for he has failed even to make himself the Tupper of Painting.

Sententiæ: Artis: First Principles of Art for Painters and Picture Lovers. By Harry Quilter, M.A. (Isbister.)

[A reply to this review appeared on November 23.]

A SENTIMENTAL JOURNEY THROUGH LITERATURE

(*Pall Mall Gazette*, December 1, 1886.)

This is undoubtedly an interesting book, not merely through its eloquence and earnestness, but also through the wonderful catholicity of taste that it displays. Mr. Noel has a passion for panegyric. His eulogy on Keats is closely followed by a eulogy on Whitman, and his praise of Lord Tennyson is equalled only by his praise of Mr. Robert Buchanan. Sometimes, we admit, we would like a little more fineness of discrimination, a little more delicacy of perception. Sincerity of utterance is valuable in a critic, but sanity of judgment is more valuable still, and Mr. Noel's judgments are not always distinguished by their sobriety. Many of the essays, however, are well worth reading. The best is certainly that on *The Poetic Interpretation of Nature*, in which Mr. Noel claims that what is called by Mr. Ruskin the 'pathetic fallacy of literature' is in reality a vital emotional truth; but the essays on Hugo and Mr. Browning are good also; the little paper entitled *Rambles by the Cornish Seas* is a real marvel of delightful description, and the monograph on Chatterton has a good deal of merit, though we must protest very strongly against Mr. Noel's idea that Chatterton must be modernised before he can be appreciated. Mr. Noel has absolutely no right whatsoever to alter Chatterton's' yonge damoyselles' and '*anlace* fell' into 'youthful damsels' and '*weapon* fell,' for Chatterton's archaisms were an essential part of his inspiration and his method. Mr. Noel in one of his essays speaks with much severity of those who prefer sound to sense in poetry and, no doubt, this is a very wicked thing to do; but he himself is guilty of a much graver sin against art when, in his desire to emphasise the meaning of Chatterton, he destroys Chatterton's music. In the modernised version he gives of the wonderful *Songe to Ælla*, he mars by his corrections the poem's metrical beauty, ruins the rhymes and robs the music of its echo. Nineteenth-century restorations have done quite enough harm to English architecture without English poetry being treated in the same manner, and we hope that when Mr. Noel writes again about Chatterton he will quote from the poet's verse, not from a publisher's version.

This, however, is not by any means the chief blot on Mr. Noel's book. The fault of his book is that it tells us far more about his own personal feelings than it does about the qualities of the various works of art that are criticised. It is in fact a diary of the emotions suggested by literature, rather than any real addition to literary criticism, and we fancy that many of the poets about whom he writes so eloquently would be not a little surprised at the qualities he finds in their work. Byron, for instance, who spoke with such contempt of what he called 'twaddling about trees and babbling o' green fields'; Byron who cried, 'Away with this cant about nature! A good poet can imbue a pack of cards with more poetry than inhabits the forests of America,' is claimed by Mr. Noel as a true nature-worshipper and Pantheist along with Wordsworth and Shelley; and we wonder what Keats would have thought of a critic who gravely suggests that *Endymion* is 'a parable of the development of the individual soul.' There are two ways of misunderstanding a poem. One is to misunderstand it and the other to praise it for qualities that it does not possess. The latter is Mr. Noel's method, and in his anxiety to glorify the artist he often does so at the expense of the work of art.

Mr. Noel also is constantly the victim of his own eloquence. So facile is his style that it constantly betrays him into crude and extravagant statements. Rhetoric and over-emphasis are the dangers that Mr. Noel has not always succeeded in avoiding. It is extravagant, for instance, to say that all great poetry has been 'pictorial,' or that Coleridge's *Knight's Grave* is worth many *Kubla Khans*, or that Byron has 'the splendid imperfection of an Æschylus,' or that we had lately 'one dramatist living in England, and only one, who could be compared to Hugo, and that was Richard Hengist Horne,' and that 'to find an English dramatist of the same order before him we must go back to Sheridan if not to Otway.' Mr. Noel, again, has a curious habit of classing together the most incongruous names and comparing the most incongruous works of art. What is gained by telling us that 'Sardanapalus' is perhaps hardly equal to 'Sheridan,' that Lord Tennyson's ballad of *The Revenge* and his *Ode on the Death of the Duke of Wellington* are worthy of a place beside Thomson's *Rule Britannia*, that Edgar Allan Poe, Disraeli and Mr. Alfred Austin are artists of note whom we may affiliate on Byron, and that if Sappho and Milton 'had not high genius, they would be justly reproached as sensational'? And surely it is a crude judgment that classes Baudelaire, of all poets, with Marini and mediæval troubadours, and a crude style that writes of 'Goethe, Shelley, Scott, and Wilson,' for a mortal should not thus intrude upon the immortals, even though he be guilty of holding with them that *Cain* is 'one of the finest poems in the English language.' It is only fair, however, to add that Mr. Noel subsequently makes more than ample amends for having opened Parnassus to the public in this reckless manner, by calling Wilson an 'offal-feeder,' on the ground that he once wrote a severe criticism of some of Lord Tennyson's early poems. For Mr. Noel does not mince his words. On the contrary, he speaks with much scorn of all euphuism and delicacy of expression and, preferring the affectation of nature to the affectation of art, he thinks nothing of calling other people 'Laura Bridgmans,' 'Jackasses' and the like. This, we think, is to be regretted, especially in a writer so cultured as Mr. Noel. For, though indignation may make a great poet, bad temper always makes a poor critic.

On the whole, Mr. Noel's book has an emotional rather than an intellectual interest. It is simply a record of the moods of a man of letters, and its criticisms merely reveal the critic without illuminating what he would criticise for us. The best that we can say of it is that it is a Sentimental Journey through Literature, the worst that any one could say of it is that it has all the merits of such an expedition.

Essays on Poetry and Poets. By the Hon. Roden Noel. (Kegan Paul.)

COMMON-SENSE IN ART

(*Pall Mall Gazette*, January 8, 1887.)

At this critical moment in the artistic development of England Mr. John Collier has come forward as the champion of common-sense in art. It will be remembered that Mr. Quilter, in one of his most vivid and picturesque metaphors, compared Mr. Collier's method as a painter to that of a shampooer in a Turkish bath. {119} As a writer Mr. Collier is no less interesting. It is true that he is not eloquent, but then he censures with just severity 'the meaningless eloquence of the writers on æsthetics'; we admit that he is not subtle, but then he is careful to remind us that Leonardo da Vinci's views on painting are nonsensical; his qualities are of a solid, indeed we may say of a stolid order; he is thoroughly honest, sturdy and downright, and he advises us, if we want to know anything about art, to study the works of 'Helmholtz, Stokes, or Tyndall,' to which we hope we may be allowed to add Mr. Collier's own *Manual of Oil Painting*.

For this art of painting is a very simple thing indeed, according to Mr. Collier. It consists merely in the 'representation of natural objects by means of pigments on a flat surface.' There is nothing, he tells us, 'so very mysterious' in it after all. 'Every natural object appears to us as a sort of pattern of different shades and colours,' and 'the task of the artist is so to arrange his shades and colours on his canvas that a similar pattern is produced.' This is obviously pure common-sense, and it is clear that art-definitions of this character can be comprehended by the very meanest capacity and, indeed, may be said to appeal to it. For the perfect development, however, of this pattern-producing faculty a severe training is necessary. The art student must begin by painting china, crockery, and 'still life' generally. He should rule his straight lines and employ actual measurements wherever it is possible. He will also find that a plumb-line comes in very useful. Then he should proceed to Greek sculpture, for from pottery to Phidias is only one step. Ultimately he will arrive at the living model, and as soon as he can 'faithfully represent any object that he has before him' he is a painter. After this there is, of course, only one thing to be considered, the important question of subject. Subjects, Mr. Collier tells us, are of two kinds, ancient and modern. Modern subjects are more healthy than ancient subjects, but the real difficulty of modernity in art is that the artist passes his life with respectable people, and that respectable people are unpictorial. 'For picturesqueness,' consequently, he should go to 'the rural poor,' and for pathos to the London slums. Ancient subjects offer the artist a very much wider field. If he is fond of 'rich stuffs and costly accessories' he should study the Middle Ages; if he wishes to paint beautiful people, 'untrammelled by any considerations of historical accuracy,' he should turn to the Greek and Roman mythology; and if he is a 'mediocre painter,' he should choose his 'subject from the Old and New Testament,' a recommendation, by the way, that many of our Royal Academicians seem already to have carried out. To paint a real historical picture one requires the assistance of a theatrical costumier and a photographer. From the former one hires the dresses and the latter supplies one with the true background. Besides subject-pictures there are also portraits and landscapes. Portrait painting, Mr. Collier tells us, 'makes no demands on the imagination.' As is the sitter, so is the work of art. If the sitter be commonplace, for instance, it would be 'contrary to the fundamental principles of portraiture to make the picture other than commonplace.' There are, however, certain rules that should be followed. One of the most important of these is that the artist should always consult his sitter's relations before he begins the picture. If they want a profile he must do them a profile; if they require a full face he must give them a full face; and he should be careful also to get their opinion as to the costume the sitter should wear and 'the sort of expression he should put on.' 'After all,' says Mr. Collier pathetically, 'it is they who have to live with the picture.'

Besides the difficulty of pleasing the victim's family, however, there is the difficulty of pleasing the victim. According to Mr. Collier, and he is, of course, a high authority on the matter, portrait painters bore their sitters very much. The true artist consequently should encourage his sitter to converse, or get some one to read to him; for if the sitter is bored the portrait will look sad. Still, if the sitter has not got an amiable expression naturally the artist is not bound to give him one, nor 'if he is essentially ungraceful' should the artist ever 'put him in a graceful attitude.' As regards landscape painting, Mr. Collier tells us that 'a great deal of nonsense has been talked about the impossibility of reproducing nature,' but that there is nothing really to prevent a picture giving to the eye exactly the same impression that an actual scene gives, for that when he visited 'the celebrated panorama of the Siege of Paris' he could hardly distinguish the painted from the real cannons! The whole passage is extremely interesting, and is really one out of many examples we might give of the swift and simple manner in which the common-sense method solves the great problems of art. The book concludes with a detailed exposition of the undulatory theory of light according to the most ancient scientific discoveries. Mr. Collier points out how important it is for an artist to hold sound views on the subject of ether waves, and his own thorough appreciation of Science may be estimated by the definition he gives of it as being 'neither more nor less than knowledge.'

Mr. Collier has done his work with much industry and earnestness. Indeed, nothing but the most conscientious seriousness, combined with real labour, could have produced such a book, and the exact value of common-sense in art has never before been so clearly demonstrated.

A Manual of Oil Painting. By the Hon. John Collier. (Cassell and Co.)

MINER AND MINOR POETS

(*Pall Mall Gazette*, February 1, 1887.)

The conditions that precede artistic production are so constantly treated as qualities of the work of art itself that one sometimes is tempted to wish that all art were anonymous. Yet there are certain forms of art so individual in their utterance, so purely personal in their expression, that for a full appreciation of their style and manner some knowledge of the artist's life is necessary. To this class belongs Mr. Skipsey's *Carols from the Coal-Fields*, a volume of intense human interest and high literary merit, and we are consequently glad to see that Dr. Spence Watson has added a short biography of his friend to his friend's poems, for the life and the literature are too indissolubly wedded ever really to be separated. Joseph Skipsey, Dr. Watson tells us, was sent into the coal pits at Percy Main, near North Shields, when he was seven years of age. Young as he was he had to work from twelve to sixteen hours in the day, generally in the pitch dark, and in the dreary winter months he saw the sun only upon Sundays. When he went to work he had learned the alphabet and to put words of two letters together, but he was really his own schoolmaster, and 'taught himself to write, for example, by copying the letters from printed bills or notices, when he could get a candle end,—his paper being the trapdoor, which it was his duty to open and shut as the wagons passed through, and his pen a piece of chalk.' The first book he really read was the Bible, and not content with reading it, he learned by heart the chapters which specially pleased him. When sixteen years old he was presented with a copy of Lindley Murray's Grammar, by the aid of which he gained some knowledge of the structural rules of English. He had already become acquainted with *Paradise Lost*, and was another proof of Matthew Prior's axiom, 'Who often reads will sometimes want to write,' for he had begun to write verse when only 'a bonnie pit lad.' For more than forty years of his life he laboured in 'the coal-dark underground,' and is now the caretaker of a Board-school in Newcastle-upon-Tyne. As for the qualities of his poetry, they are its directness and its natural grace. He has an intellectual as well as a metrical affinity with Blake, and possesses something of Blake's marvellous power of making simple things seem strange to us, and strange things seem simple. How delightful, for instance, is this little poem:

'Get up!' the caller calls, 'Get up!'
And in the dead of night,
To win the bairns their bite and sup,
 I rise a weary wight.

 My flannel dudden donn'd, thrice o'er
 My birds are kiss'd, and then
I with a whistle shut the door
 I may not ope again.

How exquisite and fanciful this stray lyric:

The wind comes from the west to-night;
 So sweetly down the lane he bloweth
Upon my lips, with pure delight
 From head to foot my body gloweth.

 Where did the wind, the magic find
 To charm me thus? say, heart that knoweth!
'Within a rose on which he blows
 Before upon thy lips he bloweth!'

We admit that Mr. Skipsey's work is extremely unequal, but when it is at its best it is full of sweetness and strength; and though he has carefully studied the artistic capabilities of language, he never makes his form formal by over-polishing. Beauty with him seems to be an unconscious result rather than a conscious aim; his style has all the delicate charm of chance. We have already pointed out his affinity to Blake, but with Burns also he may be said to have a spiritual kinship, and in the songs of the Northumbrian miner we meet with something of the Ayrshire peasant's wild gaiety and mad humour. He gives himself up freely to his impressions, and there is a fine, careless rapture in his laughter. The whole book deserves to be read, and much of it deserves to be loved. Mr. Skipsey can find music for every mood, whether he is dealing with the real experiences of the pitman or with the imaginative experiences of the poet, and his verse has a rich vitality about it. In these latter days of shallow rhymes it is pleasant to come across some one to whom poetry is a passion not a profession.

Mr. F. B. Doveton belongs to a different school. In his amazing versatility he reminds us of the gentleman who wrote the immortal handbills for Mrs. Jarley, for his subjects range from Dr. Carter Moffatt and the Ammoniaphone to Mr. Whiteley, Lady Bicyclists, and the Immortality of the Soul. His verses in praise of Zoedone are a fine example of didactic poetry, his elegy on the death of Jumbo is quite up to the level of the subject, and the stanzas on a watering-place,

Who of its merits can e'er think meanly?
Scattering ozone to all the land!

are well worthy of a place in any shilling guidebook. Mr. Doveton divides his poems into grave and gay, but we like him least when he is amusing, for in his merriment there is but little melody, and he makes his muse grin through a horse-collar. When he is serious he is much better, and his descriptive poems show that he has completely mastered the most approved poetical phraseology. Our old friend Boreas is as 'burly' as ever, 'zephyrs' are consistently 'amorous,' and 'the welkin rings' upon the smallest provocation; birds are 'the feathered host' or 'the sylvan throng,' the wind 'wantons o'er the lea,' 'vernal gales' murmur to 'crystal rills,' and Lemprière's Dictionary supplies the Latin names for the sun and the moon. Armed with these daring and novel expressions Mr. Doveton indulges in fierce moods of nature-worship, and botanises recklessly through the provinces. Now and then, however, we come across some pleasing passages. Mr. Doveton apparently is an enthusiastic fisherman, and sings merrily of the 'enchanting grayling' and the 'crimson and gold trout' that rise to the crafty angler's 'feathered wile.' Still, we fear that he will never produce any real good work till he has made up his mind whether destiny intends him for a poet or for an advertising agent, and we venture to hope that should he ever publish another volume he will find some other rhyme to 'vision' than 'Elysian,' a dissonance that occurs five times in this well-meaning but tedious volume.

As for Mr. Ashby-Sterry, those who object to the nude in art should at once read his lays of *The Lazy Minstrel* and be converted, for over these poems the milliner, not the muse, presides, and the result is a little alarming. As the Chelsea sage investigated the philosophy of clothes, so Mr. Ashby-Sterry has set himself to discover the poetry of petticoats, and seems to find much consolation in the thought that, though art is long, skirts are worn short. He is the only pedlar who has climbed Parnassus since Autolycus sang of

Lawn as white as driven snow,
'Cypress black as e'er was crow,

and his details are as amazing as his diminutives. He is capable of penning a canto to a crinoline, and has a pathetic monody on a mackintosh. He sings of pretty puckers and pliant pleats, and is eloquent on frills, frocks and chemisettes. The latest French fashions stir him to a fine frenzy, and the sight of a pair of Balmoral boots thrills him with absolute ecstasy. He writes rondels on ribbons, lyrics on linen and lace, and his most ambitious ode is addressed to a Tomboy in Trouserettes! Yet his verse is often dainty and delicate, and many of his poems are full of sweet and pretty conceits. Indeed, of the Thames at summer time he writes so charmingly, and with such felicitous grace of epithet, that we cannot but regret that he has chosen to make himself the Poet of Petticoats and the Troubadour of Trouserettes.

(1) *Carols from the Coal-Fields, and Other Songs and Ballads.* By Joseph Skipsey. (Walter Scott.)

(2) *Sketches in Prose and Verse.* By F. B. Doveton. (Sampson Low, Marston and Co.)

(3) *The Lazy Minstrel.* By J. Ashby-Sterry. (Fisher Unwin.)

A NEW CALENDAR

(*Pall Mall Gazette*, February 17, 1887.)

Most modern calendars mar the sweet simplicity of our lives by reminding us that each day that passes is the anniversary of some perfectly uninteresting event. Their compilers display a degraded passion for chronicling small beer, and rake out the dust-heap of history in an ardent search after rubbish. Mr. Walter Scott, however, has made a new departure and has published a calendar in which every day of the year is made beautiful for us by means of an elegant extract from the poems of Mr. Alfred Austin. This, undoubtedly, is a step in the right direction. It is true that such aphorisms as

Graves are a mother's dimples
When we complain,

or

The primrose wears a constant smile,
And captive takes the heart,

can hardly be said to belong to the very highest order of poetry, still, they are preferable, on the whole, to the date of Hannah More's birth, or of the burning down of Exeter Change, or of the opening of the Great Exhibition; and though it would be dangerous to make calendars the basis of Culture, we should all be much improved if we began each day with a fine passage of English poetry. How far this desirable result can be attained by a use of the volume now before us is, perhaps, open to question, but it must be admitted that its anonymous compiler has done his work very conscientiously, nor will we quarrel with him for the fact that he constantly repeats the same quotation twice over. No doubt it was difficult to find in Mr. Austin's work three hundred and sixty-five different passages really worthy of insertion in an almanac, and, besides, our climate has so degenerated of late that there is no reason at all why a motto perfectly suitable for February should not be equally appropriate when August has set in with its usual severity. For the misprints there is less excuse. Even the most uninteresting poet cannot survive bad editing.

Prefixed to the Calendar is an introductory note from the pen of Mr. William Sharp, written in that involved and affected style which is Mr. Sharp's distinguishing characteristic, and displaying that intimate acquaintance with Sappho's lost poems which is the privilege only of those who are not acquainted with Greek literature. As a criticism it is not of much value, but as an advertisement it is quite excellent. Indeed, Mr. Sharp hints mysteriously at secret political influence, and tells us that though Mr. Austin 'sings with Tityrus' yet he 'has conversed with Æneas,' which, we suppose, is a euphemistic method of alluding to the fact that Mr. Austin once lunched with Lord Beaconsfield. It is for the poet, however, not for the politician, that Mr. Sharp reserves his loftiest panegyric and, in his anxiety to smuggle the author of *Leszko the Bastard* and *Grandmother's Teaching* into the charmed circle of the Immortals, he leaves no adjective unturned, quoting and misquoting Mr. Austin with a recklessness that is absolutely fatal to the cause he pleads. For mediocre critics are usually safe in their generalities; it is in their reasons and examples that they come so lamentably to grief. When, for instance, Mr. Sharp tells us that lines with the 'natural magic' of Shakespeare, Keats and Coleridge are 'far from infrequent' in Mr. Austin's poems, all that we can say is that we have never come across any lines of the kind in Mr. Austin's published works, but it is difficult to help smiling when Mr. Sharp gravely calls upon us to note 'the illuminative significance' of such a commonplace verse as

My manhood keeps the dew of morn,
    And what have I to give;
Being right glad that I was born,
    And thankful that I live.

Nor do Mr. Sharp's constant misquotations really help him out of his difficulties. Such a line as

A meadow ribbed with drying swathes of hay,

has at least the merit of being a simple, straightforward description of an ordinary scene in an English landscape, but not much can be said in favour of

A meadow ribbed with dying swathes of hay,

which is Mr. Sharp's own version, and one that he finds 'delightfully suggestive.' It is indeed suggestive, but only of that want of care that comes from want of taste.

On the whole, Mr. Sharp has attempted an impossible task. Mr. Austin is neither an Olympian nor a Titan, and all the puffing in Paternoster Row cannot set him on Parnassus.

His verse is devoid of all real rhythmical life; it may have the metre of poetry, but it has not often got its music, nor can there be any true delicacy in the ear that tolerates such rhymes as 'chord' and 'abroad.' Even the claim that Mr. Sharp puts forward for him, that his muse takes her impressions directly from nature and owes nothing to books, cannot be sustained for a moment. Wordsworth is a great poet, but bad echoes of Wordsworth are extremely depressing, and when Mr. Austin calls the cuckoo a

Voyaging voice

and tells us that

The stockdove broods
Low to itself,

we must really enter a protest against such silly plagiarisms.

Perhaps, however, we are treating Mr. Sharp too seriously. He admits himself that it was at the special request of the compiler of the Calendar that he wrote the preface at all, and though he courteously adds that the task is agreeable to him, still he shows only too clearly that he considers it a task and, like a clever lawyer or a popular clergyman, tries to atone for his lack of sincerity by a pleasing over-emphasis. Nor is there any reason why this Calendar should not be a great success. If published as a broad-sheet, with a picture of Mr. Austin 'conversing with Æneas,' it might gladden many a simple cottage home and prove a source of innocent amusement to the Conservative working-man.

Days of the Year: A Poetic Calendar from the Works of Alfred Austin. Selected and edited by A. S. With Introduction by William Sharp. (Walter Scott.)

THE POETS' CORNER—II

(*Pall Mall Gazette*, March 8, 1837.)

A little schoolboy was once asked to explain the difference between prose and poetry. After some consideration he replied, '"blue violets" is prose, and "violets blue" is poetry.' The distinction, we admit, is not exhaustive, but it seems to be the one that is extremely popular with our minor poets. Opening at random *The Queens Innocent* we come across passages like this:

    Full gladly would I sit
Of such a potent magus at the feet,

    and this:

    The third, while yet a youth,
Espoused a lady noble but not royal,
One only son who gave him—Pharamond—

lines that, apparently, rest their claim to be regarded as poetry on their unnecessary and awkward inversions. Yet this poem is not without beauty, and the character of Nardi, the little prince who is treated as the Court fool, shows a delicate grace of fancy, and is both tender and true. The most delightful thing in the whole volume is a little lyric called *April*, which is like a picture set to music.

The Chimneypiece of Bruges is a narrative poem in blank verse, and tells us of a young artist who, having been unjustly convicted of his wife's murder, spends his life in carving on the great chimneypiece of the prison the whole story of his love and suffering. The poem is full of colour, but the blank verse is somewhat heavy in movement. There are some pretty things in the book, and a poet without hysterics is rare.

Dr. Dawson Burns's *Oliver Cromwell* is a pleasant panegyric on the Protector, and reads like a prize poem by a nice sixth-form boy. The verses on *The Good Old Times* should be sent as a leaflet to all Tories of Mr. Chaplin's school, and the lines on Bunker's Hill, beginning,

I stand on Bunker's towering pile,

are sure to be popular in America.

K. E. V.'s little volume is a series of poems on the Saints. Each poem is preceded by a brief biography of the Saint it celebrates—which is a very necessary precaution, as few of them ever existed. It does not display much poetic power, and such lines as these on St. Stephen,—

Did ever man before so fall asleep?
A cruel shower of stones his only bed,
For lullaby the curses loud and deep,
His covering with blood red—

may be said to add another horror to martyrdom. Still it is a thoroughly well-intentioned book and eminently suitable for invalids.

Mr. Foskett's poems are very serious and deliberate. One of the best of them, *Harold Glynde*, is a Cantata for Total Abstainers, and has already been set to music. *A Hindoo Tragedy* is the story of an enthusiastic Brahmin reformer who tries to break down the prohibition against widows marrying, and there are other interesting tales. Mr. Foskett has apparently forgotten to insert the rhymes in his sonnet to Wordsworth; but, as he tells us elsewhere that 'Poesy is uninspired by Art,' perhaps he is only heralding a new and formless form. He is always sincere in his feelings, and his apostrophe to Canon Farrar is equalled only by his apostrophe to Shakespeare.

The Pilgrimage of Memory suffers a good deal by being printed as poetry, and Mr. Barker should republish it at once as a prose work. Take, for instance, this description of a lady on a runaway horse:—

Her screams alarmed the Squire, who seeing the peril of his daughter, rode frantic after her. I saw at once the danger, and stepping from the footpath, show'd myself before the startled animal, which forthwith slackened pace, and darting up adroitly, I seized the rein, and in another moment, had released the maiden's foot, and held her, all insensible, within my arms. Poor girl, her head and face were sorely bruised, and I tried hard to staunch the blood which flowed from many a scalp-wound, and wipe away the dust that disfigured her lovely features. In another moment the Squire was by my side. 'Poor child,' he cried, alarmed, 'is she dead?' 'No, sir; not dead, I think,' said I, 'but sorely bruised and injured.'

There is clearly nothing to be gained by dividing the sentences of this simple and straightforward narrative into lines of unequal length, and Mr. Barker's own arrangement of the metre,

In another moment,
The Squire was by my side.
'Poor child,' he cried, alarmed, 'is she dead?'
'No, sir; not dead, I think,' said I,
'But sorely bruised and injured,'

seems to us to be quite inferior to ours. We beg that the second edition of *The Pilgrimage of Memory* may be issued as a novel in prose.

Mr. Gladstone Turner believes that we are on the verge of a great social cataclysm, and warns us that our *cradles* are even now being rocked by *slumbering volcanoes*! We hope that there is no truth in this statement, and that it is merely a startling metaphor introduced for the sake of effect, for elsewhere in the volume there is a great deal of beauty which we should be sorry to think was doomed to immediate extinction. *The Choice*, for instance, is a charming poem, and the sonnet on *Evening* would be almost perfect if it were not for an unpleasant assonance in the fifth line. Indeed, so good is much of Mr. Gladstone Turner's work that we trust he will give up rhyming 'real' to 'steal' and 'feel,' as such bad habits are apt to grow on careless poets and to blunt their ear for music.

Nivalis is a five-act tragedy in blank verse. Most plays that are written to be read, not to be acted, miss that condensation and directness of expression which is one of the secrets of true dramatic diction, and Mr. Schwartz's tragedy is consequently somewhat verbose. Still, it is full of fine lines and noble scenes. It is essentially a work of art, and though, as far as language is concerned, the personages all speak through the lips of the poet, yet in passion and purpose their characters are clearly differentiated, and the Queen Nivalis and her lover Giulio are drawn with real psychological power. We hope that some day Mr. Schwartz will write a play for the stage, as he has the dramatic instinct and the dramatic imagination, and can make life pass into literature without robbing it of its reality.

(1) *The Queen's Innocent, with Other Poems.* By Elise Cooper. (David Stott.)

(2) *The Chimneypiece of Bruges and Other Poems.* By Constance E. Dixon. (Elliot Stock.)

(3) *Oliver Cromwell and Other Poems.* By Dawson Burns, D.D. (Partridge and Co.)

(4) *The Circle of Saints.* By K. E. V. (Swan Sonnenschein and Co.)

(5) *Poems.* By Edward Foskett. (Kegan Paul.)

(6) *The Pilgrimage of Memory.* By John Thomas Barker. (Simpkin, Marshall and Co.)

(7) *Errata.* By G. Gladstone Turner. (Longmans, Green and Co.)

(8) *Nivalis.* By J. M. W. Schwartz. (Kegan Paul.)

GREAT WRITERS BY LITTLE MEN

(*Pall Mall Gazette*, March 28, 1887.)

In an introductory note prefixed to the initial volume of 'Great Writers,' a series of literary monographs now being issued by Mr. Walter Scott, the publisher himself comes forward in the kindest manner possible to give his authors the requisite 'puff preliminary,' and ventures to express the modest opinion that such original and valuable works 'have never before been produced in any part of the world at a price so low as a shilling a volume.' Far be it from us to make any heartless allusion to the fact that Shakespeare's *Sonnets* were brought out at fivepence, or that for fourpence-halfpenny one could have bought a Martial in ancient Rome. Every man, a cynical American tells us, has the right to beat a drum before his booth. Still, we must acknowledge that Mr. Walter Scott would have been much better employed in correcting some of the more obvious errors that appear in his series. When, for instance, we come across such a phrase as 'the brotherly liberality of the brothers *Wedgewood*,' the awkwardness of the expression is hardly atoned for by the fact that the name of the great potter is misspelt; Longfellow is so essentially poor in rhymes that it is unfair to rob him even of one, and the misquotation on page 77 is absolutely unkind; the joke Coleridge himself made upon the subject should have been sufficient to remind any one that 'Comberbach' (*sic*) was not the name under which he enlisted, and no real beauty is added to the first line of his pathetic *Work Without Hope* by printing 'lare' (*sic*) instead of 'lair.' The truth is that all premature panegyrics bring their own punishment upon themselves and, in the present case, though the series has only just entered upon existence, already a great deal of the work done is careless, disappointing, unequal and tedious.

Mr. Eric Robertson's *Longfellow* is a most depressing book. No one survives being over-estimated, nor is there any surer way of destroying an author's reputation than to glorify him without judgment and to praise him without tact. Henry Wadsworth Longfellow was one of the first true men of letters America produced, and as such deserves a high place in any history of American civilisation. To a land out of breath in its greed for gain he showed the example of a life devoted entirely to the study of literature; his lectures, though not by any means brilliant, were still productive of much good; he had a most charming and gracious personality, and he wrote some pretty poems. But his poems are not of the kind that call for intellectual analysis or for elaborate description or, indeed, for any serious discussion at all. They are as unsuited for panegyric as they are unworthy of censure, and it is difficult to help smiling when Mr. Robertson gravely tells us that few modern poets have given utterance to a faith so comprehensive as that expressed in the *Psalm of Life*, or that *Evangeline* should confer on Longfellow the title of 'Golden-mouthed,' and that the style of metre adopted 'carries the ear back to times in the world's history when grand simplicities were sung.' Surely Mr. Robertson does not believe that there is any connection at all between Longfellow's unrhymed dactylics and the hexameter of Greece and Rome, or that any one reading *Evangeline* would be reminded of Homer's or Virgil's line? Where also lies the advantage of confusing popularity with poetic power? Though the *Psalm of Life* be shouted from Maine to California, that would not make it true poetry. Why call upon us to admire a bad misquotation from the *Midnight Mass for the Dying Year*, and why talk of Longfellow's 'hundreds of imitators'? Longfellow has no imitators, for of echoes themselves there are no echoes and it is only style that makes a school.

Now and then, however, Mr. Robertson considers it necessary to assume a critical attitude. He tells us, for instance, that whether or not Longfellow was a genius of the first order, it must be admitted that he loved social pleasures and was a good eater and judge of wines, admiring 'Bass's ale' more than anything else he had seen in England! The remarks on *Excelsior* are even still more amazing. *Excelsior*, says Mr. Robertson, is not a ballad because a ballad deals either with real or with supernatural people, and the hero of the poem cannot be brought under either category. For, 'were he of human flesh, his madcap notion of scaling a mountain with the purpose of getting to the sky would be simply drivelling lunacy,' to say nothing of the fact that the peak in question is much frequented by tourists, while, on the other hand, 'it would be absurd to suppose him a spirit . . . for no spirit would be so silly as climb a snowy mountain for nothing'! It is really painful to have to read such preposterous nonsense, and if Mr. Walter Scott imagines that work of this kind is 'original and valuable' he has much to learn. Nor are Mr. Robertson's criticisms upon other poets at all more felicitous. The casual allusion to Herrick's 'confectioneries of verse' is, of course, quite explicable, coming as it does from an editor who excluded Herrick from an anthology of the child-poems of our literature in favour of Mr. Ashby-Sterry and Mr. William Sharp, but when Mr. Robertson tells us that Poe's 'loftiest flights of imagination in verse . . . rise into no more empyreal realm than the *fantastic*,' we can only recommend him to read as soon as possible the marvellous lines *To Helen*, a poem as beautiful as a Greek gem and as musical as Apollo's lute. The remarks, too, on Poe's critical estimate of his own work show that Mr. Robertson has never really studied the poet on whom he pronounces such glib and shallow judgments, and exemplify very clearly the fact that even dogmatism is no excuse for ignorance.

After reading Mr. Hall Caine's *Coleridge* we are irresistibly reminded of what Wordsworth once said about a bust that had been done of himself. After contemplating it for some time, he remarked, 'It is not a bad Wordsworth, but it is not the real Wordsworth; it is not Wordsworth the poet, it is the sort of Wordsworth who might be Chancellor of the Exchequer.' Mr. Caine's Coleridge is certainly not the sort of Coleridge who might have been Chancellor of the Exchequer, for the author of *Christabel* was not by any means remarkable as a financier; but, for all that, it is not the real Coleridge, it is not Coleridge the poet. The incidents of the life are duly recounted; the gunpowder plot at Cambridge, the egg-hot and oronokoo at the little tavern in Newgate Street, the blue coat and white waistcoat that so amazed the worthy Unitarians, and the terrible smoking experiment at Birmingham are all carefully chronicled, as no doubt they should be in every popular biography; but of the spiritual progress of the man's soul we hear absolutely nothing. Never for one single instant are we brought near to Coleridge; the magic of that wonderful personality is hidden from us by a cloud of mean details, an unholy jungle of facts, and the 'critical history' promised to us by Mr. Walter Scott in his unfortunate preface is conspicuous only by its absence.

Carlyle once proposed in jest to write a life of Michael Angelo without making any reference to his art, and Mr. Caine has shown that such a project is perfectly feasible. He has written the life of a great peripatetic philosopher and chronicled only the peripatetics. He has tried to tell us about a poet, and his book might be the biography of the famous tallow-chandler who would not appreciate the *Watchman*. The real events of Coleridge's life are not his gig excursions and his walking tours; they are his thoughts, dreams and passions, his moments of creative impulse, their source and secret, his moods of imaginative joy, their marvel and their meaning, and not his moods merely but the music and the melancholy that they brought him; the lyric loveliness of his voice when he sang, the sterile sorrow of the years when he was silent. It is said that every man's life is a Soul's Tragedy. Coleridge's certainly was so, and though we may not be able to pluck out the heart of his mystery, still let us recognise that mystery is there; and that the goings-out and comings-in of a man, his places of sojourn and his roads of travel are but idle things to chronicle, if that which is the man be left unrecorded. So mediocre is Mr. Caine's book that even accuracy could not make it better.

On the whole, then, Mr. Walter Scott cannot be congratulated on the success of his venture so far, The one really admirable feature of the series is the bibliography that is appended to each volume. These bibliographies are compiled by Mr. Anderson, of the British Museum, and are so valuable to the student, as well as interesting in themselves, that it is much to be regretted that they should be accompanied by such tedious letterpress.

(1) *Life of Henry Wadsworth Longfellow*. By Eric S. Robertson.

(2) *Life of Samuel Taylor Coleridge*. By Hall Caine. 'Great Writers' Series. (Walter Scott.)

A NEW BOOK ON DICKENS

(*Pall Mall Gazette*, March 31, 1887.)

Mr. Marzials' *Dickens* is a great improvement on the *Longfellow* and *Coleridge* of his predecessors. It is certainly a little sad to find our old friend the manager of the Theatre Royal, Portsmouth, appearing as 'Mr. Vincent Crumules' (*sic*), but such misprints are not by any means uncommon in Mr. Walter Scott's publications, and, on the whole, this is a very pleasant book indeed. It is brightly and cleverly written, admirably constructed, and gives a most vivid and graphic picture of that strange modern drama, the drama of Dickens's life. The earlier chapters are quite excellent, and, though the story of the famous novelist's boyhood has been often told before, Mr. Marzials shows that it can be told again without losing any of the charm of its interest, while the account of Dickens in the plenitude of his glory is most appreciative and genial. We are really brought close to the man with his indomitable energy, his extraordinary capacity for work, his high spirits, his fascinating, tyrannous personality. The description of his method of reading is admirable, and the amazing stump-campaign in America attains, in Mr. Marzials' hands, to the dignity of a mock-heroic poem. One side of Dickens's character, however, is left almost entirely untouched, and yet it is one in every way deserving of close study. That Dickens should have felt bitterly towards his father and mother is quite explicable, but that, while feeling so bitterly, he should have caricatured them for the amusement of the public, with an evident delight in his own humour, has always seemed to us a most curious psychological problem. We are far from complaining that he did so. Good novelists are much rarer than good sons, and none of us would part readily with Micawber and Mrs. Nickleby. Still, the fact remains that a man who was affectionate and loving to his children, generous and warm-hearted to his friends, and whose books are the very bacchanalia of benevolence, pilloried his parents to make the groundlings laugh, and this fact every biographer of Dickens should face and, if possible, explain.

As for Mr. Marzials' critical estimate of Dickens as a writer, he tells us quite frankly that he believes that Dickens at his best was 'one of the greatest masters of pathos who ever lived,' a remark that seems to us an excellent example of what novelists call 'the fine courage of despair.' Of course, no biographer of Dickens could say anything else, just at present. A popular series is bound to express popular views, and cheap criticisms may be excused in cheap books. Besides, it is always open to every one to accept G. H. Lewes's unfortunate maxim that any author who makes one cry possesses the gift of pathos and, indeed, there is something very flattering in being told that one's own emotions are the ultimate test of literature. When Mr. Marzials discusses Dickens's power of drawing human nature we are upon somewhat safer ground, and we cannot but admire the cleverness with which he passes over his hero's innumerable failures. For, in some respects, Dickens might be likened to those old sculptors of our Gothic cathedrals who could give form to the most fantastic fancy, and crowd with grotesque monsters a curious world of dreams, but saw little of the grace and dignity of the men and women among whom they lived, and whose art, lacking sanity, was therefore incomplete. Yet they at least knew the limitations of their art, while Dickens never knew the limitations of his. When he tries to be serious he succeeds only in being dull, when he aims at truth he reaches merely platitude. Shakespeare could place Ferdinand and Miranda by the side of Caliban, and Life recognises them all as her own, but Dickens's Mirandas are the young ladies out of a fashion-book, and his Ferdinands the walking gentlemen of an unsuccessful company of third-rate players. So little sanity, indeed, had Dickens's art that he was never able even to satirise: he could only caricature; and so little does Mr. Marzials realise where Dickens's true strength and weakness lie, that he actually complains that Cruikshank's illustrations are too much exaggerated and that he could never draw either a lady or a gentleman.

The latter was hardly a disqualification for illustrating Dickens as few such characters occur in his books, unless we are to regard Lord Frederick Verisopht and Sir Mulberry Hawk as valuable studies of high life; and, for our own part, we have always considered that the greatest injustice ever done to Dickens has been done by those who have tried to illustrate him seriously.

In conclusion, Mr. Marzials expresses his belief that a century hence Dickens will be read as much as we now read Scott, and says rather prettily that as long as he is read 'there will be one gentle and humanising influence the more at work among men,' which is always a useful tag to append to the life of any popular author. Remembering that of all forms of error prophecy is the most gratuitous, we will not take upon ourselves to decide the question of Dickens's immortality. If our descendants do not read him they will miss a great source of amusement, and if they do, we hope they will not model their style upon his. Of this, however, there is but little danger, for no age ever borrows the slang of its predecessor. As for 'the gentle and humanising influence,' this is taking Dickens just a little too seriously.

Life of Charles Dickens. By Frank T. Marzials. 'Great Writers' Series. (Walter Scott.)

OUR BOOK-SHELF

(*Pall Mall Gazette*, April 12, 1887.)

The Master Of Tanagra is certainly one of Ernst von Wildenbruch's most delightful productions. It presents an exceedingly pretty picture of the bright external side of ancient Greek life, and tells how a handsome young Tanagrian left his home for the sake of art, and returned to it for love's sake—an old story, no doubt, but one which gains a new charm from its new setting. The historical characters of the book, such as Praxiteles and Phryne, seem somehow less real than those that are purely imaginary, but this is usually the case in all novels that would recreate the past for us, and is a form of penalty that Romance has often to pay when she tries to blend fact with fancy, and to turn the great personages of history into puppets for a little play. The translation, which is from the pen of the Baroness von Lauer, reads very pleasantly, and some of the illustrations are good, though it is impossible to reproduce by any process the delicate and exquisite charm of the Tanagra figurines.

M. Paul Stapfer in his book *Molière et Shakespeare* shows very clearly that the French have not yet forgiven Schlegel for having threatened that, as a reprisal for the atrocities committed by Napoleon, he would prove that Molière was no poet. Indeed, M. Stapfer, while admitting that one should be fair 'envers tout le monde, même envers les Allemands,' charges down upon the German critics with the brilliancy and dash of a French cuirassier, and mocks at them for their dulness, at the very moment that he is annexing their erudition, an achievement for which the French genius is justly renowned. As for the relative merits of Molière and Shakespeare, M. Stapfer has no hesitation in placing the author of *Le Misanthrope* by the side of the author of *Hamlet*. Shakespeare's comedies seem to him somewhat wilful and fantastic; he prefers Orgon and Tartuffe to Oberon and Titania, and can hardly forgive Beatrice for having been 'born to speak all mirth, and no matter.'

Perhaps he hardly realises that it is as a poet, not as a playwright, that we love Shakespeare in England, and that Ariel singing by the yellow sands, or fairies hiding in a wood near Athens, may be as real as Alceste in his wooing of Célimène, and as true as Harpagon weeping for his money-box; still, his book is full of interesting suggestion, many of his remarks on literature are quite excellent, and his style has the qualities of grace, distinction, and ease of movement.

Not so much can be said for *Annals of the Life of Shakespeare*, which is a dull though well-meaning little book. What we do not know about Shakespeare is a most fascinating subject, and one that would fill a volume, but what we do know about him is so meagre and inadequate that when it is collected together the result is rather depressing. However, there are many people, no doubt, who find a great source of interest in the fact that the author of *The Merchant of Venice* once brought an action for the sum of £1, 15s. 10d. and gained his suit, and for these this volume will have considerable charm. It is a pity that the finest line Ben Jonson ever wrote about Shakespeare should be misquoted at the very beginning of the book, and the illustration of Shakespeare's monument gives the inscription very badly indeed. Also, it was Ben Jonson's stepfather, not his 'father-in-law,' as stated, who was the bricklayer; but it is quite useless to dwell upon these things, as nobody nowadays seems to have any time either to correct proofs or to consult authorities.

One of the most pleasing volumes that has appeared as yet in the Canterbury Series is the collection of Allan Ramsay's poems. Ramsay, whose profession was the making of periwigs, and whose pleasure was the making of poetry, is always delightful reading, except when he tries to write English and to imitate Pope. His *Gentle Shepherd* is a charming pastoral play, full of humour and romance; his *Vision* has a good deal of natural fire; and some of his songs, such as *The Yellow-hair'd Laddie* and *The Lass of Patie's Mill*, might rank beside those of Burns. The preface to this attractive little edition is from the pen of Mr. J. Logie Robertson, and the simple, straightforward style in which it is written contrasts favourably with the silly pompous manner affected by so many of the other editors of the series.

Ramsay's life is worth telling well, and Mr. Robertson tells it well, and gives us a really capital picture of Edinburgh society in the early half of the last century.

Dante for Beginners, by Miss Arabella Shore, is a sort of literary guide-book. What Virgil was to the great Florentine, Miss Shore would be to the British public, and her modest little volume can do no possible harm to Dante, which is more than one can say of many commentaries on the *Divine Comedy*.

Miss Phillimore's *Studies in Italian Literature* is a much more elaborate work, and displays a good deal of erudition. Indeed, the erudition is sometimes displayed a little too much, and we should like to see the lead of learning transmuted more often into the gold of thought. The essays on Petrarch and Tasso are tedious, but those on Aleardi and Count Arrivabene are excellent, particularly the former. Aleardi was a poet of wonderful descriptive power, and though, as he said himself, he subordinated his love of poetry to his love of country, yet in such service he found perfect freedom.

The article on Edoardo Fusco also is full of interest, and is a timely tribute to the memory of one who did so much for the education and culture of modern Italy. On the whole, the book is well worth reading; so well worth reading, indeed, that we hope that the foolish remarks on the Greek Drama will be amended in a second edition, or, which would be better still, struck out altogether. They show a want of knowledge that must be the result of years of study.

(1) *The Master of Tanagra*. Translated from the German of Ernst von Wildenbruch by the Baroness von Lauer. (H. Grevel and Co.)

(2) *Molière et Shakespeare*. By Paul Stapfer. (Hachette.)

(3) *Annals of the Life of Shakespeare*. (Sampson Low, Marston and Co.)

(4) *Poems by Allan Ramsay*. Selected and arranged, with a Biographical Sketch of the Poet, by J. Logie Robertson, M.A. 'Canterbury Poets.' (Walter Scott.)

(5) *Dante for Beginners*. By Arabella Shore. (Chapman and Hall.)

(6) *Studies in Italian Literature*. By Miss Phillimore. (Sampson Low, Marston and Co.)

A CHEAP EDITION OF A GREAT MAN

(*Pall Mall Gazette*, April 18, 1887.)

43

Formerly we used to canonise our great men; nowadays we vulgarise them. The vulgarisation of Rossetti has been going on for some time past with really remarkable success, and there seems no probability at present of the process being discontinued. The grass was hardly green upon the quiet grave in Birchington churchyard when Mr. Hall Caine and Mr. William Sharp rushed into print with their Memoirs and Recollections. Then came the usual mob of magazine-hacks with their various views and attitudes, and now Mr. Joseph Knight has produced for the edification of the British public a popular biography of the poet of the Blessed Damozel, the painter of Dante's Dream.

It is only fair to state that Mr. Knight's work is much better than that of his predecessors in the same field. His book is, on the whole, modestly and simply written; whatever its other faults may be, it is at least free from affectation of any kind; and it makes no serious pretence at being either exhaustive or definitive. Yet the best we can say of it is that it is just the sort of biography Guildenstern might have written of Hamlet. Nor does its unsatisfactory character come merely from the ludicrous inadequacy of the materials at Mr. Knight's disposal; it is the whole scheme and method of the book that is radically wrong. Rossetti's was a great personality, and personalities such as his do not easily survive shilling primers. Sooner or later they have inevitably to come down to the level of their biographers, and in the present instance nothing could be more absolutely commonplace than the picture Mr. Knight gives us of the wonderful seer and singer whose life he has so recklessly essayed to write.

No doubt there are many people who will be deeply interested to know that Rossetti was once chased round his garden by an infuriated zebu he was trying to exhibit to Mr. Whistler, or that he had a great affection for a dog called 'Dizzy,' or that 'sloshy' was one of his favourite words of contempt, or that Mr. Gosse thought him very like Chaucer in appearance, or that he had 'an absolute disqualification' for whist-playing, or that he was very fond of quoting the *Bab Ballads*, or that he once said that if he could live by writing poetry he would see painting d---d! For our part, however, we cannot help expressing our regret that such a shallow and superficial biography as this should ever have been published. It is but a sorry task to rip the twisted ravel from the worn garment of life and to turn the grout in a drained cup. Better, after all, that we knew a painter only through his vision and a poet through his song, than that the image of a great man should be marred and made mean for us by the clumsy geniality of good intentions. A true artist, and such Rossetti undoubtedly was, reveals himself so perfectly in his work, that unless a biographer has something more valuable to give us than idle anecdotes and unmeaning tales, his labour is misspent and his industry misdirected.

Bad, however, as is Mr. Knight's treatment of Rossetti's life, his treatment of Rossetti's poetry is infinitely worse. Considering the small size of the volume, and the consequently limited number of extracts, the amount of misquotation is almost incredible, and puts all recent achievements in this sphere of modern literature completely into the shade. The fine line in the first canto of *Rose Mary*:

What glints there like a lance that flees?

appears as:

What glints there like a glance that flees?

which is very painful nonsense; in the description of that graceful and fanciful sonnet *Autumn Idleness*, the deer are represented as '*grazing* from hillock eaves' instead of gazing from hillock-eaves; the opening of *Dantis Tenebræ* is rendered quite incomprehensible by the substitution of 'my' for 'thy' in the second line; even such a well-known ballad as *Sister Helen* is misquoted, and, indeed, from the *Burden of Nineveh*, the *Blessed Damozel*, the *King's Tragedy* and Guido Cavalcanti's lovely *ballata*, down to the *Portrait* and such sonnets as *Love-sweetness*, *Farewell to the Glen*, and *A Match with the Moon*, there is not one single poem that does not display some careless error or some stupid misprint.

As for Rossetti's elaborate system of punctuation, Mr. Knight pays no attention to it whatsoever. Indeed, he shows quite a rollicking indifference to all the secrets and subtleties of style, and inserts or removes stops in a manner that is absolutely destructive to the lyrical beauty of the verse. The hyphen, also, so constantly employed by Rossetti in the case of such expressions as 'hillock-eaves' quoted above, 'hill-fire,' 'birth-hour,' and the like, is almost invariably disregarded, and by the brilliant omission of a semicolon Mr. Knight has succeeded in spoiling one of the best stanzas in *The Staff and Scrip*—a poem, by the way, that he speaks of as *The Staff and the Scrip* (*sic*). After this tedious comedy of errors it seems almost unnecessary to point out that the earliest Italian poet is not called Ciullo D'Alcano (*sic*), or that *The Bothie of Toper-na-Fuosich* (*sic*) is not the title of Clough's boisterous epic, or that *Dante and his Cycle* (*sic*) is not the name Rossetti gave to his collection of translations; and why *Troy Town* should appear in the index as *Tory Town* is really quite inexplicable, unless it is intended as a compliment to Mr. Hall Caine who once dedicated, or rather tried to dedicate, to Rossetti a lecture on the relations of poets to politics. We are sorry, too, to find an English dramatic critic misquoting Shakespeare, as we had always been of opinion that this was a privilege reserved specially for our English actors. We sincerely hope that there will soon be an end to all biographies of this kind. They rob life of much of its dignity and its wonder, add to death itself a new terror, and make one wish that all art were anonymous. Nor could there have been any more unfortunate choice of a subject for popular treatment than that to which we owe the memoir that now lies before us. A pillar of fire to the few who knew him, and of cloud to the many who knew him not, Dante Gabriel Rossetti lived apart from the gossip and tittle-tattle of a shallow age. He never trafficked with the merchants for his soul, nor brought his wares into the market-place for the idle to gape at. Passionate and romantic though he was, yet there was in his nature something of high austerity. He loved seclusion, and hated notoriety, and would have shuddered at the idea that within a few years after his death he was to make his appearance in a series of popular biographies, sandwiched between the author of *Pickwick* and the Great Lexicographer. One man alone, the friend his verse won for him, did he desire should write his life, and it is to Mr. Theodore Watts that we, too, must look to give us the real Rossetti. It may be admitted at once that Mr. Watts's subject has for the moment been a little spoiled for him. Rude hands have touched it, and unmusical voices have made it sound almost common in our ears. Yet none the less is it for him to tell us of the marvel of this man whose art he has analysed with such exquisite insight, whose life he knows as no one else can know it, whom he so loyally loved and tended, and by whom he was so loyally beloved in turn. As for the others, the scribblers and nibblers of literature, if they indeed reverence Rossetti's memory, let them pay him the one homage he would most have valued, the gracious homage of silence. 'Though you can fret me, yet you cannot play upon me,' says Hamlet to his false friend, and even so might Rossetti speak to those well-intentioned mediocrities who would seem to know his stops and would sound him to the top of his compass. True, they cannot fret him now, for he has passed beyond the possibility of pain; yet they cannot play upon him either; it is not for them to pluck out the heart of his mystery.

There is, however, one feature of this book that deserves unstinted praise. Mr. Anderson's bibliography will be found of immense use by every student of Rossetti's work and influence. Perhaps Young's very powerful attack on Pre-Raphaelitism, as expounded by Mr. Ruskin (Longmans, 1857), might be included, but, in all other respects, it seems quite complete, and the chronological list of paintings and drawings is really admirable. When this unfortunate 'Great Writers' Series comes to an end, Mr. Anderson's bibliographies should be collected together and published in a separate volume. At present they are in a very second-rate company indeed.

Life of Dante Gabriel Rossetti. By Joseph Knight. 'Great Writers' Series. (Walter Scott.)

MR. MORRIS'S ODYSSEY

(*Pall Mall Gazette*, April 26, 1887.)

Of all our modern poets, Mr. William Morris is the one best qualified by nature and by art to translate for us the marvellous epic of the wanderings of Odysseus. For he is our only true story-singer since Chaucer; if he is a Socialist, he is also a Saga-man; and there was a time when he was never wearied of telling us strange legends of gods and men, wonderful tales of chivalry and romance. Master as he is of decorative and descriptive verse, he has all the Greek's joy in the visible aspect of things, all the Greek's sense of delicate and delightful detail, all the Greek's pleasure in beautiful textures and exquisite materials and imaginative designs; nor can any one have a keener sympathy with the Homeric admiration for the workers and the craftsmen in the various arts, from the stainers in white ivory and the embroiderers in purple and fold, to the weaver sitting by the loom and the dyer dipping in the vat, the chaser of shield and helmet, the carver of wood or stone. And to all this is added the true temper of high romance, the power to make the past as real to us as the present, the subtle instinct to discern passion, the swift impulse to portray life.

It is no wonder the lovers of Greek literature have so eagerly looked forward to Mr. Morris's version of the Odyssean epic, and now that the first volume has appeared, it is not extravagant to say that of all our English translations this is the most perfect and the most satisfying. In spite of Coleridge's well-known views on the subject, we have always held that Chapman's *Odyssey* is immeasurably inferior to his *Iliad*, the mere difference of metre alone being sufficient to set the former in a secondary place; Pope's *Odyssey*, with its glittering rhetoric and smart antithesis, has nothing of the grand manner of the original; Cowper is dull, and Bryant dreadful, and Worsley too full of Spenserian prettinesses; while excellent though Messrs. Butcher and Lang's version undoubtedly is in many respects, still, on the whole, it gives us merely the facts of the *Odyssey* without providing anything of its artistic effect. Avia's translation even, though better than almost all its predecessors in the same field, is not worthy of taking rank beside Mr. Morris's, for here we have a true work of art, a rendering not merely of language into language, but of poetry into poetry, and though the new spirit added in the transfusion may seem to many rather Norse than Greek, and, perhaps at times, more boisterous than beautiful, there is yet a vigour of life in every line, a splendid ardour through each canto, that stirs the blood while one reads like the sound of a trumpet, and that, producing a physical as well as a spiritual delight, exults the senses no less than it exalts the soul. It may be admitted at once that, here and there, Mr. Morris has missed something of the marvellous dignity of the Homeric verse, and that, in his desire for rushing and ringing metre, he has occasionally sacrificed majesty to movement, and made stateliness give place to speed; but it is really only in such blank verse as Milton's that this effect of calm and lofty music can be attained, and in all other respects blank verse is the most inadequate medium for reproducing the full flow and fervour of the Greek hexameter. One merit, at any rate, Mr. Morris's version entirely and absolutely possesses. It is, in no sense of the word, literary; it seems to deal immediately with life itself, and to take from the reality of things its own form and colour; it is always direct and simple, and at its best has something of the 'large utterance of the early gods.'

As for individual passages of beauty, nothing could be better than the wonderful description of the house of the Phœacian king, or the whole telling of the lovely legend of Circe, or the manner in which the pageant of the pale phantoms in Hades is brought before our eyes. Perhaps the huge epic humour of the escape from the Cyclops is hardly realised, but there is always a linguistic difficulty about rendering this fascinating story into English, and where we are given so much poetry we should not complain about losing a pun; and the exquisite idyll of the meeting and parting with the daughter of Alcinous is really delightfully told. How good, for instance, is this passage taken at random from the Sixth Book:

But therewith unto the handmaids goodly Odysseus spake:
'Stand off I bid you, damsels, while the work in hand I take,
And wash the brine from my shoulders, and sleek them all around.
Since verily now this long while sweet oil they have not found.
But before you nought will I wash me, for shame I have indeed,
Amidst of fair-tressed damsels to be all bare of weed.'
So he spake and aloof they gat them, and thereof they told the may,
But Odysseus with the river from his body washed away
The brine from his back and his shoulders wrought broad and mightily,
And from his head was he wiping the foam of the untilled sea;
But when he had throughly washed him, and the oil about him had shed
He did upon the raiment the gift of the maid unwed.
But Athene, Zeus-begotten, dealt with him in such wise
That bigger yet was his seeming, and mightier to all eyes,
With the hair on his head crisp curling as the bloom of the daffodil.
And as when the silver with gold is o'erlaid by a man of skill,

Yea, a craftsman whom Hephæstus and Pallas Athene have taught
To be master over masters, and lovely work he hath wrought;
So she round his head and his shoulders shed grace abundantly.

It may be objected by some that the line

With the hair on his head crisp curling as the bloom of the daffodil,

is a rather fanciful version of

ουλας ηκε κομας, νακινθινω ανθει ομοιας

and it certainly seems probable that the allusion is to the dark colour of the hero's hair; still, the point is not one of much importance, though it may be worth noting that a similar expression occurs in Ogilby's superbly illustrated translation of the *Odyssey*, published in 1665, where Charles II.'s Master of the Revels in Ireland gives the passage thus:

Minerva renders him more tall and fair,
Curling in rings like daffodils his hair.

No anthology, however, can show the true merit of Mr. Morris's translation, whose real merit does not depend on stray beauties, nor is revealed by chance selections, but lies in the absolute rightness and coherence of the whole, in its purity and justice of touch, its freedom from affectation and commonplace, its harmony of form and matter. It is sufficient to say that this is a poet's version of a poet, and for such surely we should be thankful. In these latter days of coarse and vulgar literature, it is something to have made the great sea-epic of the South native and natural to our northern isle, something to have shown that our English speech may be a pipe through which Greek lips can blow, something to have taught Nausicaa to speak the same language as Perdita.

The Odyssey of Homer. Done into English Verse by William Morris, author of *The Earthly Paradise*. In two volumes. Volume I. (Reeves and Turner.)

For review of Volume II. see *Mr. Morris's Completion of the Odyssey*, page 215.

A BATCH OF NOVELS

(*Pall Mall Gazette*, May 2, 1887.)

Of the three great Russian novelists of our time Tourgenieff is by far the finest artist. He has that spirit of exquisite selection, that delicate choice of detail, which is the essence of style; his work is entirely free from any personal intention; and by taking existence at its most fiery-coloured moments he can distil into a few pages of perfect prose the moods and passions of many lives.

Count Tolstoi's method is much larger, and his field of vision more extended. He reminds us sometimes of Paul Veronese, and, like that great painter, can crowd, without over-crowding, the giant canvas on which he works. We may not at first gain from his works that artistic unity of impression which is Tourgenieff's chief charm, but once that we have mastered the details the whole seems to have the grandeur and the simplicity of an epic. Dostoieffski differs widely from both his rivals. He is not so fine an artist as Tourgenieff, for he deals more with the facts than with the effects of life; nor has he Tolstoi's largeness of vision and epic dignity; but he has qualities that are distinctively and absolutely his own, such as a fierce intensity of passion and concentration of impulse, a power of dealing with the deepest mysteries of psychology and the most hidden springs of life, and a realism that is pitiless in its fidelity, and terrible because it is true. Some time ago we had occasion to draw attention to his marvellous novel *Crime and Punishment*, where in the haunt of impurity and vice a harlot and an assassin meet together to read the story of Dives and Lazarus, and the outcast girl leads the sinner to make atonement for his sin; nor is the book entitled *Injury and Insult* at all inferior to that great masterpiece. Mean and ordinary though the surroundings of the story may seem, the heroine Natasha is like one of the noble victims of Greek tragedy; she is Antigone with the passion of Phædra, and it is impossible to approach her without a feeling of awe. Greek also is the gloom of Nemesis that hangs over each character, only it is a Nemesis that does not stand outside of life, but is part of our own nature and of the same material as life itself. Aleósha, the beautiful young lad whom Natasha follows to her doom, is a second Tito Melema, and has all Tito's charm and grace and fascination. Yet he is different. He would never have denied Baldassare in the Square at Florence, nor lied to Romola about Tessa. He has a magnificent, momentary sincerity, a boyish unconsciousness of all that life signifies, an ardent enthusiasm for all that life cannot give. There is nothing calculating about him. He never thinks evil, he only does it. From a psychological point of view he is one of the most interesting characters of modern fiction, as from an artistic he is one of the most attractive. As we grow to know him he stirs strange questions for us, and makes us feel that it is not the wicked only who do wrong, nor the bad alone who work evil.

And by what a subtle objective method does Dostoieffski show us his characters! He never tickets them with a list nor labels them with a description. We grow to know them very gradually, as we know people whom we meet in society, at first by little tricks of manner, personal appearance, fancies in dress, and the like; and afterwards by their deeds and words; and even then they constantly elude us, for though Dostoieffski may lay bare for us the secrets of their nature, yet he never explains his personages away; they are always surprising us by something that they say or do, and keep to the end the eternal mystery of life.

Irrespective of its value as a work of art, this novel possesses a deep autobiographical interest also, as the character of Vania, the poor student who loves Natasha through all her sin and shame, is Dostoieffski's study of himself. Goethe once had to delay the completion of one of his novels till experience had furnished him with new situations, but almost before he had arrived at manhood Dostoieffski knew life in its most real forms; poverty and suffering, pain and misery, prison, exile, and love, were soon familiar to him, and by the lips of Vania he has told his own story. This note of personal feeling, this harsh reality of actual experience, undoubtedly gives the book something of its strange fervour and terrible passion, yet it has not made it egotistic; we see things from every point of view, and we feel, not that fiction has been trammelled by fact, but that fact itself has become ideal and imaginative. Pitiless, too, though Dostoieffski is in his method as an artist, as a man he is full of human pity for all, for those who do evil as well as for those who suffer it, for the selfish no less than for those whose lives are wrecked for others and whose sacrifice is in vain. Since *Adam Bede* and *Le Père Goriot* no more powerful novel has been written than *Insult and Injury*.

Mr. Hardinge's book *Willow Garth* deals, strangely enough, with something like the same idea, though the treatment is, of course, entirely different. A girl of high birth falls passionately in love with a young farm-bailiff who is a sort of Arcadian Antinous and a very Ganymede in gaiters. Social difficulties naturally intervene, so she drowns her handsome rustic in a convenient pond. Mr. Hardinge has a most charming style, and, as a writer, possesses both distinction and grace. The book is a delightful combination of romance and satire, and the heroine's crime is treated in the most picturesque manner possible.

Marcella Grace tells of modern life in Ireland, and is one of the best books Miss Mulholland has ever published. In its artistic reserve, and the perfect simplicity of its style, it is an excellent model for all lady-novelists to follow, and the scene where the heroine finds the man, who has been sent to shoot her, lying fever-stricken behind a hedge with his gun by his side, is really remarkable. Nor could anything be better than Miss Mulholland's treatment of external nature. She never shrieks over scenery like a tourist, nor wearies us with sunsets like the Scotch school; but all through her book there is a subtle atmosphere of purple hills and silent moorland; she makes us live with nature and not merely look at it.

The accomplished authoress of *Soap* was once compared to George Eliot by the *Court Journal*, and to Carlyle by the *Daily News*, but we fear that we cannot compete with our contemporaries in these daring comparisons. Her present book is very clever, rather vulgar, and contains some fine examples of bad French.

As for *A Marked Man*, *That Winter Night*, and *Driven Home*, the first shows some power of description and treatment, but is sadly incomplete; the second is quite unworthy of any man of letters, and the third is absolutely silly. We sincerely hope that a few more novels like these will be published, as the public will then find out that a bad book is very dear at a shilling.

(1) *Injury and Insult*. By Fedor Dostoieffski. Translated from the Russian by Frederick Whishaw. (Vizetelly and Co.)

(2) *The Willow Garth*. By W. M. Hardinge. (Bentley and Son.)

(3) *Marcella Grace*. By Rosa Mulholland. (Macmillan and Co.)

(4) *Soap*. By Constance MacEwen. (Arrowsmith.)

(5) *A Marked Man*. By Faucet Streets. (Hamilton and Adams.)

(6) *That Winter Night*. By Robert Buchanan. (Arrowsmith.)

(7) *Driven Home*. By Evelyn Owen. (Arrowsmith.)

SOME NOVELS

(*Saturday Review*, May 7, 1887.)

The only form of fiction in which real characters do not seem out of place is history. In novels they are detestable, and *Miss Bayle's Romance* is entirely spoiled as a realistic presentation of life by the author's attempt to introduce into her story a whole mob of modern celebrities and notorieties, including the Heir Apparent and Mr. Edmund Yates. The identity of the latter personage is delicately veiled under the pseudonym of 'Mr. Atlas, editor of the *World*,' but the former appears as 'The Prince of Wales' *pur et simple*, and is represented as spending his time yachting in the Channel and junketing at Homburg with a second-rate American family who, by the way, always address him as 'Prince,' and show in other respects an ignorance that even their ignorance cannot excuse. Indeed, His Royal Highness is no mere spectator of the story; he is one of the chief actors in it, and it is through his influence that the noisy Chicago *belle*, whose lack of romance gives the book its title, achieves her chief social success. As for the conversation with which the Prince is credited, it is of the most amazing kind. We find him on one page gravely discussing the depression of trade with Mr. Ezra P. Bayle, a shoddy American millionaire, who promptly replies, 'Depression of fiddle-sticks, Prince'; in another passage he naïvely inquires of the same shrewd speculator whether the thunderstorms and prairie fires of the West are still 'on so grand a scale' as when he visited Illinois; and we are told in the second volume that, after contemplating the magnificent view from St. Ives he exclaimed with enthusiasm, 'Surely Mr. Brett must have had a scene like this in his eye when he painted *Britannia's Realm*? I never saw anything more beautiful.' Even Her Majesty figures in this extraordinary story in spite of the excellent aphorism *ne touchez pas à la reine*; and when Miss Alma J. Bayle is married to the Duke of Windsor's second son she receives from the hands of royalty not merely the customary Cashmere shawl of Court tradition, but also a copy of *Diaries in the Highlands* inscribed 'To *the* Lady Plowden Eton, with the kindest wishes of Victoria R.I.', a mistake that the Queen, of all persons in the world, is the least likely to have committed. Perhaps, however, we are treating *Miss Bayle's Romance* too seriously. The book has really no claim to be regarded as a novel at all. It is simply a society paragraph expanded into three volumes and, like most paragraphs of the kind, is in the worst possible taste. We are not by any means surprised that the author, while making free with the names of others, has chosen to conceal his own name; for no reputation could possibly survive the production of such silly, stupid work; but we must say that we are surprised that this book has been brought out by the Publishers in Ordinary to Her Majesty the Queen. We do not know what the duties attaching to this office are, but we should not have thought that the issuing of vulgar stories about the Royal Family was one of them.

From Heather Hills is very pleasant reading indeed. It is healthy without being affected; and though Mrs. Perks gives us many descriptions of Scotch scenery we are glad to say that she has not adopted the common chromo-lithographic method of those popular North British novelists who have never yet fully realised the difference between colour and colours, and who imagine that by emptying a paint box over every page they can bring before us the magic of mist and mountain, the wonder of sea or glen. Mrs. Perks has a grace and delicacy of touch that is quite charming, and she can deal with nature without either botanising or being blatant, which nowadays is a somewhat rare accomplishment. The interest of the story centres on Margaret Dalrymple, a lovely Scotch girl who is brought to London by her aunt, takes every one by storm and falls in love with young Lord Erinwood, who is on the brink of proposing to her when he is dissuaded from doing so by a philosophic man of the world who thinks that a woodland Artemis is a bad wife for an English peer, and that no woman who has a habit of saying exactly what she means can possibly get on in smart society. The would-be philosopher is ultimately hoist with his own petard, as he falls in love himself with Margaret Dalrymple, and as for the weak young hero he is promptly snatched up, rather against his will, by a sort of Becky Sharp, who succeeds in becoming Lady Erinwood. However, a convenient railway accident, the *deus ex machina* of nineteenth-century novels, carries Miss Norma Novello off; and everybody is finally made happy, except, of course, the philosopher, who gets only a lesson where he wanted to get love. There is just one part of the novel to which we must take exception. The whole story of Alice Morgan is not merely needlessly painful, but it is of very little artistic value. A tragedy may be the basis of a story, but it should never be simply a casual episode. At least, if it is so, it entirely fails to produce any artistic effect. We hope, too, that in Mrs. Perks's next novel she will not allow her hero to misquote English poetry. This is a privilege reserved for Mrs. Malaprop.

A constancy that lasts through three volumes is often rather tedious, so that we are glad to make the acquaintance of Miss Lilian Ufford, the heroine of Mrs. Houston's *A Heart on Fire*. This young lady begins by being desperately in love with Mr. Frank Thorburn, a struggling schoolmaster, and ends by being desperately in love with Colonel Dallas, a rich country gentleman who spends most of his time and his money in preaching a crusade against beer. After she gets engaged to the Colonel she discovers that Mr. Thorburn is in reality Lord Netherby's son and heir, and for the moment she seems to have a true woman's regret at having given up a pretty title; but all ends well, and the story is brightly and pleasantly told. The Colonel is a middle-aged Romeo of the most impassioned character, and as it is his heart that is 'on fire,' he may serve as a psychological pendant to *La Femme de Quarante Ans.*

Mr. G. Manville Fenn's *A Bag of Diamonds* belongs to the Drury Lane School of Fiction and is a sort of fireside melodrama for the family circle. It is evidently written to thrill Bayswater, and no doubt Bayswater will be thrilled. Indeed, there is a great deal that is exciting in the book, and the scene in which a kindly policeman assists two murderers to convey their unconscious victim into a four-wheeled cab, under the impression that they are a party of guests returning from a convivial supper in Bloomsbury, is quite excellent of its kind, and, on the whole, not too improbable, considering that shilling literature is always making demands on our credulity without ever appealing to our imagination.

The Great Hesper, by Mr. Frank Barrett, has at least the merit of introducing into fiction an entirely new character. The villain is Nyctalops, and, though we are not prepared to say that there is any necessary connection between Nyctalopy and crime, we are quite ready to accept Mr. Barrett's picture of Jan Van Hoeck as an interesting example of the modern method of dealing with life. For, Pathology is rapidly becoming the basis of sensational literature, and in art, as in politics, there is a great future for monsters. What a Nyctalops is we leave Mr. Barrett to explain. His novel belongs to a class of book that many people might read once for curiosity but nobody could read a second time for pleasure.

A Day after the Fair is an account of a holiday tour through Scotland taken by two young barristers, one of whom rescues a pretty girl from drowning, falls in love with her, and is rewarded for his heroism by seeing her married to his friend. The idea of the book is not bad, but the treatment is very unsatisfactory, and combines the triviality of the tourist with the dulness of good intentions.

'Mr. Winter' is always amusing and audacious, though we cannot say that we entirely approve of the names he gives to his stories. *Bootle's Baby* was a masterpiece, but *Houp-la* was a terrible title, and *That Imp* is not much better. The book, however, is undoubtedly clever, and the Imp in question is not a Nyctalops nor a specimen for a travelling museum, but a very pretty girl who, because an officer has kissed her without any serious matrimonial intentions, exerts all her fascinations to bring the unfortunate Lovelace to her feet and, having succeeded in doing so, promptly rejects him with a virtuous indignation that is as delightful as it is out of place. We must confess that we have a good deal of sympathy for 'Driver' Dallas, of the Royal Horse, who suffers fearful agonies at what he imagines is a heartless flirtation on the part of the lady of his dreams; but the story is told from the Imp's point of view, and as such we must accept it. There is a very brilliant description of a battle in the Soudan, and the account of barrack life is, of course, admirable. So admirable indeed is it that we hope that 'Mr. Winter' will soon turn his attention to new topics and try to handle fresh subjects. It would be sad if such a clever and observant writer became merely the garrison hack of literature. We would also earnestly beg 'Mr. Winter' not to write foolish prefaces about unappreciative critics; for it is only mediocrities and old maids who consider it a grievance to be misunderstood.

(1) *Miss Bayle's Romance: A Story of To-Day.* (Bentley and Son, Publishers in Ordinary to Her Majesty the Queen.)

(2) *From Heather Hills.* By Mrs. J. Hartley Perks. (Hurst and Blackett.)

(3) *A Heart on Fire.* By Mrs. Houston. (F. V. White and Co.)

(4) *A Bag of Diamonds.* By George Manville Fenn. (Ward and Downey.)

(5) *The Great Hesper.* By Frank Barrett. (Ward and Downey.)

(6) *A Day after the Fair.* By William Cairns. (Swan Sonnenschein and Co.)

(7) *That Imp.* By John Strange Winter, Author of *Booties' Baby*, etc. (F. V. White and Co.)

THE POETS' CORNER—III

(*Pall Mall Gazette*, May 30, 1887.)

Such a pseudonym for a poet as 'Glenessa' reminds us of the good old days of the Della Cruscans, but it would not be fair to attribute Glenessa's poetry to any known school of literature, either past or present. Whatever qualities it possesses are entirely its own. Glenessa's most ambitious work, and the one that gives the title to his book, is a poetic drama about the Garden of Eden. The subject is undoubtedly interesting, but the execution can hardly be said to be quite worthy of it. Devils, on account of their inherent wickedness, may be excused for singing—

Then we'll rally—rally—rally—
Yes, we'll rally—rally O!—

but such scenes as—

Enter ADAM.

ADAM (excitedly). Eve, where art thou?

EVE (surprised). Oh!

ADAM (in astonishment). Eve! my God, she's there
Beside that fatal tree;

or—

Enter ADAM and EVE.

EVE (in astonishment). Well, is not this surprising?

ADAM (distracted). It is—

seem to belong rather to the sphere of comedy than to that of serious verse. Poor Glenessa! the gods have not made him poetical, and we hope he will abandon his wooing of the muse. He is fitted, not for better, but for other things.

Vortigern and Rowena is a cantata about the Britons and the Danes. There is a Druid priestess who sings of Cynthia and Endymion, and a chorus of jubilant Vikings. It is charmingly printed, and as a libretto for music quite above the average.

As truly religious people are resigned to everything, even to mediocre poetry, there is no reason at all why Madame Guyon's verses should not be popular with a large section of the community. Their editor, Mr. Dyer, has reprinted the translations Cowper made for Mr. Bull, added some versions of his own and written a pleasing preface about this gentle seventeenth-century saint whose life was her best, indeed her only true poem.

Mr. Pierce has discovered a tenth muse and writes impassioned verses to the Goddess of Chess whom he apostrophises as 'Sublime Caissa'! Zukertort and Steinitz are his heroes, and he is as melodious on mates as he is graceful on gambits. We are glad to say, however, that he has other subjects, and one of his poems beginning:

Cedar boxes deeply cut,
China bowls of quaint device,
Heap'd with rosy leaves and spice,
Violets in old volumes shut—

is very dainty and musical.

Mr. Clifford Harrison is well known as the most poetic of our reciters, but as a writer himself of poetry he is not so famous. Yet his little volume *In Hours of Leisure* contains some charming pieces, and many of the short fourteen-line poems are really pretty, though they are very defective in form. Indeed, of form Mr. Harrison is curiously careless. Such rhymes as 'calm' and 'charm,' 'baize' and 'place,' '*jeu*' and 'knew,' are quite dreadful, while 'operas' and 'stars,' 'Gaútama' and 'afar' are too bad even for Steinway Hall. Those who have Keats's genius may borrow Keats's cockneyisms, but from minor poets we have a right to expect some regard to the ordinary technique of verse. However, if Mr. Harrison has not always form, at least he has always feeling. He has a wonderful command over all the egotistic emotions, is quite conscious of the artistic value of remorse, and displays a sincere sympathy with his own moments of sadness, playing upon his moods as a young lady plays upon the piano. Now and then we come across some delicate descriptive touches, such as

The cuckoo knew its latest day had come,
And told its name once more to all the hills,

and whenever Mr. Harrison writes about nature he is certainly pleasing and picturesque but, as a rule, he is over-anxious about himself and forgets that the personal expression of joy or sorrow is not poetry, though it may afford excellent material for a sentimental diary.

The daily increasing class of readers that likes unintelligible poetry should study *Æonial*. It is in many ways a really remarkable production. Very fantastic, very daring, crowded with strange metaphor and clouded by monstrous imagery, it has a sort of turbid splendour about it, and should the author some day add meaning to his music he may give us a true work of art. At present he hardly realises that an artist should be articulate.

Seymour's Inheritance is a short novel in blank verse. On the whole, it is very harmless both in manner and matter, but we must protest against such lines as

And in the windows of his heart the blinds
Of happiness had been drawn down by Grief,

for a simile committing suicide is always a depressing spectacle. Some of the other poems are so simple and modest that we hope Mr. Ross will not carry out his threat of issuing a 'more pretentious volume.' Pretentious volumes of poetry are very common and very worthless.

Mr. Brodie's *Lyrics of the Sea* are spirited and manly, and show a certain freedom of rhythmical movement, pleasant in days of wooden verse. He is at his best, however, in his sonnets. Their architecture is not always of the finest order but, here and there, one meets with lines that are graceful and felicitous.

Like silver swallows on a summer morn
Cutting the air with momentary wings,

is pretty, and on flowers Mr. Brodie writes quite charmingly. The only thoroughly bad piece in the book is *The Workman's Song*. Nothing can be said in favour of

Is there a bit of blue, boys?
Is there a bit of blue?

In heaven's leaden hue, boys?

   'Tis hope's eye peeping through . . .

for optimism of this kind is far more dispiriting than Schopenhauer or Hartmann at their worst, nor are there really any grounds for supposing that the British workman enjoys third-rate poetry.

(1) *The Discovery and Other Poems.* By Glenessa. (National Publishing Co.)

(2) *Vortigern and Rowena: A Dramatic Cantata.* By Edwin Ellis Griffin. (Hutchings and Crowsley.)

(3) *The Poems of Madame de la Mothe Guyon.* Edited and arranged by the Rev. A. Saunders Dyer, M.A. (Bryce and Son.)

(4) *Stanzas and Sonnets.* By J. Pierce, M.A. (Longmans, Green and Co.)

(5) *In Hours of Leisure.* By Clifford Harrison. (Kegan Paul.)

(6) *Æonial.* By the Author of *The White Africans.* (Elliot Stock.)

(7) *Seymour's Inheritance.* By James Ross. (Arrowsmith.)

(8) *Lyrics of the Sea.* By E. H. Brodie. (Bell and Sons.)

MR. PATER'S IMAGINARY PORTRAITS

(*Pall Mall Gazette*, June 11, 1887.)

   To convey ideas through the medium of images has always been the aim of those who are artists as well as thinkers in literature, and it is to a desire to give a sensuous environment to intellectual concepts that we owe Mr. Pater's last volume. For these Imaginary or, as we should prefer to call them, Imaginative Portraits of his, form a series of philosophic studies in which the philosophy is tempered by personality, and the thought shown under varying conditions of mood and manner, the very permanence of each principle gaining something through the change and colour of the life through which it finds expression. The most fascinating of all these pictures is undoubtedly that of Sebastian Van Storck. The account of Watteau is perhaps a little too fanciful, and the description of him as one who was 'always a seeker after something in the world, that is there in no satisfying measure, or not at all,' seems to us more applicable to him who saw Mona Lisa sitting among the rocks than to the gay and debonair *peintre des fêtes galantes.* But Sebastian, the grave young Dutch philosopher, is charmingly drawn. From the first glimpse we get of him, skating over the water-meadows with his plume of squirrel's tail and his fur muff, in all the modest pleasantness of boyhood, down to his strange death in the desolate house amid the sands of the Helder, we seem to see him, to know him, almost to hear the low music of his voice. He is a dreamer, as the common phrase goes, and yet he is poetical in this sense, that his theorems shape life for him, directly. Early in youth he is stirred by a fine saying of Spinoza, and sets himself to realise the ideal of an intellectual disinterestedness, separating himself more and more from the transient world of sensation, accident and even affection, till what is finite and relative becomes of no interest to him, and he feels that as nature is but a thought of his, so he himself is but a passing thought of God. This conception, of the power of a mere metaphysical abstraction over the mind of one so fortunately endowed for the reception of the sensible world, is exceedingly delightful, and Mr. Pater has never written a more subtle psychological study, the fact that Sebastian dies in an attempt to save the life of a little child giving to the whole story a touch of poignant pathos and sad irony.

   Denys l'Auxerrois is suggested by a figure found, or said to be found, on some old tapestries in Auxerre, the figure of a 'flaxen and flowery creature, sometimes wellnigh naked among the vine-leaves, sometimes muffled in skins against the cold, sometimes in the dress of a monk, but always with a strong impress of real character and incident from the veritable streets' of the town itself. From this strange design Mr. Pater has fashioned a curious mediæval myth of the return of Dionysus among men, a myth steeped in colour and passion and old romance, full of wonder and full of worship, Denys himself being half animal and half god, making the world mad with a new ecstasy of living, stirring the artists simply by his visible presence, drawing the marvel of music from reed and pipe, and slain at last in a stage-play by those who had loved him. In its rich affluence of imagery this story is like a picture by Mantegna, and indeed Mantegna might have suggested the description of the pageant in which Denys rides upon a gaily-painted chariot, in soft silken raiment and, for head-dress, a strange elephant scalp with gilded tusks.

   If *Denys l'Auxerrois* symbolises the passion of the senses and *Sebastian Van Storck* the philosophic passion, as they certainly seem to do, though no mere formula or definition can adequately express the freedom and variety of the life that they portray, the passion for the imaginative world of art is the basis of the story of *Duke Carl of Rosenmold.* Duke Carl is not unlike the late King of Bavaria, in his love of France, his admiration for the *Grand Monarque* and his fantastic desire to amaze and to bewilder, but the resemblance is possibly only a chance one. In fact Mr. Pater's young hero is the precursor of the *Aufklärung* of the last century, the German precursor of Herder and Lessing and Goethe himself, and finds the forms of art ready to his hand without any national spirit to fill them or make them vital and responsive. He too dies, trampled to death by the soldiers of the country he so much admired, on the night of his marriage with a peasant girl, the very failure of his life lending him a certain melancholy grace and dramatic interest.

   On the whole, then, this is a singularly attractive book. Mr. Pater is an intellectual impressionist. He does not weary us with any definite doctrine or seek to suit life to any formal creed. He is always looking for exquisite moments and, when he has found them, he analyses them with delicate and delightful art and then passes on, often to the opposite pole of thought or feeling, knowing that every mood has its own quality and charm and is justified by its mere existence. He has taken the sensationalism of Greek philosophy and made it a new method of art criticism. As for his style, it is curiously ascetic. Now and then, we come across phrases with a strange sensuousness of expression, as when he tells us how Denys l'Auxerrois, on his return from a long journey, 'ate flesh for the first time, tearing the hot, red morsels with his delicate fingers in a kind of wild greed,' but such passages are rare. Asceticism is the keynote of Mr. Pater's prose; at times it is almost too severe in its self-control and makes us long for a little more freedom. For indeed, the danger of such prose as his is that it is apt to become somewhat laborious. Here and there, one is tempted to say of Mr. Pater that he is 'a seeker after something in language, that is there in no satisfying measure, or not at all.' The continual preoccupation with phrase and epithet has its drawbacks as well as its virtues. And yet, when all is said, what wonderful prose it is, with its subtle preferences, its fastidious purity, its rejection of what is common or ordinary! Mr. Pater has the true spirit of selection, the true tact of omission. If he be not among the greatest prose writers of our literature he is, at least, our greatest artist in prose; and though it may be admitted that the best style is that which seems an unconscious result rather than a conscious aim, still in these latter days when violent rhetoric does duty for eloquence and vulgarity usurps the name of nature, we should be grateful for a style that deliberately aims at perfection of form, that seeks to produce its effect by artistic means and sets before itself an ideal of grave and chastened beauty.

Imaginary Portraits. By Walter Pater, M.A., Fellow of Brasenose College, Oxford. (Macmillan and Co.)

A GOOD HISTORICAL NOVEL

(*Pall Mall Gazette*, August 8, 1887.)

Most modern Russian novelists look upon the historical novel as a *faux genre*, or a sort of fancy dress ball in literature, a mere puppet show, not a true picture of life. Yet their own history is full of such wonderful scenes and situations, ready for dramatist or novelist to treat of, that we are not surprised that, in spite of the dogmas of the *école naturaliste*, Mr. Stephen Coleridge has taken the Russia of the sixteenth century as the background for his strange tale. Indeed, there is much to be said in favour of a form remote from actual experience. Passion itself gains something from picturesqueness of surroundings; distance of time, unlike distance of space, makes objects larger and more vivid; over the common things of contemporary life there hangs a mist of familiarity that often makes their meaning obscure. There are also moments when we feel that but little artistic pleasure is to be gained from the study of the modern realistic school. Its works are powerful but they are painful, and after a time we tire of their harshness, their violence and their crudity. They exaggerate the importance of facts and underrate the importance of fiction. Such, at any rate, is the mood—and what is criticism itself but a mood?—produced in us by a perusal of Mr. Coleridge's *Demetrius*. It is the story of a young lad of unknown parentage who is brought up in the household of a Polish noble. He is a tall, fair-looking youth, by name Alexis, with a pride of bearing and grace of manner that seem strange in one of such low station. Suddenly he is recognised by an exiled Russian noble as Demetrius, the son of Ivan the Terrible who was supposed to have been murdered by the usurper Boris. His identity is still further established by a strange cross of seven emeralds that he wears round his neck, and by a Greek inscription in his book of prayers which discloses the secret of his birth and the story of his rescue. He himself feels that the blood of kings beats in his veins, and appeals to the nobles of the Polish Diet to espouse his cause. By his passionate utterance he makes them acknowledge him as the true Tsar and invades Russia at the head of a large army. The people throng to him from every side, and Marfa, the widow of Ivan the Terrible, escapes from the convent in which she has been immured by Boris and comes to meet her son. At first she seems not to recognise him, but the music of his voice and the wonderful eloquence of his pleading win her over, and she embraces him in presence of the army and admits him to be her child. The usurper, terrified at the tidings, and deserted by his soldiers, commits suicide, and Alexis enters Moscow in triumph, and is crowned in the Kremlin. Yet he is not the true Demetrius, after all. He is deceived himself and he deceives others. Mr. Coleridge has drawn his character with delicate subtlety and quick insight, and the scene in which he discovers that he is no son of Ivan's and has no right to the name he claims, is exceedingly powerful and dramatic. One point of resemblance does exist between Alexis and the real Demetrius. Both of them are murdered, and with the death of this strange hero Mr. Coleridge ends his remarkable story.

On the whole, Mr. Coleridge has written a really good historical novel and may be congratulated on his success. The style is particularly interesting, and the narrative parts of the book are deserving of high praise for their clearness, dignity and sobriety. The speeches and passages of dialogue are not so fortunate, as they have an awkward tendency to lapse into bad blank verse. Here, for instance, is a speech printed by Mr. Coleridge as prose, in which the true music of prose is sacrificed to a false metrical system which is at once monotonous and tiresome:

But Death, who brings us freedom from all falsehood,
Who heals the heart when the physician fails,
Who comforts all whom life cannot console,
Who stretches out in sleep the tired watchers;
He takes the King and proves him but a beggar!
He speaks, and we, deaf to our Maker's voice,
Hear and obey the call of our destroyer!
Then let us murmur not at anything;
For if our ills are curable, 'tis idle,
And if they are past remedy, 'tis vain.
The worst our strongest enemy can do
Is take from us our life, and this indeed
Is in the power of the weakest also.

This is not good prose; it is merely blank verse of an inferior quality, and we hope that Mr. Coleridge in his next novel will not ask us to accept second-rate poetry as musical prose. For, that Mr. Coleridge is a young writer of great ability and culture cannot be doubted and, indeed, in spite of the error we have pointed out, *Demetrius* remains one of the most fascinating and delightful novels that has appeared this season.

Demetrius. By the Hon. Stephen Coleridge. (Kegan Paul.)

NEW NOVELS

(*Saturday Review*, August 20, 1887.)

Teutonic fiction, as a rule, is somewhat heavy and very sentimental; but Werner's *Her Son*, excellently translated by Miss Tyrrell, is really a capital story and would make a capital play. Old Count Steinrück has two grandsons, Raoul and Michael. The latter is brought up like a peasant's child, cruelly treated by his grandfather and by the peasant to whose care he is confided, his mother, the Countess Louis Steinrück, having married an adventurer and a gambler. He is the rough hero of the tale, the Saint Michael of that war with evil which is life; while Raoul, spoiled by his grandfather and his French mother, betrays his country and tarnishes his name. At every step in the narrative these two young men come into collision. There is a war of character, a clash of personalities. Michael is proud, stern and noble. Raoul is weak, charming and evil. Michael has the world against him and conquers. Raoul has the world on his side and loses. The whole story is full of movement and life, and the psychology of the characters is displayed by action not by analysis, by deeds not by description. Though there are three long volumes, we do not tire of the tale. It has truth, passion and power, and there are no better things than these in fiction.

The interest of Mr. Sale Lloyd's *Scamp* depends on one of those misunderstandings which is the stock-in-trade of second-rate novelists. Captain Egerton falls in love with Miss Adela Thorndyke, who is a sort of feeble echo of some of Miss Broughton's heroines, but will not marry her because he has seen her talking with a young man who lives in the neighbourhood and is one of his oldest friends. We are sorry to say that Miss Thorndyke remains quite faithful to Captain Egerton, and goes so far as to refuse for his sake the rector of the parish, a local baronet, and a real live lord. There are endless pages of five o'clock tea-prattle and a good many tedious characters. Such novels as *Scamp* are possibly more easy to write than they are to read.

James Hepburn belongs to a very different class of book. It is not a mere chaos of conversation, but a strong story of real life, and it cannot fail to give Miss Veitch a prominent position among modern novelists. James Hepburn is the Free Church minister of Mossgiel, and presides over a congregation of pleasant sinners and serious hypocrites. Two people interest him, Lady Ellinor Farquharson and a handsome young vagabond called Robert Blackwood. Through his efforts to save Lady Ellinor from shame and ruin he is accused of being her lover; through his intimacy with Robert Blackwood he is suspected of having murdered a young girl in his household. A meeting of the elders and office-bearers of the church is held to consider the question of the minister's resignation, at which, to the amazement of every one, Robert Blackwood comes forth and confesses to the crime of which Hepburn is accused. The whole story is exceedingly powerful, and there is no extravagant use of the Scotch dialect, which is a great advantage to the reader.

The title-page of *Tiff* informs us that it was written by the author of *Lucy; or, a Great Mistake*, which seems to us a form of anonymity, as we have never heard of the novel in question. We hope, however, that it was better than *Tiff*, for *Tiff* is undeniably tedious. It is the story of a beautiful girl who has many lovers and loses them, and of an ugly girl who has one lover and keeps him. It is a rather confused tale, and there are far too many love-scenes in it. If this 'Favourite Fiction' Series, in which *Tiff* appears, is to be continued, we would entreat the publisher to alter the type and the binding. The former is far too small: while, as for the cover, it is of sham crocodile leather adorned with a blue spider and a vulgar illustration of the heroine in the arms of a young man in evening dress. Dull as *Tiff* is—and its dulness is quite remarkable—it does not deserve so detestable a binding.

(1) *Her Son*. Translated from the German of E. Werner by Christina Tyrrell. (Richard Bentley and Son.)

(2) *Scamp*. By J. Sale Lloyd. (White and Co.)

(3) *James Hepburn*. By Sophie Veitch. (Alexander Gardner.)

(4) *Tiff*. By the Author of *Lucy; or, A Great Mistake*. 'Favourite Fiction' Series. (William Stevens.)

TWO BIOGRAPHIES OF KEATS

(*Pall Mall Gazette*, September 27, 1887.)

A poet, said Keats once, 'is the most unpoetical of all God's creatures,' and whether the aphorism be universally true or not, this is certainly the impression produced by the two last biographies that have appeared of Keats himself. It cannot be said that either Mr. Colvin or Mr. William Rossetti makes us love Keats more or understand him better. In both these books there is much that is like 'chaff in the mouth,' and in Mr. Rossetti's there is not a little that is like 'brass on the palate.' To a certain degree this is, no doubt, inevitable nowadays. Everybody pays a penalty for peeping through keyholes, and the keyhole and the backstairs are essential parts of the method of the modern biographers. It is only fair, however, to state at the outset that Mr. Colvin has done his work much better than Mr. Rossetti. The account Mr. Colvin gives of Keats's boyhood, for instance, is very pleasing, and so is the sketch of Keats's circle of friends, both Leigh Hunt and Haydon being admirably drawn. Here and there, trivial family details are introduced without much regard to proportion, and the posthumous panegyrics of devoted friends are not really of so much value, in helping us to form any true estimate of Keats's actual character, as Mr. Colvin seems to imagine. We have no doubt that when Bailey wrote to Lord Houghton that common-sense and gentleness were Keats's two special characteristics the worthy Archdeacon meant extremely well, but we prefer the real Keats, with his passionate wilfulness, his fantastic moods and his fine inconsistence. Part of Keats's charm as a man is his fascinating incompleteness. We do not want him reduced to a sand-paper smoothness or made perfect by the addition of popular virtues. Still, if Mr. Colvin has not given us a very true picture of Keats's character, he has certainly told the story of his life in a pleasant and readable manner. He may not write with the ease and grace of a man of letters, but he is never pretentious and not often pedantic.

Mr. Rossetti's book is a great failure. To begin with, Mr. Rossetti commits the great mistake of separating the man from the artist. The facts of Keats's life are interesting only when they are shown in their relation to his creative activity. The moment they are isolated they are either uninteresting or painful. Mr. Rossetti complains that the early part of Keats's life is uneventful and the latter part depressing, but the fault lies with the biographer, not with the subject.

The book opens with a detailed account of Keats's life, in which he spares us nothing, from what he calls the 'sexual misadventure at Oxford' down to the six weeks' dissipation after the appearance of the *Blackwood* article and the hysterical and morbid ravings of the dying man. No doubt, most if not all of the things Mr. Rossetti tells us are facts; but there is neither tact shown in the selection that is made of the facts nor sympathy in the use to which they are put. When Mr. Rossetti writes of the man he forgets the poet, and when he criticises the poet he shows that he does not understand the man. His first error, as we have said, is isolating the life from the work; his second error is his treatment of the work itself. Take, for instance, his criticism of that wonderful *Ode to a Nightingale*, with all its marvellous magic of music, colour and form. He begins by saying that 'the first point of weakness' in the poem is the 'surfeit of mythological allusions,' a statement which is absolutely untrue, as out of the eight stanzas of the poem only three contain any mythological allusions at all, and of these not one is either forced or remote. Then coming to the second verse,

> Oh for a draught of vintage, that hath been
> Cool'd a long age in the deep-delvèd earth,
> Tasting of Flora and the country-green,
> Dance, and Provençal song, and sunburnt mirth!

Mr. Rossetti exclaims in a fine fit of 'Blue Ribbon' enthusiasm: 'Surely nobody wants wine as a preparation for enjoying a nightingale's music, whether in a literal or in a fanciful relation'! 'To call wine "the true, the blushful Hippocrene" . . . seems' to him 'both stilted and repulsive'; 'the phrase "with beaded bubbles winking at the brim" is (though picturesque) trivial'; 'the succeeding image, "Not charioted by Bacchus and his pards"' is 'far worse'; while such an expression as 'light-winged Dryad of the trees' is an obvious pleonasm, for Dryad really means *Oak*-nymph! As for that superb burst of passion,

> Thou wast not born for death, immortal Bird!
> No hungry generations tread thee down;
> The voice I hear this passing night was heard
> In ancient days by emperor and clown:

Mr. Rossetti tells us that it is a palpable, or rather 'palpaple (*sic*) fact that this address . . . is a logical solecism,' as men live longer than nightingales. As Mr. Colvin makes very much the same criticism, talking of 'a breach of logic which is also . . . a flaw in the poetry,' it may be worth while to point out to these two last critics of Keats's work that what Keats meant to convey was the contrast between the permanence of beauty and the change and decay of human life, an idea which receives its fullest expression in the *Ode on a Grecian Urn*. Nor do the other poems fare much better at Mr. Rossetti's hands. The fine invocation in *Isabella*—

> Moan hither, all ye syllables of woe,
> From the deep throat of sad Melpomene!
> Through bronzèd lyre in tragic order go,
> And touch the strings into a mystery,

seems to him 'a *fadeur*'; the Indian Bacchante of the fourth book of *Endymion* he calls a 'sentimental and beguiling wine-bibber,' and, as for Endymion himself, he declares that he cannot understand 'how his human organism, *with respirative and digestive processes*, continues to exist,' and gives us his own idea of how Keats should have treated the subject. An eminent French critic once exclaimed in despair, '*Je trouve des physiologistes partout*!'; but it has been reserved for Mr. Rossetti to speculate on Endymion's digestion, and we readily accord to him all the distinction of the position. Even where Mr. Rossetti seeks to praise, he spoils what he praises. To speak of *Hyperion* as 'a monument of Cyclopean architecture in verse' is bad enough, but to call it 'a Stonehenge of reverberance' is absolutely detestable; nor do we learn much about *The Eve of St. Mark* by being told that its 'simplicity is full-blooded as well as quaint.' What is the meaning, also, of stating that Keats's *Notes on Shakespeare* are 'somewhat strained and *bloated*'? and is there nothing better to be said of Madeline in *The Eve of St. Agnes* than that 'she is made a very charming and loveable figure, *although she does nothing very particular except to undress without looking behind her, and to elope*'? There is no necessity to follow Mr. Rossetti any further as he flounders about through the quagmire that he has made for his own feet. A critic who can say that 'not many of Keats's poems are highly admirable' need not be too seriously treated. Mr. Rossetti is an industrious man and a painstaking writer, but he entirely lacks the temper necessary for the interpretation of such poetry as was written by John Keats.

It is pleasant to turn again to Mr. Colvin, who criticises always with modesty and often with acumen. We do not agree with him when he accepts Mrs. Owens's theory of a symbolic and allegoric meaning underlying *Endymion*, his final judgment on Keats as 'the most Shaksperean spirit that has lived since Shakspere' is not very fortunate, and we are surprised to find him suggesting, on the evidence of a rather silly story of Severn's, that Sir Walter Scott was privy to the *Blackwood* article. There is nothing, however, about his estimate of the poet's work that is harsh, irritating or uncouth. The true Marcellus of English song has not yet found his Virgil, but Mr. Colvin makes a tolerable Statius.

(1) *Keats*. By Sidney Colvin. 'English Men of Letters' Series. (Macmillan and Co.)

(2) *Life of John Keats*. By William Michael Rossetti. 'Great Writers' Series. (Walter Scott.)

A SCOTCHMAN ON SCOTTISH POETRY

(*Pall Mall Gazette*, October 24, 1887.)

A distinguished living critic, born south of the Tweed, once whispered in confidence to a friend that he believed that the Scotch knew really very little about their own national literature. He quite admitted that they love their 'Robbie Burns' and their 'Sir Walter' with a patriotic enthusiasm that makes them extremely severe upon any unfortunate southron who ventures to praise either in their presence, but he claimed that the works of such great national poets as Dunbar, Henryson and Sir David Lyndsay are sealed books to the majority of the reading public in Edinburgh, Aberdeen and Glasgow, and that few Scotch people have any idea of the wonderful outburst of poetry that took place in their country during the fifteenth and sixteenth centuries, at a time when there was little corresponding development in England. Whether this terrible accusation be absolutely true, or not, it is needless to discuss at present. It is probable that the archaism of language alone will always prevent a poet like Dunbar from being popular in the ordinary acceptation of the word. Professor Veitch's book, however, shows that there are some, at any rate, in the 'land o' cakes' who can admire and appreciate their marvellous early singers, and whose admiration for *The Lord of the Isles* and the verses *To a Mountain Daisy* does not blind them to the exquisite beauties of *The Testament of Cresseid*, *The Thistle and the Rose*, and the *Dialog betwix Experience and ane Courteour*.

Taking as the subject of his two interesting volumes the feeling for Nature in Scottish Poetry, Professor Veitch starts with a historical disquisition on the growth of the sentiment in humanity. The primitive state he regards as being simply a sort of 'open-air feeling.' The chief sources of pleasure are the warmth of the sunshine, the cool of the breeze and the general fresh aspect of the earth and sky, connecting itself with a consciousness of life and sensuous enjoyment; while darkness, storm and cold are regarded as repulsive. This is followed by the pastoral stage in which we find the love of green meadows and of shady trees and of all things that make life pleasant and comfortable. This, again, by the stage of agriculture, the era of the war with earth, when men take pleasure in the cornfield and in the garden, but hate everything that is opposed to tillage, such as woodland and rock, or that cannot be subdued to utility, such as mountain and sea. Finally we come to the pure nature-feeling, the free delight in the mere contemplation of the external world, the joy in sense-impressions irrespective of all questions of Nature's utility and beneficence. But here the growth does not stop. The Greek, desiring to make Nature one with humanity, peopled the grove and hillside with beautiful and fantastic forms, saw the god hiding in the thicket, and the naiad drifting with the stream. The modern Wordsworthian, desiring to make man one with Nature, finds in external things 'the symbols of our inner life, the workings of a spirit akin to our own.' There is much that is suggestive in these early chapters of Professor Veitch's book, but we cannot agree with him in the view he takes of the primitive attitude towards Nature. The 'open-air feeling,' of which he talks, seems to us comparatively modern. The earliest Nature-myths tell us, not of man's 'sensuous enjoyment' of Nature, but of the terror that Nature inspires. Nor are darkness and storm regarded by the primitive man as 'simply repulsive'; they are to him divine and supernatural things, full of wonder and full of awe. Some reference, also, should have been made to the influence of towns on the development of the nature-feeling, for, paradox though it may seem, it is none the less true that it is largely to the creation of cities that we owe the love of the country.

Professor Veitch is on a safer ground when he comes to deal with the growth and manifestations of this feeling as displayed in Scotch poetry. The early singers, as he points out, had all the mediæval love of gardens, all the artistic delight in the bright colours of flowers and the pleasant song of birds, but they felt no sympathy for the wild solitary moorland, with its purple heather, its grey rocks and its waving bracken. Montgomerie was the first to wander out on the banks and braes and to listen to the music of the burns, and it was reserved for Drummond of Hawthornden to sing of flood and forest and to notice the beauty of the mists on the hillside and the snow on the mountain tops. Then came Allan Ramsay with his honest homely pastorals; Thomson, who writes about Nature like an eloquent auctioneer, and yet was a keen observer, with a fresh eye and an open heart; Beattie, who approached the problems that Wordsworth afterwards solved; the great Celtic epic of Ossian, such an important factor in the romantic movement of Germany and France; Fergusson, to whom Burns is so much indebted; Burns himself, Leyden, Sir Walter Scott, James Hogg and (*longo intervallo*) Christopher North and the late Professor Shairp. On nearly all these poets Professor Veitch writes with fine judgment and delicate feeling, and even his admiration for Burns has nothing absolutely aggressive about it. He shows, however, a certain lack of the true sense of literary proportion in the amount of space he devotes to the two last writers on our list. Christopher North was undoubtedly an interesting personality to the Edinburgh of his day, but he has not left behind him anything of real permanent value. There was too much noise in his criticism, too little music in his poetry. As for Professor Shairp, looked on as a critic he was a tragic example of the unfortunate influence of Wordsworth, for he was always confusing ethical with æsthetical questions, and never had the slightest idea how to approach such poets as Shelley and Rossetti whom it was his mission to interpret to young Oxford in his later years; {189} while, considered as a poet, he deserves hardly more than a passing reference. Professor Veitch gravely tells us that one of the descriptions of *Kilmahoe* is 'not surpassed in the language for real presence, felicity of epithet, and purity of reproduction,' and statements of this kind serve to remind us of the fact that a criticism which is based on patriotism is always provincial in its result. But it is only fair to add that it is very rarely that Professor Veitch is so extravagant and so grotesque. His judgment and taste are, as a rule, excellent, and his book is, on the whole, a very fascinating and delightful contribution to the history of literature.

The Feeling for Nature in Scottish Poetry. By John Veitch, Professor of Logic and Rhetoric in the University of Glasgow. (Blackwood and Son.)

LITERARY AND OTHER NOTES—I

(*Woman's World*, November 1887.)

The Princess Christian's translation of the *Memoirs of Wilhelmine, Margravine of Baireuth*, is a most fascinating and delightful book. The Margravine and her brother, Frederick the Great, were, as the Princess herself points out in an admirably written introduction, 'among the first of those questioning minds that strove after spiritual freedom' in the last century. 'They had studied,' says the Princess, 'the English philosophers, Newton, Locke, and Shaftesbury, and were roused to enthusiasm by the writings of Voltaire and Rousseau. Their whole lives bore the impress of the influence of French thought on the burning questions of the day. In the eighteenth century began that great struggle of philosophy against tyranny and worn-out abuses which culminated in the French Revolution. The noblest minds were engaged in the struggle, and, like most reformers, they pushed their conclusions to extremes, and too often lost sight of the need of a due proportion in things. The Margravine's influence on the intellectual development of her country is untold. She formed at Baireuth a centre of culture and learning which had before been undreamt of in Germany.'

The historical value of these *Memoirs* is, of course, well known. Carlyle speaks of them as being 'by far the best authority' on the early life of Frederick the Great. But considered merely as the autobiography of a clever and charming woman, they are no less interesting, and even those who care nothing for eighteenth-century politics, and look upon history itself as an unattractive form of fiction, cannot fail to be fascinated by the Margravine's wit, vivacity and humour, by her keen powers of observation, and by her brilliant and assertive egotism. Not that her life was by any means a happy one. Her father, to quote the Princess Christian, 'ruled his family with the same harsh despotism with which he ruled his country, taking pleasure in making his power felt by all in the most galling manner,' and the Margravine and her brother 'had much to suffer, not only from his ungovernable temper, but also from the real privations to which they were subjected.' Indeed, the picture the Margravine gives of the King is quite extraordinary. 'He despised all learning,' she writes, 'and wished me to occupy myself with nothing but needlework and household duties or details. Had he found me writing or reading, he would probably have whipped me.' He 'considered music a capital offence, and maintained that every one should devote himself to one object: men to the military service, and women to their household duties. Science and the arts he counted among the "seven deadly sins."' Sometimes he took to religion, 'and then,' says the Margravine, 'we lived like Trappists, to the great grief of my brother and myself. Every afternoon the King preached a sermon, to which we had to listen as attentively as if it proceeded from an Apostle. My brother and I were often seized with such an intense sense of the ridiculous that we burst out laughing, upon which an apostolic curse was poured out on our heads, which we had to accept with a show of humility and penitence.' Economy and soldiers were his only topics of conversation; his chief social amusement was to make his guests intoxicated; and as for his temper, the accounts the Margravine gives of it would be almost incredible if they were not amply corroborated from other sources. Suetonius has written of the strange madness that comes on kings, but even in his melodramatic chronicles there is hardly anything that rivals what the Margravine has to tell us. Here is one of her pictures of family life at a Royal Court in the last century, and it is not by any means the worst scene she describes:

On one occasion, when his temper was more than usually bad, he told the Queen that he had received letters from Anspach, in which the Margrave announced his arrival at Berlin for the beginning of May. He was coming there for the purpose of marrying my sister, and one of his ministers would arrive previously with the betrothal ring. My father asked my sister whether she were pleased at this prospect, and how she would arrange her household. Now my sister had always made a point of telling him whatever came into her head, even the greatest home-truths, and he had never taken her outspokenness amiss. On this occasion, therefore, relying on former experience, she answered him as follows: 'When I have a house of my own, I shall take care to have a well-appointed dinner-table, better than yours is, and if I have children of my own, I shall not plague them as you do yours, and force them to eat things they thoroughly dislike!'

'What is amiss with my dinner-table?' the King enquired, getting very red in the face.

'You ask what is the matter with it,' my sister replied; 'there is not enough on it for us to eat, and what there is is cabbage and carrots, which we detest.' Her first answer had already angered my father, but now he gave vent to his fury. But instead of punishing my sister he poured it all on my mother, my brother, and myself. To begin with he threw his plate at my brother's head, who would have been struck had he not got out of the way; a second one he threw at me, which I also happily escaped; then torrents of abuse followed these first signs of hostility. He reproached the Queen with having brought up her children so badly. 'You will curse your mother,' he said to my brother, 'for having made you such a good-for-nothing creature.' . . . As my brother and I passed near him to leave the room, he hit out at us with his crutch. Happily we escaped the blow; for it would certainly have struck us down, and we at last escaped without harm.

Yet, as the Princess Christian remarks, 'despite the almost cruel treatment Wilhelmine received from her father, it is noticeable that throughout her memoirs she speaks of him with the greatest affection. She makes constant reference to his "good heart"'; and says that his faults 'were more those of temper than of nature.' Nor could all the misery and wretchedness of her home life dull the brightness of her intellect. What would have made others morbid, made her satirical. Instead of weeping over her own personal tragedies, she laughs at the general comedy of life. Here, for instance, is her description of Peter the Great and his wife, who arrived at Berlin in 1718:

The Czarina was small, broad, and brown-looking, without the slightest dignity or appearance. You had only to look at her to detect her low origin. She might have passed for a German actress, she had decked herself out in such a manner. Her dress had been bought second-hand, and was trimmed with some dirty looking silver embroidery; the bodice was trimmed with precious stones, arranged in such a manner as to represent the double eagle. She wore a dozen orders; and round the bottom of her dress hung quantities of relics and pictures of saints, which rattled when she walked, and reminded one of a smartly harnessed mule. The orders too made a great noise, knocking against each other.

The Czar, on the other hand, was tall and well grown, with a handsome face, but his expression was coarse, and impressed one with fear. He wore a simple sailor's dress. His wife, who spoke German very badly, called her court jester to her aid, and spoke Russian with her. This poor creature was a Princess Gallizin, who had been obliged to undertake this sorry office to save her life, as she had been mixed up in a conspiracy against the Czar, and had twice been flogged with the knout!

* * * * * *

The following day [the Czar] visited all the sights of Berlin, amongst others the very curious collection of coins and antiques. Amongst these last named was a statue, representing a heathen god. It was anything but attractive, but was the most valuable in the collection. The Czar admired it very much, and insisted on the Czarina kissing it. On her refusing, he said to her in bad German that she should lose her head if she did not at once obey him. Being terrified at the Czar's anger she immediately complied with his orders without the least hesitation. The Czar asked the King to give him this and other statues, a request which he could not refuse. The same thing happened about a cupboard, inlaid with amber. It was the only one of its kind, and had cost King Frederick I. an enormous sum, and the consternation was general on its having to be sent to Petersburg.

This barbarous Court happily left after two days. The Queen rushed at once to Monbijou, which she found in a state resembling that of the fall of Jerusalem. I never saw such a sight. Everything was destroyed, so that the Queen was obliged to rebuild the whole house.

55

Nor are the Margravine's descriptions of her reception as a bride in the principality of Baireuth less amusing. Hof was the first town she came to, and a deputation of nobles was waiting there to welcome her. This is her account of them:

Their faces would have frightened little children, and, to add to their beauty, they had arranged their hair to resemble the wigs that were then in fashion. Their dresses clearly denoted the antiquity of their families, as they were composed of heirlooms, and were cut accordingly, so that most of them did not fit. In spite of their costumes being the 'Court Dresses,' the gold and silver trimmings were so black that you had a difficulty in making out of what they were made. The manners of these nobles suited their faces and their clothes. They might have passed for peasants. I could scarcely restrain my laughter when I first beheld these strange figures. I spoke to each in turn, but none of them understood what I said, and their replies sounded to me like Hebrew, because the dialect of the Empire is quite different from that spoken in Brandenburg.

The clergy also presented themselves. These were totally different creatures. Round their necks they wore great ruffs, which resembled washing baskets. They spoke very slowly, so that I might be able to understand them better. They said the most foolish things, and it was only with much difficulty that I was able to prevent myself from laughing. At last I got rid of all these people, and we sat down to dinner. I tried my best to converse with those at table, but it was useless. At last I touched on agricultural topics, and then they began to thaw. I was at once informed of all their different farmsteads and herds of cattle. An almost interesting discussion took place as to whether the oxen in the upper part of the country were fatter than those in the lowlands.

* * * * *

I was told that as the next day was Sunday, I must spend it at Hof, and listen to a sermon. Never before had I heard such a sermon! The clergyman began by giving us an account of all the marriages that had taken place from Adam's time to that of Noah. We were spared no detail, so that the gentlemen all laughed and the poor ladies blushed. The dinner went off as on the previous day. In the afternoon all the ladies came to pay me their respects. Gracious heavens! What ladies, too! They were all as ugly as the gentlemen, and their head-dresses were so curious that swallows might have built their nests in them.

As for Baireuth itself, and its petty Court, the picture she gives of it is exceedingly curious. Her father-in-law, the reigning Margrave, was a narrow-minded mediocrity, whose conversation 'resembled that of a sermon read aloud for the purpose of sending the listener to sleep,' and he had only two topics, Telemachus, and Amelot de la Houssaye's *Roman History*. The Ministers, from Baron von Stein, who always said 'yes' to everything, to Baron von Voit, who always said 'no,' were not by any means an intellectual set of men. 'Their chief amusement,' says the Margravine, 'was drinking from morning till night,' and horses and cattle were all they talked about. The palace itself was shabby, decayed and dirty. 'I was like a lamb among wolves,' cries the poor Margravine; 'I was settled in a strange country, at a Court which more resembled a peasant's farm, surrounded by coarse, bad, dangerous, and tiresome people.'

Yet her *esprit* never deserted her. She is always clever, witty, and entertaining. Her stories about the endless squabbles over precedence are extremely amusing. The society of her day cared very little for good manners, knew, indeed, very little about them, but all questions of etiquette were of vital importance, and the Margravine herself, though she saw the shallowness of the whole system, was far too proud not to assert her rights when circumstances demanded it, as the description she gives of her visit to the Empress of Germany shows very clearly. When this meeting was first proposed, the Margravine declined positively to entertain the idea. 'There was no precedent,' she writes, 'of a King's daughter and the Empress having met, and I did not know to what rights I ought to lay claim.' Finally, however, she is induced to consent, but she lays down three conditions for her reception:

I desired first of all that the Empress's Court should receive me at the foot of the stairs, secondly, that she should meet me at the door of her bedroom, and, thirdly, that she should offer me an armchair to sit on.

* * * * *

They disputed all day over the conditions I had made. The two first were granted me, but all that could be obtained with respect to the third was, that the Empress would use quite a small armchair, whilst she gave me a chair.

Next day I saw this Royal personage. I own that had I been in her place I would have made all the rules of etiquette and ceremony the excuse for not being obliged to appear. The Empress was small and stout, round as a ball, very ugly, and without dignity or manner. Her mind corresponded to her body. She was terribly bigoted, and spent her whole day praying. The old and ugly are generally the Almighty's portion. She received me trembling all over, and was so upset that she could not say a word.

After some silence I began the conversation in French. She answered me in her Austrian dialect that she could not speak in that language, and begged I would speak in German. The conversation did not last long, for the Austrian and low Saxon tongues are so different from each other that to those acquainted with only one the other is unintelligible. This is what happened to us. A third person would have laughed at our misunderstandings, for we caught only a word here and there, and had to guess the rest. The poor Empress was such a slave to etiquette that she would have thought it high treason had she spoken to me in a foreign language, though she understood French quite well.

Many other extracts might be given from this delightful book, but from the few that have been selected some idea can be formed of the vivacity and picturesqueness of the Margravine's style. As for her character, it is very well summed up by the Princess Christian, who, while admitting that she often appears almost heartless and inconsiderate, yet claims that, 'taken as a whole, she stands out in marked prominence among the most gifted women of the eighteenth century, not only by her mental powers, but by her goodness of heart, her self-sacrificing devotion, and true friendship.' An interesting sequel to her *Memoirs* would be her correspondence with Voltaire, and it is to be hoped that we may shortly see a translation of these letters from the same accomplished pen to which we owe the present volume. {198}

* * * * *

Women's Voices is an anthology of the most characteristic poems by English, Scotch and Irish women, selected and arranged by Mrs. William Sharp. 'The idea of making this anthology,' says Mrs. Sharp, in her preface, 'arose primarily from the conviction that our women-poets had never been collectively represented with anything like adequate justice; that the works of many are not so widely known as they deserve to be; and that at least some fine fugitive poetry could be thus rescued from oblivion'; and Mrs. Sharp proceeds to claim that the 'selections will further emphasise the value of women's work in poetry for those who are already well acquainted with English Literature, and that they will convince many it is as possible to form an anthology of "pure poetry" from the writings of women as from those of men.' It is somewhat difficult to define what 'pure poetry' really is, but the collection is certainly extremely interesting, extending, as it does, over nearly three centuries of our literature. It opens with *Revenge*, a poem by the 'learned, virtuous, and truly noble Ladie,' Elizabeth Carew, who published a *Tragedie of Marian, the faire Queene of Iewry*, in 1613, from which *Revenge* is taken. Then come some very pretty verses by Margaret, Duchess of Newcastle, who produced a volume of poems in 1653. They are supposed to be sung by a sea-goddess, and their fantastic charm and the graceful wilfulness of their fancy are well worthy of note, as these first stanzas show:

My cabinets are oyster-shells,
In which I keep my Orient pearls;
And modest coral I do wear,
Which blushes when it touches air.

On silvery waves I sit and sing,
And then the fish lie listening:
Then resting on a rocky stone
I comb my hair with fishes' bone;

The whilst Apollo with his beams
Doth dry my hair from soaking streams,
His light doth glaze the water's face,
And make the sea my looking-glass.

Then follow *Friendship's Mystery*, by 'The Matchless Orinda,' Mrs. Katherine Philips; *A Song*, by Mrs. Aphra Behn, 'the first English woman who adopted literature as a profession'; and the Countess of Winchelsea's *Nocturnal Reverie*. Wordsworth once said that, with the exception of this poem and Pope's *Windsor Forest*, 'the poetry of the period intervening between *Paradise Lost* and *The Seasons* does not contain a single new image of external nature,' and though the statement is hardly accurate, as it leaves Gay entirely out of account, it must be admitted that the simple naturalism of Lady Winchelsea's description is extremely remarkable. Passing on through Mrs. Sharp's collection, we come across poems by Lady Grisell Baillie; by Jean Adams, a poor 'sewing-maid in a Scotch manse,' who died in the Greenock Workhouse; by Isobel Pagan, 'an Ayrshire lucky, who kept an alehouse, and sold whiskey without a license,' 'and sang her own songs as a means of subsistence'; by Mrs. Thrale, Dr. Johnson's friend; by Mrs. Hunter, the wife of the great anatomist; by the worthy Mrs. Barbauld; and by the excellent Mrs. Hannah More. Here is Miss Anna Seward, 'called by her admirers "the Swan of Lichfield,"' who was so angry with Dr. Darwin for plagiarising some of her verses; Lady Anne Barnard, whose *Auld Robin Gray* was described by Sir Walter Scott as 'worth all the dialogues Corydon and Phyllis have together spoken from the days of Theocritus downwards'; Jean Glover, a Scottish weaver's daughter, who 'married a strolling player and became the best singer and actor of his troop'; Joanna Baillie, whose tedious dramas thrilled our grandfathers; Mrs. Tighe, whose *Psyche* was very much admired by Keats in his youthful days; Frances Kemble, Mrs. Siddons's niece; poor L. E. L., whom Disraeli described as 'the personification of Brompton, pink satin dress, white satin shoes, red cheeks, snub nose, and her hair *à la* Sappho'; the two beautiful sisters, Lady Dufferin and Mrs. Norton; Emily Bronte, whose poems are instinct with tragic power and quite terrible in their bitter intensity of passion, the fierce fire of feeling seeming almost to consume the raiment of form; Eliza Cook, a kindly, vulgar writer; George Eliot, whose poetry is too abstract, and lacks all rhythmical life; Mrs. Carlyle, who wrote much better poetry than her husband, though this is hardly high praise; and Mrs. Browning, the first really great poetess in our literature. Nor are contemporary writers forgotten. Christina Rossetti, some of whose poems are quite priceless in their beauty; Mrs. Augusta Webster, Mrs. Hamilton King, Miss Mary Robinson, Mrs. Craik; Jean Ingelow, whose sonnet on *An Ancient Chess King* is like an exquisitely carved gem; Mrs. Pfeiffer; Miss May Probyn, a poetess with the true lyrical impulse of song, whose work is as delicate as it is delightful; Mrs. Nesbit, a very pure and perfect artist; Miss Rosa Mulholland, Miss Katharine Tynan, Lady Charlotte Elliot, and many other well-known writers, are duly and adequately represented. On the whole, Mrs. Sharp's collection is very pleasant reading indeed, and the extracts given from the works of living poetesses are extremely remarkable, not merely for their absolute artistic excellence, but also for the light they throw upon the spirit of modern culture.

It is not, however, by any means a complete anthology. Dame Juliana Berners is possibly too antiquated in style to be suitable to a modern audience. But where is Anne Askew, who wrote a ballad in Newgate; and where is Queen Elizabeth, whose 'most sweet and sententious ditty' on Mary Stuart is so highly praised by Puttenham as an example of 'Exargasia,' or The Gorgeous in Literature? Why is the Countess of Pembroke excluded? Sidney's sister should surely have a place in any anthology of English verse. Where is Sidney's niece, Lady Mary Wroth, to whom Ben Jonson dedicated *The Alchemist*? Where is 'the noble ladie Diana Primrose,' who wrote *A Chain of Pearl, or a memorial of the peerless graces and heroic virtues of Queen Elizabeth, of glorious memory*? Where is Mary Morpeth, the friend and admirer of Drummond of Hawthornden? Where is the Princess Elizabeth, daughter of James I., and where is Anne Killigrew, maid of honour to the Duchess of York? The Marchioness of Wharton, whose poems were praised by Waller; Lady Chudleigh, whose lines beginning—

Wife and servant are the same,
But only differ in the name,

are very curious and interesting; Rachel Lady Russell, Constantia Grierson, Mary Barber, Lætitia Pilkington; Eliza Haywood, whom Pope honoured by a place in *The Dunciad*; Lady Luxborough, Lord Bolingbroke's half-sister; Lady Mary Wortley Montagu; Lady Temple, whose poems were printed by Horace Walpole; Perdita, whose lines on the snowdrop are very pathetic; the beautiful Duchess of Devonshire, of whom Gibbon said that 'she was made for something better than a Duchess'; Mrs. Ratcliffe, Mrs. Chapone, and Amelia Opie, all deserve a place on historical, if not on artistic, grounds. In fact, the space given by Mrs. Sharp to modern and living poetesses is somewhat disproportionate, and I am sure that those on whose brows the laurels are still green would not grudge a little room to those the green of whose laurels is withered and the music of whose lyres is mute.

Reviews

* * * * *

One of the most powerful and pathetic novels that has recently appeared is *A Village Tragedy* by Margaret L. Woods. To find any parallel to this lurid little story, one must go to Dostoieffski or to Guy de Maupassant. Not that Mrs. Woods can be said to have taken either of these two great masters of fiction as her model, but there is something in her work that recalls their method; she has not a little of their fierce intensity, their terrible concentration, their passionless yet poignant objectivity; like them, she seems to allow life to suggest its own mode of presentation; and, like them, she recognises that a frank acceptance of the facts of life is the true basis of all modern imitative art. The scene of Mrs. Woods's story lies in one of the villages near Oxford; the characters are very few in number, and the plot is extremely simple. It is a romance of modern Arcadia—a tale of the love of a farm-labourer for a girl who, though slightly above him in social station and education, is yet herself also a servant on a farm. True Arcadians they are, both of them, and their ignorance and isolation serve only to intensify the tragedy that gives the story its title. It is the fashion nowadays to label literature, so, no doubt, Mrs. Woods's novel will be spoken of as 'realistic.' Its realism, however, is the realism of the artist, not of the reporter; its tact of treatment, subtlety of perception, and fine distinction of style, make it rather a poem than a *procès-verbal*; and though it lays bare to us the mere misery of life, it suggests something of life's mystery also. Very delicate, too, is the handling of external Nature. There are no formal guide-book descriptions of scenery, nor anything of what Byron petulantly called 'twaddling about trees,' but we seem to breathe the atmosphere of the country, to catch the exquisite scent of the beanfields, so familiar to all who have ever wandered through the Oxfordshire lanes in June; to hear the birds singing in the thicket, and the sheep-bells tinkling from the hill. Characterisation, that enemy of literary form, is such an essential part of the method of the modern writer of fiction, that Nature has almost become to the novelist what light and shade are to the painter—the one permanent element of style; and if the power of *A Village Tragedy* be due to its portrayal of human life, no small portion of its charm comes from its Theocritean setting.

* * * * *

It is, however, not merely in fiction and in poetry that the women of this century are making their mark. Their appearance amongst the prominent speakers at the Church Congress, some weeks ago, was in itself a very remarkable proof of the growing influence of women's opinions on all matters connected with the elevation of our national life, and the amelioration of our social conditions. When the Bishops left the platform to their wives, it may be said that a new era began, and the change will, no doubt, be productive of much good. The Apostolic dictum, that women should not be suffered to teach, is no longer applicable to a society such as ours, with its solidarity of interests, its recognition of natural rights, and its universal education, however suitable it may have been to the Greek cities under Roman rule. Nothing in the United States struck me more than the fact that the remarkable intellectual progress of that country is very largely due to the efforts of American women, who edit many of the most powerful magazines and newspapers, take part in the discussion of every question of public interest, and exercise an important influence upon the growth and tendencies of literature and art. Indeed, the women of America are the one class in the community that enjoys that leisure which is so necessary for culture. The men are, as a rule, so absorbed in business, that the task of bringing some element of form into the chaos of daily life is left almost entirely to the opposite sex, and an eminent Bostonian once assured me that in the twentieth century the whole culture of his country would be in petticoats. By that time, however, it is probable that the dress of the two sexes will be assimilated, as similarity of costume always follows similarity of pursuits.

* * * * *

In a recent article in *La France*, M. Sarcey puts this point very well. The further we advance, he says, the more apparent does it become that women are to take their share as bread-winners in the world. The task is no longer monopolised by men, and will, perhaps, be equally shared by the sexes in another hundred years. It will be necessary, however, for women to invent a suitable costume, as their present style of dress is quite inappropriate to any kind of mechanical labour, and must be radically changed before they can compete with men upon their own ground. As to the question of desirability, M. Sarcey refuses to speak. 'I shall not see the end of this revolution,' he remarks, 'and I am glad of it.' But, as is pointed out in a very sensible article in the *Daily News*, there is no doubt that M. Sarcey has reason and common-sense on his side with regard to the absolute unsuitability of ordinary feminine attire to any sort of handicraft, or even to any occupation which necessitates a daily walk to business and back again in all kinds of weather. Women's dress can easily be modified and adapted to any exigencies of the kind; but most women refuse to modify or adapt it. They must follow the fashion, whether it be convenient or the reverse. And, after all, what is a fashion? From the artistic point of view, it is usually a form of ugliness so intolerable that we have to alter it every six months. From the point of view of science, it not unfrequently violates every law of health, every principle of hygiene. While from the point of view of simple ease and comfort, it is not too much to say that, with the exception of M. Felix's charming tea-gowns, and a few English tailor-made costumes, there is not a single form of really fashionable dress that can be worn without a certain amount of absolute misery to the wearer. The contortion of the feet of the Chinese beauty, said Dr. Naftel at the last International Medical Congress, held at Washington, is no more barbarous or unnatural than the panoply of the *femme du monde*.

And yet how sensible is the dress of the London milk-woman, of the Irish or Scotch fishwife, of the North-Country factory-girl! An attempt was made recently to prevent the pit-women from working, on the ground that their costume was unsuited to their sex, but it is really only the idle classes who dress badly. Wherever physical labour of any kind is required, the costume used is, as a rule, absolutely right, for labour necessitates freedom, and without freedom there is no such thing as beauty in dress at all. In fact, the beauty of dress depends on the beauty of the human figure, and whatever limits, constrains, and mutilates is essentially ugly, though the eyes of many are so blinded by custom that they do not notice the ugliness till it has become unfashionable.

What women's dress will be in the future it is difficult to say. The writer of the *Daily News* article is of opinion that skirts will always be worn as distinctive of the sex, and it is obvious that men's dress, in its present condition, is not by any means an example of a perfectly rational costume. It is more than probable, however, that the dress of the twentieth century will emphasise distinctions of occupation, not distinctions of sex.

* * * * *

It is hardly too much to say that, by the death of the author of *John Halifax, Gentleman*, our literature has sustained a heavy loss. Mrs. Craik was one of the finest of our women-writers, and though her art had always what Keats called 'a palpable intention upon one,' still its imaginative qualities were of no mean order. There is hardly one of her books that has not some distinction of style; there is certainly not one of them that does not show an ardent love of all that is beautiful and good in life. The good she, perhaps, loved somewhat more than the beautiful, but her heart had room for both. Her first novel appeared in 1849, the year of the publication of Charlotte Bronte's *Jane Eyre*, and Mrs. Gaskell's *Ruth*, and her last work was done for the magazine which I have the honour to edit. She was very much interested in the scheme for the foundation of the *Woman's World*, suggested its title, and promised to be one of its warmest supporters. One article from her pen is already in proof and will appear next month, and in a letter I received from her, a few days before she died, she told me that she had almost finished a second, to be called *Between Schooldays and Marriage*. Few women have enjoyed a greater popularity than Mrs. Craik, or have better deserved it. It is sometimes said that John Halifax is not a real man, but only a woman's ideal of a man. Well, let us be grateful for such ideals. No one can read the story of which John Halifax is the hero without being the better for it. Mrs. Craik will live long in the affectionate memory of all who knew her, and one of her novels, at any rate, will always have a high and honourable place in English fiction. Indeed, for simple narrative power, some of the chapters of *John Halifax, Gentleman*, are almost unequalled in our prose literature.

* * * * *

The news of the death of Lady Brassey has been also received by the English people with every expression of sorrow and sympathy. Though her books were not remarkable for any perfection of literary style, they had the charm of brightness, vivacity, and unconventionality. They revealed a fascinating personality, and their touches of domesticity made them classics in many an English household. In all modern movements Lady Brassey took a keen interest. She gained a first-class certificate in the South Kensington School of Cookery, scullery department and all; was one of the most energetic members of the St. John's Ambulance Association, many branches of which she succeeded in founding; and, whether at Normanhurst or in Park Lane, always managed to devote some portion of her day to useful and practical work. It is sad to have to chronicle in the first number of the *Woman's World* the death of two of the most remarkable Englishwomen of our day.

(1) *Memoirs of Wilhelmine Margravine of Baireuth*. Translated and edited by Her Royal Highness Princess Christian of Schleswig-Holstein, Princess of Great Britain and Ireland. (David Stott.)

(2) *Women's Voices*: *An Anthology of the most Characteristic Poems by English, Scotch, and Irish Women*. Selected, edited, and arranged by Mrs. William Sharp. (Walter Scott.)

(3) *A Village Tragedy*. By Margaret L. Woods. (Bentley and Son.)

MR. MAHAFFY'S NEW BOOK

(*Pall Mall Gazette*, November 9, 1887.)

Mr. Mahaffy's new book will be a great disappointment to everybody except the Paper-Unionists and the members of the Primrose League. His subject, the history of *Greek Life and Thought: from the Age of Alexander to the Roman Conquest*, is extremely interesting, but the manner in which the subject is treated is quite unworthy of a scholar, nor can there be anything more depressing than Mr. Mahaffy's continual efforts to degrade history to the level of the ordinary political pamphlet of contemporary party warfare. There is, of course, no reason why Mr. Mahaffy should be called upon to express any sympathy with the aspirations of the old Greek cities for freedom and autonomy. The personal preferences of modern historians on these points are matters of no import whatsoever. But in his attempts to treat the Hellenic world as 'Tipperary writ large,' to use Alexander the Great as a means of whitewashing Mr. Smith, and to finish the battle of Chæronea on the plains of Mitchelstown, Mr. Mahaffy shows an amount of political bias and literary blindness that is quite extraordinary. He might have made his book a work of solid and enduring interest, but he has chosen to give it a merely ephemeral value and to substitute for the scientific temper of the true historian the prejudice, the flippancy, and the violence of the platform partisan. For the flippancy parallels can, no doubt, be found in some of Mr. Mahaffy's earlier books, but the prejudice and the violence are new, and their appearance is very much to be regretted. There is always something peculiarly impotent about the violence of a literary man. It seems to bear no reference to facts, for it is never kept in check by action. It is simply a question of adjectives and rhetoric, of exaggeration and over-emphasis. Mr. Balfour is very anxious that Mr. William O'Brien should wear prison clothes, sleep on a plank bed, and be subjected to other indignities, but Mr. Mahaffy goes far beyond such mild measures as these, and begins his history by frankly expressing his regret that Demosthenes was not summarily put to death for his attempt to keep the spirit of patriotism alive among the citizens of Athens! Indeed, he has no patience with what he calls 'the foolish and senseless opposition to Macedonia'; regards the revolt of the Spartans against 'Alexander's Lord Lieutenant for Greece' as an example of 'parochial politics'; indulges in Primrose League platitudes against a low franchise and the iniquity of allowing 'every pauper' to have a vote; and tells us that the 'demagogues' and 'pretended patriots' were so lost to shame that they actually preached to the parasitic mob of Athens the doctrine of autonomy—'not now extinct,' Mr. Mahaffy adds regretfully—and propounded, as a principle of political economy, the curious idea that people should be allowed to manage their own affairs! As for the personal character of the despots, Mr. Mahaffy admits that if he had to judge by the accounts in the Greek historians, from Herodotus downwards, he 'would certainly have said that the ineffaceable passion for autonomy, which marks every epoch of Greek history, and every canton within its limits, must have arisen from the excesses committed by the officers of foreign potentates, or local tyrants,' but a careful study of the cartoons published in *United Ireland* has convinced him 'that a ruler may be the soberest, the most conscientious, the most considerate, and yet have terrible things said of him by mere political malcontents.' In fact, since Mr. Balfour has been caricatured, Greek history must be entirely rewritten! This is the pass to which the distinguished professor of a distinguished university has been brought. Nor can anything equal Mr. Mahaffy's prejudice against the Greek patriots, unless it be his contempt for those few fine Romans who, sympathising with Hellenic civilisation and culture, recognised the political value of autonomy and the intellectual importance of a healthy national life. He mocks at what he calls their 'vulgar mawkishness about Greek liberties, their anxiety to redress historical wrongs,' and congratulates his readers that this feeling was not intensified by the remorse that their own forefathers had been the oppressors. Luckily, says Mr. Mahaffy, the old Greeks had conquered Troy, and so the pangs of conscience which now so deeply afflict a Gladstone and a Morley for the sins of their ancestors could hardly affect a Marcius or a Quinctius! It is quite unnecessary to comment on the silliness and bad taste of passages of this kind, but it is interesting to note that the facts of history are too strong even for Mr. Mahaffy. In spite of his sneers at the provinciality of national feeling and his vague panegyrics on cosmopolitan culture, he is compelled to admit that 'however patriotism may be superseded in stray individuals by larger benevolence, bodies of men who abandon it will only replace it by meaner motives,' and cannot help expressing his regret that the better classes among the Greek communities were so entirely devoid of public spirit that they squandered 'as idle absentees, or still idler residents, the time and means given them to benefit their country,' and failed to recognise their opportunity of founding a Hellenic Federal Empire. Even when he comes to deal with art, he cannot help admitting that the noblest sculpture of the time was that which expressed the spirit of the first great *national* struggle, the repulse of the Gallic hordes which overran Greece in 278 B.C., and that to the patriotic feeling evoked at this crisis we owe the *Belvedere Apollo*, the *Artemis* of the Vatican, the *Dying Gaul*, and the finest achievements of the Perganene school. In literature, also, Mr. Mahaffy is loud in his lamentations over what he considers to be the shallow society tendencies of the new comedy, and misses the fine freedom of Aristophanes, with his intense patriotism, his vital interest in politics, his large issues and his delight in vigorous national life. He confesses the decay of oratory under the blighting influences of imperialism, and the sterility of those pedantic disquisitions upon style which are the inevitable consequence of the lack of healthy subject-matter. Indeed, on the last page of his history Mr. Mahaffy makes a formal recantation of most of his political prejudices. He is still of opinion that Demosthenes should have been put to death for resisting the Macedonian invasion, but admits that the imperialism of Rome, which followed the imperialism of Alexander, produced incalculable mischief, beginning with intellectual decay, and ending with financial ruin. 'The touch of Rome,' he says, 'numbed Greece and Egypt, Syria and Asia Minor, and if there are great buildings attesting the splendour of the Empire, where are the signs of intellectual and moral vigour, if we except that stronghold of nationality, the little land of Palestine?' This palinode is, no doubt, intended to give a plausible air of fairness to the book, but such a death-bed repentance comes too late, and makes the whole preceding history seem not fair but foolish.

It is a relief to turn to the few chapters that deal directly with the social life and thought of the Greeks. Here Mr. Mahaffy is very pleasant reading indeed. His account of the colleges at Athens and Alexandria, for instance, is extremely interesting, and so is his estimate of the schools of Zeno, of Epicurus, and of Pyrrho. Excellent, too, in many points is the description of the literature and art of the period. We do not agree with Mr. Mahaffy in his panegyric of the Laocoon, and we are surprised to find a writer, who is very indignant at what he considers to be the modern indifference to Alexandrine poetry, gravely stating that no study is 'more wearisome and profitless' than that of the *Greek Anthology.*

The criticism of the new comedy, also, seems to us somewhat pedantic. The aim of social comedy, in Menander no less than in Sheridan, is to mirror the manners, not to reform the morals, of its day, and the censure of the Puritan, whether real or affected, is always out of place in literary criticism, and shows a want of recognition of the essential distinction between art and life. After all, it is only the Philistine who thinks of blaming Jack Absolute for his deception, Bob Acres for his cowardice, and Charles Surface for his extravagance, and there is very little use in airing one's moral sense at the expense of one's artistic appreciation. Valuable, also, though modernity of expression undoubtedly is, still it requires to be used with tact and judgment. There is no objection to Mr. Mahaffy's describing Philopœmen as the Garibaldi, and Antigonus Doson as the Victor Emmanuel of his age. Such comparisons have, no doubt, a certain cheap popular value. But, on the other hand, a phrase like 'Greek Pre-Raphaelitism' is rather awkward; not much is gained by dragging in an allusion to Mr. Shorthouse's *John Inglesant* in a description of the *Argonautics* of Apollonius Rhodius; and when we are told that the superb Pavilion erected in Alexandria by Ptolemy Philadelphus was a 'sort of glorified Holborn Restaurant,' we must say that the elaborate description of the building given in Athenæus could have been summed up in a better and a more intelligible epigram.

On the whole, however, Mr. Mahaffy's book may have the effect of drawing attention to a very important and interesting period in the history of Hellenism. We can only regret that, just as he has spoiled his account of Greek politics by a foolish partisan bias, so he should have marred the value of some of his remarks on literature by a bias that is quite as unmeaning. It is uncouth and harsh to say that 'the superannuated schoolboy who holds fellowships and masterships at English colleges' knows nothing of the period in question except what he reads in Theocritus, or that a man may be considered in England a distinguished Greek professor 'who does not know a single date in Greek history between the death of Alexander and the battle of Cynoscephalæ'; and the statement that Lucian, Plutarch, and the four Gospels are excluded from English school and college studies in consequence of the pedantry of 'pure scholars, as they are pleased to call themselves,' is, of course, quite inaccurate. In fact, not merely does Mr. Mahaffy miss the spirit of the true historian, but he often seems entirely devoid of the temper of the true man of letters. He is clever, and, at times, even brilliant, but he lacks reasonableness, moderation, style and charm. He seems to have no sense of literary proportion, and, as a rule, spoils his case by overstating it. With all his passion for imperialism, there is something about Mr. Mahaffy that is, if not parochial, at least provincial, and we cannot say that this last book of his will add anything to his reputation either as an historian, a critic, or a man of taste.

Greek Life and Thought: from the Age of Alexander to the Roman Conquest. By J. P. Mahaffy, Fellow of Trinity College, Dublin. (Macmillan and Co.)

MR. MORRIS'S COMPLETION OF THE ODYSSEY

(*Pall Mall Gazette*, November 24, 1887.)

Mr. Morris's second volume brings the great romantic epic of Greek literature to its perfect conclusion, and although there can never be an ultimate translation of either *Iliad* or *Odyssey*, as each successive age is sure to find pleasure in rendering the two poems in its own manner and according to its own canons of taste, still it is not too much to say that Mr. Morris's version will always be a true classic amongst our classical translations. It is not, of course, flawless. In our notice of the first volume we ventured to say that Mr. Morris was sometimes far more Norse than Greek, nor does the volume that now lies before us make us alter that opinion. The particular metre, also, selected by Mr. Morris, although admirably adapted to express 'the strong-winged music of Homer,' as far as its flow and freedom are concerned, misses something of its dignity and calm. Here, it must be admitted, we feel a distinct loss, for there is in Homer not a little of Milton's lofty manner, and if swiftness be an essential of the Greek hexameter, stateliness is one of its distinguishing qualities in Homer's hands. This defect, however, if we must call it a defect, seems almost unavoidable, as for certain metrical reasons a majestic movement in English verse is necessarily a slow movement; and, after all that can be said is said, how really admirable is this whole translation! If we set aside its noble qualities as a poem and look on it purely from the scholar's point of view, how straightforward it is, how honest and direct! Its fidelity to the original is far beyond that of any other verse-translation in our literature, and yet it is not the fidelity of a pedant to his text but rather the fine loyalty of poet to poet.

When Mr. Morris's first volume appeared many of the critics complained that his occasional use of archaic words and unusual expressions robbed his version of the true Homeric simplicity. This, however, is not a very felicitous criticism, for while Homer is undoubtedly simple in his clearness and largeness of vision, his wonderful power of direct narration, his wholesome sanity, and the purity and precision of his method, simple in language he undoubtedly is not. What he was to his contemporaries we have, of course, no means of judging, but we know that the Athenian of the fifth century B.C. found him in many places difficult to understand, and when the creative age was succeeded by the age of criticism and Alexandria began to take the place of Athens as the centre of culture for the Hellenistic world, Homeric dictionaries and glossaries seem to have been constantly published. Indeed, Athenæus tells us of a wonderful Byzantine blue-stocking, a *précieuse* from the Propontis, who wrote a long hexameter poem, called *Mnemosyne*, full of ingenious commentaries on difficulties in Homer, and in fact, it is evident that, as far as the language is concerned, such a phrase as 'Homeric simplicity' would have rather amazed an ancient Greek. As for Mr. Morris's tendency to emphasise the etymological meaning of words, a point commented on with somewhat flippant severity in a recent number of *Macmillan's Magazine*, here Mr. Morris seems to us to be in complete accord, not merely with the spirit of Homer, but with the spirit of all early poetry. It is quite true that language is apt to degenerate into a system of almost algebraic symbols, and the modern city-man who takes a ticket for Blackfriars Bridge, naturally never thinks of the Dominican monks who once had their monastery by Thames-side, and after whom the spot is named. But in earlier times it was not so. Men were then keenly conscious of the real meaning of words, and early poetry, especially, is full of this feeling, and, indeed, may be said to owe to it no small portion of its poetic power and charm. These old words, then, and this old use of words which we find in Mr. Morris's *Odyssey* can be amply justified upon historical grounds, and as for their artistic effect, it is quite excellent. Pope tried to put Homer into the ordinary language of his day, with what result we know only too well; but Mr. Morris, who uses his archaisms with the tact of a true artist, and to whom indeed they seem to come absolutely naturally, has succeeded in giving to his version by their aid that touch, not of 'quaintness,' for Homer is never quaint, but of old-world romance and old-world beauty, which we moderns find so pleasurable, and to which the Greeks themselves were so keenly sensitive.

As for individual passages of special merit, Mr. Morris's translation is no robe of rags sewn with purple patches for critics to sample. Its real value lies in the absolute rightness and coherence of the whole, in the grand architecture of the swift, strong verse, and in the fact that the standard is not merely high but everywhere sustained. It is impossible, however, to resist the temptation of quoting Mr. Morris's rendering of that famous passage in the twenty-third book of the epic, in which Odysseus eludes the trap laid for him by Penelope, whose very faith in the certainty of her husband's return makes her sceptical of his identity when he stands before her; an instance, by the way, of Homer's wonderful psychological knowledge of human nature, as it is always the dreamer himself who is most surprised when his dream comes true.

Thus she spake to prove her husband; but Odysseus, grieved at heart,
Spake thus unto his bed-mate well-skilled in gainful art:
'O woman, thou sayest a word exceeding grievous to me!
Who hath otherwhere shifted my bedstead? full hard for him should it be,
For as deft as he were, unless soothly a very God come here,
Who easily, if he willed it, might shift it otherwhere.
But no mortal man is living, how strong soe'er in his youth,
Who shall lightly hale it elsewhere, since a mighty wonder forsooth
Is wrought in that fashioned bedstead, and I wrought it, and I alone.
In the close grew a thicket of olive, a long-leaved tree full-grown,
That flourished and grew goodly as big as a pillar about,
So round it I built my bride-room, till I did the work right out
With ashlar stone close-fitting; and I roofed it overhead,
And thereto joined doors I made me, well-fitting in their stead.
Then I lopped away the boughs of the long-leafed olive-tree,
And shearing the bole from the root up full well and cunningly,
I planed it about with the brass, and set the rule thereto,
And shaping thereof a bed-post, with the wimble I bored it through.
So beginning, I wrought out the bedstead, and finished it utterly,
And with gold enwrought it about, and with silver and ivory,
And stretched on it a thong of oxhide with the purple dye made bright.
Thus then the sign I have shown thee; nor, woman, know I aright
If my bed yet bideth steadfast, or if to another place
Some man hath moved it, and smitten the olive-bole from its base.'

These last twelve books of the *Odyssey* have not the same marvel of romance, adventure and colour that we find in the earlier part of the epic. There is nothing in them that we can compare to the exquisite idyll of Nausicaa or to the Titanic humour of the episode in the Cyclops' cave. Penelope has not the glamour of Circe, and the song of the Sirens may sound sweeter than the whizz of the arrows of

Odysseus as he stands on the threshold of his hall. Yet, for sheer intensity of passionate power, for concentration of intellectual interest and for masterly dramatic construction, these latter books are quite unequalled. Indeed, they show very clearly how it was that, as Greek art developed, the epos passed into the drama. The whole scheme of the argument, the return of the hero in disguise, his disclosure of himself to his son, his terrible vengeance on his enemies and his final recognition by his wife, reminds us of the plot of more than one Greek play, and shows us what the great Athenian poet meant when he said that his own dramas were merely scraps from Homer's table. In rendering this splendid poem into English verse, Mr. Morris has done our literature a service that can hardly be over-estimated, and it is pleasant to think that, even should the classics be entirely excluded from our educational systems, the English boy will still be able to know something of Homer's delightful tales, to catch an echo of his grand music and to wander with the wise Odysseus round 'the shores of old romance.'

The Odyssey of Homer. Done into English Verse by William Morris, Author of *The Earthly Paradise*. Volume II. (Reeves and Turner.)

SIR CHARLES BOWEN'S VIRGIL

(*Pall Mall Gazette*, November 30, 1887.)

Sir Charles Bowen's translation of the *Eclogues* and the first six books of the *Æneid* is hardly the work of a poet, but it is a very charming version for all that, combining as it does the fine loyalty and learning of a scholar with the graceful style of a man of letters, two essential qualifications for any one who would render in English verse the picturesque pastorals of Italian provincial life, or the stately and polished epic of Imperial Rome. Dryden was a true poet, but, for some reason or other, he failed to catch the real Virgilian spirit. His own qualities became defects when he accepted the task of a translator. He is too robust, too manly, too strong. He misses Virgil's strange and subtle sweetness and has but little of his exquisite melody. Professor Conington, on the other hand, was an admirable and painstaking scholar, but he was so entirely devoid of literary tact and artistic insight that he thought that the majesty of Virgil could be rendered in the jingling manner of *Marmion*, and though there is certainly far more of the mediæval knight than of the moss-trooper about Æneas, even Mr. Morris's version is not by any means perfect. Compared with professor Conington's bad ballad it is, of course, as gold to brass; considered simply as a poem it has noble and enduring qualities of beauty, music and strength; but it hardly conveys to us the sense that the *Æneid* is the literary epic of a literary age. There is more of Homer in it than of Virgil, and the ordinary reader would hardly realise from the flow and spirit of its swinging lines that Virgil was a self-conscious artist, the Laureate of a cultured Court. The *Æneid* bears almost the same relation to the *Iliad* that the *Idylls of the King* do to the old Celtic romances of Arthur. Like them it is full of felicitous modernisms, of exquisite literary echoes and of delicate and delightful pictures; as Lord Tennyson loves England so did Virgil love Rome; the pageants of history and the purple of empire are equally dear to both poets; but neither of them has the grand simplicity or the large humanity of the early singers, and, as a hero, Æneas is no less a failure than Arthur. Sir Charles Bowen's version hardly gives us this peculiar literary quality of Virgil's verse, and, now and then, it reminds us, by some awkward inversion, of the fact that it is a translation; still, on the whole, it is extremely pleasant to read, and, if it does not absolutely mirror Virgil, it at least brings us many charming memories of him.

The metre Sir Charles Bowen has selected is a form of English hexameter, with the final dissyllable shortened into a foot of a single syllable only. It is, of course, accentual not quantitative, and though it misses that element of sustained strength which is given by the dissyllabic ending of the Latin verse, and has consequently a tendency to fall into couplets, the increased facility of rhyming gained by the change is of no small value. To any English metre that aims at swiftness of movement rhyme seems to be an absolute essential, and there are not enough double rhymes in our language to admit of the retention of this final dissyllabic foot.

As an example of Sir Charles Bowen's method we would take his rendering of the famous passage in the fifth *Eclogue* on the death of Daphnis:

All of the nymphs went weeping for Daphnis cruelly slain:
Ye were witnesses, hazels and river waves, of the pain
When to her son's sad body the mother clave with a cry,
Calling the great gods cruel, and cruel the stars of the sky.
None upon those dark days their pastured oxen did lead,
Daphnis, to drink of the cold clear rivulet; never a steed
Tasted the flowing waters, or cropped one blade in the mead.
Over thy grave how the lions of Carthage roared in despair,
Daphnis, the echoes of mountain wild and of forest declare.
Daphnis was first who taught us to guide, with a chariot rein,
Far Armenia's tigers, the chorus of Iacchus to train,
Led us with foliage waving the pliant spear to entwine.
As to the tree her vine is a glory, her grapes to the vine,
Bull to the horned herd, and the corn to a fruitful plain,
Thou to thine own wert beauty; and since fate robbed us of thee,
Pales herself, and Apollo are gone from meadow and lea.

'Calling the great gods cruel, and cruel the stars of the sky' is a very felicitous rendering of 'Atque deos atque astra vocat crudelia mater,' and so is 'Thou to thine own wert beauty' for 'Tu decus omne tuis.' This passage, too, from the fourth book of the *Æneid* is good:

Now was the night. Tired limbs upon earth were folded to sleep,
Silent the forests and fierce sea-waves; in the firmament deep
Midway rolled heaven's stars; no sound on the meadow stirred;
Every beast of the field, each bright-hued feathery bird
Haunting the limpid lakes, or the tangled briary glade,

Under the silent night in sleep were peacefully laid:
All but the grieving Queen. She yields her never to rest,
Takes not the quiet night to her eyelids or wearied breast.

And this from the sixth book is worth quoting:

'Never again such hopes shall a youth of the lineage of Troy
Rouse in his great forefathers of Latium! Never a boy
Nobler pride shall inspire in the ancient Romulus land!
Ah, for his filial love! for his old-world faith! for his hand
Matchless in battle! Unharmed what foemen had offered to stand
Forth in his path, when charging on foot for the enemy's ranks
Or when plunging the spur in his foam-flecked courser's flanks!
Child of a nation's sorrow! if thou canst baffle the Fates'
Bitter decrees, and break for a while their barrier gates,
Thine to become Marcellus! I pray thee bring me anon
Handfuls of lilies, that I bright flowers may strew on my son,
Heap on the shade of the boy unborn these gifts at the least,
Doing the dead, though vainly, the last sad service.'

He ceased.

'Thine to become Marcellus' has hardly the simple pathos of 'Tu Marcellus eris,' but 'Child of a nation's sorrow' is a graceful rendering of 'Heu, miserande puer.' Indeed, there is a great deal of feeling in the whole translation, and the tendency of the metre to run into couplets, of which we have spoken before, is corrected to a certain degree in the passage quoted above from the *Eclogues* by the occasional use of the triplet, as, elsewhere, by the introduction of alternate, not successive, rhymes.

Sir Charles Bowen is to be congratulated on the success of his version. It has both style and fidelity to recommend it. The metre he has chosen seems to us more suited to the sustained majesty of the *Æneid* than it is to the pastoral note of the *Eclogues*. It can bring us something of the strength of the lyre but has hardly caught the sweetness of the pipe. Still, it is in many points a very charming translation, and we gladly welcome it as a most valuable addition to the literature of echoes.

Virgil in English Verse. Eclogues and Æneid I.-VI. By the Right Hon. Sir Charles Bowen, one of Her Majesty's Lords Justices of Appeal. (John Murray.)

LITERARY AND OTHER NOTES—II

(*Woman's World*, December 1887.)

Lady Bellairs's *Gossips with Girls and Maidens* contains some very interesting essays, and a quite extraordinary amount of useful information on all matters connected with the mental and physical training of women. It is very difficult to give good advice without being irritating, and almost impossible to be at once didactic and delightful; but Lady Bellairs manages very cleverly to steer a middle course between the Charybdis of dulness and the Scylla of flippancy. There is a pleasing *intimité* about her style, and almost everything that she says has both good sense and good humour to recommend it. Nor does she confine herself to those broad generalisations on morals, which are so easy to make, so difficult to apply. Indeed, she seems to have a wholesome contempt for the cheap severity of abstract ethics, enters into the most minute details for the guidance of conduct, and draws out elaborate lists of what girls should avoid, and what they should cultivate.

Here are some specimens of 'What to Avoid':—

A loud, weak, affected, whining, harsh, or shrill tone of voice.
Extravagancies in conversation—such phrases as 'Awfully this,' 'Beastly that,' 'Loads of time,' 'Don't you know,' 'hate' for 'dislike,' etc.
Sudden exclamations of annoyance, surprise, or joy—often dangerously approaching to 'female swearing'—as
'Bother!' 'Gracious!' 'How jolly!'
Yawning when listening to any one.
Talking on family matters, even to your bosom friends.
Attempting any vocal or instrumental piece of music that you cannot execute with ease.
Crossing your letters.
Making a short, sharp nod with the head, intended to do duty for a bow.
All nonsense in the shape of belief in dreams, omens, presentiments, ghosts, spiritualism, palmistry, etc.
Entertaining wild flights of the imagination, or empty idealistic aspirations.

I am afraid that I have a good deal of sympathy with what are called 'empty idealistic aspirations'; and 'wild flights of the imagination' are so extremely rare in the nineteenth century that they seem to me deserving rather of praise than of censure. The exclamation 'Bother!' also, though certainly lacking in beauty, might, I think, be permitted under circumstances of extreme aggravation, such as, for instance, the rejection of a manuscript by the editor of a magazine; but in all other respects the list seems to be quite excellent. As for 'What to Cultivate,' nothing could be better than the following:

An unaffected, low, distinct, silver-toned voice.
The art of pleasing those around you, and seeming pleased with them, and all they may do for you.
The charm of making little sacrifices quite naturally, as if of no account to yourself.

The habit of making allowances for the opinions, feelings, or prejudices of others.
An erect carriage—that is, a sound body.
A good memory for faces, and facts connected with them—thus avoiding giving offence through not recognising or bowing to people, or saying to them what had best been left unsaid.
The art of listening without impatience to prosy talkers, and smiling at the twice told tale or joke.

I cannot help thinking that the last aphorism aims at too high a standard. There is always a certain amount of danger in any attempt to cultivate impossible virtues. However, it is only fair to add that Lady Bellairs recognises the importance of self-development quite as much as the importance of self-denial; and there is a great deal of sound sense in everything that she says about the gradual growth and formation of character. Indeed, those who have not read Aristotle upon this point might with advantage read Lady Bellairs.

Miss Constance Naden's little volume, *A Modern Apostle and Other Poems*, shows both culture and courage—culture in its use of language, courage in its selection of subject-matter. The modern apostle of whom Miss Naden sings is a young clergyman who preaches Pantheistic Socialism in the Free Church of some provincial manufacturing town, converts everybody, except the woman whom he loves, and is killed in a street riot. The story is exceedingly powerful, but seems more suitable for prose than for verse. It is right that a poet should be full of the spirit of his age, but the external forms of modern life are hardly, as yet, expressive of that spirit. They are truths of fact, not truths of the imagination, and though they may give the poet an opportunity for realism, they often rob the poem of the reality that is so essential to it. Art, however, is a matter of result, not of theory, and if the fruit is pleasant, we should not quarrel about the tree. Miss Naden's work is distinguished by rich imagery, fine colour, and sweet music, and these are things for which we should be grateful, wherever we find them. In point of mere technical skill, her longer poems are the best; but some of the shorter poems are very fascinating. This, for instance, is pretty:

The copyist group was gathered round
A time-worn fresco, world-renowned,
Whose central glory once had been
The face of Christ, the Nazarene.

And every copyist of the crowd
With his own soul that face endowed,
Gentle, severe, majestic, mean;
But which was Christ, the Nazarene?

Then one who watched them made complaint,
And marvelled, saying, 'Wherefore paint
Till ye be sure your eyes have seen
The face of Christ, the Nazarene?'

And this sonnet is full of suggestion:

The wine-flushed monarch slept, but in his ear
An angel breathed—'Repent, or choose the flame
Quenchless.' In dread he woke, but not in shame,
Deep musing—'Sin I love, yet hell I fear.'

Wherefore he left his feasts and minions dear,
And justly ruled, and died a saint in name.
But when his hasting spirit heavenward came,
A stern voice cried—'O Soul! what dost thou here?'

'Love I forswore, and wine, and kept my vow
To live a just and joyless life, and now
I crave reward.' The voice came like a knell—
'Fool! dost thou hope to find again thy mirth,
And those foul joys thou didst renounce on earth?
Yea, enter in! My heaven shall be thy hell.'

Miss Constance Naden deserves a high place among our living poetesses, and this, as Mrs. Sharp has shown lately in her volume, entitled *Women's Voices*, is no mean distinction.

Phyllis Browne's Life of Mrs. Somerville forms part of a very interesting little series, called 'The World's Workers'—a collection of short biographies catholic enough to include personalities so widely different as Turner and Richard Cobden, Handel and Sir Titus Salt, Robert Stephenson and Florence Nightingale, and yet possessing a certain definite aim. As a mathematician and a scientist, the translator and populariser of *La Mécanique Céleste*, and the author of an important book on physical geography, Mrs. Somerville is, of course, well known. The scientific bodies of Europe covered her with honours; her bust stands in the hall of the Royal Society, and one of the Women's Colleges at Oxford bears her name. Yet, considered simply in the light of a wife and a mother, she is no less admirable; and those who consider that stupidity is the proper basis for the domestic virtues, and that intellectual women must of necessity be helpless with their hands, cannot do better than read Phyllis Browne's pleasant little book, in which they will find that the greatest woman-mathematician of any age was a clever needlewoman, a good housekeeper, and a most skilful cook. Indeed, Mrs. Somerville seems to have been quite renowned for her cookery. The discoverers of the North-West Passage christened an island 'Somerville,' not as a tribute to the distinguished mathematician, but as a recognition of the excellence of some orange marmalade which the distinguished mathematician had prepared with her own hands and presented to the ships before they left England; and to the fact that she was able to make currant jelly at a very critical moment she owed the affection of some of her husband's relatives, who up to that time had been rather prejudiced against her on the ground that she was merely an unpractical Blue-stocking.

Nor did her scientific knowledge ever warp or dull the tenderness and humanity of her nature. For birds and animals she had always a great love. We hear of her as a little girl watching with eager eyes the swallows as they built their nests in summer or prepared for their flight in the autumn; and when snow was on the ground she used to open the windows to let the robins hop in and pick crumbs on the breakfast-table. On one occasion she went with her father on a tour in the Highlands, and found on her return that a pet goldfinch, which had been left in the charge of the servants, had been neglected by them and had died of starvation. She was almost heart-broken at the event, and in writing her *Recollections*, seventy years after, she mentioned it and said that, as she wrote, she felt deep pain. Her chief pet in her old age was a mountain sparrow, which used to perch on her arm and go to sleep there while she was writing. One day the sparrow fell into the water-jug and was drowned, to the great grief of its mistress who could hardly be consoled for its loss, though later on we hear of a beautiful paroquet taking the place of *le moineau d'Uranie*, and becoming Mrs. Somerville's constant companion. She was also very energetic, Phyllis Browne tells us, in trying to get a law passed in the Italian Parliament for the protection of animals, and said once, with reference to this subject, 'We English cannot boast of humanity so long as our sportsmen find pleasure in shooting down tame pigeons as they fly terrified out of a cage'—a remark with which I entirely agree. Mr. Herbert's Bill for the protection of land birds gave her immense pleasure, though, to quote her own words, she was 'grieved to find that "the lark, which at heaven's gate sings," is thought unworthy of man's protection'; and she took a great fancy to a gentleman who, on being told of the number of singing birds that is eaten in Italy— nightingales, goldfinches, and robins—exclaimed in horror, 'What! robins! our household birds! I would as soon eat a child!' Indeed, she believed to some extent in the immortality of animals on the ground that, if animals have no future, it would seem as if some were created for uncompensated misery—an idea which does not seem to me to be either extravagant or fantastic, though it must be admitted that the optimism on which it is based receives absolutely no support from science.

On the whole, Phyllis Browne's book is very pleasant reading. Its only fault is that it is far too short, and this is a fault so rare in modern literature that it almost amounts to a distinction. However, Phyllis Browne has managed to crowd into the narrow limits at her disposal a great many interesting anecdotes. The picture she gives of Mrs. Somerville working away at her translation of Laplace in the same room with her children is very charming, and reminds one of what is told of George Sand; there is an amusing account of Mrs. Somerville's visit to the widow of the young Pretender, the Countess of Albany, who, after talking with her for some time, exclaimed, 'So you don't speak Italian. You must have had a very bad education'! And this story about the Waverley Novels may possibly be new to some of my readers:

A very amusing circumstance in connection with Mrs. Somerville's acquaintance with Sir Walter arose out of the childish inquisitiveness of Woronzow Greig, Mrs. Somerville's little boy.

During the time Mrs. Somerville was visiting Abbotsford the Waverley Novels were appearing, and were creating a great sensation; yet even Scott's intimate friends did not know that he was the author; he enjoyed keeping the affair a mystery. But little Woronzow discovered what he was about. One day when Mrs. Somerville was talking about a novel that had just been published, Woronzow said, 'I knew all these stories long ago, for Mr. Scott writes on the dinner-table; when he has finished he puts the green cloth with the papers in a corner of the dining-room, and when he goes out Charlie Scott and I read the stories.'

Phyllis Browne remarks that this incident shows 'that persons who want to keep a secret ought to be very careful when children are about'; but the story seems to me to be far too charming to require any moral of the kind.

Bound up in the same volume is a Life of Miss Mary Carpenter, also written by Phyllis Browne. Miss Carpenter does not seem to me to have the charm and fascination of Mrs. Somerville. There is always something about her that is formal, limited, and precise. When she was about two years old she insisted on being called 'Doctor Carpenter' in the nursery; at the age of twelve she is described by a friend as a sedate little girl, who always spoke like a book; and before she entered on her educational schemes she wrote down a solemn dedication of herself to the service of humanity. However, she was one of the practical, hardworking saints of the nineteenth century, and it is no doubt quite right that the saints should take themselves very seriously. It is only fair also to remember that her work of rescue and reformation was carried on under great difficulties. Here, for instance, is the picture Miss Cobbe gives us of one of the Bristol night-schools:

It was a wonderful spectacle to see Mary Carpenter sitting patiently before the large school gallery in St. James's Back, teaching, singing, and praying with the wild street-boys, in spite of endless interruptions caused by such proceedings as shooting marbles at any object behind her, whistling, stamping, fighting, shrieking out 'Amen' in the middle of a prayer, and sometimes rising en masse and tearing like a troop of bisons in hob-nailed shoes down from the gallery, round the great schoolroom, and down the stairs, and into the street. These irrepressible outbreaks she bore with infinite good humour.

Her own account is somewhat pleasanter, and shows that 'the troop of bisons in hob-nailed shoes' was not always so barbarous.

I had taken to my class on the preceding week some specimens of ferns neatly gummed on white paper. . . . This time I took a piece of coal-shale, with impressions of ferns, to show them. . . . I told each to examine the specimen, and tell me what he thought it was. W. gave so bright a smile that I saw he knew; none of the others could tell; he said they were ferns, like what I showed them last week, but he thought they were chiselled on the stone. Their surprise and pleasure were great when I explained the matter to them.

The history of Joseph: they all found a difficulty in realising that this had actually occurred. One asked if Egypt existed now, and if people lived in it. When I told them that buildings now stood which had been erected about the time of Joseph, one said that it was impossible, as they must have fallen down ere this. I showed them the form of a pyramid, and they were satisfied. One asked if all books were true.

The story of Macbeth impressed them very much. They knew the name of Shakespeare, having seen his name over a public-house.

A boy defined conscience as 'a thing a gentleman hasn't got, who, when a boy finds his purse and gives it back to him, doesn't give the boy sixpence.'

Another boy was asked, after a Sunday evening lecture on 'Thankfulness,' what pleasure he enjoyed most in the course of a year. He replied candidly, 'Cock-fightin', ma'am; there's a pit up by the "Black Boy" as is worth anythink in Brissel.'

There is something a little pathetic in the attempt to civilise the rough street-boy by means of the refining influence of ferns and fossils, and it is difficult to help feeling that Miss Carpenter rather overestimated the value of elementary education. The poor are not to be fed upon facts. Even Shakespeare and the Pyramids are not sufficient; nor is there much use in giving them the results of culture, unless we also give them those conditions under which culture can be realised. In these cold, crowded cities of the North, the proper basis for morals, using the word in its wide Hellenic signification, is to be found in architecture, not in books.

Still, it would be ungenerous not to recognise that Mary Carpenter gave to the children of the poor not merely her learning, but her love. In early life, her biographer tells us, she had longed for the happiness of being a wife and a mother; but later she became content that her affection could be freely given to all who needed it, and the verse in the prophecies, 'I have given thee children whom thou hast not borne,' seemed to her to indicate what was to be her true mission. Indeed, she rather inclined to Bacon's opinion, that unmarried people do the best public work. 'It is quite striking,' she says in one of her letters, 'to observe how much the useful power and influence of woman has developed of late years. Unattached ladies, such as widows and unmarried women, have quite ample work to do in the world for the good of others to absorb all their powers. Wives and mothers have a very noble work given them by God, and want no more.' The whole passage is extremely interesting, and the phrase 'unattached ladies' is quite delightful, and reminds one of Charles Lamb.

* * * * *

Ismay's Children is by the clever authoress of that wonderful little story *Flitters, Tatters, and the Counsellor*, a story which delighted the realists by its truth, fascinated Mr. Ruskin by its beauty, and remains to the present day the most perfect picture of street-arab life in all English prose fiction. The scene of the novel is laid in the south of Ireland, and the plot is extremely dramatic and ingenious. Godfrey Mauleverer, a reckless young Irishman, runs away with Ismay D'Arcy, a pretty, penniless governess, and is privately married to her in Scotland. Some time after the birth of her third child, Ismay died, and her husband, who had never made his marriage public, nor taken any pains to establish the legitimacy of his children, is drowned while yachting off the coast of France. The care of Ismay's children then devolves on an old aunt, Miss Juliet D'Arcy, who brings them back to Ireland to claim their inheritance for them. But a sudden stroke of paralysis deprives her of her memory, and she forgets the name of the little Scotch village in which Ismay's informal marriage took place. So Tighe O'Malley holds Barrettstown, and Ismay's children live in an old mill close to the great park of which they are the rightful heirs. The boy, who is called Godfrey after his father, is a fascinating study, with his swarthy foreign beauty, his fierce moods of love and hate, his passionate pride, and his passionate tenderness. The account of his midnight ride to warn his enemy of an impending attack of Moonlighters is most powerful and spirited; and it is pleasant to meet in modern fiction a character that has all the fine inconsistencies of life, and is neither too fantastic an exception to be true, nor too ordinary a type to be common. Excellent also, in its direct simplicity of rendering, is the picture of Miss Juliet D'Arcy; and the scene in which, at the moment of her death, the old woman's memory returns to her is quite admirable, both in conception and in treatment. To me, however, the chief interest of the book lies in the little lifelike sketches of Irish character with which it abounds. Modern realistic art has not yet produced a Hamlet, but at least it may claim to have studied Guildenstern and Rosencrantz very closely; and, for pure fidelity and truth to nature, nothing could be better than the minor characters in *Ismay's Children*. Here we have the kindly old priest who arranges all the marriages in his parish, and has a strong objection to people who insist on making long confessions; the important young curate fresh from Maynooth, who gives himself more airs than a bishop, and has to be kept in order; the professional beggars, with their devout faith, their grotesque humour, and their incorrigible laziness; the shrewd shopkeeper, who imports arms in flour-barrels for the use of the Moonlighters and, as soon as he has got rid of them, gives information of their whereabouts to the police; the young men who go out at night to be drilled by an Irish-American; the farmers with their wild land-hunger, bidding secretly against each other for every vacant field; the dispensary doctor, who is always regretting that he has not got a Trinity College degree; the plain girls, who want to go into convents; the pretty girls, who want to get married; and the shopkeepers' daughters, who want to be thought young ladies. There is a whole pell-mell of men and women, a complete panorama of provincial life, an absolutely faithful picture of the peasant in his own home. This note of realism in dealing with national types of character has always been a distinguishing characteristic of Irish fiction, from the days of Miss Edgeworth down to our own days, and it is not difficult to see in *Ismay's Children* some traces of the influence of *Castle Rack-rent*. I fear, however, that few people read Miss Edgeworth nowadays, though both Scott and Tourgénieff acknowledged their indebtedness to her novels, and her style is always admirable in its clearness and precision.

* * * * *

Miss Leffler-Arnim's statement, in a lecture delivered recently at St. Saviour's Hospital, that 'she had heard of instances where ladies were so determined not to exceed the fashionable measurement that they had actually held on to a cross-bar while their maids fastened the fifteen-inch corset,' has excited a good deal of incredulity, but there is nothing really improbable in it. From the sixteenth century to our own day there is hardly any form of torture that has not been inflicted on girls, and endured by women, in obedience to the dictates of an unreasonable and monstrous Fashion. 'In order to obtain a real Spanish figure,' says Montaigne, 'what a Gehenna of suffering will not women endure, drawn in and compressed by great *coches* entering the flesh; nay, sometimes they even die thereof.' 'A few days after my arrival at school,' Mrs. Somerville tells us in her memoirs, 'although perfectly straight and well made, I was enclosed in stiff stays, with a steel busk in front; while above my frock, bands drew my shoulders back till the shoulder-blades met. Then a steel rod with a semicircle, which went under my chin, was clasped to the steel busk in my stays. In this constrained state I and most of the younger girls had to prepare our lessons'; and in the life of Miss Edgeworth we read that, being sent to a certain fashionable establishment, 'she underwent all the usual tortures of back-boards, iron collars and dumbs, and also (because she was a very tiny person) the unusual one of being hung by the neck to draw out the muscles and increase the growth,' a signal failure in her case. Indeed, instances of absolute mutilation and misery are so common in the past that it is unnecessary to multiply them; but it is really sad to think that in our own day a civilised woman can hang on to a cross-bar while her maid laces her waist into a fifteen-inch circle. To begin with, the waist is not a circle at all, but an oval; nor can there be any greater error than to imagine that an unnaturally small waist gives an air of grace, or even of slightness, to the whole figure. Its effect, as a rule, is simply to exaggerate the width of the shoulders and the hips; and those whose figures possess that stateliness which is called stoutness by the vulgar, convert what is a quality into a defect by yielding to the silly edicts of Fashion on the subject of tight-lacing. The fashionable English waist, also, is not merely far too small, and consequently quite out of proportion to the rest of the figure, but it is worn far too low down. I use the expression 'worn' advisedly, for a waist nowadays seems to be regarded as an article of apparel to be put on when and where one likes. A long waist always implies shortness of the lower limbs, and, from the artistic point of view, has the effect of diminishing the height; and I am glad to see that many of the most charming women in Paris are returning to the idea of the Directoire style of dress. This style is not by any means perfect, but at least it has the merit of indicating the proper position of the waist. I feel quite sure that all English women of culture and position will set their faces against such stupid and dangerous practices as are related by Miss Leffler-Arnim. Fashion's motto is: *Il faut souffrir pour être belle*; but the motto of art and of common-sense is: *Il faut être bête pour souffrir*.

* * * * *

Talking of Fashion, a critic in the *Pall Mall Gazette* expresses his surprise that I should have allowed an illustration of a hat, covered with 'the bodies of dead birds,' to appear in the first number of the *Woman's World*; and as I have received many letters on the subject, it is only right that I should state my exact position in the matter. Fashion is such an essential part of the *mundus muliebris* of our day, that it seems to me absolutely necessary that its growth, development, and phases should be duly chronicled; and the historical and practical value of such a record depends entirely upon its perfect fidelity to fact. Besides, it is quite easy for the children of light to adapt almost any fashionable form of dress to the requirements of utility and the demands of good taste. The Sarah Bernhardt tea-gown, for instance, figured in the present issue, has many good points about it, and the gigantic dress-improver does not appear to me to be really essential to the mode; and though the Postillion costume of the fancy dress ball is absolutely detestable in its silliness and vulgarity, the so-called Late Georgian costume in the same plate is rather pleasing. I must, however, protest against the idea that to chronicle the development of Fashion implies any approval of the particular forms that Fashion may adopt.

* * * * *

Mrs. Craik's article on the condition of the English stage will, I feel sure, be read with great interest by all who are watching the development of dramatic art in this country. It was the last thing written by the author of *John Halifax, Gentleman*, and reached me only a few days before her lamented death. That the state of things is such as Mrs. Craik describes, few will be inclined to deny; though, for my own part, I must acknowledge that I see more vulgarity than vice in the tendencies of the modern stage; nor do I think it possible to elevate dramatic art by limiting its subject-matter. *On tue une littérature quand on lui interdit la vérité humaine.* As far as the serious presentation of life is concerned, what we require is more imaginative treatment, greater freedom from theatric language and theatric convention. It may be questioned, also, whether the consistent reward of virtue and punishment of wickedness be really the healthiest ideal for an art that claims to mirror nature. However, it is impossible not to recognise the fine feeling that actuates every line of Mrs. Craik's article; and though one may venture to disagree with the proposed method, one cannot but sympathise with the purity and delicacy of the thought, and the high nobility of the aim.

* * * * *

The French Minister of Education, M. Spuller, has paid Racine a very graceful and appropriate compliment, in naming after him the second college that has been opened in Paris for the higher education of girls. Racine was one of the privileged few who was allowed to read the celebrated *Traité de l'Education des Filles* before it appeared in print; he was charged, along with Boileau, with the task of revising the text of the constitution and rules of Madame de Maintenon's great college; it was for the Demoiselles de St. Cyr that he composed *Athalie*; and he devoted a great deal of his time to the education of his own children. The Lycée Racine will, no doubt, become as important an institution as the Lycée Fénelon, and the speech delivered by M. Spuller on the occasion of its opening was full of the happiest augury for the future. M. Spuller dwelt at great length on the value of Goethe's aphorism, that the test of a good wife is her capacity to take her husband's place and to become a father to his children, and mentioned that the thing that struck him most in America was the wonderful Brooklyn Bridge, a superb titanic structure, which was completed under the direction of the engineer's wife, the engineer himself having died while the building of the bridge was in progress. 'Il me semble,' said M. Spuller, 'que la femme de l'ingénieur du pont de Brooklyn a réalisé la pensée de Goethe, et que non seulement elle est devenue un père pour ses enfants, mais un autre père pour l'œuvre admirable, vraiment unique, qui a immortalisé le nom qu'elle portait avec son mari.' M. Spuller also laid great stress on the necessity of a thoroughly practical education, and was extremely severe on the 'Blue-stockings' of literature. 'Il ne s'agit pas de former ici des "femmes savantes." Les "femmes savantes" ont été marquées pour jamais par un des plus grands génies de notre race d'une légère teinte de ridicule. Non, ce n'est pas des femmes savantes que nous voulons: ce sont tout simplement des femmes: des femmes dignes de ce pays de France, qui est la patrie du bons sens, de la mesure, et de la grâce; des femmes ayant la notion juste et le sens exquis du rôle qui doit leur appartenir dans la société moderne.' There is, no doubt, a great deal of truth in M. Spuller's observations, but we must not mistake a caricature for the reality. After all, *Les Précieuses Ridicules* contrasted very favourably with the ordinary type of womanhood of their day, not merely in France, but also in England; and an uncritical love of sonnets is preferable, on the whole, to coarseness, vulgarity and ignorance.

* * * * *

I am glad to see that Miss Ramsay's brilliant success at Cambridge is not destined to remain an isolated instance of what women can do in intellectual competitions with men. At the Royal University in Ireland, the Literature Scholarship of £100 a year for five years has been won by Miss Story, the daughter of a North of Ireland clergyman. It is pleasant to be able to chronicle an item of Irish news that has nothing to do with the violence of party politics or party feeling, and that shows how worthy women are of that higher culture and education which has been so tardily and, in some instances, so grudgingly granted to them.

* * * * *

The Empress of Japan has been ordering a whole wardrobe of fashionable dresses in Paris for her own use and the use of her ladies-in-waiting. The chrysanthemum (the imperial flower of Japan) has suggested the tints of most of the Empress's own gowns, and in accordance with the colour-schemes of other flowers the rest of the costumes have been designed. The same steamer, however, that carries out the masterpieces of M. Worth and M. Felix to the Land of the Rising Sun, also brings to the Empress a letter of formal and respectful remonstrance from the English Rational Dress Society. I trust that, even if the Empress rejects the sensible arguments of this important Society, her own artistic feeling may induce her to reconsider her resolution to abandon Eastern for Western costume.

* * * * *

I hope that some of my readers will interest themselves in the Ministering Children's League for which Mr. Walter Crane has done the beautiful and suggestive design of *The Young Knight*. The best way to make children good is to make them happy, and happiness seems to me an essential part of Lady Meath's admirable scheme.

(1) *Gossips with Girls and Maidens Betrothed and Free*. By Lady Bellairs. (Blackwood and Sons.)

(2) *A Modern Apostle and Other Poems*. By Constance Naden. (Kegan Paul.)

(3) *Mrs. Somerville* and *Mary Carpenter*. By Phyllis Browne, Author of *What Girls Can Do*, etc. (Cassell and Co.)

(4) *Ismay's Children*. By the Author of *Hogan, M.P.*; *Flitters, Tatters, and the Counsellor*, etc. (Macmillan and Co.)

ARISTOTLE AT AFTERNOON TEA

(*Pall Mall Gazette*, December 16, 1887.)

In society, says Mr. Mahaffy, every civilised man and woman ought to feel it their duty to say something, even when there is hardly anything to be said, and, in order to encourage this delightful art of brilliant chatter, he has published a social guide without which no *débutante* or dandy should ever dream of going out to dine. Not that Mr. Mahaffy's book can be said to be, in any sense of the word, popular. In discussing this important subject of conversation, he has not merely followed the scientific method of Aristotle which is, perhaps, excusable, but he has adopted the literary style of Aristotle for which no excuse is possible. There is, also, hardly a single anecdote, hardly a single illustration, and the reader is left to put the Professor's abstract rules into practice, without either the examples or the warnings of history to encourage or to dissuade him in his reckless career. Still, the book can be warmly recommended to all who propose to substitute the vice of verbosity for the stupidity of silence. It fascinates in spite of its form and pleases in spite of its pedantry, and is the nearest approach, that we know of, in modern literature to meeting Aristotle at an afternoon tea.

As regards physical conditions, the only one that is considered by Mr. Mahaffy as being absolutely essential to a good conversationalist, is the possession of a musical voice. Some learned writers have been of opinion that a slight stammer often gives peculiar zest to conversation, but Mr. Mahaffy rejects this view and is extremely severe on every eccentricity from a native brogue to an artificial catchword. With his remarks on the latter point, the meaningless repetition of phrases, we entirely agree. Nothing can be more irritating than the scientific person who is always saying '*Exactly* so,' or the commonplace person who ends every sentence with '*Don't you know*?' or the pseudo-artistic person who murmurs '*Charming, charming*,' on the smallest provocation. It is, however, with the mental and moral qualifications for conversation that Mr. Mahaffy specially deals. Knowledge he, naturally, regards as an absolute essential, for, as he most justly observes, 'an ignorant man is seldom agreeable, except as a butt.' Upon the other hand, strict accuracy should be avoided. 'Even a consummate liar,' says Mr. Mahaffy, is a better ingredient in a company than 'the scrupulously truthful man, who weighs every statement, questions every fact, and corrects every inaccuracy.' The liar at any rate recognises that recreation, not instruction, is the aim of conversation, and is a far more civilised being than the blockhead who loudly expresses his disbelief in a story which is told simply for the amusement of the company. Mr. Mahaffy, however, makes an exception in favour of the eminent specialist and tells us that intelligent questions addressed to an astronomer, or a pure mathematician, will elicit many curious facts which will pleasantly beguile the time. Here, in the interest of Society, we feel bound to enter a formal protest. Nobody, even in the provinces, should ever be allowed to ask an intelligent question about pure mathematics across a dinner-table. A question of this kind is quite as bad as inquiring suddenly about the state of a man's soul, a sort of *coup* which, as Mr. Mahaffy remarks elsewhere, 'many pious people have actually thought a decent introduction to a conversation.'

As for the moral qualifications of a good talker, Mr. Mahaffy, following the example of his great master, warns us against any disproportionate excess of virtue. Modesty, for instance, may easily become a social vice, and to be continually apologising for one's ignorance or stupidity is a grave injury to conversation, for, 'what we want to learn from each member is his free opinion on the subject in hand, not his own estimate of the value of that opinion.' Simplicity, too, is not without its dangers. The *enfant terrible*, with his shameless love of truth, the raw country-bred girl who always says what she means, and the plain, blunt man who makes a point of speaking his mind on every possible occasion, without ever considering whether he has a mind at all, are the fatal examples of what simplicity leads to. Shyness may be a form of vanity, and reserve a development of pride, and as for sympathy, what can be more detestable than the man, or woman, who insists on agreeing with everybody, and so makes 'a discussion, which implies differences in opinion,' absolutely impossible? Even the unselfish listener is apt to become a bore. 'These silent people,' says Mr. Mahaffy, 'not only take all they can get in Society for nothing, but they take it without the smallest gratitude, and have the audacity afterwards to censure those who have laboured for their amusement.' Tact, which is an exquisite sense of the symmetry of things, is, according to Mr. Mahaffy, the highest and best of all the moral conditions for conversation. The man of tact, he most wisely remarks, 'will instinctively avoid jokes about Blue Beard' in the company of a woman who is a man's third wife; he will never be guilty of talking like a book, but will rather avoid too careful an attention to grammar and the rounding of periods; he will cultivate the art of graceful interruption, so as to prevent a subject being worn threadbare by the aged or the inexperienced; and should he be desirous of telling a story, he will look round and consider each member of the party, and if there be a single stranger present will forgo the pleasure of anecdotage rather than make the social mistake of hurting even one of the guests. As for prepared or premeditated art, Mr. Mahaffy has a great contempt for it and tells us of a certain college don (let us hope not at Oxford or Cambridge) who always carried a jest-book in his pocket and had to refer to it when he wished to make a repartee. Great wits, too, are often very cruel, and great humourists often very vulgar, so it will be better to try and 'make good conversation without any large help from these brilliant but dangerous gifts.'

In a *tête-à-tête* one should talk about persons, and in general Society about things. The state of the weather is always an excusable exordium, but it is convenient to have a paradox or heresy on the subject always ready so as to direct the conversation into other channels. Really domestic people are almost invariably bad talkers as their very virtues in home life have dulled their interest in outer things. The very best mothers will insist on chattering of their babies and prattling about infant education. In fact, most women do not take sufficient interest in politics, just as most men are deficient in general reading. Still, anybody can be made to talk, except the very obstinate, and even a commercial traveller may be drawn out and become quite interesting. As for Society small talk, it is impossible, Mr. Mahaffy tells us, for any sound theory of conversation to depreciate gossip, 'which is perhaps the main factor in agreeable talk throughout Society.' The retailing of small personal points about great people always gives pleasure, and if one is not fortunate enough to be an Arctic traveller or an escaped Nihilist, the best thing one can do is to relate some anecdote of 'Prince Bismarck, or King Victor Emmanuel, or Mr. Gladstone.' In the case of meeting a genius and a Duke at dinner, the good talker will try to raise himself to the level of the former and to bring the latter down to his own level. To succeed among one's social superiors one must have no hesitation in contradicting them. Indeed, one should make bold criticisms and introduce a bright and free tone into a Society whose grandeur and extreme respectability make it, Mr. Mahaffy remarks, as pathetically as inaccurately, 'perhaps somewhat dull.' The best conversationalists are those whose ancestors have been bilingual, like the French and Irish, but the art of conversation is really within the reach of almost every one, except those who are morbidly truthful, or whose high moral worth requires to be sustained by a permanent gravity of demeanour and a general dulness of mind.

These are the broad principles contained in Mr. Mahaffy's clever little book, and many of them will, no doubt, commend themselves to our readers. The maxim, 'If you find the company dull, blame yourself,' seems to us somewhat optimistic, and we have no sympathy at all with the professional story-teller who is really a great bore at a dinner-table; but Mr. Mahaffy is quite right in insisting that no bright social intercourse is possible without equality, and it is no objection to his book to say that it will not teach people how to talk cleverly. It is not logic that makes men reasonable, nor the science of ethics that makes men good, but it is always useful to analyse, to formularise and to investigate. The only thing to be regretted in the volume is the arid and jejune character of the style. If Mr. Mahaffy would only write as he talks, his book would be much pleasanter reading.

The Principles of the Art of Conversation: *A Social Essay.* By J. P. Mahaffy. (Macmillan and Co.)

EARLY CHRISTIAN ART IN IRELAND

(*Pall Mall Gazette*, December 17, 1887.)

The want of a good series of popular handbooks on Irish art has long been felt, the works of Sir William Wilde, Petrie and others being somewhat too elaborate for the ordinary student; so we are glad to notice the appearance, under the auspices of the Committee of Council on Education, of Miss Margaret Stokes's useful little volume on the early Christian art of her country. There is, of course, nothing particularly original in Miss Stokes's book, nor can she be said to be a very attractive or pleasing writer, but it is unfair to look for originality in primers, and the charm of the illustrations fully atones for the somewhat heavy and pedantic character of the style.

This early Christian art of Ireland is full of interest to the artist, the archæologist and the historian. In its rudest forms, such as the little iron hand-bell, the plain stone chalice and the rough wooden staff, it brings us back to the simplicity of the primitive Christian Church, while to the period of its highest development we owe the great masterpieces of Celtic metal-work. The stone chalice is now replaced by the chalice of silver and gold; the iron bell has its jewel-studded shrine, and the rough staff its gorgeous casing; rich caskets and splendid bindings preserve the holy books of the Saints and, instead of the rudely carved symbol of the early missionaries, we have such beautiful works of art as the processional cross of Cong Abbey. Beautiful this cross certainly is with its delicate intricacy of ornamentation, its grace of proportion and its marvel of mere workmanship, nor is there any doubt about its history. From the inscriptions on it, which are corroborated by the annals of Innisfallen and the book of Clonmacnoise, we learn that it was made for King Turlough O'Connor by a native artist under the superintendence of Bishop O'Duffy, its primary object being to enshrine a portion of the true cross that was sent to the king in 1123. Brought to Cong some years afterwards, probably by the archbishop, who died there in 1150, it was concealed at the time of the Reformation, but at the beginning of the present century was still in the possession of the last abbot, and at his death it was purchased by professor MacCullagh and presented by him to the museum of the Royal Irish Academy. This wonderful work is alone well worth a visit to Dublin, but not less lovely is the chalice of Ardagh, a two-handled silver cup, absolutely classical in its perfect purity of form, and decorated with gold and amber and crystal and with varieties of *cloisonné* and *champlevé* enamel. There is no mention of this cup, or of the so-called Tara brooch, in ancient Irish history. All that we know of them is that they were found accidentally, the former by a boy who was digging potatoes near the old Rath of Ardagh, the latter by a poor child who picked it up near the seashore. They both, however, belong probably to the tenth century.

Of all these works, as well as of the bell shrines, book-covers, sculptured crosses and illuminated designs in manuscripts, excellent pictures are given in Miss Stokes's handbook. The extremely interesting *Fiachal Phadrig*, or shrine of St. Patrick's tooth, might have been figured and noted as an interesting example of the survival of ornament, and one of the old miniatures of the scribe or Evangelist writing would have given an additional interest to the chapter on Irish MSS. On the whole, however, the book is wonderfully well illustrated, and the ordinary art student will be able to get some useful suggestions from it. Indeed, Miss Stokes, echoing the aspirations of many of the great Irish archæologists, looks forward to the revival of a native Irish school in architecture, sculpture, metal-work and painting. Such an aspiration is, of course, very laudable, but there is always a danger of these revivals being merely artificial reproductions, and it may be questioned whether the peculiar forms of Irish ornamentation could be made at all expressive of the modern spirit. A recent writer on house decoration has gravely suggested that the British householder should take his meals in a Celtic dining-room adorned with a dado of Ogham inscriptions, and such wicked proposals may serve as a warning to all who fancy that the reproduction of a form necessarily implies a revival of the spirit that gave the form life and meaning, and who fail to recognise the difference between art and anachronisms. Miss Stokes's proposal for an ark-shaped church in which the mural painter is to repeat the arcades and 'follow the architectural compositions of the grand pages of the Eusebian canons in the Book of Kells,' has, of course, nothing grotesque about it, but it is not probable that the artistic genius of the Irish people will, even when 'the land has rest,' find in such interesting imitations its healthiest or best expression. Still, there are certain elements of beauty in ancient Irish art that the modern artist would do well to study. The value of the intricate illuminations in the Book of Kells, as far as their adaptability to modern designs and modern material goes, has been very much overrated, but in the ancient Irish torques, brooches, pins, clasps and the like, the modern goldsmith will find a rich and, comparatively speaking, an untouched field; and now that the Celtic spirit has become the leaven of our politics, there is no reason why it should not contribute something to our decorative art. This result, however, will not be obtained by a patriotic misuse of old designs, and even the most enthusiastic Home Ruler must not be allowed to decorate his dining-room with a dado of Oghams.

Early Christian Art in Ireland. By Margaret Stokes. (Published for the Committee of Council on Education by Chapman and Hall.)

LITERARY AND OTHER NOTES—III

(*Woman's World*, January 1888.)

Madame Ristori's *Etudes et Souvenirs* is one of the most delightful books on the stage that has appeared since Lady Martin's charming volume on the Shakespearian heroines. It is often said that actors leave nothing behind them but a barren name and a withered wreath; that they subsist simply upon the applause of the moment; that they are ultimately doomed to the oblivion of old play-bills; and that their art, in a word, dies with them, and shares their own mortality. 'Chippendale, the cabinet-maker,' says the clever author of *Obiter Dicta*, 'is more potent than Garrick the actor. The vivacity of the latter no longer charms (save in Boswell); the chairs of the former still render rest impossible in a hundred homes.' This view, however, seems to me to be exaggerated. It rests on the assumption that acting is simply a mimetic art, and takes no account of its imaginative and intellectual basis. It is quite true, of course, that the personality of the player passes away, and with it that pleasure-giving power by virtue of which the arts exist. Yet the artistic method of a great actor survives. It lives on in tradition, and becomes part of the science of a school. It has all the intellectual life of a principle. In England, at the present moment, the influence of Garrick on our actors is far stronger than that of Reynolds on our painters of portraits, and if we turn to France it is easy to discern the tradition of Talma, but where is the tradition of David?

Madame Ristori's memoirs, then, have not merely the charm that always attaches to the autobiography of a brilliant and beautiful woman, but have also a definite and distinct artistic value. Her analysis of the character of Lady Macbeth, for instance, is full of psychological interest, and shows us that the subtleties of Shakespearian criticism are not necessarily confined to those who have views on weak endings and rhyming tags, but may also be suggested by the art of acting itself. The author of *Obiter Dicta* seeks to deny to actors all critical insight and all literary appreciation. The actor, he tells us, is art's slave, not her child, and lives entirely outside literature, 'with its words for ever on his lips, and none of its truths engraven on his heart.' But this seems to me to be a harsh and reckless generalisation. Indeed, so far from agreeing with it, I would be inclined to say that the mere artistic process of acting, the translation of literature back again into life, and the presentation of thought under the conditions of action, is in itself a critical method of a very high order; nor do I think that a study of the careers of our great English actors will really sustain the charge of want of literary appreciation. It may be true that actors pass too quickly away from the form, in order to get at the feeling that gives the form beauty and colour, and that, where the literary critic studies the language, the actor looks simply for the life; and yet, how well the great actors have appreciated that marvellous music of words which in Shakespeare, at any rate, is so vital an element of poetic power, if, indeed, it be not equally so in the case of all who have any claim to be regarded as true poets. 'The sensual life of verse,' says Keats, in a dramatic criticism published in the *Champion*, 'springs warm from the lips of Kean, and to one learned in Shakespearian hieroglyphics, learned in the spiritual portion of those lines to which Kean adds a sensual grandeur, his tongue must seem to have robbed the Hybla bees and left them honeyless.' This particular feeling, of which Keats speaks, is familiar to all who have heard Salvini, Sarah Bernhardt, Ristori, or any of the great artists of our day, and it is a feeling that one cannot, I think, gain merely by reading the passage to oneself. For my own part, I must confess that it was not until I heard Sarah Bernhardt in *Phèdre* that I absolutely realised the sweetness of the music of Racine. As for Mr. Birrell's statement that actors have the words of literature for ever on their lips, but none of its truths engraven on their hearts, all that one can say is that, if it be true, it is a defect which actors share with the majority of literary critics.

The account Madame Ristori gives of her own struggles, voyages and adventures, is very pleasant reading indeed. The child of poor actors, she made her first appearance when she was three months old, being brought on in a hamper as a New Year's gift to a selfish old gentleman who would not forgive his daughter for having married for love. As, however, she began to cry long before the hamper was opened, the comedy became a farce, to the immense amusement of the public. She next appeared in a mediæval melodrama, being then three years of age, and was so terrified at the machinations of the villain that she ran away at the most critical moment. However, her stage-fright seems to have disappeared, and we find her playing Silvio Pellico's *Francesco, da Rimini* at fifteen, and at eighteen making her *début* as Marie Stuart. At this time the naturalism of the French method was gradually displacing the artificial elocution and academic poses of the Italian school of acting. Madame Ristori seems to have tried to combine simplicity with style, and the passion of nature with the self-restraint of the artist. 'J'ai voulu fondre les deux manières,' she tells us, 'car je sentais que toutes choses étant susceptibles de progrès, l'art dramatique aussi était appelé à subir des transformations.' The natural development, however, of the Italian drama was almost arrested by the ridiculous censorship of plays then existing in each town under Austrian or Papal rule. The slightest allusion to the sentiment of nationality or the spirit of freedom was prohibited. Even the word *patria* was regarded as treasonable, and Madame Ristori tells us an amusing story of the indignation of a censor who was asked to license a play, in which a dumb man returns home after an absence of many years, and on his entrance upon the stage makes gestures expressive of his joy in seeing his native land once more. 'Gestures of this kind,' said the censor, 'are obviously of a very revolutionary tendency, and cannot possibly be allowed. The only gestures that I could think of permitting would be gestures expressive of a dumb man's delight in scenery generally.'

The stage directions were accordingly altered, and the word 'landscape' substituted for 'native land'! Another censor was extremely severe on an unfortunate poet who had used the expression 'the beautiful Italian sky,' and explained to him that 'the beautiful Lombardo-Venetian sky' was the proper official expression to use. Poor Gregory in *Romeo and Juliet* had to be rechristened, because Gregory is a name dear to the Popes; and the

Here I have a pilot's thumb,
Wrecked as homeward he did come,

of the first witch in *Macbeth* was ruthlessly struck out as containing an obvious allusion to the steersman of St. Peter's bark. Finally, bored and bothered by the political and theological Dogberrys of the day, with their inane prejudices, their solemn stupidity, and their entire ignorance of the conditions necessary for the growth of sane and healthy art, Madame Ristori made up her mind to leave the stage. She, however, was extremely anxious to appear once before a Parisian audience, Paris being at that time the centre of dramatic activity, and after some consideration left Italy for France in the year 1855. There she seems to have been a great success, particularly in the part of Myrrha; classical without being cold, artistic without being academic, she brought to the interpretation of the character of Alfieri's great heroine the colour-element of passion, the form-element of style. Jules Janin was loud in his praises, the Emperor begged Ristori to join the troupe of the Comédie Française, and Rachel, with the strange narrow jealousy of her nature, trembled for her laurels. Myrrha was followed by Marie Stuart, and Marie Stuart by Medea. In the latter part Madame Ristori excited the greatest enthusiasm. Ary Scheffer designed her costumes for her; and the Niobe that stands in the Uffizzi Gallery at Florence, suggested to Madame Ristori her famous pose in the scene with the children. She would not consent, however, to remain in France, and we find her subsequently playing in almost every country in the world from Egypt to Mexico, from Denmark to Honolulu. Her representations of classical plays seem to have been always immensely admired. When she played at Athens, the King offered to arrange for a performance in the beautiful old theatre of Dionysos, and during her tour in Portugal she produced *Medea* before the University of Coimbra. Her description of the latter engagement is extremely interesting. On her arrival at the University, she was received by the entire body of the undergraduates, who still wear a costume almost mediæval in character. Some of them came on the stage in the course of the play as the handmaidens of Creusa, hiding their black beards beneath heavy veils, and as soon as they had finished their parts they took their places gravely among the audience, to Madame Ristori's horror, still in their Greek dress, but with their veils thrown back, and smoking long cigars. 'Ce n'est pas la première fois,' she says, 'que j'ai dû empêcher, par un effort de volonté, la tragédie de se terminer en farce.' Very interesting, also, is her account of the production of Montanelli's *Camma*, and she tells an amusing story of the arrest of the author by the French police on the charge of murder, in consequence of a telegram she sent to him in which the words 'body of the victim' occurred. Indeed, the whole book is full of cleverly written stories, and admirable criticisms on dramatic art. I have quoted from the French version, which happens to be the one that lies before me, but whether in French or Italian the book is one of the most fascinating autobiographies that has appeared for some time, even in an age like ours when literary egotism has been brought to such an exquisite pitch of perfection.

* * * * *

The New Purgatory and Other Poems, by Miss E. R. Chapman, is, in some respects, a very remarkable little volume. It used to be said that women were too poetical by nature to make great poets, too receptive to be really creative, too well satisfied with mere feeling to search after the marble splendour of form. But we must not judge of woman's poetic power by her achievements in days when education was denied to her, for where there is no faculty of expression no art is possible. Mrs. Browning, the first great English poetess, was also an admirable scholar, though she may not have put the accents on her Greek, and even in those poems that seem most remote from classical life, such as *Aurora Leigh*, for instance, it is not difficult to trace the fine literary influence of a classical training. Since Mrs. Browning's time, education has become, not the privilege of a few women, but the inalienable inheritance of all; and, as a natural consequence of the increased faculty of expression thereby gained, the women poets of our day hold a very high literary position. Curiously enough, their poetry is, as a rule, more distinguished for strength than for beauty; they seem to love to grapple with the big intellectual problems of modern life; science, philosophy and metaphysics form a large portion of their ordinary subject-matter; they leave the triviality of triolets to men, and try to read the writing on the wall, and to solve the last secret of the Sphinx. Hence Robert Browning, not Keats, is their idol; *Sordello* moves them more than the *Ode on a Grecian Urn*; and all Lord Tennyson's magic and music seems to them as nothing compared with the psychological subtleties of *The Ring and the Book*, or the pregnant questions stirred in the dialogue between Blougram and Gigadibs. Indeed I remember hearing a charming young Girtonian, forgetting for a moment the exquisite lyrics in *Pippa Passes*, and the superb blank verse of *Men and Women*, state quite seriously that the reason she admired the author of *Red-Cotton Night-Cap Country* was that he had headed a reaction against beauty in poetry!

Miss Chapman is probably one of Mr. Browning's disciples. She does not imitate him, but it is easy to discern his influence on her verse, and she has caught something of his fine, strange faith. Take, for instance, her poem, *A Strong-minded Woman*:

See her? Oh, yes!—Come this way—hush! this way,
  Here she is lying,
Sweet—with the smile her face wore yesterday,
  As she lay dying.
Calm, the mind-fever gone, and, praise God! gone
  All the heart-hunger;
Looking the merest girl at forty-one—
  You guessed her younger?
Well, she'd the flower-bloom that children have,
  Was lithe and pliant,
With eyes as innocent blue as they were brave,
  Resolved, defiant.
Yourself—you worship art! Well, at that shrine
  She too bowed lowly,
Drank thirstily of beauty, as of wine,
  Proclaimed it holy.
But could you follow her when, in a breath,
  She knelt to science,

Vowing to truth true service to the death,
  And heart-reliance?
Nay,—then for you she underwent eclipse,
  Appeared as alien
As once, before he prayed, those ivory lips
  Seemed to Pygmalion.
    * * * * *

  Hear from your heaven, my dear, my lost delight,
    You who were woman
To your heart's heart, and not more pure, more white,
  Than warmly human.
How shall I answer? How express, reveal
  Your true life-story?
How utter, if they cannot guess—not feel
  Your crowning glory?
This way. Attend my words. The rich, we know,
  Do into heaven
Enter but hardly; to the poor, the low,
  God's kingdom's given.
Well, there's another heaven—a heaven on earth—
  (That's love's fruition)
Whereto a certain lack—a certain dearth—
  Gains best admission.
Here, too, she was too rich—ah, God! if less
  Love had been lent her!—
Into the realm of human happiness
  These look—not enter.

Well, here we have, if not quite an echo, at least a reminiscence of the metre of *The Grammarian's Funeral*; and the peculiar blending together of lyrical and dramatic forms, seems essentially characteristic of Mr. Browning's method. Yet there is a distinct personal note running all through the poem, and true originality is to be found rather in the use made of a model than in the rejection of all models and masters. *Dans l'art comme dans la nature on est toujours fils de quelqu'un*, and we should not quarrel with the reed if it whispers to us the music of the lyre. A little child once asked me if it was the nightingale who taught the linnets how to sing.

Miss Chapman's other poems contain a great deal that is interesting. The most ambitious is *The New Purgatory*, to which the book owes its title. It is a vision of a strange garden in which, cleansed and purified of all stain and shame, walk Judas of Cherioth, Nero the Lord of Rome, Ysabel the wife of Ahab, and others, around whose names cling terrible memories of horror, or awful splendours of sin. The conception is fine, but the treatment is hardly adequate. There are, however, some good strong lines in it, and, indeed, almost all of Miss Chapman's poems are worth reading, if not for their absolute beauty, at least for their intellectual intention.
    * * * * *

Nothing is more interesting than to watch the change and development of the art of novel-writing in this nineteenth century—'this so-called nineteenth century,' as an impassioned young orator once termed it, after a contemptuous diatribe against the evils of modern civilisation. In France they have had one great genius, Balzac, who invented the modern method of looking at life; and one great artist, Flaubert, who is the impeccable master of style; and to the influence of these two men we may trace almost all contemporary French fiction. But in England we have had no schools worth speaking of. The fiery torch lit by the Brontës has not been passed on to other hands; Dickens has influenced only journalism; Thackeray's delightful superficial philosophy, superb narrative power, and clever social satire have found no echoes; nor has Trollope left any direct successors behind him—a fact which is not much to be regretted, however, as, admirable though Trollope undoubtedly is for rainy afternoons and tedious railway journeys, from the point of view of literature he is merely the perpetual curate of Pudlington Parva. As for George Meredith, who could hope to reproduce him? His style is chaos illumined by brilliant flashes of lightning. As a writer he has mastered everything, except language; as a novelist he can do everything, except tell a story; as an artist he is everything, except articulate. Too strange to be popular, too individual to have imitators, the author of *Richard Feverel* stands absolutely alone. It is easy to disarm criticism, but he has disarmed the disciple. He gives us his philosophy through the medium of wit, and is never so pathetic as when he is humorous. To turn truth into a paradox is not difficult, but George Meredith makes all his paradoxes truths, and no Theseus can thread his labyrinth, no Œdipus solve his secret.

However, it is only fair to acknowledge that there are some signs of a school springing up amongst us. This school is not native, nor does it seek to reproduce any English master. It may be described as the result of the realism of Paris filtered through the refining influence of Boston. Analysis, not action, is its aim; it has more psychology than passion, and it plays very cleverly upon one string, and this is the commonplace.
    * * * * *

As a reaction against this school, it is pleasant to come across a novel like Lady Augusta Noel's *Hithersea Mere*. If this story has any definite defect, it comes from its delicacy and lightness of treatment. An industrious Bostonian would have made half a dozen novels out of it, and have had enough left for a serial. Lady Augusta Noel is content to vivify her characters, and does not care about vivisection; she suggests rather than explains; and she does not seek to make life too obviously rational. Romance, picturesqueness, charm—these are the qualities of her book. As for its plot, it has so many plots that it is difficult to describe them. We have the story of Rhona Somerville, the daughter of a great popular preacher, who tries to write her father's life, and, on looking over his papers and early diaries, finds struggle where she expected calm, and doubt where she looked for faith, and is afraid to keep back the truth, and yet dares not publish it. Rhona is quite charming; she is like a little flower that takes itself very seriously, and she shows us how thoroughly nice and natural a narrow-minded girl may be. Then we have the two brothers, John and Adrian Mowbray. John is the hard-working, vigorous clergyman, who is impatient of all theories, brings his faith to the test of action, not of intellect, lives what he believes, and has no sympathy for those who waver or question—a thoroughly admirable, practical, and extremely irritating man. Adrian is the fascinating *dilettante*, the philosophic doubter, a sort of romantic rationalist with a taste for art. Of course, Rhona marries the brother who needs conversion, and their gradual influence on each other is indicated by a few subtle touches. Then we have the curious story of Olga, Adrian Mowbray's first love. She is a wonderful and mystical girl, like a little maiden out of the Sagas, with the blue eyes and fair hair of the North. An old Norwegian nurse is always at her side, a sort of Lapland witch who teaches her how to see visions and to interpret dreams. Adrian mocks at this superstition, as he calls it, but as a consequence of disregarding it, Olga's only brother is drowned skating, and she never speaks to Adrian again. The whole story is told in the most suggestive way, the mere delicacy of the touch making what is strange seem real. The most delightful character in the whole book, however, is a girl called Hilary Marston, and hers also is the most tragic tale of all. Hilary is like a little woodland faun, half Greek and half gipsy; she knows the note of every bird, and the haunt of every animal; she is terribly out of place in a drawing-room, but is on intimate terms with every young poacher in the district; squirrels come and sit on her shoulder, which is pretty, and she carries ferrets in her pockets, which is dreadful; she never reads a book, and has not got a single accomplishment, but she is fascinating and fearless, and wiser, in her own way, than any pedant or bookworm. This poor little English Dryad falls passionately in love with a great blind helpless hero, who regards her as a sort of pleasant tom-boy; and her death is most touching and pathetic. Lady Augusta Noel has a charming and winning style, her descriptions of Nature are quite admirable, and her book is one of the most pleasantly-written novels that has appeared this winter.

Miss Alice Corkran's *Margery Merton's Girlhood* has the same lightness of touch and grace of treatment. Though ostensibly meant for young people, it is a story that all can read with pleasure, for it is true without being harsh, and beautiful without being affected, and its rejection of the stronger and more violent passions of life is artistic rather than ascetic. In a word, it is a little piece of true literature, as dainty as it is delicate, and as sweet as it is simple. Margery Merton is brought up in Paris by an old maiden aunt, who has an elaborate theory of education, and strict ideas about discipline. Her system is an excellent one, being founded on the science of Darwin and the wisdom of Solomon, but it comes to terrible grief when put into practice; and finally she has to procure a governess, Madame Réville, the widow of a great and unappreciated French painter. From her Margery gets her first feeling for art, and the chief interest of the book centres round a competition for an art scholarship, into which Margery and the other girls of the convent school enter. Margery selects Joan of Arc as her subject; and, rather to the horror of the good nuns, who think that the saint should have her golden aureole, and be as gorgeous and as ecclesiastical as bright paints and bad drawing can make her, the picture represents a common peasant girl, standing in an old orchard, and listening in ignorant terror to the strange voices whispering in her ear. The scene in which she shows her sketch for the first time to the art master and the Mother Superior is very cleverly rendered indeed, and shows considerable dramatic power.

Of course, a good deal of opposition takes place, but ultimately Margery has her own way and, in spite of a wicked plot set on foot by a jealous competitor, who persuades the Mother Superior that the picture is not Margery's own work, she succeeds in winning the prize. The whole account of the gradual development of the conception in the girl's mind, and the various attempts she makes to give her dream its perfect form, is extremely interesting and, indeed, the book deserves a place among what Sir George Trevelyan has happily termed 'the art-literature' of our day. Mr. Ruskin in prose, and Mr. Browning in poetry, were the first who drew for us the workings of the artist soul, the first who led us from the painting or statue to the hand that fashioned it, and the brain that gave it life. They seem to have made art more expressive for us, to have shown us a passionate humanity lying behind line and colour. Theirs was the seed of this new literature, and theirs, too, is its flower; but it is pleasant to note their influence on Miss Corkran's little story, in which the creation of a picture forms the dominant *motif.*

* * * * *

Mrs. Pfeiffer's *Women and Work* is a collection of most interesting essays on the relation to health and physical development of the higher education of girls, and the intellectual or more systematised effort of woman. Mrs. Pfeiffer, who writes a most admirable prose style, deals in succession with the sentimental difficulty, with the economic problem, and with the arguments of physiologists. She boldly grapples with Professor Romanes, whose recent article in the *Nineteenth Century*, on the leading characters which mentally differentiate men and women, attracted so much attention, and produces some very valuable statistics from America, where the influence of education on health has been most carefully studied. Her book is a most important contribution to the discussion of one of the great social problems of our day. The extended activity of women is now an accomplished fact; its results are on their trial; and Mrs. Pfeiffer's excellent essays sum up the situation very completely, and show the rational and scientific basis of the movement more clearly and more logically than any other treatise I have as yet seen.

* * * * *

It is interesting to note that many of the most advanced modern ideas on the subject of the education of women are anticipated by Defoe in his wonderful *Essay upon Projects*, where he proposes that a college for women should be erected in every county in England, and ten colleges of the kind in London. 'I have often thought of it, 'he says,' as one of the most barbarous customs in the world that we deny the advantages of learning to women. Their youth is spent to teach them to stitch and sew, or make baubles. They are taught to read, indeed, and perhaps to write their names or so, and that is the height of a woman's education. And I would but ask any who slight the sex for their understanding, "What is a man (a gentleman I mean) good for that is taught no more?" What has the woman done to forfeit the privilege of being taught? Shall we upbraid women with folly when it is only the error of this inhuman custom that hindered them being made wiser?' Defoe then proceeds to elaborate his scheme for the foundation of women's colleges, and enters into minute details about the architecture, the general curriculum, and the discipline. His suggestion that the penalty of death should be inflicted on any man who ventured to make a proposal of marriage to any of the girl students during term time possibly suggested the plot of Lord Tennyson's *Princess*, so its harshness may be excused, and in all other respects his ideas are admirable. I am glad to see that this curious little volume forms one of the National Library series. In its anticipations of many of our most modern inventions it shows how thoroughly practical all dreamers are.

* * * * *

I am sorry to see that Mrs. Fawcett deprecates the engagement of ladies of education as dressmakers and milliners, and speaks of it as being detrimental to those who have fewer educational advantages. I myself would like to see dressmaking regarded not merely as a learned profession, but as a fine art. To construct a costume that will be at once rational and beautiful requires an accurate knowledge of the principles of proportion, a thorough acquaintance with the laws of health, a subtle sense of colour, and a quick appreciation of the proper use of materials, and the proper qualities of pattern and design. The health of a nation depends very largely on its mode of dress; the artistic feeling of a nation should find expression in its costume quite as much as in its architecture; and just as the upholstering tradesman has had to give place to the decorative artist, so the ordinary milliner, with her lack of taste and lack of knowledge, her foolish fashions and her feeble inventions, will have to make way for the scientific and artistic dress designer. Indeed, so far from it being wise to discourage women of education from taking up the profession of dressmakers, it is exactly women of education who are needed, and I am glad to see in the new technical college for women at Bedford, millinery and dressmaking are to be taught as part of the ordinary curriculum. There has also been started in London a Society of Lady Dressmakers for the purpose of teaching educated girls and women, and the Scientific Dress Association is, I hear, doing very good work in the same direction.

* * * * *

I have received some very beautiful specimens of Christmas books from Messrs. Griffith and Farran. *Treasures of Art and Song*, edited by Robert Ellice Mack, is a real *édition de luxe* of pretty poems and pretty pictures; and *Through the Year* is a wonderfully artistic calendar.

Messrs. Hildesheimer and Faulkner have also sent me *Rhymes and Roses*, illustrated by Ernest Wilson and St. Clair Simmons; *Cape Town Dicky*, a child's book, with some very lovely pictures by Miss Alice Havers; a wonderful edition of *The Deserted Village*, illustrated by Mr. Charles Gregory and Mr. Hines; and some really charming Christmas cards, those by Miss Alice Havers, Miss Edwards, and Miss Dealy being especially good.

* * * * *

The most perfect and the most poisonous of all modern French poets once remarked that a man can live for three days without bread, but that no one can live for three days without poetry. This, however, can hardly be said to be a popular view, or one that commends itself to that curiously uncommon quality which is called common-sense. I fancy that most people, if they do not actually prefer a salmis to a sonnet, certainly like their culture to repose on a basis of good cookery, and as there is something to be said for this attitude, I am glad to see that several ladies are interesting themselves in cookery classes. Mrs. Marshall's brilliant lectures are, of course, well known, and besides her there is Madame Lebour-Fawssett, who holds weekly classes in Kensington. Madame Fawssett is the author of an admirable little book, entitled *Economical French Cookery for Ladies*, and I am glad to hear that her lectures are so successful. I was talking the other day to a lady who works a great deal at the East End of London, and she told me that no small part of the permanent misery of the poor is due to their entire ignorance of the cleanliness and economy necessary for good cooking.

* * * * *

The Popular Ballad Concert Society has been reorganised under the name of the Popular Musical Union. Its object will be to train the working classes thoroughly in the enjoyment and performance of music, and to provide the inhabitants of the crowded districts of the East End with concerts and oratorios, to be performed as far as possible by trained members of the working classes; and, though money is urgently required, it is proposed to make the Society to a certain degree self-supporting by giving something in the form of high-class concerts in return for subscriptions and donations. The whole scheme is an excellent one, and I hope that the readers of the *Woman's World* will give it their valuable support. Mrs. Ernest Hart is the secretary, and the treasurer is the Rev. S. Barnett.

(1) *Etudes et Souvenirs.* By Madame Ristori. (Paul Ollendorff.)

(2) *The New Purgatory and Other Poems.* By Elizabeth Rachel Chapman. (Fisher Unwin.)

(3) *Hithersea Mere.* By Lady Augusta Noel, Author of *Wandering Willie, From Generation to Generation, etc.* (Macmillan and Co.)

(4) *Margery Merton's Girlhood.* By Alice Corkran. (Blackie and Son.)

(5) *Women and Work.* By Emily Pfeiffer. (Trübner and Co.)

(6) *Treasures of Art and Song.* Edited by Robert Ellice Mack. (Griffith and Farren.)

(7) *Rhymes and Roses.* Illustrated by Ernest Wilson and St. Clair Simons. *Cape Town Dicky.* Illustrated by Alice Havers. *The Deserted Pillage.* Illustrated by Charles Gregory and John Hines. (Hildesheimer and Faulkner.)

THE POETS' CORNER—IV

(*Pall Mall Gazette*, January 20, 1888.)

A cynical critic once remarked that no great poet is intelligible and no little poet worth understanding, but that otherwise poetry is an admirable thing. This, however, seems to us a somewhat harsh view of the subject. Little poets are an extremely interesting study. The best of them have often some new beauty to show us, and though the worst of them may bore yet they rarely brutalise. *Poor Folks' Lives*, for instance, by the Rev. Frederick Langbridge, is a volume that could do no possible harm to any one. These poems display a healthy, rollicking, G. R. Sims tone of feeling, an almost unbounded regard for the converted drunkard, and a strong sympathy with the sufferings of the poor. As for their theology, it is of that honest, downright and popular kind, which in these rationalistic days is probably quite as useful as any other form of theological thought. Here is the opening of a poem called *A Street Sermon*, which is an interesting example of what muscular Christianity can do in the sphere of verse-making:

What, God fight shy of the city?
    He's t' other side up I guess;
If you ever want to find Him,
    Whitechapel's the right address.

Those who prefer pseudo-poetical prose to really prosaic poetry will wish that Mr. Dalziel had converted most of his *Pictures in the Fire* into leaders for the *Daily Telegraph*, as, from the literary point of view, they have all the qualities dear to the Asiatic school. What a splendid leader the young lions of Fleet Street would have made out of *The Prestige of England*, for instance, a poem suggested by the opening of the Zulu war in 1879.

Now away sail our ships far away o'er the sea,
    Far away with our gallant and brave;
The loud war-cry is sounding like wild revelriè,
    And our heroes dash on to their grave;
For the fierce Zulu tribes have arisen in their might,
    And in thousands swept down on our few;
But these braves only yielded when crushed in the fight,
    Man to man to their colours were true.

The conception of the war-cry sounding 'like wild revelriè' is quite in the true Asiatic spirit, and indeed the whole poem is full of the daring English of a special correspondent. Personally, we prefer Mr. Dalziel when he is not quite so military. *The Fairies*, for instance, is a very pretty poem, and reminds us of some of Dicky Doyle's charming drawings, and *Nat Bentley* is a capital ballad in its way. The Irish poems, however, are rather vulgar and should be expunged. The Celtic element in literature is extremely valuable, but there is absolutely no excuse for shrieking 'Shillelagh!' and 'O Gorrah!'

Women must Weep, by Professor Harald Williams, has the most dreadful cover of any book that we have come across for some time past. It is possibly intended to symbolise the sorrow of the world, but it merely suggests the decorative tendencies of an undertaker and is as depressing as it is detestable. However, as the cowl does not make the monk, so the binding, in the case of the Savile Club school, does not make the poet, and we open the volume without prejudice. The first poem that we come to is a vigorous attack on those wicked and misguided people who believe that Beauty is its own reason for existing, and that Art should have no other aim but her own perfection. Here are some of the Professor's gravest accusations:

Why do they patch, in their fatal choice,
    When at secrets such the angels quake,
But a play of the Vision and the Voice?—
    Oh, it's all for Art's sake.

Why do they gather what should be left,
    And leave behind what they ought to take,
And exult in the basest blank or theft?—
    Oh, it's all for Art's sake.

It certainly must be admitted that to 'patch' or to 'exult in the basest blank' is a form of conduct quite unbefitting an artist, the very obscurity and incomprehensible character of such a crime adding something to its horror. However, while fully recognising the wickedness of 'patching' we cannot but think that Professor Harald Williams is happier in his criticism of life than he is in his art criticism. His poem *Between the Banks*, for instance, has a touch of sincerity and fine feeling that almost atones for its over-emphasis.

Mr. Buchan's blank verse drama *Joseph and His Brethren* bears no resemblance to that strange play on the same subject which Mr. Swinburne so much admires. Indeed, it may be said to possess all the fatal originality of inexperience. However, Mr. Buchan does not leave us in any doubt about his particular method of writing. 'As to the dialogue,' he says, 'I have put the language of real life into the mouths of the speakers, except when they may be supposed to be under strong emotion; then their utterances become more rapid—broken—figurative—in short more poetical.' Well, here is the speech of Potiphar's wife under strong emotion:

ZULEEKHA (seizing him). Love me! or death!
Ha! dost thou think thou wilt not, and yet live?
By Isis, no. And thou wilt turn away,
Iron, marble mockman! Ah! I hold thy life!
Love feeds on death. It swallows up all life,
Hugging, or killing. I to woo, and thou—
Unhappy me! Oh!

The language here is certainly rapid and broken, and the expression 'marble mockman' is, we suppose, figurative, but the passage can scarcely be described as poetical, though it fulfils all Mr. Buchan's conditions. Still, tedious as Zuleekha and Joseph are, the Chorus of Ancients is much worse. These 'ideal spectators' seem to spend their lives in uttering those solemn platitudes that with the aged pass for wisdom. The chief offenders are the members of what Mr. Buchan calls 'The 2nd.—Semi-chorus,' who have absolutely no hesitation in interrupting the progress of the play with observations of this kind:

2ND.—semi-chorus

Ah! but favour extreme shown to one
    Among equals who yet stand apart,
        Awakeneth, say ye, if naturally,
            The demons—jealousy, envy, hate,—
        In the breast of those passed by.

It is a curious thing that when minor poets write choruses to a play they should always consider it necessary to adopt the style and language of a bad translator. We fear that Mr. Bohn has much to answer for.

God's Garden is a well-meaning attempt to use Nature for theological and educational purposes. It belongs to that antiquated school of thought that, in spite of the discoveries of modern science, invites the sluggard to look at the ant, and the idle to imitate the bee. It is full of false analogies and dull eighteenth-century didactics. It tells us that the flowering cactus should remind us that a dwarf may possess mental and moral qualities, that the mountain ash should teach us the precious fruits of affliction, and that a fond father should learn from the example of the chestnut that the most beautiful children often turn out badly! We must admit that we have no sympathy with this point of view, and we strongly protest against the idea that

The flaming poppy, with its black core, tells
Of anger's flushing face, and heart of sin.

The worst use that man can make of Nature is to turn her into a mirror for his own vices, nor are Nature's secrets ever disclosed to those who approach her in this spirit. However, the author of this irritating little volume is not always botanising and moralising in this reckless and improper fashion. He has better moments, and those who sympathise with the Duke of Westminster's efforts to provide open spaces for the people, will no doubt join in the aspiration—

God bless wise Grosvenors whose hearts incline,
Workmen to fête, and grateful souls refine;

though they may regret that so noble a sentiment is expressed in so inadequate a form.

It is difficult to understand why Mr. Cyrus Thornton should have called his volume *Voices of the Street*. However, poets have a perfect right to christen their own children, and if the wine is good no one should quarrel with the bush. Mr. Thornton's verse is often graceful and melodious, and some of his lines, such as—

And the wise old Roman bondsman saw no terror in the dead—
Children when the play was over, going softly home to bed,

have a pleasant Tennysonian ring. The *Ballad of the Old Year* is rather depressing. 'Bury the Old Year Solemnly' has been said far too often, and the sentiment is suitable only for Christmas crackers. The best thing in the book is *The Poet's Vision of Death*, which is quite above the average.

Mrs. Dobell informs us that she has already published sixteen volumes of poetry and that she intends to publish two more. The volume that now lies before us is entitled *In the Watches of the Night*, most of the poems that it contains having been composed 'in the neighbourhood of the sea, between the hours of ten and two o'clock.' Judging from the following extract we cannot say that we consider this a very favourable time for inspiration, at any rate in the case of Mrs. Dobell:

Were Anthony Trollope and George Eliot
Alive—which unfortunately they are not—
As regards the subject of 'quack-snubbing,' you know,
To support me I am sure they hadn't been slow—
For they, too, hated the wretched parasite
That fattens on the freshest, the most bright
Of the blossoms springing from the—Public Press!—
And that oft are flowers that even our quacks should bless!

(1) *Poor Folks' Lives.* By the Rev. Frederick Langbridge. (Simpkin, Marshall and Co.)

(2) *Pictures in the Fire.* By George Dalziel. (Privately Printed.)

(3) *Women Must Weep.* By Professor F. Harald Williams. (Swan Sonnenschein and Co.)

(4) *Joseph and His Brethren: a Trilogy.* By Alexander Buchan. (Digby and Long.)

(5) *God's Garden.* By Heartsease. (James Nisbet and Co.)

(6) *Voices of the Street.* By Cyrus Thornton. (Elliot Stock.)

(7) *In the Watches of the Night.* By Mrs. Horace Dobell. (Remington and Co.)

LITERARY AND OTHER NOTES—IV

(*Woman's World*, February 1888.)

Canute The Great, by Michael Field, is in many respects a really remarkable work of art. Its tragic element is to be found in life, not in death; in the hero's psychological development, not in his moral declension or in any physical calamity; and the author has borrowed from modern science the idea that in the evolutionary struggle for existence the true tragedy may be that of the survivor. Canute, the rough generous Viking, finds himself alienated from his gods, his forefathers, his very dreams. With centuries of Pagan blood in his veins, he sets himself to the task of becoming a great Christian governor and lawgiver to men; and yet he is fully conscious that, while he has abandoned the noble impulses of his race, he still retains that which in his nature is most fierce or fearful. It is not by faith that he reaches the new creed, nor through gentleness that he seeks after the new culture. The beautiful Christian woman whom he has made queen of his life and lands teaches him no mercy, and knows nothing of forgiveness. It is sin and not suffering that purifies him—mere sin itself. 'Be not afraid,' he says in the last great scene of the play:

'Be not afraid;
I have learnt this, sin is a mighty bond

'Twixt God and man. Love that has ne'er forgiven
Is virgin and untender; spousal passion
Becomes acquainted with life's vilest things,
Transmutes them, and exalts. Oh, wonderful,
This touch of pardon,—all the shame cast out;
The heart a-ripple with the gaiety,
The leaping consciousness that Heaven knows all,
And yet esteems us royal. Think of it—
The joy, the hope!'

This strange and powerful conception is worked out in a manner as strong as it is subtle; and, indeed, almost every character in the play seems to suggest some new psychological problem. The mere handling of the verse is essentially characteristic of our modern introspective method, as it presents to us, not thought in its perfected form, but the involutions of thought seeking for expression. We seem to witness the very workings of the mind, and to watch the passion struggling for utterance. In plays of this kind (plays that are meant to be read, not to be acted) it must be admitted that we often miss that narrative and descriptive element which in the epic is so great a charm, and, indeed, may be said to be almost essential to the perfect literary presentation of any story. This element the Greek managed to retain by the introduction of chorus and messenger; but we seem to have been unable to invent any substitute for it. That there is here a distinct loss cannot, I think, be denied. There is something harsh, abrupt, and inartistic in such a stage-direction as 'Canute strangles Edric, flings his body into the stream, and gazes out.' It strikes no dramatic note, it conveys no picture, it is meagre and inadequate. If acted it might be fine; but as read, it is unimpressive. However, there is no form of art that has not got its limitations, and though it is sad to see the action of a play relegated to a formal footnote, still there is undoubtedly a certain gain in psychological analysis and psychological concentration.

It is a far cry from the Knutlinga Saga to Rossetti's note-book, but Michael Field passes from one to the other without any loss of power. Indeed, most readers will probably prefer *The Cup of Water*, which is the second play in this volume, to the earlier historical drama. It is more purely poetical; and if it has less power, it has certainly more beauty. Rossetti conceived the idea of a story in which a young king falls passionately in love with a little peasant girl who gives him a cup of water, and is by her beloved in turn, but being betrothed to a noble lady, he yields her in marriage to his friend, on condition that once a year—on the anniversary of their meeting—she brings him a cup of water. The girl dies in childbirth, leaving a daughter who grows into her mother's perfect likeness, and comes to meet the king when he is hunting. Just, however, as he is about to take the cup from her hand, a second figure, in her exact likeness, but dressed in peasant's clothes, steps to her side, looks in the king's face, and kisses him on the mouth. He falls forward on his horse's neck, and is lifted up dead. Michael Field has struck out the supernatural element so characteristic of Rossetti's genius, and in some other respects modified for dramatic purposes material Rossetti left unused. The result is a poem of exquisite and pathetic grace. Cara, the peasant girl, is a creation as delicate as it is delightful, and it deserves to rank beside the Faun of *Callirhöe*. As for the young king who loses all the happiness of his life through one noble moment of unselfishness, and who recognised as he stands over Cara's dead body that

women are not chattels,
To deal with as one's generosity
May prompt or straiten, . . .

and that

we must learn
To drink life's pleasures if we would be pure,

he is one of the most romantic figures in all modern dramatic work. Looked at from a purely technical point of view, Michael Field's verse is sometimes lacking in music, and has no sustained grandeur of movement; but it is extremely dramatic, and its method is admirably suited to express those swift touches of nature and sudden flashes of thought which are Michael Field's distinguishing qualities. As for the moral contained in these plays, work that has the rich vitality of life has always something of life's mystery also; it cannot be narrowed down to a formal creed, nor summed up in a platitude; it has many answers, and more than one secret.

* * * * *

Miss Frances Martin's *Life of Elizabeth Gilbert* is an extremely interesting book. Elizabeth Gilbert was born at a time when, as her biographer reminds us, kindly and intelligent men and women could gravely implore the Almighty to 'take away' a child merely because it was blind; when they could argue that to teach the blind to read, or to attempt to teach them to work, was to fly in the face of Providence; and her whole life was given to the endeavour to overcome this prejudice and superstition; to show that blindness, though a great privation, is not necessarily a disqualification; and that blind men and women can learn, labour, and fulfil all the duties of life. Before her day all that the blind were taught was to commit texts from the Bible to memory. She saw that they could learn handicrafts, and be made industrious and self-supporting. She began with a small cellar in Holborn, at the rent of eighteenpence a week, but before her death she could point to large and well-appointed workshops in almost every city of England where blind men and women are employed, where tools have been invented by or modified for them, and where agencies have been established for the sale of their work. The whole story of her life is full of pathos and of beauty. She was not born blind, but lost her sight through an attack of scarlet fever when she was three years old. For a long time she could not realise her position, and we hear of the little child making earnest appeals to be taken 'out of the dark room,' or to have a candle lighted; and once she whispered to her father, 'If I am a very good little girl, may I see my doll to-morrow?' However, all memory of vision seems to have faded from her before she left the sick-room, though, taught by those around her, she soon began to take an imaginary interest in colour, and a very real one in form and texture. An old nurse is still alive who remembers making a pink frock for her when she was a child, her delight at its being pink and her pleasure in stroking down the folds; and when in 1835 the young Princess Victoria visited Oxford with her mother, Bessie, as she was always called, came running home, exclaiming, 'Oh, mamma, I have seen the Duchess of Kent, and she had on a brown silk dress.' Her youthful admiration of Wordsworth was based chiefly upon his love of flowers, but also on personal knowledge. When she was about ten years old, Wordsworth went to Oxford to receive the honorary degree of D.C.L.

from the University. He stayed with Dr. Gilbert, then Principal of Brasenose, and won Bessie's heart the first day by telling at the dinner table how he had almost leapt off the coach in Bagley Wood to gather the blue veronica. But she had a better reason for remembering that visit. One day she was in the drawing-room alone, and Wordsworth entered. For a moment he stood silent before the blind child, the little sensitive face, with its wondering, inquiring look, turned towards him. Then he gravely said, 'Madam, I hope I do not disturb you.' She never forgot that 'Madam'—grave, solemn, almost reverential.

As for the great practical work of her life, the amelioration of the condition of the blind, Miss Martin gives a wonderful account of her noble efforts and her noble success; and the volume contains a great many interesting letters from eminent people, of which the following characteristic note from Mr. Ruskin is not the least interesting:

DENMARK HILL, 2nd September 1871.

MADAM,—I am obliged by your letter, and I deeply sympathise with the objects of the institution over which you preside. But one of my main principles of work is that every one must do their best, and spend their all in their own work, and mine is with a much lower race of sufferers than you plead for—with those who 'have eyes and see not.'—I am, Madam, your faithful servant, J. Ruskin.

Miss Martin is a most sympathetic biographer, and her book should be read by all who care to know the history of one of the remarkable women of our century.

* * * * *

Ourselves and Our Neighbours is a pleasant volume of social essays from the pen of one of the most graceful and attractive of all American poetesses, Mrs. Louise Chandler Moulton. Mrs. Moulton, who has a very light literary touch, discusses every important modern problem—from Society rosebuds and old bachelors, down to the latest fashions in bonnets and in sonnets. The best chapter in the book is that entitled 'The Gospel of Good Gowns,' which contains some very excellent remarks on the ethics of dress. Mrs. Moulton sums up her position in the following passage:—

The desire to please is a natural characteristic of unspoiled womanhood. 'If I lived in the woods, I should dress for the trees,' said a woman widely known for taste and for culture. Every woman's dress should be, and if she has any ideality will be, an expression of herself. . . . The true gospel of dress is that of fitness and taste. Pictures are painted, and music is written, and flowers are fostered, that life may be made beautiful. Let women delight our eyes like pictures, be harmonious as music, and fragrant as flowers, that they also may fulfil their mission of grace and of beauty. By companionship with beautiful thoughts shall their tastes be so formed that their toilets will never be out of harmony with their means or their position. They will be clothed almost as unconsciously as the lilies of the field; but each one will be herself, and there will be no more uniformity in their attire than in their faces.

The modern Dryad who is ready to 'dress for the trees' seems to me a charming type; but I hardly think that Mrs. Moulton is right when she says that the woman of the future will be clothed 'almost as unconsciously as the lilies of the field.' Possibly, however, she means merely to emphasise the distinction between dressing and dressing-up, a distinction which is often forgotten.

* * * * *

Warring' Angels is a very sad and suggestive story. It contains no impossible heroine and no improbable hero, but is simply a faithful transcript from life, a truthful picture of men and women as they are. Darwin could not have enjoyed it, as it does not end happily. There is, at least, no distribution of cakes and ale in the last chapter. But, then, scientific people are not always the best judges of literature. They seem to think that the sole aim of art should be to amuse, and had they been consulted on the subject would have banished Melpomene from Parnassus. It may be admitted, however, that not a little of our modern art is somewhat harsh and painful. Our Castaly is very salt with tears, and we have bound the brows of the Muses with cypress and with yew. We are often told that we are a shallow age, yet we have certainly the saddest literature of all the ages, for we have made Truth and not Beauty the aim of art, and seem to value imitation more than imagination. This tendency is, of course, more marked in fiction than it is in poetry. Beauty of form is always in itself a source of joy; the mere *technique* of verse has an imaginative and spiritual element; and life must, to a certain degree, be transfigured before it can find its expression in music. But ordinary fiction, rejecting the beauty of form in order to realise the facts of life, seems often to lack the vital element of delight, to miss that pleasure-giving power in virtue of which the arts exist. It would not, however, be fair to regard *Warring Angels* simply as a specimen of literary photography. It has a marked distinction of style, a definite grace and simplicity of manner. There is nothing crude in it, though it is to a certain degree inexperienced; nothing violent, though it is often strong. The story it has to tell has frequently been told before, but the treatment makes it new; and Lady Flower, for whose white soul the angels of good and evil are at war, is admirably conceived, and admirably drawn.

* * * * *

A Song of Jubilee and Other Poems contains some pretty, picturesque verses. Its author is Mrs. De Courcy Laffan, who, under the name of Mrs. Leith Adams, is well known as a novelist and story writer. The Jubilee Ode is quite as good as most of the Jubilee Odes have been, and some of the short poems are graceful. This from *The First Butterfly* is pretty:

O little bird without a song! I love
Thy silent presence, floating in the light—
A living, perfect thing, when scarcely yet
The snow-white blossom crawls along the wall,
And not a daisy shows its star-like head
Amid the grass.

Miss Bella Duffy's *Life of Madame de Staël* forms part of that admirable 'Eminent Women' Series, which is so well edited by Mr. John H. Ingram. There is nothing absolutely new in Miss Duffy's book, but this was not to be expected. Unpublished correspondence, that delight of the eager biographer, is not to be had in the case of Madame de Staël, the De Broglie family having either destroyed or successfully concealed all the papers which might have revealed any facts not already in the possession of the world. Upon the other hand, the book has the excellent quality of condensation, and gives us in less than two hundred pages a very good picture of Madame de Staël and her day. Miss Duffy's criticism of *Corinne* is worth quoting:

Corinne is a classic of which everybody is bound to speak with respect. The enormous admiration which it exacted at the time of its appearance may seem somewhat strange in this year of grace; but then it must be remembered that Italy was not the over-written country it has since become. Besides this, Madame de Staël was the most conspicuous personage of her day. Except Chateaubriand, she had nobody to dispute with her the palm of literary glory in France. Her exile, her literary circle, her courageous opinions, had kept the eyes of Europe fixed on her for years, so that any work from her pen was sure to excite the liveliest curiosity.

Corinne is a kind of glorified guide-book, with some of the qualities of a good novel. It is very long winded, but the appetite of the age was robust in that respect, and the highly-strung emotions of the hero and heroine could not shock a taste which had been formed by the Sorrows of Werther. It is extremely moral, deeply sentimental, and of a deadly earnestness—three characteristics which could not fail to recommend it to a dreary and ponderous generation, the most deficient in taste that ever trod the earth.

But it is artistic in the sense that the interest is concentrated from first to last on the central figure, and the drama, such as it is, unfolds itself naturally from its starting point, which is the contrast between the characters of Oswald and Corinne.

The 'dreary and ponderous generation, the most deficient in taste that ever trod the earth,' seems to me a somewhat exaggerated mode of expression, but 'glorified guide-book' is a not unfelicitous description of the novel that once thrilled Europe. Miss Duffy sums up her opinion of Madame de Staël as a writer in the following passage:

Her mind was strong of grasp and wide in range, but continuous effort fatigued it. She could strike out isolated sentences alternately brilliant, exhaustive, and profound, but she could not link them to other sentences so as to form an organic whole. Her thought was definite singly, but vague as a whole. She always saw things separately, and tried to combine them arbitrarily, and it is generally difficult to follow out any idea of hers from its origin to its end. Her thoughts are like pearls of price profusely scattered, or carelessly strung together, but not set in any design. On closing one of her books, the reader is left with no continuous impression. He has been dazzled and delighted, enlightened also by flashes; but the horizons disclosed have vanished again, and the outlook is enriched by no new vistas.

Then she was deficient in the higher qualities of the imagination. She could analyse, but not characterise; construct, but not create. She could take one defect like selfishness, or one passion like love, and display its workings; or she could describe a whole character, like Napoleon's, with marvellous penetration; but she could not make her personages talk, or act like human beings. She lacked pathos, and had no sense of humour. In short, hers was a mind endowed with enormous powers of comprehension, and an amazing richness of ideas, but deficient in perception of beauty, in poetry, and in true originality. She was a great social personage, but her influence on literature was not destined to be lasting, because, in spite of foreseeing too much, she had not the true prophetic sense of proportion, and confused the things of the present with those of the future—the accidental with the enduring.

I cannot but think that in this passage Miss Duffy rather underrates Madame de Staël's influence on the literature of the nineteenth century. It is true that she gave our literature no new form, but she was one of those who gave it a new spirit, and the romantic movement owes her no small debt. However, a biography should be read for its pictures more than for its criticisms, and Miss Duffy shows a remarkable narrative power, and tells with a good deal of *esprit* the wonderful adventures of the brilliant woman whom Heine termed 'a whirlwind in petticoats.'

* * * * *

Mr. Harcourt's reprint of John Evelyn's *Life of Mrs. Godolphin* is a welcome addition to the list of charming library books. Mr. Harcourt's grandfather, the Archbishop of York, himself John Evelyn's great-great-grandson, inherited the manuscript from his distinguished ancestor, and in 1847 entrusted it for publication to Samuel Wilberforce, then Bishop of Oxford. As the book has been for a long time out of print, this new edition is sure to awake fresh interest in the life of the noble and virtuous lady whom John Evelyn so much admired. Margaret Godolphin was one of the Queen's Maids of Honour at the Court of Charles II., and was distinguished for the delicate purity of her nature, as well as for her high intellectual attainments. Some of the extracts Evelyn gives from her Diary seem to show an austere, formal, almost ascetic spirit; but it was inevitable that a nature so refined as hers should have turned in horror from such ideals of life as were presented by men like Buckingham and Rochester, like Etheridge, Killigrew, and Sedley, like the King himself, to whom she could scarcely bring herself to speak. After her marriage she seems to have become happier and brighter, and her early death makes her a pathetic and interesting figure in the history of the time. Evelyn can see no fault in her, and his life of her is the most wonderful of all panegyrics.

* * * * *

Amongst the Maids-of-Honour mentioned by John Evelyn is Frances Jennings, the elder sister of the great Duchess of Marlborough. Miss Jennings, who was one of the most beautiful women of her day, married first Sir George Hamilton, brother of the author of the *Mémoires de Grammont*, and afterwards Richard Talbot, who was made Duke of Tyrconnel by James II. William's successful occupation of Ireland, where her husband was Lord Deputy, reduced her to poverty and obscurity, and she was probably the first Peeress who ever took to millinery as a livelihood. She had a dressmaker's shop in the Strand, and, not wishing to be detected, sat in a white mask and a white dress, and was known by the name of the 'White Widow.'

I was reminded of the Duchess when I read Miss Emily Faithfull's admirable article in *Gralignani* on 'Ladies as Shopkeepers.' 'The most daring innovation in England at this moment,' says Miss Faithfull, 'is the lady shopkeeper. At present but few people have had the courage to brave the current social prejudice. We draw such fine distinctions between the wholesale and retail traders that our cotton-spinners, calico-makers, and general merchants seem to think that they belong to a totally different sphere, from which they look down on the lady who has had sufficient brains, capital, and courage to open a shop. But the old world moves faster than it did in former days, and before the end of the nineteenth century it is probable that a gentlewoman will be recognised in spite of her having entered on commercial pursuits, especially as we are growing accustomed to see scions of our noblest families on our Stock Exchange and in tea-merchants' houses; one Peer of the realm is now doing an extensive business in coals, and another is a cab proprietor.' Miss Faithfull then proceeds to give a most interesting account of the London dairy opened by the Hon. Mrs. Maberley, of Madame Isabel's millinery establishment, and of the wonderful work done by Miss Charlotte Robinson, who has recently been appointed Decorator to the Queen. About three years ago, Miss Faithfull tells us, Miss Robinson came to Manchester, and opened a shop in King Street, and, regardless of that bugbear which terrifies most women—the loss of social status—she put up her own name over the door, and without the least self-assertion quietly entered into competition with the sterner sex. The result has been eminently satisfactory. This year Miss Robinson has exhibited at Saltaire and at Manchester, and next year she proposes to exhibit at Glasgow, and, possibly, at Brussels. At first she had some difficulty in making people understand that her work is really commercial, not charitable; she feels that, until a healthy public opinion is created, women will pose as 'destitute ladies,' and never take a dignified position in any calling they adopt. Gentlemen who earn their own living are not spoken of as 'destitute,' and we must banish this idea in connection with ladies who are engaged in an equally honourable manner. Miss Faithfull concludes her most valuable article as follows: 'The more highly educated our women of business are, the better for themselves, their work, and the whole community. Many of the professions to which ladies have hitherto turned are overcrowded, and when once the fear of losing social position is boldy disregarded, it will be found that commercial life offers a variety of more or less lucrative employments to ladies of birth and capital, who find it more congenial to their tastes and requirements to invest their money and spend their energies in a business which yields a fair return rather than sit at home content with a scanty pittance.'

I myself entirely agree with Miss Faithfull, though I feel that there is something to be said in favour of the view put forward by Lady Shrewsbury in the *Woman's World*, {289} and a great deal to be said in favour of Mrs. Joyce's scheme for emigration. Mr. Walter Besant, if we are to judge from his last novel, is of Lady Shrewsbury's way of thinking.

* * * * *

I hope that some of my readers will be interested in Miss Beatrice Crane's little poem, *Blush-Roses*, for which her father, Mr. Walter Crane, has done so lovely and graceful a design. Mrs. Simon, of Birkdale Park, Southport, tells me that she offered a prize last term at her school for the best sonnet on any work of art. The poems were sent to Professor Dowden, who awarded the prize to the youthful authoress of the following sonnet on Mr. Watts's picture of *Hope*:

She sits with drooping form and fair bent head,
Low-bent to hear the faintly-sounding strain
That thrills her with the sweet uncertain pain
Of timid trust and restful tears unshed.
Around she feels vast spaces. Awe and dread
　Encompass her.
And the dark doubt she fain
Would banish, sees the shuddering fear remain,
And ever presses near with stealthy tread.
　But not for ever will the misty space
Close down upon her meekly-patient eyes.
The steady light within them soon will ope
Their heavy lids, and then the sweet fair face,
Uplifted in a sudden glad surprise,
Will find the bright reward which comes to Hope.

I myself am rather inclined to prefer this sonnet on Mr. Watts's *Psyche*. The sixth line is deficient; but, in spite of the faulty *technique*, there is a great deal that is suggestive in it:

　Unfathomable boundless mystery,
Last work of the Creator, deathless, vast,
Soul—essence moulded of a changeful past;
Thou art the offspring of Eternity;
Breath of his breath, by his vitality
Engendered, in his image cast,
Part of the Nature-song whereof the last
Chord soundeth never in the harmony.
'Psyche'! Thy form is shadowed o'er with pain
Born of intensest longing, and the rain
Of a world's weeping lieth like a sea
Of silent soundless sorrow in thine eyes.
Yet grief is not eternal, for clouds rise
From out the ocean everlastingly.

I have to thank Mr. William Rossetti for kindly allowing me to reproduce Dante Gabriel Rossetti's drawing of the authoress of *Goblin Market*; and thanks are also due to Mr. Lafayette, of Dublin, for the use of his photograph of H.R.H. the Princess of Wales in her Academic Robes as Doctor of Music, which served as our frontispiece last month, and to Messrs. Hills and Saunders, of Oxford, and Mr. Lord and Mr. Blanchard, of Cambridge, for a similar courtesy in the case of the article on *Greek Plays at the Universities*.

(1) *Canute the Great*. By Michael Field. (Bell and Sons.)

(2) *Life of Elizabeth Gilbert*. By Frances Martin. (Macmillan and Co.)

(3) *Ourselves and Our Neighbours*. By Louise Chandler Moulton. (Ward and Downey.)

(4) *Warring Angels*. (Fisher Unwin.)

(5) *A Song of Jubilee and Other Poems*. By Mrs. De Courcy Laffan. (Kegan Paul.)

(6) *Life of Madame de Staël*. By Bella Duffy. 'Eminent Women' Series.

(7) *Life of Mrs. Godolphin*. By John Evelyn, Esq., of Wooton. Edited by William Harcourt of Nuneham. (Sampson Low, Marston and Co.)

THE POETS' CORNER—V

(*Pall Mall Gazette*, February 15, 1888.)

Mr. Heywood's *Salome* seems to have thrilled the critics of the United States. From a collection of press notices prefixed to the volume we learn that *Putnam's Magazine* has found in it 'the simplicity and grace of naked Grecian statues,' and that Dr. Jos. G. Cogswell, LL.D., has declared that it will live to be appreciated 'as long as the English language endures.' Remembering that prophecy is the most gratuitous form of error, we will not attempt to argue with Dr. Jos. G. Cogswell, LL.D., but will content ourselves with protesting against such a detestable expression as 'naked Grecian statues.' If this be the literary style of the future the English language will not endure very long. As for the poem itself, the best that one can say of it is that it is a triumph of conscientious industry. From an artistic point of view it is a very commonplace production indeed, and we must protest against such blank verse as the following:

From the hour I saw her first, I was entranced,
Or embosomed in a charmed world, circumscribed
By its proper circumambient atmosphere,
Herself its centre, and wide pervading spirit.
The air all beauty of colour held dissolved,
And tints distilled as dew are shed by heaven.

Mr. Griffiths' *Sonnets and Other Poems* are very simple, which is a good thing, and very sentimental, which is a thing not quite so good. As a general rule, his verse is full of pretty echoes of other writers, but in one sonnet he makes a distinct attempt to be original and the result is extremely depressing.

Earth wears her grandest robe, by autumn spun,
Like some stout matron who of youth has run
The course, . . .

is the most dreadful simile we have ever come across even in poetry. Mr. Griffiths should beware of originality. Like beauty, it is a fatal gift.

Imitators of Mr. Browning are, unfortunately, common enough, but imitators of Mr. and Mrs. Browning combined are so very rare that we have read Mr. Francis Prevost's *Fires of Green Wood* with great interest. Here is a curious reproduction of the manner of *Aurora Leigh*:

But Spring! that part at least our unchaste eyes
Infer from some wind-blown philactery,
(It wears its breast bare also)—chestnut buds,
Pack'd in white wool as though sent here from heaven,
Stretching wild stems to reach each climbing lark
That shouts against the fading stars.

And here is a copy of Mr. Browning's mannerisms. We do not like it quite so well:

If another
Save all bother,
Hold that perhaps loaves grow like parsnips:
Call the baker
Heaven's care-taker,
Live, die; Death may show him where the farce nips.
Not I; truly
He may duly
Into church or church-day shunt God;
Chink his pocket,
Win your locket;—
Down we go together to confront God.

Yet, in spite of these ingenious caricatures there are some good poems, or perhaps we should say some good passages, in Mr. Prevost's volume. *The Whitening of the Thorn-tree*, for instance, opens admirably, and is, in some respects, a rather remarkable story. We have no doubt that some day Mr. Prevost will be able to study the great masters without stealing from them.

Mr. John Cameron Grant has christened himself 'England's Empire Poet,' and, lest we should have any doubts upon the subject, tells us that he 'dare not lie,' a statement which in a poet seems to show a great want of courage. Protection and Paper-Unionism are the gods of Mr. Grant's idolatry, and his verse is full of such fine fallacies and masterly misrepresentations that he should be made Laureate to the Primrose League at once. Such a stanza as—

Ask the ruined Sugar-worker if he loves the foreign beet—
Rather, one can hear him answer, would I see my children eat—

would thrill any Tory tea-party in the provinces, and it would be difficult for the advocates of Coercion to find a more appropriate or a more characteristic peroration for a stump speech than

We have not to do with justice, right depends on point of view,
The one question for our thought is, what's our neighbour going to do.

The hymn to the Union Jack, also, would make a capital leaflet for distribution in boroughs where the science of heraldry is absolutely unknown, and the sonnet on Mr. Gladstone is sure to be popular with all who admire violence and vulgarity in literature. It is quite worthy of Thersites at his best.

Mr. Evans's *Cæsar Borgia* is a very tedious tragedy. Some of the passages are in the true 'Ercles' vein,' like the following:

CÆSAR (starting up).
Help, Michelotto, help! Begone! Begone!
Fiends! torments! devils! Gandia! What, Gandia?
O turn those staring eyes away. See! See
He bleeds to death! O fly! Who are those fiends
That tug me by the throat? O! O! O! O! (Pauses.)

But, as a rule, the style is of a more commonplace character. The other poems in the volume are comparatively harmless, though it is sad to find Shakespeare's 'Bacchus with pink eyne' reappearing as 'pinky-eyed Silenus.'

The Cross and the Grail is a collection of poems on the subject of temperance. Compared to real poetry these verses are as 'water unto wine,' but no doubt this was the effect intended. The illustrations are quite dreadful, especially one of an angel appearing to a young man from Chicago who seems to be drinking brown sherry.

Juvenal in Piccadilly and *The Excellent Mystery* are two fierce social satires and, like most satires, they are the product of the corruption they pillory. The first is written on a very convenient principle. Blank spaces are left for the names of the victims and these the reader can fill up as he wishes.

Must—bluster,—give the lie,
—wear the night out,—sneer!

is an example of this anonymous method. It does not seem to us very effective. *The Excellent Mystery* is much better. It is full of clever epigrammatic lines, and its wit fully atones for its bitterness. It is hardly a poem to quote but it is certainly a poem to read.

The Chronicle of Mites is a mock-heroic poem about the inhabitants of a decaying cheese who speculate about the origin of their species and hold learned discussions upon the meaning of evolution and the Gospel according to Darwin. This cheese-epic is a rather unsavoury production and the style is at times so monstrous and so realistic that the author should be called the Gorgon-Zola of literature.

(1) *Salome*. By J. C. Heywood. (Kegan Paul.)

(2) *Sonnets and Other Poems*. By William Griffiths. (Digby and Long.)

(3) *Fires of Green Wood*. By Francis Prevost. (Kegan Paul.)

(4) *Vanclin and Other Verses*. By John Cameron Grant. (E. W. Allen.)

(5) *Cæsar Borgia*. By W. Evans, M.A. (William Maxwell and Son.)

(6) *The Cross and the Grail*. (Women's Temperance Association, Chicago.)

(7) *Juvenal in Piccadilly*. By Oxoniensis. (Vizetelly and Co.)

(8) *The Excellent Mystery: A Matrimonial Satire*. By Lord Pimlico. (Vizetelly and Co.)

(9) *The Chronicle of Mites*. By James Aitchison. (Kegan Paul.)

VENUS OR VICTORY

(*Pall Mall Gazette*, February 24, 1888.)

There are certain problems in archæology that seem to possess a real romantic interest, and foremost among these is the question of the so-called Venus of Melos. Who is she, this marble mutilated goddess whom Gautier loved, to whom Heine bent his knee? What sculptor wrought her, and for what shrine? Whose hands walled her up in that rude niche where the Melian peasant found her? What symbol of her divinity did she carry? Was it apple of gold or shield of bronze? Where is her city and what was her name among gods and men? The last writer on this fascinating subject is Mr. Stillman, who in a most interesting book recently published in America, claims that the work of art in question is no sea-born and foam-born Aphrodite, but the very Victory Without Wings that once stood in the little chapel outside the gates of the Acropolis at Athens. So long ago as 1826, that is to say six years after the discovery of the statue, the Venus hypothesis was violently attacked by Millingen, and from that time to this the battle of the archæologists has never ceased. Mr. Stillman, who fights, of course, under Millingen's banner, points out that the statue is not of the Venus type at all, being far too heroic in character to correspond to the Greek conception of Aphrodite at any period of their artistic development, but that it agrees distinctly with certain well-known statues of Victory, such as the celebrated 'Victory of Brescia.' The latter is in bronze, is later, and has the wings, but the type is unmistakable, and though not a reproduction it is certainly a recollection of the Melian statue. The representation of Victory on the coin of Agathocles is also obviously of the Melian type, and in the museum of Naples is a terra-cotta Victory in almost the identical action and drapery. As for Dumont d'Urville's statement that, when the statue was discovered, one hand held an apple and the other a fold of the drapery, the latter is obviously a mistake, and the whole evidence on the subject is so contradictory that no reliance can be placed on the statement made by the French Consul and the French naval officers, none of whom seems to have taken the trouble to ascertain whether the arm and hand now in the Louvre were really found in the same niche as the statue at all. At any rate, these fragments seem to be of extremely inferior workmanship, and they are so imperfect that they are quite worthless as data for measure or opinion. So far, Mr. Stillman is on old ground. His real artistic discovery is this. In working about the Acropolis of Athens, some years ago, he photographed among other sculptures the mutilated Victories in the Temple of Nikè Apteros, the 'Wingless Victory,' the little Ionic temple in which stood that statue of Victory of which it was said that '*the Athenians made her without wings that she might never leave Athens.*' Looking over the photographs afterwards, when the impression of the comparatively diminutive size had passed, he was struck with the close resemblance of the type to that of the Melian statue. Now, this resemblance is so striking that it cannot be questioned by any one who has an eye for form. There are the same large heroic proportions, the same ampleness of physical development, and the same treatment of drapery, and there is also that perfect spiritual kinship which, to any true antiquarian, is one of the most valuable modes of evidence. Now it is generally admitted on both sides that the Melian statue is probably Attic in its origin, and belongs certainly to the period between Phidias and Praxiteles, that is to say, to the age of Scopas, if it be not actually the work of Scopas himself; and as it is to Scopas that these bas-reliefs have been always attributed, the similarity of style can, on Mr. Stillman's hypothesis, be easily accounted for.

As regards the appearance of the statue in Melos, Mr. Stillman points out that Melos belonged to Athens as late as she had any Greek allegiance, and that it is probable that the statue was sent there for concealment on the occasion of some siege or invasion. When this took place, Mr. Stillman does not pretend to decide with any degree of certainty, but it is evident that it must have been subsequent to the establishment of the Roman hegemony, as the brickwork of the niche in which the statue was found is clearly Roman in character, and before the time of Pausanias and Pliny, as neither of these antiquaries mentions the statue. Accepting, then, the statue as that of the Victory Without Wings, Mr. Stillman agrees with Millingen in supposing that in her left hand she held a bronze shield, the lower rim of which rested on the left knee where some marks of the kind are easily recognisable, while with her right hand she traced, or had just finished tracing, the names of the great heroes of Athens. Valentin's objection, that if this were so the left thigh would incline outwards so as to secure a balance, Mr. Stillman meets partly by the analogy of the Victory of Brescia and partly by the evidence of Nature herself; for he has had a model photographed in the same position as the statue and holding a shield in the manner he proposes in his restoration. The result is precisely the contrary to that which Valentin assumes. Of course, Mr. Stillman's solution of the whole matter must not be regarded as an absolutely scientific demonstration. It is simply an induction in which a kind of artistic instinct, not communicable or equally valuable to all people, has had the greatest part, but to this mode of interpretation archæologists as a class have been far too indifferent; and it is certain that in the present case it has given us a theory which is most fruitful and suggestive.

The little temple of Nikè Apteros has had, as Mr. Stillman reminds us, a destiny unique of its kind. Like the Parthenon, it was standing little more than two hundred years ago, but during the Turkish occupation it was razed, and its stones all built into the great bastion which covered the front of the Acropolis and blocked up the staircase to the Propylæa. It was dug out and restored, nearly every stone in its place, by two German architects during the reign of Otho, and it stands again just as Pausanias described it on the spot where old Ægeus watched for the return of Theseus from Crete. In the distance are Salamis and Ægina, and beyond the purple hills lies Marathon. If the Melian statue be indeed the Victory Without Wings, she had no unworthy shrine.

There are some other interesting essays in Mr. Stillman's book on the wonderful topographical knowledge of Ithaca displayed in the *Odyssey*, and discussions of this kind are always interesting as long as there is no attempt to represent Homer as the ordinary literary man; but the article on the Melian statue is by far the most important and the most delightful. Some people will, no doubt, regret the possibility of the disappearance of the old name, and as Venus not as Victory will still worship the stately goddess, but there are others who will be glad to see in her the image and ideal of that spiritual enthusiasm to which Athens owed her liberty, and by which alone can liberty be won.

On the Track of Ulysses; together with an Excursion in Quest of the So-called Venus of Melos. By W. J. Stillman. (Houghton, Mifflin and Co., Boston.)

LITERARY AND OTHER NOTES—V

(*Woman's World*, March 1888.)

The Princess Emily Ruete of Oman and Zanzibar, whose efforts to introduce women doctors into the East are so well known, has just published a most interesting account of her life, under the title of *Memoirs of an Arabian Princess*. The Princess is the daughter of the celebrated Sejid Saîd, Imam of Mesket and Sultan of Zanzibar, and her long residence in Germany has given her the opportunity of comparing Eastern with Western civilisation. She writes in a very simple and unaffected manner; and though she has many grievances against her brother, the present Sultan (who seems never to have forgiven her for her conversion to Christianity and her marriage with a German subject), she has too much tact, *esprit*, and good humour to trouble her readers with any dreary record of family quarrels and domestic differences. Her book throws a great deal of light on the question of the position of women in the East, and shows that much of what has been written on this subject is quite inaccurate. One of the most curious passages is that in which the Princess gives an account of her mother:

My mother was a Circassian by birth, who in early youth had been torn away from her home. Her father had been a farmer, and she had always lived peacefully with her parents and her little brother and sister. War broke out suddenly, and the country was overrun by marauding bands. On their approach, the family fled into an underground place, as my mother called it—she probably meant a cellar, which is not known in Zanzibar. Their place of refuge was, however, invaded by a merciless horde, the parents were slain, and the children carried off by three mounted Arnauts.

She came into my father's possession when quite a child, probably at the tender age of seven or eight years, as she cast her first tooth in our house. She was at once adopted as playmate by two of my sisters, her own age, with whom she was educated and brought up. Together with them she learnt to read, which raised her a good deal above her equals, who, as a rule, became members of our family at the age of sixteen or eighteen years, or older still, when they had outgrown whatever taste they might once have had for schooling. She could scarcely be called pretty; but she was tall and shapely, had black eyes, and hair down to her knees. Of a very gentle disposition, her greatest pleasure consisted in assisting other people, in looking after and nursing any sick person in the house; and I well remember her going about with her books from one patient to another, reading prayers to them.

She was in great favour with my father, who never refused her anything, though she interceded mostly for others; and when she came to see him, he always rose to meet her half-way—a distinction he conferred but very rarely. She was as kind and pious as she was modest, and in all her dealings frank and open. She had another daughter besides myself, who had died quite young. Her mental powers were not great, but she was very clever at needlework. She had always been a tender and loving mother to me, but this did not hinder her from punishing me severely when she deemed it necessary.

She had many friends at Bet-il-Mtoni, which is rarely to be met with in an Arab harem. She had the most unshaken and firmest trust in God. When I was about five years old, I remember a fire breaking out in the stables close by, one night while my father was at his city residence. A false alarm spread over the house that we, too, were in imminent danger; upon which the good woman hastened to take me on her arm, and her big kurân (we pronounce the word thus) on the other, and hurried into the open air. On the rest of her possessions she set no value in this hour of danger.

Here is a description of Schesade, the Sultan's second legitimate wife:

She was a Persian Princess of entrancing beauty, and of inordinate extravagance. Her little retinue was composed of one hundred and fifty cavaliers, all Persians, who lived on the ground floor; with them she hunted and rode in the broad day—rather contrary to Arab notions. The Persian women are subjected to quite a Spartan training in bodily exercise; they enjoy great liberty, much more so than Arab women, but they are also more rude in mind and action.

Schesade is said to have carried on her extravagant style of life beyond bounds; her dresses, cut always after the Persian fashion, were literally covered with embroideries of pearls. A great many of these were picked up nearly every morning by the servants in her rooms, where she had dropped them from her garments, but the Princess would never take any of these precious jewels back again. She did not only drain my father's exchequer most wantonly, but violated many of our sacred laws; in fact, she had only married him for his high station and wealth, and had loved some one else all the time. Such a state of things could, of course, only end in a divorce; fortunately Schesade had no children of her own. There is a rumour still current among us that beautiful Schesade was observed, some years after this event, when my father carried on war in Persia, and had the good fortune of taking the fortress of Bender Abbâs on the Persian Gulf, heading her troops, and taking aim at the members of our family herself.

Another of the remarkable women mentioned by the Princess was her stepmother, Azze-bint-Zef, who seems to have completely ruled the Sultan, and to have settled all questions of home and foreign policy; while her great-aunt, the Princess Asche, was regent of the empire during the Sultan's minority, and was the heroine of the siege of Mesket. Of her the Princess gives the following account:

Dressed in man's clothes, she inspected the outposts herself at night, she watched and encouraged the soldiers in all exposed places, and was saved several times only by the speed of her horse in unforeseen attacks. One night she rode out, oppressed with care, having just received information that the enemy was about to attempt an entrance into the city by means of bribery that night, and with intent to massacre all; and now she went to convince herself of the loyalty of her troops. Very cautiously she rode up to a guard, requesting to speak to the 'Akîd' (the officer in charge), and did all in her power to seduce him from his duty by great offers of reward on the part of the besiegers. The indignation of the brave man, however, completely allayed her fears as to the fidelity of the troops, but the experiment nearly cost her her own life. The soldiers were about to massacre the supposed spy on the spot, and it required all her presence of mind to make good her escape.

The situation grew, however, to be very critical at Mesket. Famine at last broke out, and the people were well-nigh distracted, as no assistance or relief could be expected from without. It was therefore decided to attempt a last sortie in order to die at least with glory. There was just sufficient powder left for one more attack, but there was no more lead for either guns or muskets. In this emergency the regent ordered iron nails and pebbles to be used in place of balls. The guns were loaded with all the old iron and brass that could be collected, and she opened her treasury to have bullets made out of her own silver dollars. Every nerve was strained, and the sally succeeded beyond all hope. The enemy was completely taken by surprise and fled in all directions, leaving more than half their men dead and wounded on the field. Mesket was saved, and, delivered out of her deep distress, the brave woman knelt down on the battlefield and thanked God in fervent prayer.

From that time her Government was a peaceful one, and she ruled so wisely that she was able to transfer to her nephew, my father, an empire so unimpaired as to place him in a position to extend the empire by the conquest of Zanzibar. It is to my great-aunt, therefore, that we owe, and not to an inconsiderable degree, the acquisition of this second empire.

She, too, was an Eastern woman!

All through her book the Princess protests against the idea that Oriental women are degraded or oppressed, and in the following passage she points out how difficult it is for foreigners to get any real information on the subject:

The education of the children is left entirely to the mother, whether she be legitimate wife or purchased slave, and it constitutes her chief happiness. Some fashionable mothers in Europe shift this duty on to the nurse, and, by-and-by, on the governess, and are quite satisfied with looking up their children, or receiving their visits, once a day. In France the child is sent to be nursed in the country, and left to the care of strangers. An Arab mother, on the other hand, looks continually after her children. She watches and nurses them with the greatest affection, and never leaves them as long as they may stand in need of her motherly care, for which she is rewarded by the fondest filial love.

If foreigners had more frequent opportunities to observe the cheerfulness, the exuberance of spirits even, of Eastern women, they would soon and more easily be convinced of the untruth of all those stories afloat about the degraded, oppressed, and listless state of their life. It is impossible to gain a true insight into the actual domesticity in a few moments' visit; and the conversation carried on, on those formal occasions, hardly deserves that name; there is barely more than the exchange of a few commonplace remarks—and it is questionable if even these have been correctly interpreted.

Notwithstanding his innate hospitality, the Arab has the greatest possible objection to having his home pried into by those of another land and creed. Whenever, therefore, a European lady called on us, the enormous circumference of her hoops (which were the fashion then, and took up the entire width of the stairs) was the first thing to strike us dumb with wonder; after which, the very meagre conversation generally confined itself on both sides to the mysteries of different costumes; and the lady retired as wise as she was when she came, after having been sprinkled over with attar of roses, and being the richer for some parting presents. It is true she had entered a harem; she had seen the much-pitied Oriental ladies (though only through their veils); she had with her own eyes seen our dresses, our jewellery, the nimbleness with which we sat down on the floor—and that was all. She could not boast of having seen more than any other foreign lady who had called before her. She is conducted upstairs and downstairs, and is watched all the time. Rarely she sees more than the reception-room, and more rarely still can she guess or find out who the veiled lady is with whom she conversed. In short, she has had no opportunity whatsoever of learning anything of domestic life, or the position of Eastern women.

No one who is interested in the social position of women in the East should fail to read these pleasantly-written memoirs. The Princess is herself a woman of high culture, and the story of her life is as instructive as history and as fascinating as fiction.

* * * * *

Mrs. Oliphant's *Makers of Venice* is an admirable literary *pendant* to the same writer's charming book on Florence, though there is a wide difference between the beautiful Tuscan city and the sea-city of the Adriatic. Florence, as Mrs. Oliphant points out, is a city full of memories of the great figures of the past. The traveller cannot pass along her streets without treading in the very traces of Dante, without stepping on soil made memorable by footprints never to be effaced. The greatness of the surroundings, the palaces, churches, and frowning mediæval castles in the midst of the city, are all thrown into the background by the greatness, the individuality, the living power and vigour of the men who are their originators, and at the same time their inspiring soul. But when we turn to Venice the effect is very different. We do not think of the makers of that marvellous city, but rather of what they made. The idealised image of Venice herself meets us everywhere. The mother is not overshadowed by the too great glory of any of her sons. In her records the city is everything—the republic, the worshipped ideal of a community in which every man for the common glory seems to have been willing to sink his own. We know that Dante stood within the red walls of the arsenal, and saw the galleys making and mending, and the pitch flaming up to heaven; Petrarch came to visit the great Mistress of the Sea, taking refuge there, 'in this city, true home of the human race,' from trouble, war and pestilence outside; and Byron, with his facile enthusiasms and fervent eloquence, made his home for a time in one of the stately, decaying palaces; but with these exceptions no great poet has ever associated himself with the life of Venice. She had architects, sculptors and painters, but no singer of her own. The arts through which she gave her message to the world were visible and imitative. Mrs. Oliphant, in her bright, picturesque style, tells the story of Venice pleasantly and well. Her account of the two Bellinis is especially charming; and the chapters on Titian and Tintoret are admirably written. She concludes her interesting and useful history with the following words, which are well worthy of quotation, though I must confess that the 'alien modernisms' trouble me not a little:

The critics of recent days have had much to say as to the deterioration of Venice in her new activity, and the introduction of alien modernisms, in the shape of steamboats and other new industrial agents, into her canals and lagoons. But in this adoption of every new development of power, Venice is only proving herself the most faithful representative of the vigorous republic of old. Whatever prejudice or angry love may say, we cannot doubt that the Michiels, the Dandolos, the Foscari, the great rulers who formed Venice, had steamboats existed in their day, serving their purpose better than their barges and peati, would have adopted them without hesitation, without a thought of what any critics might say. The wonderful new impulse which has made Italy a great power has justly put strength and life before those old traditions of beauty, which made her not only the 'woman country' of Europe, but a sort of Odalisque trading upon her charms, rather than the nursing mother of a noble and independent nation. That in her recoil from that somewhat degrading position, she may here and there have proved too regardless of the claims of antiquity, we need not attempt to deny; the new spring of life in her is too genuine and great to keep her entirely free from this evident danger. But it is strange that any one who loves Italy, and sincerely rejoices in her amazing resurrection, should fail to recognise how venial is this fault.

Miss Mabel Robinson's last novel, *The Plan of Campaign*, is a very powerful study of modern political life. As a concession to humanity, each of the politicians is made to fall in love, and the charm of their various romances fully atones for the soundness of the author's theory of rent. Miss Robinson dissects, describes, and discourses with keen scientific insight and minute observation. Her style, though somewhat lacking in grace, is, at its best, simple and strong. Richard Talbot and Elinor Fetherston are admirably conceived and admirably drawn, and the whole account of the murder of Lord Roeglass is most dramatic.

A Year in Eden, by Harriet Waters Preston, is a chronicle of New England life, and is full of the elaborate subtlety of the American school of fiction. The Eden in question is the little village of Pierpont, and the Eve of this provincial paradise is a beautiful girl called Monza Middleton, a fascinating, fearless creature, who brings ruin and misery on all who love her. Miss Preston writes an admirable prose style, and the minor characters in the book are wonderfully lifelike and true.

The Englishwoman's Year-Book contains a really extraordinary amount of useful information on every subject connected with woman's work. In the census taken in 1831 (six years before the Queen ascended the Throne), no occupation whatever was specified as appertaining to women, except that of domestic service; but in the census of 1881, the number of occupations mentioned as followed by women is upwards of three hundred and thirty. The most popular occupations seem to be those of domestic service, school teaching, and dressmaking; the lowest numbers on the list are those of bankers, gardeners, and persons engaged in scientific pursuits. Besides these, the *Year-Book* makes mention of stockbroking and conveyancing as professions that women are beginning to adopt. The historical account of the literary work done by Englishwomen in this century, as given in the *Year-Book*, is curiously inadequate, and the list of women's magazines is not complete, but in all other respects the publication seems a most useful and excellent one.

* * * * *

Wordsworth, in one of his interesting letters to Lady Beaumont, says that it is 'an awful truth that there neither is nor can be any genuine enjoyment of poetry among nineteen out of twenty of those persons who live or wish to live in the broad light of the world—among those who either are, or are striving to make themselves, people of consideration in society,' adding that the mission of poetry is 'to console the afflicted; to add sunshine to daylight by making the happy happier; to teach the young and the gracious of every age to see, to think, and feel, and, therefore, to become more actively and securely virtuous.' I am, however, rather disposed to think that the age in which we live is one that has a very genuine enjoyment of poetry, though we may no longer agree with Wordsworth's ideas on the subject of the poet's proper mission; and it is interesting to note that this enjoyment manifests itself by creation even more than by criticism. To realise the popularity of the great poets, one should turn to the minor poets and see whom they follow, what master they select, whose music they echo. At present, there seems to be a reaction in favour of Lord Tennyson, if we are to judge by *Rachel and Other Poems*, which is a rather remarkable little volume in its way. The poem that gives its title to the book is full of strong lines and good images; and, in spite of its Tennysonian echoes, there is something attractive in such verses as the following:

Day by day along the Orient faintly glows the tender dawn,
Day by day the pearly dewdrops tremble on the upland lawn:

Day by day the star of morning pales before the coming ray,
And the first faint streak of radiance brightens to the perfect day.

Day by day the rosebud gathers to itself, from earth and sky,
Fragrant stores and ampler beauty, lovelier form and deeper dye:

Day by day a richer crimson mantles in its glowing breast—
Every golden hour conferring some sweet grace that crowns the rest.

And thou canst not tell the moment when the day ascends her throne,
When the morning star hath vanished, and the rose is fully blown.

So each day fulfils its purpose, calm, unresting, strong, and sure,
Moving onward to completion, doth the work of God endure.

How unlike man's toil and hurry! how unlike the noise, the strife,
All the pain of incompleteness, all the weariness of life!

Ye look upward and take courage. He who leads the golden hours,
Feeds the birds, and clothes the lily, made these human hearts of ours:

Knows their need, and will supply it, manna falling day by day,
Bread from heaven, and food of angels, all along the desert way.

The Secretary of the International Technical College at Bedford has issued a most interesting prospectus of the aims and objects of the Institution. The College seems to be intended chiefly for ladies who have completed their ordinary course of English studies, and it will be divided into two departments, Educational and Industrial. In the latter, classes will be held for various decorative and technical arts, and for wood-carving, etching, and photography, as well as sick-nursing, dressmaking, cookery, physiology, poultry-rearing, and the cultivation of flowers. The curriculum certainly embraces a wonderful amount of subjects, and I have no doubt that the College will supply a real want.

* * * * *

The Ladies' Employment Society has been so successful that it has moved to new premises in Park Street, Grosvenor Square, where there are some very pretty and useful things for sale. The children's smocks are quite charming, and seem very inexpensive. The subscription to the Society is one guinea a year, and a commission of five per cent. is charged on each thing sold.

* * * * *

Miss May Morris, whose exquisite needle-work is well known, has just completed a pair of curtains for a house in Boston. They are amongst the most perfect specimens of modern embroidery that I have seen, and are from Miss Morris's own design. I am glad to hear that Miss Morris has determined to give lessons in embroidery. She has a thorough knowledge of the art, her sense of beauty is as rare as it is refined, and her power of design is quite remarkable.

Mrs. Jopling's life-classes for ladies have been such a success that a similar class has been started in Chelsea by Mr. Clegg Wilkinson at the Carlyle Studios, King's Road. Mr. Wilkinson (who is a very brilliant young painter) is strongly of opinion that life should be studied from life itself, and not from that abstract presentation of life which we find in Greek marbles—a position which I have always held very strongly myself.

(1) *Memoirs of an Arabian Princess*. By the Princess Emily Ruete of Oman and Zanzibar. (Ward and Downey.)

(2) *Makers of Venice*. By Mrs. Oliphant. (Macmillan and Co.)

(3) *The Plan of Campaign*. By Mabel Robinson. (Vizetelly and Co.)

(4) *A Year in Eden*. By Harriet Waters Preston. (Fisher Unwin.)

(5) *The Englishwoman's Year-Book*, 1888. (Hatchards.)

(6) *Rachel and Other Poems*. (Cornish Brothers.)

THE POETS' CORNER—VI

(*Pall Mall Gazette*, April 6, 1888.)

David Westren, by Mr. Alfred Hayes, is a long narrative poem in Tennysonian blank verse, a sort of serious novel set to music. It is somewhat lacking in actuality, and the picturesque style in which it is written rather contributes to this effect, lending the story beauty but robbing it of truth. Still, it is not without power, and cultured verse is certainly a pleasanter medium for story-telling than coarse and common prose. The hero of the poem is a young clergyman of the muscular Christian school:

A lover of good cheer; a bubbling source
Of jest and tale; a monarch of the gun;
A dreader tyrant of the darting trout
Than that bright bird whose azure lightning threads
The brooklet's bowery windings; the red fox
Did well to seek the boulder-strewn hill-side,
When Westren cheered her dappled foes; the otter
Had cause to rue the dawn when Westren's form
Loomed through the streaming bracken, to waylay
Her late return from plunder, the rough pack
Barking a jealous welcome round their friend.

One day he meets on the river a lovely girl who is angling, and helps her to land

A gallant fish, all flashing in the sun
In silver mail inlaid with scarlet gems,
His back thick-sprinkled as a leopard's hide
With rich brown spots, and belly of bright gold.

They naturally fall in love with each other and marry, and for many years David Westren leads a perfectly happy life. Suddenly calamity comes upon him, his wife and children die and he finds himself alone and desolate. Then begins his struggle. Like Job, he cries out against the injustice of things, and his own personal sorrow makes him realise the sorrow and misery of the world. But the answer that satisfied Job does not satisfy him. He finds no comfort in contemplating Leviathan:

As if we lacked reminding of brute force,
As if we never felt the clumsy hoof,
As if the bulk of twenty million whales
Were worth one pleading soul, or all the laws
That rule the lifeless suns could soothe the sense
Of outrage in a loving human heart!
Sublime? majestic? Ay, but when our trust
Totters, and faith is shattered to the base,
Grand words will not uprear it.

Mr. Hayes states the problem of life extremely well, but his solution is sadly inadequate both from a psychological and from a dramatic point of view. David Westren ultimately becomes a mild Unitarian, a sort of pastoral Stopford Brooke with leanings towards Positivism, and we leave him preaching platitudes to a village congregation. However, in spite of this commonplace conclusion there is a great deal in Mr. Hayes's poem that is strong and fine, and he undoubtedly possesses a fair ear for music and a remarkable faculty of poetical expression. Some of his descriptive touches of nature, such as

In meeting woods, whereon a film of mist
Slept like the bloom upon the purple grape,

are very graceful and suggestive, and he will probably make his mark in literature.

There is much that is fascinating in Mr. Rennell Rodd's last volume, *The Unknown Madonna and Other Poems*. Mr. Rodd looks at life with all the charming optimism of a young man, though he is quite conscious of the fact that a stray note of melancholy, here and there, has an artistic as well as a popular value; he has a keen sense of the pleasurableness of colour, and his verse is distinguished by a certain refinement and purity of outline; though not passionate he can play very prettily with the words of passion, and his emotions are quite healthy and quite harmless. *In Excelsis*, the most ambitious poem in the book, is somewhat too abstract and metaphysical, and such lines as

Lift thee o'er thy 'here' and 'now,'
Look beyond thine 'I' and 'thou,'

are excessively tedious. But when Mr. Rodd leaves the problem of the Unconditioned to take care of itself, and makes no attempt to solve the mysteries of the Ego and the non-Ego, he is very pleasant reading indeed. A *Mazurka of Chopin* is charming, in spite of the awkwardness of the fifth line, and so are the verses on Assisi, and those on San Servolo at Venice. These last have all the brilliancy of a clever pastel. The prettiest thing in the whole volume is this little lyric on Spring:

Such blue of sky, so palely fair,
Such glow of earth, such lucid air!
Such purple on the mountain lines,
Such deep new verdure in the pines!
The live light strikes the broken towers,
The crocus bulbs burst into flowers,
The sap strikes up the black vine stock,
And the lizard wakes in the splintered rock,
And the wheat's young green peeps through the sod,
And the heart is touched with a thought of God;

The very silence seems to sing,
It must be Spring, it must be Spring!

We do not care for 'palely fair' in the first line, and the repetition of the word 'strikes' is not very felicitous, but the grace of movement and delicacy of touch are pleasing.

The Wind, by Mr. James Ross, is a rather gusty ode, written apparently without any definite scheme of metre, and not very impressive as it lacks both the strength of the blizzard and the sweetness of Zephyr. Here is the opening:

The roaming, tentless wind
No rest can ever find—
From east, and west, and south, and north
He is for ever driven forth!
From the chill east
Where fierce hyænas seek their awful feast:
From the warm west,
By beams of glitt'ring summer blest.

Nothing could be much worse than this, and if the line 'Where fierce hyænas seek their awful feast' is intended to frighten us, it entirely misses its effect. The ode is followed by some sonnets which are destined, we fear, to be *ludibria ventis*. Immortality, even in the nineteenth century, is not granted to those who rhyme 'awe' and 'war' together.

Mr. Isaac Sharp's *Saul of Tarsus* is an interesting, and, in some respects, a fine poem.

Saul of Tarsus, silently,
With a silent company,
To Damascus' gates drew nigh.
* * * * *
And his eyes, too, and his mien
Were, as are the eagles, keen;
All the man was aquiline—

are two strong, simple verses, and indeed the spirit of the whole poem is dignified and stately. The rest of the volume, however, is disappointing. Ordinary theology has long since converted its gold into lead, and words and phrases that once touched the heart of the world have become wearisome and meaningless through repetition. If Theology desires to move us, she must re-write her formulas.

There is something very pleasant in coming across a poet who can apostrophise Byron as

transcendent star
That gems the firmament of poesy,

and can speak of Longfellow as a 'mighty Titan.' Reckless panegyrics of this kind show a kindly nature and a good heart, and Mr. Mackenzie's *Highland Daydreams* could not possibly offend any one. It must be admitted that they are rather old-fashioned, but this is usually the case with natural spontaneous verse. It takes a great artist to be thoroughly modern. Nature is always a little behind the age.

The Story of the Cross, an attempt to versify the Gospel narratives, is a strange survival of the Tate and Brady school of poetry. Mr. Nash, who styles himself 'a humble soldier in the army of Faith,' expresses a hope that his book may 'invigorate devotional feeling, especially among the young, to whom verse is perhaps more attractive than to their elders,' but we should be sorry to think that people of any age could admire such a paraphrase as the following:

Foxes have holes, in which to slink for rest,
The birds of air find shelter in the nest;
But He, the Son of Man and Lord of all,
Has no abiding place His own to call.

It is a curious fact that the worst work is always done with the best intentions, and that people are never so trivial as when they take themselves very seriously.

(1) *David Westren*. By Alfred Hayes, M.A. New Coll., Oxon. (Birmingham: Cornish Brothers.)

(2) *The Unknown Madonna and Other Poems*. By Rennell Rodd. (David Stott.)

(3) *The Wind and Six Sonnets*. By James Ross. (Bristol: J. W. Arrowsmith.)

(4) *Saul of Tarsus*. By Isaac Sharp. (Kegan Paul.)

(5) *Highland Daydreams*. By George Mackenzie. (Inverness: Office of the *Northern Chronicle*.)

(6) *The Story of the Cross*. By Charles Nash. (Elliot Stock.)

M. CARO ON GEORGE SAND

(*Pall Mall Gazette*, April 14, 1888.)

The biography of a very great man from the pen of a very ladylike writer—this is the best description we can give of M. Caro's Life of George Sand. The late Professor of the Sorbonne could chatter charmingly about culture, and had all the fascinating insincerity of an accomplished phrase-maker; being an extremely superior person he had a great contempt for Democracy and its doings, but he was always popular with the Duchesses of the Faubourg, as there was nothing in history or in literature that he could not explain away for their edification; having never done anything remarkable he was naturally elected a member of the Academy, and he always remained loyal to the traditions of that thoroughly respectable and thoroughly pretentious institution. In fact, he was just the sort of man who should never have attempted to write a Life of George Sand or to interpret George Sand's genius. He was too feminine to appreciate the grandeur of that large womanly nature, too much of a *dilettante* to realise the masculine force of that strong and ardent mind. He never gets at the secret of George Sand, and never brings us near to her wonderful personality. He looks on her simply as a littérateur, as a writer of pretty stories of country life and of charming, if somewhat exaggerated, romances. But George Sand was much more than this. Beautiful as are such books as *Consuelo* and *Mauprat*, *François le Champi* and *La Mare au Diable*, yet in none of them is she adequately expressed, by none of them is she adequately revealed. As Mr. Matthew Arnold said, many years ago, 'We do not know George Sand unless we feel the spirit which goes through her work as a whole.' With this spirit, however, M. Caro has no sympathy. Madame Sand's doctrines are antediluvian, he tells us, her philosophy is quite dead and her ideas of social regeneration are Utopian, incoherent and absurd. The best thing for us to do is to forget these silly dreams and to read *Teverino* and *Le Secrétaire Intime*. Poor M. Caro! This spirit, which he treats with such airy flippancy, is the very leaven of modern life. It is remoulding the world for us and fashioning our age anew. If it is antediluvian, it is so because the deluge is yet to come; if it is Utopian, then Utopia must be added to our geographies. To what curious straits M. Caro is driven by his violent prejudices may be estimated by the fact that he tries to class George Sand's novels with the old *Chansons de geste*, the stories of adventure characteristic of primitive literatures; whereas in using fiction as a vehicle of thought, and romance as a means of influencing the social ideals of her age, George Sand was merely carrying out the traditions of Voltaire and Rousseau, of Diderot and of Chateaubriand. The novel, says M. Caro, must be allied either to poetry or to science. That it has found in philosophy one of its strongest allies seems not to have occurred to him. In an English critic such a view might possibly be excusable. Our greatest novelists, such as Fielding, Scott and Thackeray cared little for the philosophy of their age. But coming, as it does, from a French critic, the statement seems to show a strange want of recognition of one of the most important elements of French fiction. Nor, even in the narrow limits that he has imposed upon himself, can M. Caro be said to be a very fortunate or felicitous critic. To take merely one instance out of many, he says nothing of George Sand's delightful treatment of art and the artist's life. And yet how exquisitely does she analyse each separate art and present it to us in its relation to life! In *Consuelo* she tells us of music; in *Horace* of authorship; in *Le Château des Désertes* of acting; in *Les Maîtres Mosaïstes* of mosaic work; in *Le Château de Pictordu* of portrait painting; and in *La Daniella* of the painting of landscape. What Mr. Ruskin and Mr. Browning have done for England she did for France. She invented an art literature. It is unnecessary, however, to discuss any of M. Caro's minor failings, for the whole effect of the book, so far as it attempts to portray for us the scope and character of George Sand's genius, is entirely spoiled by the false attitude assumed from the beginning, and though the dictum may seem to many harsh and exclusive, we cannot help feeling that an absolute incapacity for appreciating the spirit of a great writer is no qualification for writing a treatise on the subject.

As for Madame Sand's private life, which is so intimately connected with her art (for, like Goethe, she had to live her romances before she could write them), M. Caro says hardly anything about it. He passes it over with a modesty that almost makes one blush, and for fear of wounding the susceptibilities of those *grandes dames* whose passions M. Paul Bourget analyses with such subtlety, he transforms her mother, who was a typical French *grisette*, into 'a very amiable and *spirituelle* milliner'! It must be admitted that Joseph Surface himself could hardly show greater tact and delicacy, though we ourselves must plead guilty to preferring Madame Sand's own description of her as an 'enfant du vieux pavé de Paris.'

As regards the English version, which is by M. Gustave Masson, it may be up to the intellectual requirements of the Harrow schoolboys, but it will hardly satisfy those who consider that accuracy, lucidity and ease are essential to a good translation. Its carelessness is absolutely astounding, and it is difficult to understand how a publisher like Mr. Routledge could have allowed such a piece of work to issue from his press. 'Il descend avec le sourire d'un Machiavel' appears as 'he descends into the smile of a Machiavelli'; George Sand's remark to Flaubert about literary style, 'tu la considères comme un but, elle n'est qu'un effet' is translated 'you consider it an end, it is merely *an effort*'; and such a simple phrase as 'ainsi le veut l'esthe'tique du roman' is converted into 'so the æsthetes of the world would have it.' 'Il faudra relâcher mes Économies' is 'I will have to draw upon my savings,' not 'my economies will assuredly be relaxed'; 'cassures résineuses' is not 'cleavages full of rosin,' and 'Mme. Sand ne réussit que deux fois' is hardly 'Madame Sand was not twice successful.' 'Querelles d'école' does not mean 'school disputations'; 'ceux qui se font une sorte d'esthétique de l'indifférence absolue' is not 'those of which the æsthetics seem to be an absolute indifference'; 'chimère' should not be translated 'chimera,' nor 'lettres inéditées' 'inedited letters'; 'ridicules' means absurdities, not 'ridicules,' and 'qui pourra définir sa pensée?' is not 'who can clearly despise her thought?' M. Masson comes to grief over even such a simple sentence as 'elle s'étonna des fureurs qui accueillirent ce livre, ne comprenant pas que l'on haïsse un auteur à travers son œuvre,' which he translates 'she was surprised at the storm which greeted this book, *not understanding that the author is hated through his work.*' Then, passing over such phrases as 'substituted by religion' instead of 'replaced by religion,' and 'vulgarisation' where 'popularisation' is meant, we come to that most irritating form of translation, the literal word-for-word style. The stream 'excites itself by the declivity which it obeys' is one of M. Masson's finest achievements in this *genre*, and it is an admirable instance of the influence of schoolboys on their masters. However, it would be tedious to make a complete 'catalogue of slips,' so we will content ourselves by saying that M. Masson's translation is not merely quite unworthy of himself, but is also quite undeserved by the public. Nowadays, the public has its feelings.

George Sand. By the late Elmé Marie Caro. Translated by Gustave Masson, B.A., Assistant Master, Harrow School. 'Great French Writers' Series. (Routledge and Sons.)

THE POETS' CORNER—VII

(*Pall Mall Gazette*, October 24, 1888.)

Mr. Ian Hamilton's *Ballad of Hádji* is undeniably clever. Hádji is a wonderful Arab horse that a reckless hunter rides to death in the pursuit of a wild boar, and the moral of the poem—for there is a moral—seems to be that an absorbing passion is a very dangerous thing and blunts the human sympathies. In the course of the chase a little child is drowned, a Brahmin maiden murdered, and an aged peasant severely wounded, but the hunter cares for none of these things and will not hear of stopping to render any assistance. Some of the stanzas are very graceful, notably one beginning

Yes—like a bubble filled with smoke—
The curd-white moon upswimming broke
The vacancy of space;

but such lines as the following, which occur in the description of the fight with the boar—

I hung as close as keepsake locket
On maiden breast—but from its socket
He wrenched my bridle arm,

are dreadful, and 'his brains festooned the thorn' is not a very happy way of telling the reader how the boar died. All through the volume we find the same curious mixture of good and bad. To say that the sun kisses the earth 'with flame-moustachoed lip' is awkward and uncouth, and yet the poem in which the expression occurs has some pretty lines. Mr. Ian Hamilton should prune. Pruning, whether in the garden or in the study, is a most healthy and useful employment. The volume is nicely printed, but Mr. Strang's frontispiece is not a great success, and most of the tail-pieces seem to have been designed without any reference to the size of the page.

Mr. Catty dedicates his book to the memory of Wordsworth, Shelley, Coleridge and Keats—a somewhat pompous signboard for such very ordinary wine—and an inscription in golden letters on the cover informs us that his poems are 'addressed to the rising generation,' whom, he tells us elsewhere, he is anxious to initiate into the great comprehensive truth that 'Virtue is no other than self-interest, deeply understood.' In order to further this laudable aim he has written a very tedious blank verse poem which he calls *The Secret of Content*, but it certainly does not convey that secret to the reader. It is heavy, abstract and prosaic, and shows how intolerably dull a man can be who has the best intentions and the most earnest beliefs. In the rest of the volume, where Mr. Catty does not take himself quite so seriously, there are some rather pleasing things. The sonnet on Shelley's room at University College would be admirable but for the unmusical character of the last line.

Green in the wizard arms
Of the foam-bearded Atlantic,
An isle of old enchantment,
A melancholy isle,
Enchanted and dreaming lies;
And there, by Shannon's flowing
In the moonlight, spectre-thin,
The spectre Erin sits.

Wail no more, lonely one, mother of exile wail no more,
Banshee of the world—no more!
Thy sorrows are the world's, thou art no more alone;
Thy wrongs the world's—

are the first and last stanzas of Mr. Todhunter's poem *The Banshee*. To throw away the natural grace of rhyme from a modern song is, as Mr. Swinburne once remarked, a wilful abdication of half the power and half the charm of verse, and we cannot say that Mr. Todhunter has given us much that consoles us for its loss. Part of his poem reads like a translation of an old Bardic song, part of it like rough material for poetry, and part of it like misshapen prose. It is an interesting specimen of poetic writing but it is not a perfect work of art. It is amorphous and inchoate, and the same must be said of the two other poems, *The Doom of the Children of Lir*, and *The Lamentation for the Sons of Turann*. Rhyme gives architecture as well as melody to song, and though the lovely lute-built walls of Thebes may have risen up to unrhymed choral metres, we have had no modern Amphion to work such wonders for us. Such a verse as—

Five were the chiefs who challenged
By their deeds the Over-kingship,
Bov Derg, the Daghda's son, Ilbrac of Assaroe,
And Lir of the White Field in the plain of Emain Macha;
And after them stood up Midhir the proud, who reigned
Upon the hills of Bri,
Of Bri the loved of Liath, Bri of the broken heart;
And last was Angus Og; all these had many voices,
But for Bov Derg were most,

has, of course, an archæological interest, but has no artistic value at all. Indeed, from the point of view of art, the few little poems at the end of the volume are worth all the ambitious pseudo-epics that Mr. Todhunter has tried to construct out of Celtic lore. A *Bacchic Day* is charming, and the sonnet on the open-air performance of *The Faithfull Shepherdesse* is most gracefully phrased and most happy in conception.

Mr. Peacock is an American poet, and Professor Thomas Danleigh Supplée, A.M., Ph.D., F.R.S., who has written a preface to his *Poems of the Plains and Songs of the Solitudes*, tells us that he is entitled to be called the Laureate of the West. Though a staunch Republican, Mr. Peacock, according to the enthusiastic Professor, is not ashamed of his ancestor King William of Holland, nor of his relatives Lord and Lady Peacock who, it seems, are natives of Scotland. He was brought up at Zanesville, Muskingum Co., Ohio, where his father edited the Zanesville *Aurora*, and he had an uncle who was 'a superior man' and edited the Wheeling *Intelligencer*. His poems seem to be extremely popular, and have been highly praised, the Professor informs us, by Victor Hugo, the *Saturday Review* and the *Commercial Advertiser*. The preface is the most amusing part of the book, but the poems also are worth studying. *The Maniac*, *The Bandit Chief*, and *The Outlaw* can hardly be called light reading, but we strongly recommend the poem on Chicago:

Chicago! great city of the West!
All that wealth, all that power invest;
Thou sprang like magic from the sand,
As touched by the magician's wand.

'Thou sprang' is slightly depressing, and the second line is rather obscure, but we should not measure by too high a standard the untutored utterances of artless nature. The opening lines of *The Vendetta* also deserve mention:

When stars are glowing through day's gloaming glow,
Reflecting from ocean's deep, mighty flow,
At twilight, when no grim shadows of night,
Like ghouls, have stalked in wake of the light.

The first line is certainly a masterpiece, and, indeed, the whole volume is full of gems of this kind. The Professor remarks in his elaborate preface that Mr. Peacock 'frequently rises to the sublime,' and the two passages quoted above show how keenly critical is his taste in these matters and how well the poet deserves his panegyric.

Mr. Alexander Skene Smith's *Holiday Recreations and Other Poems* is heralded by a preface for which Principal Cairns is responsible. Principal Cairns claims that the life-story enshrined in Mr. Smith's poems shows the wide diffusion of native fire and literary culture in all parts of Scotland, 'happily under higher auspices than those of mere poetic impulse.' This is hardly a very felicitous way of introducing a poet, nor can we say that Mr. Smith's poems are distinguished by either fire or culture. He has a placid, pleasant way of writing, and, indeed, his verses cannot do any harm, though he really should not publish such attempts at metrical versions of the Psalms as the following:

A septuagenarian
We frequently may see;
An octogenarian
If one should live to be,
He is a burden to himself
With weariness and woe
And soon he dies, and off he flies,
And leaveth all below.

The 'literary culture' that produced these lines is, we fear, not of a very high order.

'I study Poetry simply as a fine art by which I may exercise my intellect and elevate my taste,' wrote the late Mr. George Morine many years ago to a friend, and the little posthumous volume that now lies before us contains the record of his quiet literary life. One of the sonnets, that entitled *Sunset*, appeared in Mr. Waddington's anthology, about ten years after Mr. Morine's death, but this is the first time that his collected poems have been published. They are often distinguished by a grave and chastened beauty of style, and their solemn cadences have something of the 'grand manner' about them. The editor, Mr. Wilton, to whom Mr. Morine bequeathed his manuscripts, seems to have performed his task with great tact and judgment, and we hope that this little book will meet with the recognition that it deserves.

(1) *The Ballad of Hádji and Other Poems*. By Ian Hamilton. (Kegan Paul.)

(2) *Poems in the Modern Spirit, with The Secret of Content*. By Charles Catty. (Walter Scott.)

(3) *The Banshee and Other Poems*. By John Todhunter. (Kegan Paul.)

(4) *Poems of the Plain and Songs of the Solitudes*. By Thomas Bower Peacock. (G. P. Putnam's Sons.)

(5) *Holiday Recreations and Other Poems*. By Alexander Skene Smith. (Chapman and Hall.)

(6) *Poems*. By George Morine. (Bell and Son.)

A FASCINATING BOOK

(*Woman's World*, November 1888.)

Mr. Alan Cole's carefully-edited translation of M. Lefébure's history of *Embroidery and Lace* is one of the most fascinating books that has appeared on this delightful subject. M. Lefébure is one of the administrators of the Musée des Arts Décoratifs at Paris, besides being a lace manufacturer; and his work has not merely an important historical value, but as a handbook of technical instruction it will be found of the greatest service by all needle-women. Indeed, as the translator himself points out, M. Lefébure's book suggests the question whether it is not rather by the needle and the bobbin, than by the brush, the graver or the chisel, that the influence of woman should assert itself in the arts. In Europe, at any rate, woman is sovereign in the domain of art-needle-work, and few men would care to dispute with her the right of using those delicate implements so intimately associated with the dexterity of her nimble and slender fingers; nor is there any reason why the productions of embroidery should not, as Mr. Alan Cole suggests, be placed on the same level with those of painting, engraving and sculpture, though there must always be a great difference between those purely decorative arts that glorify their own material and the more imaginative arts in which the material is, as it were, annihilated, and absorbed into the creation of a new form. In the beautifying of modern houses it certainly must be admitted—indeed, it should be more generally recognised than it is—that rich embroidery on hangings and curtains, *portières*, couches and the like, produces a far more decorative and far more artistic effect than can be gained from our somewhat wearisome English practice of covering the walls with pictures and engravings; and the almost complete disappearance of embroidery from dress has robbed modern costume of one of the chief elements of grace and fancy.

That, however, a great improvement has taken place in English embroidery during the last ten or fifteen years cannot, I think, be denied. It is shown, not merely in the work of individual artists, such as Mrs. Holiday, Miss May Morris and others, but also in the admirable productions of the South Kensington School of Embroidery (the best—indeed, the only really good—school that South Kensington has produced). It is pleasant to note, on turning over the leaves of M. Lefébure's book, that in this we are merely carrying out certain old traditions of Early English art. In the seventh century, St. Ethelreda, first abbess of the Monastery of Ely, made an offering to St. Cuthbert of a sacred ornament she had worked with gold and precious stones, and the cope and maniple of St. Cuthbert, which are preserved at Durham, are considered to be specimens of *opus Anglicanum*. In the year 800, the Bishop of Durham allotted the income of a farm of two hundred acres for life to an embroideress named Eanswitha, in consideration of her keeping in repair the vestments of the clergy in his diocese. The battle standard of King Alfred was embroidered by Danish princesses; and the Anglo-Saxon Gudric gave Alcuid a piece of land, on condition that she instructed his daughter in needle-work. Queen Mathilda bequeathed to the Abbey of the Holy Trinity at Caen a tunic embroidered at Winchester by the wife of one Alderet; and when William presented himself to the English nobles, after the Battle of Hastings, he wore a mantle covered with Anglo-Saxon embroideries, which is probably, M. Lefébure suggests, the same as that mentioned in the inventory of the Bayeux Cathedral, where, after the entry relating to the *broderie à telle* (representing the conquest of England), two mantles are described—one of King William, 'all of gold, powdered with crosses and blossoms of gold, and edged along the lower border with an orphrey of figures.' The most splendid example of the *opus Anglicanum* now in existence is, of course, the Syon cope at the South Kensington Museum; but English work seems to have been celebrated all over the Continent. Pope Innocent IV. so admired the splendid vestments worn by the English clergy in 1246, that he ordered similar articles from Cistercian monasteries in England. St. Dunstan, the artistic English monk, was known as a designer for embroideries; and the stole of St. Thomas à Becket is still preserved in the cathedral at Sens, and shows us the interlaced scroll-forms used by Anglo-Saxon MS. illuminators.

How far this modern artistic revival of rich and delicate embroidery will bear fruit depends, of course, almost entirely on the energy and study that women are ready to devote to it; but I think that it must be admitted that all our decorative arts in Europe at present have, at least, this element of strength—that they are in immediate relationship with the decorative arts of Asia. Wherever we find in European history a revival of decorative art, it has, I fancy, nearly always been due to Oriental influence and contact with Oriental nations. Our own keenly intellectual art has more than once been ready to sacrifice real decorative beauty either to imitative presentation or to ideal motive. It has taken upon itself the burden of expression, and has sought to interpret the secrets of thought and passion. In its marvellous truth of presentation it has found its strength, and yet its weakness is there also. It is never with impunity that an art seeks to mirror life. If Truth has her revenge upon those who do not follow her, she is often pitiless to her worshippers. In Byzantium the two arts met—Greek art, with its intellectual sense of form, and its quick sympathy with humanity; Oriental art, with its gorgeous materialism, its frank rejection of imitation, its wonderful secrets of craft and colour, its splendid textures, its rare metals and jewels, its marvellous and priceless traditions. They had, indeed, met before, but in Byzantium they were married; and the sacred tree of the Persians, the palm of Zoroaster, was embroidered on the hem of the garments of the Western world. Even the Iconoclasts, the Philistines of theological history, who, in one of those strange outbursts of rage against Beauty that seem to occur only amongst European nations, rose up against the wonder and magnificence of the new art, served merely to distribute its secrets more widely; and in the *Liber Pontificalis*, written in 687 by Athanasius, the librarian, we read of an influx into Rome of gorgeous embroideries, the work of men who had arrived from Constantinople and from Greece. The triumph of the Mussulman gave the decorative art of Europe a new departure—that very principle of their religion that forbade the actual representation of any object in nature being of the greatest artistic service to them, though it was not, of course, strictly carried out. The Saracens introduced into Sicily the art of weaving silken and golden fabrics; and from Sicily the manufacture of fine stuffs spread to the North of Italy, and became localised in Genoa, Florence, Venice, and other towns. A still greater art-movement took place in Spain under the Moors and Saracens, who brought over workmen from Persia to make beautiful things for them. M. Lefébure tells us of Persian embroidery penetrating as far as Andalusia; and Almeria, like Palermo, had its Hotel des Tiraz, which rivalled the Hôtel des Tiraz at Bagdad, *tiraz* being the generic name for ornamental tissues and costumes made with them. Spangles (those pretty little discs of gold, silver, or polished steel, used in certain embroidery for dainty glinting effects) were a Saracenic invention; and Arabic letters often took the place of letters in the Roman characters for use in inscriptions upon embroidered robes and Middle Age tapestries, their decorative value being so much greater. The book of crafts by Etienne Boileau, provost of the merchants in 1258-1268, contains a curious enumeration of the different craft-guilds of Paris, among which we find 'the tapiciers, or makers of the *tapis sarrasinois* (or Saracen cloths), who say that their craft is for the service only of churches, or great men like kings and counts'; and, indeed, even in our own day, nearly all our words descriptive of decorative textures and decorative methods point to an Oriental origin. What the inroads of the Mohammedans did for Sicily and Spain, the return of the Crusaders did for the other countries of Europe. The nobles who left for Palestine clad in armour, came back in the rich stuffs of the East; and their costumes, pouches (*aumônières sarra-sinoises*), and caparisons excited the admiration of the needle-workers of the West. Matthew Paris says that at the sacking of Antioch, in 1098, gold, silver and priceless costumes were so equally distributed among the Crusaders, that many who the night before were famishing and imploring relief, suddenly found themselves overwhelmed with wealth; and Robert de Clair tells us of the wonderful fêtes that followed the capture of Constantinople. The thirteenth century, as M. Lefébure points out, was conspicuous for an increased demand in the West for embroidery. Many Crusaders made offerings to churches of plunder from Palestine; and St. Louis, on his return from the first Crusade, offered thanks at St. Denis to God for mercies bestowed on him during his six years' absence and travel, and presented some richly-embroidered stuffs to be used on great occasions as coverings to the reliquaries containing the relics of holy martyrs. European embroidery, having thus become possessed of new materials and wonderful methods, developed on its own intellectual and imitative lines, inclining, as it went on, to the purely pictorial, and seeking to rival painting, and to produce landscapes and figure-subjects with elaborate perspective and subtle aerial effects. A fresh Oriental influence, however, came through the Dutch and the Portuguese, and the famous *Compagnie des Grandes Indes*; and M. Lefébure gives an illustration of a door-hanging now in the Cluny Museum, where we find the French *fleurs-de-lys* intermixed with Indian ornament. The hangings of Madame de Maintenon's room at Fontainebleau, which were embroidered at St. Cyr, represent Chinese scenery upon a jonquil-yellow ground.

Clothes were sent out ready cut to the East to be embroidered, and many of the delightful coats of the period of Louis XV. and Louis XVI. owe their dainty decoration to the needles of Chinese artists. In our own day the influence of the East is strongly marked. Persia has sent us her carpets for patterns, and Cashmere her lovely shawls, and India her dainty muslins finely worked with gold thread palmates, and stitched over with iridescent beetles' wings. We are beginning now to dye by Oriental methods, and the silk robes of China and Japan have taught us new wonders of colour-combination, and new subtleties of delicate design. Whether we have yet learned to make a wise use of what we have acquired is less certain. If books produce an effect, this book of M. Lefébure should certainly make us study with still deeper interest the whole question of embroidery, and by those who already work with their needles it will be found full of most fertile suggestion and most admirable advice.

Even to read of the marvellous works of embroidery that were fashioned in bygone ages is pleasant. Time has kept a few fragments of Greek embroidery of the fourth century B.C. for us. One is figured in M. Lefébure's book—a chain-stitch embroidery of yellow flax upon a mulberry-coloured worsted material, with graceful spirals and palmetto-patterns: and another, a tapestried cloth powdered with ducks, was reproduced in the *Woman's World* some months ago for an article by Mr. Alan Cole. {334a} Now and then we find in the tomb of some dead Egyptian a piece of delicate work. In the treasury at Ratisbon is preserved a specimen of Byzantine embroidery on which the Emperor Constantine is depicted riding on a white palfrey, and receiving homage from the East and West. Metz has a red silk cope wrought with great eagles, the gift of Charlemagne, and Bayeux the needle-wrought epic of Queen Matilda. But where is the great crocus-coloured robe, wrought for Athena, on which the gods fought against the giants? Where is the huge velarium that Nero stretched across the Colosseum at Rome, on which was represented the starry sky, and Apollo driving a chariot drawn by steeds? How one would like to see the curious table-napkins wrought for Heliogabalus, on which were displayed all the dainties and viands that could be wanted for a feast; or the mortuary-cloth of King Chilperic, with its three hundred golden bees; or the fantastic robes that excited the indignation of the Bishop of Pontus, and were embroidered with 'lions, panthers, bears, dogs, forests, rocks, hunters—all, in fact, that painters can copy from nature.' Charles of Orleans had a coat, on the sleeves of which were embroidered the verses of a song beginning '*Madame, je suis tout joyeux*,' the musical accompaniment of the words being wrought in gold thread, and each note, of square shape in those days, formed with four pearls. {334b} The room prepared in the palace at Rheims for the use of Queen Joan of Burgundy was decorated with 'thirteen hundred and twenty-one *papegauts* (parrots) made in broidery and blazoned with the King's arms, and five hundred and sixty-one butterflies, whose wings were similarly ornamented with the Queen's arms—the whole worked in fine gold.' Catherine de Medicis had a mourning-bed made for her 'of black velvet embroidered with pearls and powdered with crescents and suns.' Its curtains were of damask, 'with leafy wreaths and garlands figured upon a gold and silver ground, and fringed along the edges with broideries of pearls,' and it stood in a room hung with rows of the Queen's devices in cut black velvet on cloth of silver. Louis XIV. had gold-embroidered caryatides fifteen feet high in his apartment. The state-bed of Sobieski, King of Poland, was made of Smyrna gold brocade embroidered in turquoises and pearls, with verses from the Koran; its supports were of silver-gilt, beautifully chased and profusely set with enamelled and jewelled medallions. He had taken it from the Turkish camp before Vienna, and the standard of Mahomet had stood under it. The Duchess de la Ferté wore a dress of reddish-brown velvet, the skirt of which, adjusted in graceful folds, was held up by big butterflies made of Dresden china; the front was a *tablier* of cloth of silver, upon which was embroidered an orchestra of musicians arranged in a pyramidal group, consisting of a series of six ranks of performers, with beautiful instruments wrought in raised needle-work. 'Into the night go one and all,' as Mr. Henley sings in his charming *Ballade of Dead Actors*.

Many of the facts related by M. Lefébure about the embroiderers' guilds are also extremely interesting. Etienne Boileau, in his book of crafts, to which I have already alluded, tells us that a member of the guild was prohibited from using gold of less value than 'eight sous (about 6s.) the skein; he was bound to use the best silk, and never to mix thread with silk, because that made the work false and bad.' The test or trial piece prescribed for a worker who was the son of a master-embroiderer was 'a single figure, a sixth of the natural size, to be shaded in gold'; whilst one not the son of a master was required to produce 'a complete incident with many figures.' The book of crafts also mentions 'cutters-out and stencillers and illuminators' amongst those employed in the industry of embroidery. In 1551 the Parisian Corporation of Embroiderers issued a notice that 'for the future, the colouring in representations of nude figures and faces should be done in three or four gradations of carnation-dyed silk, and not, as formerly, in white silks.' During the fifteenth century every household of any position retained the services of an embroiderer by the year. The preparation of colours also, whether for painting or for dyeing threads and textile fabrics, was a matter which, M. Lefébure points out, received close attention from the artists of the Middle Ages. Many undertook long journeys to obtain the more famous recipes, which they filed, subsequently adding to and correcting them as experience dictated. Nor were great artists above making and supplying designs for embroidery. Raphael made designs for Francis I., and Boucher for Louis XV.; and in the Ambras collection at Vienna is a superb set of sacerdotal robes from designs by the brothers Van Eyck and their pupils. Early in the sixteenth century books of embroidery designs were produced, and their success was so great that in a few years French, German, Italian, Flemish, and English publishers spread broadcast books of design made by their best engravers. In the same century, in order to give the designers opportunity of studying directly from nature, Jean Robin opened a garden with conservatories, in which he cultivated strange varieties of plants then but little known in our latitudes. The rich brocades and brocadelles of the time are characterised by the introduction of large flowery patterns, with pomegranates and other fruits with fine foliage.

The second part of M. Lefébure's book is devoted to the history of lace, and though some may not find it quite as interesting as the earlier portion it will more than repay perusal; and those who still work in this delicate and fanciful art will find many valuable suggestions in it, as well as a large number of exceedingly beautiful designs. Compared to embroidery, lace seems comparatively modern. M. Lefébure and Mr. Alan Cole tell us that there is no reliable or documentary evidence to prove the existence of lace before the fifteenth century. Of course in the East, light tissues, such as gauzes, muslins, and nets, were made at very early times, and were used as veils and scarfs after the manner of subsequent laces, and women enriched them with some sort of embroidery, or varied the openness of them by here and there drawing out threads. The threads of fringes seem also to have been plaited and knotted together, and the borders of one of the many fashions of Roman toga were of open reticulated weaving. The Egyptian Museum at the Louvre has a curious network embellished with glass beads; and the monk Reginald, who took part in opening the tomb of St. Cuthbert at Durham in the twelfth century, writes that the Saint's shroud had a fringe of linen threads an inch long, surmounted by a border, 'worked upon the threads,' with representations of birds and pairs of beasts, there being between each such pair a branching tree, a survival of the palm of Zoroaster, to which I have before alluded. Our authors, however, do not in these examples recognise lace, the production of which involves more refined and artistic methods, and postulates a combination of skill and varied execution carried to a higher degree of perfection. Lace, as we know it, seems to have had its origin in the habit of embroidering linen. White embroidery on linen has, M. Lefébure remarks, a cold and monotonous aspect; that with coloured threads is brighter and gayer in effect, but is apt to fade in frequent washing; but white embroidery relieved by open spaces in, or shapes cut from, the linen ground, is possessed of an entirely new charm; and from a sense of this the birth may be traced of an art in the result of which happy contrasts are effected between ornamental details of close texture and others of open-work.

Soon, also, was suggested the idea that, instead of laboriously withdrawing threads from stout linen, it would be more convenient to introduce a needle-made pattern into an open network ground, which was called a *lacis*. Of this kind of embroidery many specimens are extant. The Cluny Museum possesses a linen cap said to have belonged to Charles V.; and an alb of linen drawn-thread work, supposed to have been made by Anne of Bohemia (1527), is preserved in the cathedral at Prague. Catherine de Medicis had a bed draped with squares of *réseuil*, or *lacis*, and it is recorded that 'the girls and servants of her household consumed much time in making squares of *réseuil*.' The interesting pattern-books for open-ground embroidery, of which the first was published in 1527 by Pierre Quinty, of Cologne, supply us with the means of tracing the stages in the transition from white thread embroidery to needle-point lace. We meet in them with a style of needle-work which differs from embroidery in not being wrought upon a stuff foundation. It is, in fact, true lace, done, as it were, 'in the air,' both ground and pattern being entirely produced by the lace-maker.

The elaborate use of lace in costume was, of course, largely stimulated by the fashion of wearing ruffs, and their companion cuffs or sleeves. Catherine de Medicis induced one Frederic Vinciolo to come from Italy and make ruffs and gadrooned collars, the fashion of which she started in France; and Henry III. was so punctilious over his ruffs that he would iron and goffer his cuffs and collars himself rather than see their pleats limp and out of shape. The pattern-books also gave a great impulse to the art. M. Lefébure mentions German books with patterns of eagles, heraldic emblems, hunting scenes, and plants and leaves belonging to Northern vegetation; and Italian books, in which the *motifs* consist of oleander blossoms, and elegant wreaths and scrolls, landscapes with mythological scenes, and hunting episodes, less realistic than the Northern ones, in which appear fauns, and nymphs or *amorini* shooting arrows. With regard to these patterns, M. Lefébure notices a curious fact. The oldest painting in which lace is depicted is that of a lady, by Carpaccio, who died about 1523. The cuffs of the lady are edged with a narrow lace, the pattern of which reappears in Vecellio's *Corona*, a book not published until 1591. This particular pattern was, therefore, in use at least eighty years before it got into circulation with other published patterns.

It was not, however, till the seventeenth century that lace acquired a really independent character and individuality, and M. Duplessis states that the production of the more noteworthy of early laces owes more to the influence of men than to that of women. The reign of Louis XIV. witnessed the production of the most stately needle-point laces, the transformation of Venetian point, and the growth of *Points d'Alençon, d'Argentan, de Bruxelles* and *d'Angleterre*.

The king, aided by Colbert, determined to make France the centre, if possible, for lace manufacture, sending for this purpose both to Venice and to Flanders for workers. The studio of the Gobelins supplied designs. The dandies had their huge rabatos or bands falling from beneath the chin over the breast, and great prelates, like Bossuet and Fénelon, wore their wonderful albs and rochets. It is related of a collar made at Venice for Louis XIV. that the lace-workers, being unable to find sufficiently fine horse-hair, employed some of their own hairs instead, in order to secure that marvellous delicacy of work which they aimed at producing.

In the eighteenth century, Venice, finding that laces of lighter texture were sought after, set herself to make rose-point; and at the Court of Louis XV. the choice of lace was regulated by still more elaborate etiquette. The Revolution, however, ruined many of the manufactures. Alençon survived, and Napoleon encouraged it, and endeavoured to renew the old rules about the necessity of wearing point-lace at Court receptions. A wonderful piece of lace, powdered over with devices of bees, and costing 40,000 francs, was ordered. It was begun for the Empress Josephine, but in the course of its making her escutcheons were replaced by those of Marie Louise.

M. Lefébure concludes his interesting history by stating very clearly his attitude towards machine-made lace. 'It would be an obvious loss to art,' he says, 'should the making of lace by hand become extinct, for machinery, as skilfully devised as possible, cannot do what the hand does.' It can give us 'the results of processes, not the creations of artistic handicraft.' Art is absent 'where formal calculation pretends to supersede emotion'; it is absent 'where no trace can be detected of intelligence guiding handicraft, whose hesitancies even possess peculiar charm . . . cheapness is never commendable in respect of things which are not absolute necessities; it lowers artistic standard.' These are admirable remarks, and with them we take leave of this fascinating book, with its delightful illustrations, its charming anecdotes, its excellent advice. Mr. Alan Cole deserves the thanks of all who are interested in art for bringing this book before the public in so attractive and so inexpensive a form.

Embroidery and Lace: *Their Manufacture and History from the Remotest Antiquity to the Present Day*. Translated and enlarged by Alan S. Cole from the French of Ernest Lefébure. (Grevel and Co.)

THE POETS' CORNER—VIII

(*Pall Mall Gazette*, November 16, 1888.)

A few years ago some of our minor poets tried to set Science to music, to write sonnets on the survival of the fittest and odes to Natural Selection. Socialism, and the sympathy with those who are unfit, seem, if we may judge from Miss Nesbit's remarkable volume, to be the new theme of song, the fresh subject-matter for poetry. The change has some advantages. Scientific laws are at once too abstract and too clearly defined, and even the visible arts have not yet been able to translate into any symbols of beauty the discoveries of modern science. At the Arts and Crafts Exhibition we find the cosmogony of Moses, not the cosmogony of Darwin. To Mr. Burne-Jones Man is still a fallen angel, not a greater ape. Poverty and misery, upon the other hand, are terribly concrete things. We find their incarnation everywhere and, as we are discussing a matter of art, we have no hesitation in saying that they are not devoid of picturesqueness. The etcher or the painter finds in them 'a subject made to his hand,' and the poet has admirable opportunities of drawing weird and dramatic contrasts between the purple of the rich and the rags of the poor. From Miss Nesbit's book comes not merely the voice of sympathy but also the cry of revolution:

This is our vengeance day. Our masters made fat with our fasting
Shall fall before us like corn when the sickle for harvest is strong:
Old wrongs shall give might to our arm, remembrance of wrongs shall make lasting
The graves we will dig for our tyrants we bore with too much and too long.

The poem from which we take this stanza is remarkably vigorous, and the only consolation that we can offer to the timid and the Tories is that as long as so much strength is employed in blowing the trumpet, the sword, so far as Miss Nesbit is concerned, will probably remain sheathed. Personally, and looking at the matter from a purely artistic point of view, we prefer Miss Nesbit's gentler moments. Her eye for Nature is peculiarly keen. She has always an exquisite sense of colour and sometimes a most delicate ear for music. Many of her poems, such as *The Moat House, Absolution*, and *The Singing of the Magnificat* are true works of art, and *Vies Manquées* is a little gem of song, with its dainty dancing measure, its delicate and wilful fancy and the sharp poignant note of passion that suddenly strikes across it, marring its light laughter and lending its beauty a terrible and tragic meaning.

From the sonnets we take this at random:

Not Spring—too lavish of her bud and leaf—
 But Autumn with sad eyes and brows austere,
 When fields are bare, and woods are brown and sere,
And leaden skies weep their enchantless grief.
Spring is so much too bright, since Spring is brief,
 And in our hearts is Autumn all the year,
 Least sad when the wide pastures are most drear
And fields grieve most—robbed of the last gold sheaf.

These too, the opening stanzas of *The Last Envoy*, are charming:

The Wind, that through the silent woodland blows
O'er rippling corn and dreaming pastures goes
 Straight to the garden where the heart of Spring
Faints in the heart of Summer's earliest rose.

 Dimpling the meadow's grassy green and grey,
By furze that yellows all the common way,
 Gathering the gladness of the common broom,
And too persistent fragrance of the may—

 Gathering whatever is of sweet and dear,
The wandering wind has passed away from here,
 Has passed to where within your garden waits
The concentrated sweetness of the year.

But Miss Nesbit is not to be judged by mere extracts. Her work is too rich and too full for that.

Mr. Foster is an American poet who has read Hawthorne, which is wise of him, and imitated Longfellow, which is not quite so commendable. His *Rebecca the Witch* is a story of old Salem, written in the metre of *Hiawatha*, with a few rhymes thrown in, and conceived in the spirit of the author of *The Scarlet Letter*. The combination is not very satisfactory, but the poem, as a piece of fiction, has many elements of interest. Mr. Foster seems to be quite popular in America. The *Chicago Times* finds his fancies 'very playful and sunny,' and the *Indianapolis Journal* speaks of his 'tender and appreciative style.' He is certainly a clever story-teller, and *The Noah's Ark* (which 'somehow had escaped the sheriff's hand') is bright and amusing, and its pathos, like the pathos of a melodrama, is a purely picturesque element not intended to be taken too seriously. We cannot, however, recommend the definitely comic poems. They are very depressing.

Mr. John Renton Denning dedicates his book to the Duke of Connaught, who is Colonel-in-Chief of the Rifle Brigade, in which regiment Mr. Denning was once himself a private soldier. His poems show an ardent love of Keats and a profligate luxuriance of adjectives:

 And I will build a bower for thee, sweet,
A verdurous shelter from the noonday heat,
Thick rustling ivy, broad and green, and shining,
With honeysuckle creeping up and twining
Its nectared sweetness round thee; violets
And daisies with their fringèd coronets
And the white bells of tiny valley lilies,
And golden-leaved narcissi—daffodillies
Shall grow around thy dwelling—luscious fare
Of fruit on which the sun has laughed;

 this is the immature manner of *Endymion* with a vengeance and is not to be encouraged. Still, Mr. Denning is not always so anxious to reproduce the faults of his master. Sometimes he writes with wonderful grace and charm. *Sylvia*, for instance, is an exceedingly pretty poem, and *The Exile* has many powerful and picturesque lines. Mr. Denning should make a selection of his poems and publish them in better type and on better paper. The 'get-up' of his volume, to use the slang phrase of our young poets, is very bad indeed, and reflects no credit on the press of the Education Society of Bombay.

The best poem in Mr. Joseph McKim's little book is, undoubtedly, *William the Silent*. It is written in the spirited Macaulay style:

Awake, awake, ye burghers brave! shout, shout for joy and sing!
With thirty thousand at his back comes forth your hero King.
Now shake for ever from your necks the servile yoke of Spain,
And raise your arms and end for aye false Alva's cruel reign.
Ho! Maestricht, Liège, Brussels fair! pour forth your warriors brave,
And join your hands with him who comes your hearths and homes to save.

Some people like this style.

Mrs. Horace Dobell, who has arrived at her seventeenth volume of poetry, seems very angry with everybody, and writes poems to *A Human Toad* with lurid and mysterious footnotes such as—'Yet some one, *not* a friend of --- *did*! on a certain occasion of a glib utterance of calumnies, by ---! at Hampstead.' Here indeed is a Soul's Tragedy.

'In many cases I have deliberately employed alliteration, believing that the music of a line is intensified thereby,' says Mr. Kelly in the preface to his poems, and there is certainly no reason why Mr. Kelly should not employ this 'artful aid.' Alliteration is one of the many secrets of English poetry, and as long as it is kept a secret it is admirable. Mr. Kelly, it must be admitted, uses it with becoming modesty and reserve and never suffers it to trammel the white feet of his bright and buoyant muse. His volume is, in many ways, extremely interesting. Most minor poets are at their best in sonnets, but with him it is not so. His sonnets are too narrative, too diffuse, and too lyrical. They lack concentration, and concentration is the very essence of a sonnet. His longer poems, on the other hand, have many good qualities. We do not care for *Psychossolles*, which is elaborately commonplace, but *The Flight of Calliope* has many charming passages. It is a pity that Mr. Kelly has included the poems written before the age of nineteen. Youth is rarely original.

Andiatoroctè is the title of a volume of poems by the Rev. Clarence Walworth, of Albany, N.Y. It is a word borrowed from the Indians, and should, we think, be returned to them as soon as possible. The most curious poem of the book is called *Scenes at the Holy Home*:

Jesus and Joseph at work! Hurra!
Sight never to see again,
A prentice Deity plies the saw,
While the Master ploughs with the plane.

Poems of this kind were popular in the Middle Ages when the cathedrals of every Christian country served as its theatres. They are anachronisms now, and it is odd that they should come to us from the United States. In matters of this kind we should have some protection.

(1) *Lays and Legends*. By E. Nesbit. (Longmans, Green and Co.)

(2) *Rebecca the Witch and Other Tales*. By David Skaats Foster. (G. P. Putnam's Sons.)

(3) *Poems and Songs*. By John Renton Denning. (Bombay: Education Society's Press.)

(4) *Poems*. By Joseph McKim. (Kegan Paul.)

(5) *In the Watches of the Night*. Poems in eighteen volumes. By Mrs. Horace Dobell. Vol. xvii. (Remington and Co.)

(6) *Poems*. By James Kelly. (Glasgow: Reid and Coghill.)

(7) *Andiatoroctè*. By the Rev. Clarence A. Walworth. (G. P. Putnam's Sons.)

A NOTE ON SOME MODERN POETS

(*Woman's World*, December 1888.)

'If I were king,' says Mr. Henley, in one of his most modest rondeaus,

'Art should aspire, yet ugliness be dear;
Beauty, the shaft, should speed with wit for feather;
And love, sweet love, should never fall to sere,
   If I were king.'

And these lines contain, if not the best criticism of his own work, certainly a very complete statement of his aim and motive as a poet. His little *Book of Verses* reveals to us an artist who is seeking to find new methods of expression and has not merely a delicate sense of beauty and a brilliant, fantastic wit, but a real passion also for what is horrible, ugly, or grotesque. No doubt, everything that is worthy of existence is worthy also of art—at least, one would like to think so—but while echo or mirror can repeat for us a beautiful thing, to render artistically a thing that is ugly requires the most exquisite alchemy of form, the most subtle magic of transformation. To me there is more of the cry of Marsyas than of the singing of Apollo in the earlier poems of Mr. Henley's volume, *In Hospital: Rhymes and Rhythms*, as he calls them. But it is impossible to deny their power. Some of them are like bright, vivid pastels; others like charcoal drawings, with dull blacks and murky whites; others like etchings with deeply-bitten lines, and abrupt contrasts, and clever colour-suggestions. In fact, they are like anything and everything, except perfected poems—that they certainly are not. They are still in the twilight. They are preludes, experiments, inspired jottings in a note-book, and should be heralded by a design of 'Genius Making Sketches.' Rhyme gives architecture as well as melody to verse; it gives that delightful sense of limitation which in all the arts is so pleasurable, and is, indeed, one of the secrets of perfection; it will whisper, as a French critic has said, 'things unexpected and charming, things with strange and remote relations to each other,' and bind them together in indissoluble bonds of beauty; and in his constant rejection of rhyme, Mr. Henley seems to me to have abdicated half his power. He is a *roi en exil* who has thrown away some of the strings of his lute; a poet who has forgotten the fairest part of his kingdom.

However, all work criticises itself. Here is one of Mr. Henley's inspired jottings. According to the temperament of the reader, it will serve either as a model or as the reverse:

As with varnish red and glistening
Dripped his hair; his feet were rigid;
Raised, he settled stiffly sideways:
You could see the hurts were spinal.

He had fallen from an engine,
And been dragged along the metals.
It was hopeless, and they knew it;
So they covered him, and left him.

As he lay, by fits half sentient,
Inarticulately moaning,
With his stockinged feet protruded
Sharp and awkward from the blankets,

To his bed there came a woman,
Stood and looked and sighed a little,
And departed without speaking,
As himself a few hours after.

I was told she was his sweetheart.
They were on the eve of marriage.
She was quiet as a statue,
But her lip was gray and writhen.

In this poem, the rhythm and the music, such as it is, are obvious—perhaps a little too obvious. In the following I see nothing but ingeniously printed prose. It is a description—and a very accurate one—of a scene in a hospital ward. The medical students are supposed to be crowding round the doctor. What I quote is only a fragment, but the poem itself is a fragment:

So shows the ring
Seen, from behind, round a conjuror
Doing his pitch in the street.
High shoulders, low shoulders, broad shoulders, narrow ones,
Round, square, and angular, serry and shove;
While from within a voice,
Gravely and weightily fluent,
Sounds; and then ceases; and suddenly
(Look at the stress of the shoulders!)
Out of a quiver of silence,
Over the hiss of the spray,
Comes a low cry, and the sound
Of breath quick intaken through teeth
Clenched in resolve. And the master
Breaks from the crowd, and goes,
Wiping his hands,
To the next bed, with his pupils
Flocking and whispering behind him.

Now one can see.
Case Number One
Sits (rather pale) with his bedclothes
Stripped up, and showing his foot
(Alas, for God's image!)
Swaddled in wet white lint
Brilliantly hideous with red.

Théophile Gautier once said that Flaubert's style was meant to be read, and his own style to be looked at. Mr. Henley's unrhymed rhythms form very dainty designs, from a typographical point of view. From the point of view of literature, they are a series of vivid, concentrated impressions, with a keen grip of fact, a terrible actuality, and an almost masterly power of picturesque presentation. But the poetic form—what of that?

Well, let us pass to the later poems, to the rondels and rondeaus, the sonnets and quatorzains, the echoes and the ballades. How brilliant and fanciful this is! The Toyokuni colour-print that suggested it could not be more delightful. It seems to have kept all the wilful fantastic charm of the original:

Was I a Samurai renowned,
Two-sworded, fierce, immense of bow?

97

A histrion angular and profound?
A priest? a porter?—Child, although
I have forgotten clean, I know   .
That in the shade of Fujisan,
What time the cherry-orchards blow,
I loved you once in old Japan.

   As here you loiter, flowing-gowned
And hugely sashed, with pins a-row
Your quaint head as with flamelets crowned,
Demure, inviting—even so,
When merry maids in Miyako
To feel the sweet o' the year began,
And green gardens to overflow,
I loved you once in old Japan.

   Clear shine the hills; the rice-fields round
Two cranes are circling; sleepy and slow,
A blue canal the lake's blue bound
Breaks at the bamboo bridge; and lo!
Touched with the sundown's spirit and glow,
I see you turn, with flirted fan,
Against the plum-tree's bloomy snow . . .
I loved you once in old Japan!

   ENVOY.

   Dear, 'twas a dozen lives ago;
But that I was a lucky man
The Toyokuni here will show:
I loved you—once—in old Japan!

   This rondel, too—how light it is, and graceful!—

   We'll to the woods and gather may
Fresh from the footprints of the rain.
We'll to the woods, at every vein
To drink the spirit of the day.

   The winds of spring are out at play,
The needs of spring in heart and brain.
We'll to the woods and gather may
Fresh from the footprints of the rain.

   The world's too near her end, you say?
Hark to the blackbird's mad refrain!
It waits for her, the vast Inane?
Then, girls, to help her on the way
We'll to the woods and gather may.

   There are fine verses, also, scattered through this little book; some of them very strong, as—

   Out of the night that covers me,
   Black as the pit from pole to pole,
I thank whatever gods may be
   For my unconquerable soul.

   It matters not how strait the gate,
   How charged with punishments the scroll,
I am the master of my fate:
   I am the captain of my soul.

   Others with a true touch of romance, as—

   Or ever the knightly years were gone
   With the old world to the grave,
I was a king in Babylon,
   And you were a Christian slave.

   And here and there we come across such felicitous phrases as—

     In the sand
The gold prow-griffin claws a hold,

   or—

     The spires
Shine and are changed,

and many other graceful or fanciful lines, even 'the green sky's minor thirds' being perfectly right in its place, and a very refreshing bit of affectation in a volume where there is so much that is natural.

However, Mr. Henley is not to be judged by samples. Indeed, the most attractive thing in the book is no single poem that is in it, but the strong humane personality that stands behind both flawless and faulty work alike, and looks out through many masks, some of them beautiful, and some grotesque, and not a few misshapen. In the case with most of our modern poets, when we have analysed them down to an adjective, we can go no further, or we care to go no further; but with this book it is different. Through these reeds and pipes blows the very breath of life. It seems as if one could put one's hand upon the singer's heart and count its pulsations. There is something wholesome, virile and sane about the man's soul. Anybody can be reasonable, but to be sane is not common; and sane poets are as rare as blue lilies, though they may not be quite so delightful.

Let the great winds their worst and wildest blow,
Or the gold weather round us mellow slow;
We have fulfilled ourselves, and we can dare,
And we can conquer, though we may not share
In the rich quiet of the afterglow,
    What is to come,

is the concluding stanza of the last rondeau—indeed, of the last poem in the collection, and the high, serene temper displayed in these lines serves at once as keynote and keystone to the book. The very lightness and slightness of so much of the work, its careless moods and casual fancies, seem to suggest a nature that is not primarily interested in art—a nature, like Sordello's, passionately enamoured of life, one to which lyre and lute are things of less importance. From this mere joy of living, this frank delight in experience for its own sake, this lofty indifference, and momentary unregretted ardours, come all the faults and all the beauties of the volume. But there is this difference between them—the faults are deliberate, and the result of much study; the beauties have the air of fascinating impromptus. Mr. Henley's healthy, if sometimes misapplied, confidence in the myriad suggestions of life gives him his charm. He is made to sing along the highways, not to sit down and write. If he took himself more seriously, his work would become trivial.

* * * * *

Mr. William Sharp takes himself very seriously and has written a preface to his *Romantic Ballads and Poems of Phantasy*, which is, on the whole, the most interesting part of his volume. We are all, it seems, far too cultured, and lack robustness. 'There are those amongst us,' says Mr. Sharp, 'who would prefer a dexterously-turned triolet to such apparently uncouth measures as *Thomas the Rhymer*, or the ballad of *Clerk Saunders*: who would rather listen to the drawing-room music of the Villanelle than to the wild harp-playing by the mill-dams o' Binnorie, or the sough of the night-wind o'er drumly Annan water.' Such an expression as 'the drawing-room music of the Villanelle' is not very happy, and I cannot imagine any one with the smallest pretensions to culture preferring a dexterously turned triolet to a fine imaginative ballad, as it is only the Philistine who ever dreams of comparing works of art that are absolutely different in motive, in treatment, and in form. If English Poetry is in danger—and, according to Mr. Sharp, the poor nymph is in a very critical state—what she has to fear is not the fascination of dainty metre or delicate form, but the predominance of the intellectual spirit over the spirit of beauty. Lord Tennyson dethroned Wordsworth as a literary influence, and later on Mr. Swinburne filled all the mountain valleys with echoes of his own song. The influence to-day is that of Mr. Browning. And as for the triolets, and the rondels, and the careful study of metrical subtleties, these things are merely the signs of a desire for perfection in small things and of the recognition of poetry as an art. They have had certainly one good result—they have made our minor poets readable, and have not left us entirely at the mercy of geniuses.

But, says Mr. Sharp, every one is far too literary; even Rossetti is too literary. What we want is simplicity and directness of utterance; these should be the dominant characteristics of poetry. Well, is that quite so certain? Are simplicity and directness of utterance absolute essentials for poetry? I think not. They may be admirable for the drama, admirable for all those imitative forms of literature that claim to mirror life in its externals and its accidents, admirable for quiet narrative, admirable in their place; but their place is not everywhere. Poetry has many modes of music; she does not blow through one pipe alone. Directness of utterance is good, but so is the subtle recasting of thought into a new and delightful form. Simplicity is good, but complexity, mystery, strangeness, symbolism, obscurity even, these have their value. Indeed, properly speaking, there is no such thing as Style; there are merely styles, that is all.

One cannot help feeling also that everything that Mr. Sharp says in his preface was said at the beginning of the century by Wordsworth, only where Wordsworth called us back to nature, Mr. Sharp invites us to woo romance. Romance, he tells us, is 'in the air.' A new romantic movement is imminent; 'I anticipate,' he says, 'that many of our poets, especially those of the youngest generation, will shortly turn towards the "ballad" as a poetic vehicle: and that the next year or two will see much romantic poetry.'

The ballad! Well, Mr. Andrew Lang, some months ago, signed the death-warrant of the ballade, and—though I hope that in this respect Mr. Lang resembles the Queen in *Alice in Wonderland*, whose bloodthirsty orders were by general consent never carried into execution—it must be admitted that the number of ballades given to us by some of our poets was, perhaps, a little excessive. But the ballad? *Sir Patrick Spens*, *Clerk Saunders*, *Thomas the Rhymer*—are these to be our archetypes, our models, the sources of our inspiration? They are certainly great imaginative poems. In Chatterton's *Ballad of Charity*, Coleridge's *Rhyme of the Ancient Mariner*, the *La Belle Dame sans Merci* of Keats, the *Sister Helen* of Rossetti, we can see what marvellous works of art the spirit of old romance may fashion. But to preach a spirit is one thing, to propose a form is another. It is true that Mr. Sharp warns the rising generation against imitation. A ballad, he reminds them, does not necessarily denote a poem in quatrains and in antique language. But his own poems, as I think will be seen later, are, in their way, warnings, and show the danger of suggesting any definite 'poetic vehicle.' And, further, are simplicity and directness of utterance really the dominant characteristics of these old imaginative ballads that Mr. Sharp so enthusiastically, and, in some particulars, so wisely praises? It does not seem to me to be so. We are always apt to think that the voices which sang at the dawn of poetry were simpler, fresher, and more natural than ours, and that the world which the early poets looked at, and through which they walked, had a kind of poetical quality of its own, and could pass, almost without changing, into song. The snow lies thick now upon Olympus, and its scarped sides are bleak and barren, but once, we fancy, the white feet of the Muses brushed the dew from the anemones in the morning, and at evening came Apollo to sing to the shepherds in the vale. But in this we are merely lending to other ages what we desire, or think we desire, for our own. Our historical sense is at fault. Every century that produces poetry is, so far, an artificial century, and the work that seems to us the most natural and simple product of its time is probably the result of the most deliberate and self-conscious effort. For Nature is always behind the age. It takes a great artist to be thoroughly modern.

Let us turn to the poems, which have really only the preface to blame for their somewhat late appearance. The best is undoubtedly *The Weird of Michael Scott*, and these stanzas are a fair example of its power:

Then Michael Scott laughed long and loud:
'Whan shone the mune ahint yon cloud
  I speered the towers that saw my birth—
Lang, lang, sall wait my cauld grey shroud,
  Lang cauld and weet my bed o' earth!'

But as by Stair he rode full speed
His horse began to pant and bleed;
  'Win hame, win hame, my bonnie mare,
Win hame if thou wouldst rest and feed,
  Win hame, we're nigh the House of Stair!'

But, with a shrill heart-bursten yell
The white horse stumbled, plunged, and fell,
  And loud a summoning voice arose,
'Is't White-Horse Death that rides frae Hell,
  Or Michael Scott that hereby goes?'

  'Ah, Laird of Stair, I ken ye weel!
Avaunt, or I your saul sall steal,
  An' send ye howling through the wood
A wild man-wolf—aye, ye maun reel
  An' cry upon your Holy Rood!'

There is a good deal of vigour, no doubt, in these lines; but one cannot help asking whether this is to be the common tongue of the future Renaissance of Romance. Are we all to talk Scotch, and to speak of the moon as the 'mune,' and the soul as the 'saul'? I hope not. And yet if this Renaissance is to be a vital, living thing, it must have its linguistic side. Just as the spiritual development of music, and the artistic development of painting, have always been accompanied, if not occasioned, by the discovery of some new instrument or some fresh medium, so, in the case of any important literary movement, half of its strength resides in its language. If it does not bring with it a rich and novel mode of expression, it is doomed either to sterility or to imitation. Dialect, archaisms and the like, will not do. Take, for instance, another poem of Mr. Sharp's, a poem which he calls *The Deith-Tide*:

The weet saut wind is blawing
  Upon the misty shore:
As, like a stormy snawing,
  The deid go streaming o'er:—
  The wan drown'd deid sail wildly
    Frae out each drumly wave:
  It's O and O for the weary sea,
    And O for a quiet grave.

This is simply a very clever *pastiche*, nothing more, and our language is not likely to be permanently enriched by such words as 'weet,' 'saut,' 'blawing,' and 'snawing.' Even 'drumly,' an adjective of which Mr. Sharp is so fond that he uses it both in prose and verse, seems to me to be hardly an adequate basis for a new romantic movement.

However, Mr. Sharp does not always write in dialect. *The Son of Allan* can be read without any difficulty, and *Phantasy* can be read with pleasure. They are both very charming poems in their way, and none the less charming because the cadences of the one recall *Sister Helen*, and the motive of the other reminds us of *La Belle Dame sans Merci*. But those who wish thoroughly to enjoy Mr. Sharp's poems should not read his preface; just as those who approve of the preface should avoid reading the poems. I cannot help saying that I think the preface a great mistake. The work that follows it is quite inadequate, and there seems little use in heralding a dawn that rose long ago, and proclaiming a Renaissance whose first-fruits, if we are to judge them by any high standard of perfection, are of so ordinary a character.

* * * * *

Miss Mary Robinson has also written a preface to her little volume, *Poems, Ballads, and a Garden Play*, but the preface is not very serious, and does not propose any drastic change or any immediate revolution in English literature. Miss Robinson's poems have always the charm of delicate music and graceful expression; but they are, perhaps, weakest where they try to be strong, and certainly least satisfying where they seek to satisfy. Her fanciful flower-crowned Muse, with her tripping steps and pretty, wilful ways, should not write Antiphons to the Unknowable, or try to grapple with abstract intellectual problems. Hers is not the hand to unveil mysteries, nor hers the strength for the solving of secrets. She should never leave her garden, and as for her wandering out into the desert to ask the Sphinx questions, that should be sternly forbidden to her. Dürer's *Melancolia*, that serves as the frontispiece to this dainty book, looks sadly out of place. Her seat is with the sibyls, not with the nymphs. What has she to do with shepherdesses piping about Darwinism and 'The Eternal Mind'?

However, if the *Songs of the Inner Life* are not very successful, the *Spring Songs* are delightful. They follow each other like wind-blown petals, and make one feel how much more charming flower is than fruit, apple-blossom than apple. There are some artistic temperaments that should never come to maturity, that should always remain in the region of promise and should dread autumn with its harvesting more than winter with its frosts. Such seems to me the temperament that this volume reveals. The first poem of the second series, *La Belle au Bois Dormant*, is worth all the more serious and thoughtful work, and has far more chance of being remembered. It is not always to high aim and lofty ambition that the prize is given. If Daphne had gone to meet Apollo, she would never have known what laurels are.

From these fascinating spring lyrics and idylls we pass to the romantic ballads. One artistic faculty Miss Robinson certainly possesses— the faculty of imitation. There is an element of imitation in all the arts; it is to be found in literature as much as in painting, and the danger of valuing it too little is almost as great as the danger of setting too high a value upon it. To catch, by dainty mimicry, the very mood and manner of antique work, and yet to retain that touch of modern passion without which the old form would be dull and empty; to win from long-silent lips some faint echo of their music, and to add to it a music of one's own; to take the mode and fashion of a bygone age, and to experiment with it, and search curiously for its possibilities; there is a pleasure in all this. It is a kind of literary acting, and has something of the charm of the art of the stage-player. And how well, on the whole, Miss Robinson does it! Here is the opening of the ballad of Rudel:

There was in all the world of France
  No singer half so sweet:
The first note of his viol brought
  A crowd into the street.

He stepped as young, and bright, and glad
  As Angel Gabriel.
And only when we heard him sing
  Our eyes forgot Rudel.

And as he sat in Avignon,
  With princes at their wine,
In all that lusty company
  Was none so fresh and fine.

His kirtle's of the Arras-blue,
  His cap of pearls and green;
His golden curls fall tumbling round
  The fairest face I've seen.

How Gautier would have liked this from the same poem!—

Hew the timbers of sandal-wood,
  And planks of ivory;
Rear up the shining masts of gold,
  And let us put to sea.

Sew the sails with a silken thread
  That all are silken too;
Sew them with scarlet pomegranates
  Upon a sheet of blue.

Rig the ship with a rope of gold
  And let us put to sea.
And now, good-bye to good Marseilles,
  And hey for Tripoli!

The ballad of the Duke of Gueldres's wedding is very clever:

'O welcome, Mary Harcourt,
  Thrice welcome, lady mine;
There's not a knight in all the world
  Shall be as true as thine.

'There's venison in the aumbry, Mary,
  There's claret in the vat;
Come in, and breakfast in the hall
  Where once my mother sat!'

O red, red is the wine that flows,
  And sweet the minstrel's play,
But white is Mary Harcourt
  Upon her wedding-day.

O many are the wedding guests
  That sit on either side;
But pale below her crimson flowers
  And homesick is the bride.

Miss Robinson's critical sense is at once too sound and too subtle to allow her to think that any great Renaissance of Romance will necessarily follow from the adoption of the ballad-form in poetry; but her work in this style is very pretty and charming, and *The Tower of*

St. Maur, which tells of the father who built up his little son in the wall of his castle in order that the foundations should stand sure, is admirable in its way. The few touches of archaism in language that she introduces are quite sufficient for their purpose, and though she fully appreciates the importance of the Celtic spirit in literature, she does not consider it necessary to talk of 'blawing' and 'snawing.' As for the garden play, *Our Lady of the Broken Heart*, as it is called, the bright, birdlike snatches of song that break in here and there—as the singing does in *Pippa Passes*—form a very welcome relief to the somewhat ordinary movement of the blank verse, and suggest to us again where Miss Robinson's real power lies. Not a poet in the true creative sense, she is still a very perfect artist in poetry, using language as one might use a very precious material, and producing her best work by the rejection of the great themes and large intellectual motives that belong to fuller and richer song. When she essays such themes, she certainly fails. Her instrument is the reed, not the lyre. Only those should sing of Death whose song is stronger than Death is.

* * * * *

The collected poems of the author of *John Halifax, Gentleman*, have a pathetic interest as the artistic record of a very gracious and comely life. They bring us back to the days when Philip Bourke Marston was young—'Philip, my King,' as she called him in the pretty poem of that name; to the days of the Great Exhibition, with the universal piping about peace; to those later terrible Crimean days, when Alma and Balaclava were words on the lips of our poets; and to days when Leonora was considered a very romantic name.

Leonora, Leonora,
How the word rolls—Leonora.
Lion-like in full-mouthed sound,
Marching o'er the metric ground,
With a tawny tread sublime.
So your name moves, Leonora,
Down my desert rhyme.

Mrs. Craik's best poems are, on the whole, those that are written in blank verse; and these, though not prosaic, remind one that prose was her true medium of expression. But some of the rhymed poems have considerable merit. These may serve as examples of Mrs. Craik's style:

A SKETCH

Dost thou thus love me, O thou all beloved,
In whose large store the very meanest coin
Would out-buy my whole wealth? Yet here thou comest
Like a kind heiress from her purple and down
Uprising, who for pity cannot sleep,
But goes forth to the stranger at her gate—
The beggared stranger at her beauteous gate—
And clothes and feeds; scarce blest till she has blest.

But dost thou love me, O thou pure of heart,
Whose very looks are prayers? What couldst thou see
In this forsaken pool by the yew-wood's side,
To sit down at its bank, and dip thy hand,
Saying, 'It is so clear!'—and lo! ere long,
Its blackness caught the shimmer of thy wings,
Its slimes slid downward from thy stainless palm,
Its depths grew still, that there thy form might rise.

THE NOVICE

It is near morning. Ere the next night fall
I shall be made the bride of heaven. Then home
To my still marriage-chamber I shall come,
And spouseless, childless, watch the slow years crawl.

These lips will never meet a softer touch
Than the stone crucifix I kiss; no child
Will clasp this neck. Ah, virgin-mother mild,
Thy painted bliss will mock me overmuch.

This is the last time I shall twist the hair
My mother's hand wreathed, till in dust she lay:
The name, her name given on my baptism day,
This is the last time I shall ever bear.

O weary world, O heavy life, farewell!
Like a tired child that creeps into the dark
To sob itself asleep, where none will mark,—
So creep I to my silent convent cell.

Friends, lovers whom I loved not, kindly hearts
Who grieve that I should enter this still door,

Grieve not. Closing behind me evermore,
Me from all anguish, as all joy, it parts.

The volume chronicles the moods of a sweet and thoughtful nature, and though many things in it may seem somewhat old-fashioned, it is still very pleasant to read, and has a faint perfume of withered rose-leaves about it.

(1) *A Book of Verses.* By William Ernest Henley. (David Nutt.)

(2) *Romantic Ballads and Poems of Phantasy.* By William Sharp. (Walter Scott.)

(3) *Poems, Ballads, and a Garden Play.* By A. Mary F. Robinson. (Fisher Unwin.)

(4) *Poems.* By the Author of *John Halifax, Gentleman.* (Macmillan and Co.)

SIR EDWIN ARNOLD'S LAST VOLUME

(*Pall Mall Gazette*, December 11, 1888.)

Writers of poetical prose are rarely good poets. They may crowd their page with gorgeous epithet and resplendent phrase, may pile Pelions of adjectives upon Ossas of descriptions, may abandon themselves to highly coloured diction and rich luxuriance of imagery, but if their verse lacks the true rhythmical life of verse, if their method is devoid of the self-restraint of the real artist, all their efforts are of very little avail. 'Asiatic' prose is possibly useful for journalistic purposes, but 'Asiatic' poetry is not to be encouraged. Indeed, poetry may be said to need far more self-restraint than prose. Its conditions are more exquisite. It produces its effects by more subtle means. It must not be allowed to degenerate into mere rhetoric or mere eloquence. It is, in one sense, the most self-conscious of all the arts, as it is never a means to an end but always an end in itself. Sir Edwin Arnold has a very picturesque or, perhaps we should say, a very pictorial style. He knows India better than any living Englishman knows it, and Hindoostanee better than any English writer should know it. If his descriptions lack distinction, they have at least the merit of being true, and when he does not interlard his pages with an interminable and intolerable series of foreign words he is pleasant enough. But he is not a poet. He is simply a poetical writer—that is all.

However, poetical writers have their uses, and there is a good deal in Sir Edwin Arnold's last volume that will repay perusal. The scene of the story is placed in a mosque attached to the monument of the Taj-Mahal, and a group composed of a learned Mirza, two singing girls with their attendant, and an Englishman, is supposed to pass the night there reading the chapter of Sa'di upon 'Love,' and conversing upon that theme with accompaniments of music and dancing. The Englishman is, of course, Sir Edwin Arnold himself:

lover of India,
Too much her lover! for his heart lived there
How far soever wandered thence his feet.

Lady Dufferin appears as

Lady Duffreen, the mighty Queen's Vice-queen!

which is really one of the most dreadful blank-verse lines that we have come across for some time past. M. Renan is 'a priest of Frangestan,' who writes in 'glittering French'; Lord Tennyson is

One we honour for his songs—
Greater than Sa'di's self—

and the Darwinians appear as the 'Mollahs of the West,' who

hold Adam's sons
Sprung of the sea-slug.

All this is excellent fooling in its way, a kind of play-acting in literature; but the best parts of the book are the descriptions of the Taj itself, which are extremely elaborate, and the various translations from Sa'di with which the volume is interspersed. The great monument Shah Jahan built for Arjamand is

Instinct with loveliness—not masonry!
Not architecture! as all others are,
But the proud passion of an Emperor's love
Wrought into living stone, which gleams and soars
With body of beauty shrining soul and thought,
Insomuch that it haps as when some face
Divinely fair unveils before our eyes—
Some woman beautiful unspeakably—
And the blood quickens, and the spirit leaps,
And will to worship bends the half-yielded knees,
Which breath forgets to breathe: so is the Taj;
You see it with the heart, before the eyes
Have scope to gaze. All white! snow white! cloud white!

We cannot say much in praise of the sixth line:

Insomuch that it haps as when some face:

it is curiously awkward and unmusical. But this passage from Sa'di is remarkable:

When Earth, bewildered, shook in earthquake-throes,
With mountain-roots He bound her borders close;
   Turkis and ruby in her rocks He stored,
And on her green branch hung His crimson rose.

   He shapes dull seed to fair imaginings;
Who paints with moisture as He painteth things?
   Look! from the cloud He sheds one drop on ocean,
As from the Father's loins one drop He brings;—

   And out of that He forms a peerless pearl,
And, out of this, a cypress boy or girl;
   Utterly wotting all their innermosts,
For all to Him is visible! Uncurl

   Your cold coils, Snakes! Creep forth, ye thrifty Ants!
Handless and strengthless He provides your wants
   Who from the 'Is not' planned the 'Is to be,'
And Life in non-existent void implants.

Sir Edwin Arnold suffers, of course, from the inevitable comparison that one cannot help making between his work and the work of Edward Fitzgerald, and certainly Fitzgerald could never have written such a line as 'utterly wotting all their innermosts,' but it is interesting to read almost any translation of those wonderful Oriental poets with their strange blending of philosophy and sensuousness, of simple parable or fable and obscure mystic utterance. What we regret most in Sir Edwin Arnold's book is his habit of writing in what really amounts to a sort of 'pigeon English.' When we are told that 'Lady Duffreen, the mighty Queen's Vice-queen,' paces among the *charpoys* of the ward 'no whit afraid of *sitla*, or of *tap*'; when the Mirza explains—

   âg lejao!
To light the kallians for the Saheb and me,

   and the attendant obeys with '*Achcha*! *Achcha*!' when we are invited to listen to 'the *Vina* and the drum' and told about *ekkas*, *Byrâgis*, *hamals* and *Tamboora*, all that we can say is that to such *ghazals* we are not prepared to say either *Shamash* or *Afrîn*. In English poetry we do not want

   chatkis for the toes,
Jasams for elbow-bands, and gote and har,
Bala and mala.

This is not local colour; it is a sort of local discoloration. It does not add anything to the vividness of the scene. It does not bring the Orient more clearly before us. It is simply an inconvenience to the reader and a mistake on the part of the writer. It may be difficult for a poet to find English synonyms for Asiatic expressions, but even if it were impossible it is none the less a poet's duty to find them. We are sorry that a scholar and a man of culture like Sir Edwin Arnold should have been guilty of what is really an act of treason against our literature. But for this error, his book, though not in any sense a work of genius or even of high artistic merit, would still have been of some enduring value. As it is, Sir Edwin Arnold has translated Sa'di and some one must translate Sir Edwin Arnold.

With Sa'di in the Garden; *or The Book of Love*. By Sir Edwin Arnold, M.A., K.C.I.E., Author of *The Light of Asia*, etc. (Trübner and Co.)

AUSTRALIAN POETS

(*Pall Mall Gazette*, December 14, 1888.)

Mr. Sladen dedicates his anthology (or, perhaps, we should say his herbarium) of Australian song to Mr. Edmund Gosse, 'whose exquisite critical faculty is,' he tells us, 'as conspicuous in his poems as in his lectures on poetry.' After so graceful a compliment Mr. Gosse must certainly deliver a series of discourses upon Antipodean art before the Cambridge undergraduates, who will, no doubt, be very much interested on hearing about Gordon, Kendall and Domett, to say nothing of the extraordinary collection of mediocrities whom Mr. Sladen has somewhat ruthlessly dragged from their modest and well-merited obscurity. Gordon, however, is very badly represented in Mr. Sladen's book, the only three specimens of his work that are included being an unrevised fragment, his *Valedictory Poem* and *An Exile's Farewell*. The latter is, of course, touching, but then the commonplace always touches, and it is a great pity that Mr. Sladen was unable to come to any financial arrangement with the holders of Gordon's copyright. The loss to the volume that now lies before us is quite irreparable. Through Gordon Australia found her first fine utterance in song.

Still, there are some other singers here well worth studying, and it is interesting to read about poets who lie under the shadow of the gum-tree, gather wattle blossoms and buddawong and sarsaparilla for their loves, and wander through the glades of Mount Baw-baw listening to the careless raptures of the mopoke. To them November is

   The wonder with the golden wings,
Who lays one hand in Summer's, one in Spring's:

   January is full of 'breaths of myrrh, and subtle hints of rose-lands';

   She is the warm, live month of lustre—she
Makes glad the land and lulls the strong sad sea;

while February is 'the true Demeter,' and

> With rich warm vine-blood splashed from heel to knee,
> Comes radiant through the yellow woodlands.

Each month, as it passes, calls for new praise and for music different from our own. July is a 'lady, born in wind and rain'; in August

> Across the range, by every scarred black fell,
> Strong Winter blows his horn of wild farewell;

while October is 'the queen of all the year,' the 'lady of the yellow hair,' who strays 'with blossom-trammelled feet' across the 'haughty-featured hills,' and brings the Spring with her. We must certainly try to accustom ourselves to the mopoke and the sarsaparilla plant, and to make the gum-tree and the buddawong as dear to us as the olives and the narcissi of white Colonus. After all, the Muses are great travellers, and the same foot that stirred the Cumnor cowslips may some day brush the fallen gold of the wattle blossoms and tread delicately over the tawny bush-grass.

Mr. Sladen has, of course, a great belief in the possibilities of Australian poetry. There are in Australia, he tells us, far more writers capable of producing good work than has been assumed. It is only natural, he adds, that this should be so, 'for Australia has one of those delightful climates conducive to rest in the open air. The middle of the day is so hot that it is really more healthful to lounge about than to take stronger exercise.' Well, lounging in the open air is not a bad school for poets, but it largely depends on the lounger. What strikes one on reading over Mr. Sladen's collection is the depressing provinciality of mood and manner in almost every writer. Page follows page, and we find nothing but echoes without music, reflections without beauty, second-rate magazine verses and third-rate verses for Colonial newspapers. Poe seems to have had some influence—at least, there are several parodies of his method—and one or two writers have read Mr. Swinburne; but, on the whole, we have artless Nature in her most irritating form. Of course Australia is young, younger even than America whose youth is now one of her oldest and most hallowed traditions, but the entire want of originality of treatment is curious. And yet not so curious, perhaps, after all. Youth is rarely original.

There are, however, some exceptions. Henry Clarence Kendall had a true poetic gift. The series of poems on the Austral months, from which we have already quoted, is full of beautiful things; Landor's *Rose Aylmer* is a classic in its way, but Kendall's *Rose Lorraine* is in parts not unworthy to be mentioned after it; and the poem entitled *Beyond Kerguelen* has a marvellous music about it, a wonderful rhythm of words and a real richness of utterance. Some of the lines are strangely powerful, and, indeed, in spite of its exaggerated alliteration, or perhaps in consequence of it, the whole poem is a most remarkable work of art.

> Down in the South, by the waste without sail on it—
>   Far from the zone of the blossom and tree—
> Lieth, with winter and whirlwind and wail on it,
>   Ghost of a land by the ghost of a sea.
> Weird is the mist from the summit to base of it;
>   Sun of its heaven is wizened and grey;
> Phantom of light is the light on the face of it—
>   Never is night on it, never is day!
> Here is the shore without flower or bird on it;
>   Here is no litany sweet of the springs—
> Only the haughty, harsh thunder is heard on it,
>   Only the storm, with a roar in its wings!
>
> Back in the dawn of this beautiful sphere, on it—
>   Land of the dolorous, desolate face—
> Beamed the blue day; and the beautiful year on it
>   Fostered the leaf and the blossom of grace.
> Grand were the lights of its midsummer noon on it—
>   Mornings of majesty shone on its seas;
> Glitter of star and the glory of moon on it
>   Fell, in the march of the musical breeze.
> Valleys and hills, with the whisper of wing in them,
>   Dells of the daffodil—spaces impearled,
> Flowered and flashed with the splendour of spring in them,
>   Back in the morn of this wonderful world.

Mr. Sladen speaks of Alfred Domett as 'the author of one of the great poems of a century in which Shelley and Keats, Byron and Scott, Wordsworth and Tennyson have all flourished,' but the extracts he gives from *Ranolf and Amohia* hardly substantiate this claim, although the song of the Tree-God in the fourth book is clever but exasperating.

A Midsummer's Noon, by Charles Harpur, 'the grey forefather of Australian poetry,' is pretty and graceful, and Thomas Henry's *Wood-Notes* and Miss Veel's *Saturday Night* are worth reading; but, on the whole, the Australian poets are extremely dull and prosaic. There seem to be no sirens in the New World. As for Mr. Sladen himself, he has done his work very conscientiously. Indeed, in one instance he almost re-writes an entire poem in consequence of the manuscript having reached him in a mutilated condition.

> A pleasant land is the land of dreams
>   At the back of the shining air!
> It hath sunnier skies and sheenier streams,
>   And gardens than Earth's more fair,

is the first verse of this lucubration, and Mr. Sladen informs us with justifiable pride that the parts printed in italics are from his own pen! This is certainly editing with a vengeance, and we cannot help saying that it reflects more credit on Mr. Sladen's good nature than on his critical or his poetical powers. The appearance, also, in a volume of 'poems produced in Australia,' of selections from Horne's *Orion* cannot be defended, especially as we are given no specimen of the poetry Horne wrote during the time that he actually was in Australia, where he held the office of 'Warden of the Blue Mountains'—a position which, as far as the title goes, is the loveliest ever given to any poet, and would have suited Wordsworth admirably: Wordsworth, that is to say, at his best, for he not infrequently wrote like the Distributor of Stamps. However, Mr. Sladen has shown great energy in the compilation of this bulky volume which, though it does not contain much that is of any artistic value, has a certain historical interest, especially for those who care to study the conditions of intellectual life in the colonies of a great empire. The biographical notices of the enormous crowd of verse-makers which is included in this volume are chiefly from the pen of Mr. Patchett Martin. Some of them are not very satisfactory. 'Formerly of West Australia, now residing at Boston, U.S. Has published several volumes of poetry,' is a ludicrously inadequate account of such a man as John Boyle O'Reilly, while in 'poet, essayist, critic, and journalist, one of the most prominent figures in literary London,' few will recognise the industrious Mr. William Sharp.

Still, on the whole, we should be grateful for a volume that has given us specimens of Kendall's work, and perhaps Mr. Sladen will some day produce an anthology of Australian poetry, not a herbarium of Australian verse. His present book has many good qualities, but it is almost unreadable.

Australian Poets, 1788-1888. Edited by Douglas B. W. Sladen, B.A. Oxon. (Griffith, Farran and Co.)

SOME LITERARY NOTES—I

(*Woman's World*, January 1889.)

In a recent article on *English Poetesses*, {374} I ventured to suggest that our women of letters should turn their attention somewhat more to prose and somewhat less to poetry. Women seem to me to possess just what our literature wants—a light touch, a delicate hand, a graceful mode of treatment, and an unstudied felicity of phrase. We want some one who will do for our prose what Madame de Sévigné did for the prose of France. George Eliot's style was far too cumbrous, and Charlotte Brontë's too exaggerated. However, one must not forget that amongst the women of England there have been some charming letter-writers, and certainly no book can be more delightful reading than Mrs. Ross's *Three Generations of English Women*, which has recently appeared. The three Englishwomen whose memoirs and correspondence Mrs. Ross has so admirably edited are Mrs. John Taylor, Mrs. Sarah Austin, and Lady Duff Gordon, all of them remarkable personalities, and two of them women of brilliant wit and European reputation. Mrs. Taylor belonged to that great Norwich family about whom the Duke of Sussex remarked that they reversed the ordinary saying that it takes nine tailors to make a man, and was for many years one of the most distinguished figures in the famous society of her native town. Her only daughter married John Austin, the great authority on jurisprudence, and her *salon* in Paris was the centre of the intellect and culture of her day. Lucie Duff Gordon, the only child of John and Sarah Austin, inherited the talents of her parents. A beauty, a *femme d'esprit*, a traveller, and clever writer, she charmed and fascinated her age, and her premature death in Egypt was really a loss to our literature. It is to her daughter that we owe this delightful volume of memoirs.

First we are introduced to Mrs. Ross's great-grandmother, Mrs. Taylor, who 'was called, by her intimate friends, "Madame Roland of Norwich," from her likeness to the portraits of the handsome and unfortunate Frenchwoman.' We hear of her darning her boy's grey worsted stockings while holding her own with Southey and Brougham, and dancing round the Tree of Liberty with Dr. Parr when the news of the fall of the Bastille was first known. Amongst her friends were Sir James Mackintosh, the most popular man of the day, 'to whom Madame de Staël wrote, "Il n'y a pas de société sans vous." "C'est très ennuyeux de dîner sans vous; la société ne va pas quand vous n'êtes pas là";' Sir James Smith, the botanist; Crabb Robinson; the Gurneys; Mrs. Barbauld; Dr. Alderson and his charming daughter, Amelia Opie; and many other well-known people. Her letters are extremely sensible and thoughtful. 'Nothing at present,' she says in one of them, 'suits my taste so well as Susan's Latin lessons, and her philosophical old master . . . When we get to Cicero's discussions on the nature of the soul, or Virgil's fine descriptions, my mind is filled up. Life is either a dull round of eating, drinking, and sleeping, or a spark of ethereal fire just kindled. . . . The character of girls must depend upon their reading as much as upon the company they keep. Besides the intrinsic pleasure to be derived from solid knowledge, a woman ought to consider it as her best resource against poverty.' This is a somewhat caustic aphorism: 'A romantic woman is a troublesome friend, as she expects you to be as imprudent as herself, and is mortified at what she calls coldness and insensibility.' And this is admirable: 'The art of life is not to estrange oneself from society, and yet not to pay too dear for it.' This, too, is good: 'Vanity, like curiosity, is wanted as a stimulus to exertion; indolence would certainly get the better of us if it were not for these two powerful principles'; and there is a keen touch of humour in the following: 'Nothing is so gratifying as the idea that virtue and philanthropy are becoming fashionable.' Dr. James Martineau, in a letter to Mrs. Ross, gives us a pleasant picture of the old lady returning from market 'weighted by her huge basket, with the shank of a leg of mutton thrust out to betray its contents,' and talking divinely about philosophy, poets, politics, and every intellectual topic of the day. She was a woman of admirable good sense, a type of Roman matron, and quite as careful as were the Roman matrons to keep up the purity of her native tongue.

Mrs. Taylor, however, was more or less limited to Norwich. Mrs. Austin was for the world. In London, Paris, and Germany, she ruled and dominated society, loved by every one who knew her. 'She is "My best and brightest" to Lord Jeffrey; "Dear, fair and wise" to Sydney Smith; "My great ally" to Sir James Stephen; "Sunlight through waste weltering chaos" to Thomas Carlyle (while he needed her aid); "La petite mère du genre humain" to Michael Chevalier; "Liebes Mütterlein" to John Stuart Mill; and "My own Professorin" to Charles Buller, to whom she taught German, as well as to the sons of Mr. James Mill.' Jeremy Bentham, when on his deathbed, gave her a ring with his portrait and some of his hair let in behind. 'There, my dear,' he said, 'it is the only ring I ever gave a woman.' She corresponded with Guizot, Barthelemy de St. Hilaire, the Grotes, Dr. Whewell, the Master of Trinity, Nassau Senior, the Duchesse d'Orléans, Victor Cousin, and many other distinguished people. Her translation of Ranke's *History of the Popes* is admirable; indeed, all her literary work was thoroughly well done, and her edition of her husband's *Province of Jurisprudence* deserves the very highest praise. Two people more unlike than herself and her husband it would have been difficult to find. He was habitually grave and despondent; she was brilliantly handsome, fond of society, in which she shone, and 'with an almost superabundance of energy and animal spirits,' Mrs. Ross tells us. She married him because she thought him perfect, but he never produced the work of which he was worthy, and of which she knew him to be worthy. Her estimate of him in the preface to the *Jurisprudence* is wonderfully striking and simple. 'He was never sanguine. He was intolerant of any imperfection. He was always under the control of severe love of truth. He lived and died a poor man.' She was terribly disappointed in him, but she loved him. Some years after his death, she wrote to M. Guizot:

In the intervals of my study of his works I read his letters to me—forty-five years of love-letters, the last as tender and passionate as the first. And how full of noble sentiments! The midday of our lives was clouded and stormy, full of cares and disappointments; but the sunset was bright and serene—as bright as the morning, and more serene. Now it is night with me, and must remain so till the dawn of another day. I am always alone—that is, I live with him.

The most interesting letters in the book are certainly those to M. Guizot, with whom she maintained the closest intellectual friendship; but there is hardly one of them that does not contain something clever, or thoughtful, or witty, while those addressed to her, in turn, are very interesting. Carlyle writes her letters full of lamentations, the wail of a Titan in pain, superbly exaggerated for literary effect.

Literature, one's sole craft and staff of life, lies broken in abeyance; what room for music amid the braying of innumerable jackasses, the howling of innumerable hyænas whetting the tooth to eat them up? Alas for it! it is a sick disjointed time; neither shall we ever mend it; at best let us hope to mend ourselves. I declare I sometimes think of throwing down the Pen altogether as a worthless weapon; and leading out a colony of these poor starving Drudges to the waste places of their old Mother Earth, when for sweat of their brow bread will rise for them; it were perhaps the worthiest service that at this moment could be rendered our old world to throw open for it the doors of the New. Thither must they come at last, 'bursts of eloquence' will do nothing; men are starving and will try many things before they die. But poor I, ach Gott! I am no Hengist or Alaric; only a writer of Articles in bad prose; stick to thy last, O Tutor; the Pen is not worthless, it is omnipotent to those who have Faith.

Henri Beyle (Stendhal), the great, I am often tempted to think the greatest of French novelists, writes her a charming letter about *nuances*. 'It seems to me,' he says, 'that except when they read Shakespeare, Byron, or Sterne, no Englishman understands "*nuances*"; we adore them. A fool says to a woman, "I love you"; the words mean nothing, he might as well say "Olli Batachor"; it is the *nuance* which gives force to the meaning.' In 1839 Mrs. Austin writes to Victor Cousin: 'I have seen young Gladstone, a distinguished Tory who wants to re-establish education based on the Church in quite a Catholic form'; and we find her corresponding with Mr. Gladstone on the subject of education. 'If you are strong enough to provide motives and checks,' she says to him, 'you may do two blessed acts—reform your clergy and teach your people. As it is, how few of them conceive what it is to teach a people'! Mr. Gladstone replies at great length, and in many letters, from which we may quote this passage:

You are for pressing and urging the people to their profit against their inclination: so am I. You set little value upon all merely technical instruction, upon all that fails to touch the inner nature of man: so do I. And here I find ground of union broad and deep-laid . . .

I more than doubt whether your idea, namely that of raising man to social sufficiency and morality, can be accomplished, except through the ancient religion of Christ; . . . or whether the principles of eclecticism are legitimately applicable to the Gospel; or whether, if we find ourselves in a state of incapacity to work through the Church, we can remedy the defect by the adoption of principles contrary to hers . . .

But indeed I am most unfit to pursue the subject; private circumstances of no common interest are upon me, as I have become very recently engaged to Miss Glynne, and I hope your recollections will enable you in some degree to excuse me.

Lord Jeffrey has a very curious and suggestive letter on popular education, in which he denies, or at least doubts, the effect of this education on morals. He, however, supports it on the ground 'that it will increase the enjoyment of individuals,' which is certainly a very sensible claim. Humboldt writes to her about an old Indian language which was preserved by a parrot, the tribe who spoke it having been exterminated, and about 'young Darwin,' who had just published his first book. Here are some extracts from her own letters:

I heard from Lord Lansdowne two or three days ago. . . . I think he is ce que nous avons de mieux. He wants only the energy that great ambition gives. He says, 'We shall have a parliament of railway kings' . . . what can be worse than that?—The deification of money by a whole people. As Lord Brougham says, we have no right to give ourselves pharisaical airs. I must give you a story sent to me. Mrs. Hudson, the railway queen, was shown a bust of Marcus Aurelius at Lord Westminster's, on which she said, 'I suppose that is not the present Marquis.' To goûter this, you must know that the extreme vulgar (hackney coachmen, etc.) in England pronounce 'marquis' very like 'Marcus.'

Dec, 11th.—Went to Savigny's. Nobody was there but W. Grimm and his wife and a few men. Grimm told me he had received two volumes of Norwegian fairy-tales, and that they were delightful. Talking of them, I said, 'Your children appear to be the happiest in the world; they live in the midst of fairytales.' 'Ah,' said he, 'I must tell you about that. When we were at Göttingen, somebody spoke to my little son about his father's Mährchen. He had read them, but never thought of their being mine. He came running to me, and said with an offended air, "Father, they say you wrote those fairy-tales; surely you never invented such silly rubbish?" He thought it below my dignity.'

Savigny told a Volksmährchen too:

'St. Anselm was grown old and infirm, and lay on the ground among thorns and thistles. Der liebe Gott said to him, "You are very badly lodged there; why don't you build yourself a house?" "Before I take the trouble," said Anselm, "I should like to know how long I have to live." "About thirty years," said Der liebe Gott. "Oh, for so short a time," replied he, "it's not worth while," and turned himself round among the thistles.'

Dr. Franck told me a story of which I had never heard before. Voltaire had for some reason or other taken a grudge against the prophet Habakkuk, and affected to find in him things he never wrote. Somebody took the Bible and began to demonstrate to him that he was mistaken. 'C'est égal,' he said, impatiently, 'Habakkuk était capable de tout!'

Oct. 30, 1853.

I am not in love with the Richtung (tendency) of our modern novelists. There is abundance of talent; but writing a pretty, graceful, touching, yet pleasing story is the last thing our writers nowadays think of. Their novels are party pamphlets on political or social questions, like Sybil, or Alton Locke, or Mary Barton, or Uncle Tom; or they are the most minute and painful dissections of the least agreeable and beautiful parts of our nature, like those of Miss Brontë—Jane Eyre and Villette; or they are a kind of martyrology, like Mrs. Marsh's Emilia Wyndham, which makes you almost doubt whether any torments the heroine would have earned by being naughty could exceed those she incurred by her virtue.

Where, oh! where is the charming, humane, gentle spirit that dictated the Vicar of Wakefield—the spirit which Goethe so justly calls versöhnend (reconciling), with all the weaknesses and woes of humanity? . . . Have you read Thackeray's Esmond? It is a curious and very successful attempt to imitate the style of our old novelists. . . . Which of Mrs. Gore's novels are translated? They are very clever, lively, worldly, bitter, disagreeable, and entertaining. . . . Miss Austen's—are they translated? They are not new, and are Dutch paintings of every-day people—very clever, very true, very unæsthetic, but amusing. I have not seen Ruth, by Mrs. Gaskell. I hear it much admired—and blamed. It is one of the many proofs of the desire women now have to friser questionable topics, and to poser insoluble moral problems. George Sand has turned their heads in that direction. I think a few broad scenes or hearty jokes à la Fielding were very harmless in comparison. They confounded nothing. . . .

The Heir of Redcliffe I have not read. . . . I am not worthy of superhuman flights of virtue—in a novel. I want to see how people act and suffer who are as good-for-nothing as I am myself. Then I have the sinful pretension to be amused, whereas all our novelists want to reform us, and to show us what a hideous place this world is: Ma foi, je ne le sais que trap, without their help.

The Head of the Family has some merits . . . But there is too much affliction and misery and frenzy. The heroine is one of those creatures now so common (in novels), who remind me of a poor bird tied to a stake (as was once the cruel sport of boys) to be 'shyed' at (i.e. pelted) till it died; only our gentle lady-writers at the end of all untie the poor battered bird, and assure us that it is never the worse for all the blows it has had—nay, the better—and that now, with its broken wings and torn feathers and bruised body, it is going to be quite happy. No, fair ladies, you know that it is not so—resigned, if you please, but make me no shams of happiness out of such wrecks.

In politics Mrs. Austin was a philosophical Tory. Radicalism she detested, and she and most of her friends seem to have regarded it as moribund. 'The Radical party is evidently effete,' she writes to M. Victor Cousin; the probable 'leader of the Tory party' is Mr. Gladstone. 'The people must be instructed, must be guided, must be, in short, governed,' she writes elsewhere; and in a letter to Dr. Whewell, she says that the state of things in France fills 'me with the deepest anxiety on one point,—the point on which the permanency of our institutions and our salvation as a nation turn. Are our higher classes able to keep the lead of the rest? If they are, we are safe; if not, I agree with my poor dear Charles Buller—our turn must come. Now Cambridge and Oxford must really look to this.' The belief in the power of the Universities to stem the current of democracy is charming. She grew to regard Carlyle as 'one of the dissolvents of the age—as mischievous as his extravagances will let him be'; speaks of Kingsley and Maurice as 'pernicious'; and talks of John Stuart Mill as a 'demagogue.' She was no doctrinaire. 'One ounce of education demanded is worth a pound imposed. It is no use to give the meat before you give the hunger.' She was delighted at a letter of St. Hilaire's, in which he said, 'We have a system and no results; you have results and no system.' Yet she had a deep sympathy with the wants of the people. She was horrified at something Babbage told her of the population of some of the manufacturing towns who are worked out before they attain to thirty years of age. 'But I am persuaded that the remedy will not, cannot come from the people,' she adds. Many of her letters are concerned with the question of the higher education of women. She discusses Buckle's lecture on 'The Influence of Women upon the Progress of Knowledge,' admits to M. Guizot that women's intellectual life is largely coloured by the emotions, but adds: 'One is not precisely a fool because one's opinions are greatly influenced by one's affections. The opinions of men are often influenced by worse things.' Dr. Whewell consults her about lecturing women on Plato, being slightly afraid lest people should think it ridiculous; Comte writes her elaborate letters on the relation of women to progress; and Mr. Gladstone promises that Mrs. Gladstone will carry out at Hawarden the suggestions contained in one of her pamphlets. She was always very practical, and never lost her admiration for plain sewing.

All through the book we come across interesting and amusing things. She gets St. Hilaire to order a large, sensible bonnet for her in Paris, which was at once christened the 'Aristotelian,' and was supposed to be the only useful bonnet in England. Grote has to leave Paris after the coup d'état, he tells her, because he cannot bear to see the establishment of a Greek tyrant. Alfred de Vigny, Macaulay, John Stirling, Southey, Alexis de Tocqueville, Hallam, and Jean Jacques Ampère all contribute to these pleasant pages. She seems to have inspired the warmest feelings of friendship in those who knew her. Guizot writes to her: 'Madame de Staël used to say that the best thing in the world was a serious Frenchman. I turn the compliment, and say that the best thing in the world is an affectionate Englishman. How much more an Englishwoman! Given equal qualities, a woman is always more charming than a man.'

Lucie Austin, afterwards Lady Duff Gordon, was born in 1821. Her chief playfellow was John Stuart Mill, and Jeremy Bentham's garden was her playground. She was a lovely, romantic child, who was always wanting the flowers to talk to her, and used to invent the most wonderful stories about animals, of whom she was passionately fond. In 1834 Mrs. Austin decided on leaving England, and Sydney Smith wrote his immortal letter to the little girl:

Lucie, Lucie, my dear child, don't tear your frock: tearing frocks is not of itself a proof of genius. But write as your mother writes, act as your mother acts: be frank, loyal, affectionate, simple, honest, and then integrity or laceration of frock is of little import. And Lucie, dear child, mind your arithmetic. You know in the first sum of yours I ever saw there was a mistake. You had carried two (as a cab is licensed to do), and you ought, dear Lucie, to have carried but one. Is this a trifle? What would life be without arithmetic but a scene of horrors? You are going to Boulogne, the city of debts, peopled by men who have never understood arithmetic. By the time you return, I shall probably have received my first paralytic stroke, and shall have lost all recollection of you. Therefore I now give you my parting advice—don't marry anybody who has not a tolerable understanding and a thousand a year. And God bless you, dear child.

At Boulogne she sat next Heine at table d'hôte. 'He heard me speak German to my mother, and soon began to talk to me, and then said, "When you go back to England, you can tell your friends that you have seen Heinrich Heine." I replied, "And who is Heinrich Heine?" He laughed heartily and took no offence at my ignorance; and we used to lounge on the end of the pier together, where he told me stories in which fish, mermaids, water-sprites and a very funny old French fiddler with a poodle were mixed up in the most fanciful manner, sometimes humorous, and very often pathetic, especially when the water-sprites brought him greetings from the "Nord See." He was . . . so kind to me and so sarcastic to every one else.' Twenty years afterwards the little girl whose 'braune Augen' Heine had celebrated in his charming poem *Wenn ich an deinem Hause*, used to go and see the dying poet in Paris. 'It does one good,' he said to her, 'to see a woman who does not carry about a broken heart, to be mended by all sorts of men, like the women here, who do not see that a total want of heart is their real failing.' On another occasion he said to her: 'I have now made peace with the whole world, and at last also with God, who sends thee to me as a beautiful angel of death: I shall certainly soon die.' Lady Duff Gordon said to him: 'Poor Poet, do you still retain such splendid illusions, that you transform a travelling Englishwoman into Azrael? That used not to be the case, for you always disliked us.' He answered: 'Yes, I do not know what possessed me to dislike the English, . . . it really was only petulance; I never hated them, indeed, I never knew them. I was only once in England, but knew no one, and found London very dreary, and the people and the streets odious. But England has revenged herself well; she has sent me most excellent friends—thyself and Milnes, that good Milnes.'

There are delightful letters from Dicky Doyle here, with the most amusing drawings, one of the present Sir Robert Peel as he made his maiden speech in the House being excellent; and the various descriptions of Hassan's performances are extremely amusing. Hassan was a black boy, who had been turned away by his master because he was going blind, and was found by Lady Duff Gordon one night sitting on her doorstep. She took care of him, and had him cured, and he seems to have been a constant source of delight to every one. On one occasion, 'when Prince Louis Napoleon (the late Emperor of the French) came in unexpectedly, he gravely said: "Please, my Lady, I ran out and bought twopenny worth of sprats for the Prince, and for the honour of the house."' Here is an amusing letter from Mrs. Norton:

MY DEAR LUCIE,—We have never thanked you for the red Pots, which no early Christian should be without, and which add that finishing stroke to the splendour of our demesne, which was supposed to depend on a roc's egg, in less intelligent times. We have now a warm Pompeian appearance, and the constant contemplation of these classical objects favours the beauty of the facial line; for what can be deduced from the great fact, apparent in all the states of antiquity, that straight noses were the ancient custom, but the logical assumption that the constant habit of turning up the nose at unsightly objects—such as the National Gallery and other offensive and obtrusive things—has produced the modern divergence from the true and proper line of profile? I rejoice to think that we ourselves are exempt. I attribute this to our love of Pompeian Pots (on account of the beauty and distinction of this Pot's shape I spell it with a big P), which has kept us straight in a world of crookedness. The pursuit of profiles under difficulties—how much more rare than a pursuit of knowledge! Talk of setting good examples before our children! Bah! let us set good Pompeian Pots before our children, and when they grow up they will not depart from them.

Lady Duff Gordon's *Letters from the Cape*, and her brilliant translation of *The Amber Witch*, are, of course, well known. The latter book was, with Lady Wilde's translation of *Sidonia the Sorceress*, my favourite romantic reading when a boy. Her letters from Egypt are wonderfully vivid and picturesque. Here is an interesting bit of art criticism:

Sheykh Yoosuf laughed so heartily over a print in an illustrated paper from a picture of Hilton's of Rebekah at the well, with the old 'wekeel' of 'Sidi Ibraheem' (Abraham's chief servant) kneeling before the girl he was sent to fetch, like an old fool without his turban, and Rebekah and the other girls in queer fancy dresses, and the camels with snouts like pigs. 'If the painter could not go into "Es Sham" to see how the Arab really look,' said Sheykh Yoosuf, 'why did he not paint a well in England, with girls like English peasants—at least it would have looked natural to English people? and the wekeel would not seem so like a madman if he had taken off a hat!' I cordially agree with Yoosuf's art criticism. Fancy pictures of Eastern things are hopelessly absurd.

Mrs. Ross has certainly produced a most fascinating volume, and her book is one of the books of the season. It is edited with tact and judgment.

* * * * *

Caroline, by Lady Lindsay, is certainly Lady Lindsay's best work. It is written in a very clever modern style, and is as full of *esprit* and wit as it is of subtle psychological insight. Caroline is an heiress, who, coming downstairs at a Continental hotel, falls into the arms of a charming, penniless young man. The hero of the novel is the young man's friend, Lord Lexamont, who makes the 'great renunciation,' and succeeds in being fine without being priggish, and Quixotic without being ridiculous. Miss Ffoulkes, the elderly spinster, is a capital character, and, indeed, the whole book is cleverly written. It has also the advantage of being in only one volume. The influence of Mudie on literature, the baneful influence of the circulating library, is clearly on the wane. The gain to literature is incalculable. English novels were becoming very tedious with their three volumes of padding—at least, the second volume was always padding—and extremely indigestible. A reckless punster once remarked to me, *apropos* of English novels, that 'the proof of the padding is in the eating,' and certainly English fiction has been very heavy—heavy with the best intentions. Lady Lindsay's book is a sign that better things are in store for us. She is brief and bright.

* * * * *

What are the best books to give as Christmas presents to good girls who are always pretty, or to pretty girls who are occasionally good? People are so fond of giving away what they do not want themselves, that charity is largely on the increase. But with this kind of charity I have not much sympathy. If one gives away a book, it should be a charming book—so charming, that one regrets having given it, and would not take it back. Looking over the Christmas books sent to me by various publishers, I find that these are the best and the most pleasing: *Gleanings from the 'Graphic,'* by Randolph Caldecott, a most fascinating volume full of sketches that have real wit and humour of line, and are not simply dependent on what the French call the *légende*, the literary explanation; *Meg's Friend*, by Alice Corkran, one of our most delicate and graceful prose-writers in the sphere of fiction, and one whose work has the rare artistic qualities of refinement and simplicity; *Under False Colours*, by Sarah Doudney, an excellent story; *The Fisherman's Daughter*, by Florence Montgomery, the author of *Misunderstood*, a tale with real charm of idea and treatment; *Under a Cloud*, by the author of *The Atelier du Lys*, and quite worthy of its author; *The Third Miss St. Quentin*, by Mrs. Molesworth, and *A Christmas Posy* from the same fascinating pen, and with delightful illustrations by Walter Crane. Miss Rosa Mulholland's *Giannetta* and Miss Agnes Giberne's *Ralph Hardcastle's Will* are also admirable books for presents, and the bound volume of *Atalanta* has much that is delightful both in art and in literature.

The prettiest, indeed the most beautiful, book from an artistic point of view is undoubtedly Mr. Walter Crane's *Flora's Feast*. It is an imaginative Masque of Flowers, and as lovely in colour as it is exquisite in design. It shows us the whole pomp and pageant of the year, the Snowdrops like white-crested knights, the little naked Crocus kneeling to catch the sunlight in his golden chalice, the Daffodils blowing their trumpets like young hunters, the Anemones with their wind-blown raiment, the green-kirtled Marsh-marigolds, and the 'Lady-smocks all silver-white,' tripping over the meadows like Arcadian milk-maids. Buttercups are here, and the white-plumed Thorn in spiky armour, and the Crown-imperial borne in stately procession, and red-bannered Tulips, and Hyacinths with their spring bells, and Chaucer's Daisy—

small and sweet,
Si douce est la Marguerite.

Gorgeous Peonies, and Columbines 'that drew the car of Venus,' and the Rose with her lover, and the stately white-vestured Lilies, and wide staring Ox-eyes, and scarlet Poppies pass before us. There are Primroses and Corncockles, Chrysanthemums in robes of rich brocade, Sunflowers and tall Hollyhocks, and pale Christmas Roses. The designs for the Daffodils, the wild Roses, the Convolvulus, and the Hollyhock are admirable, and would be beautiful in embroidery or in any precious material. Indeed, any one who wishes to find beautiful designs cannot do better than get the book. It is, in its way, a little masterpiece, and its grace and fancy, and beauty of line and colour, cannot be over-estimated. The Greeks gave human form to wood and stream, and saw Nature best in Naiad or in Dryad. Mr. Crane, with something of Gothic fantasy, has caught the Greek feeling, the love of personification, the passion for representing things under the conditions of the human form. The flowers are to him so many knights and ladies, page-boys or shepherd-boys, divine nymphs or simple girls, and in their fair bodies or fanciful raiment one can see the flower's very form and absolute essence, so that one loves their artistic truth no less than their artistic beauty. This book contains some of the best work Mr. Crane has ever done. His art is never so successful as when it is entirely remote from life. The slightest touch of actuality seems to kill it. It lives, or should live, in a world of its own fashioning. It is decorative in its complete subordination of fact to beauty of effect, in the grandeur of its curves and lines, in its entirely imaginative treatment. Almost every page of this book gives a suggestion for some rich tapestry, some fine screen, some painted *cassone*, some carving in wood or ivory.

* * * * *

From Messrs. Hildesheimer and Faulkner I have received a large collection of Christmas cards and illustrated books. One of the latter, an *édition de luxe* of Sheridan's *Here's to the Maiden of Bashful Fifteen*, is very cleverly illustrated by Miss Alice Havers and Mr. Ernest Wilson. It seems to me, however, that there is a danger of modern illustration becoming too pictorial. What we need is good book-ornament, decorative ornament that will go with type and printing, and give to each page a harmony and unity of effect. Merely dotting a page with reproductions of water-colour drawings will not do. It is true that Japanese art, which is essentially decorative, is pictorial also. But the Japanese have the most wonderful delicacy of touch, and with a science so subtle that it gives the effect of exquisite accident, they can by mere placing make an undecorated space decorative. There is also an intimate connection between their art and their handwriting or printed characters. They both go together, and show the same feeling for form and line. Our aim should be to discover some mode of illustration that will harmonise with the shapes of our letters. At present there is a discord between our pictorial illustrations and our unpictorial type. The former are too essentially imitative in character, and often disturb a page instead of decorating it. However, I suppose we must regard most of these Christmas books merely as books of pictures, with a running accompaniment of explanatory text. As the text, as a rule, consists of poetry, this is putting the poet in a very subordinate position; but the poetry in the books of this kind is not, as a rule, of a very high order of excellence.

(1) *Three Generations of English Women. Memoirs and Correspondence of Susannah Taylor, Sarah Austin, and Lady Duff Gordon.* By Janet Ross, Author of *Italian Sketches, Land of Manfred, etc.* (Fisher Unwin.)

(2) *Caroline.* By Lady Lindsay. (Bentley and Son.)

(3) *Gleanings from the 'Graphic.'* By Randolph Caldecott. (Routledge and Sons.)

(4) *Meg's Friend.* By Alice Corkran. (Blackie and Sons.)

(5) *Under False Colours.* By Sarah Doudney. (Blackie and Sons.)

(6) *The Fisherman's Daughter.* By Florence Montgomery. (Hatchards.)

(7) *Under a Cloud.* By the Author of *The Atelier du Lys.* (Hatchards.)

(8) *The Third Miss St. Quentin.* By Mrs. Molesworth. (Hatchards.)

(9) *A Christmas Posy.* By Mrs. Molesworth. Illustrated by Walter Crane. (Hatchards.)

(10) *Giannetta. A Girl's Story of Herself.* By Rosa Mulholland. (Blackie and Sons.)

(11) *Ralph Hardcastle's Will.* By Agnes Giberne. (Hatchards.)

(12) *Flora's Feast. A Masque of Flowers.* Penned and Pictured by Walter Crane. (Cassell and Co.)

(13) *Here's to the Maiden of Bashful Fifteen.* By Richard Brinsley Sheridan. Illustrated by Alice Havers and Ernest Wilson. (Hildesheimer and Faulkner.)

POETRY AND PRISON

(*Pall Mall Gazette*, January 3, 1889.)

Prison has had an admirable effect on Mr. Wilfrid Blunt as a poet. The *Love Sonnets of Proteus*, in spite of their clever Musset-like modernities and their swift brilliant wit, were but affected or fantastic at best. They were simply the records of passing moods and moments, of which some were sad and others sweet, and not a few shameful. Their subject was not of high or serious import. They contained much that was wilful and weak. *In Vinculis*, upon the other hand, is a book that stirs one by its fine sincerity of purpose, its lofty and impassioned thought, its depth and ardour of intense feeling. 'Imprisonment,' says Mr. Blunt in his preface, 'is a reality of discipline most useful to the modern soul, lapped as it is in physical sloth and self-indulgence. Like a sickness or a spiritual retreat it purifies and ennobles; and the soul emerges from it stronger and more self-contained.' To him, certainly, it has been a mode of purification. The opening sonnets, composed in the bleak cell of Galway Gaol, and written down on the fly-leaves of the prisoner's prayer-book, are full of things nobly conceived and nobly uttered, and show that though Mr. Balfour may enforce 'plain living' by his prison regulations, he cannot prevent 'high thinking' or in any way limit or constrain the freedom of a man's soul. They are, of course, intensely personal in expression. They could not fail to be so. But the personality that they reveal has nothing petty or ignoble about it. The petulant cry of the shallow egoist which was the chief characteristic of the *Love Sonnets of Proteus* is not to be found here. In its place we have wild grief and terrible scorn, fierce rage and flame-like passion. Such a sonnet as the following comes out of the very fire of heart and brain:

God knows, 'twas not with a fore-reasoned plan
  I left the easeful dwellings of my peace,
And sought this combat with ungodly Man,
  And ceaseless still through years that do not cease
  Have warred with Powers and Principalities.
My natural soul, ere yet these strifes began,
  Was as a sister diligent to please
And loving all, and most the human clan.

  God knows it. And He knows how the world's tears
  Touched me. And He is witness of my wrath,
How it was kindled against murderers
  Who slew for gold, and how upon their path
I met them. Since which day the World in arms
Strikes at my life with angers and alarms.

And this sonnet has all the strange strength of that despair which is but the prelude to a larger hope:

I thought to do a deed of chivalry,
  An act of worth, which haply in her sight
Who was my mistress should recorded be
  And of the nations. And, when thus the fight
  Faltered and men once bold with faces white
Turned this and that way in excuse to flee,
  I only stood, and by the foeman's might
Was overborne and mangled cruelly.

  Then crawled I to her feet, in whose dear cause
  I made this venture, and 'Behold,' I said,
'How I am wounded for thee in these wars.'
  But she, 'Poor cripple, would'st thou I should wed
A limbless trunk?' and laughing turned from me.
Yet she was fair, and her name 'Liberty.'

The sonnet beginning

A prison is a convent without God—
Poverty, Chastity, Obedience
Its precepts are:

is very fine; and this, written just after entering the gaol, is powerful:

Naked I came into the world of pleasure,
  And naked come I to this house of pain.
Here at the gate I lay down my life's treasure,
  My pride, my garments and my name with men.
  The world and I henceforth shall be as twain,
No sound of me shall pierce for good or ill
  These walls of grief. Nor shall I hear the vain
Laughter and tears of those who love me still.

  Within, what new life waits me! Little ease,
  Cold lying, hunger, nights of wakefulness,
Harsh orders given, no voice to soothe or please,
  Poor thieves for friends, for books rules meaningless;
This is the grave—nay, hell. Yet, Lord of Might,
Still in Thy light my spirit shall see light.

But, indeed, all the sonnets are worth reading, and *The Canon of Aughrim*, the longest poem in the book, is a most masterly and dramatic description of the tragic life of the Irish peasant. Literature is not much indebted to Mr. Balfour for his sophistical *Defence of Philosophic Doubt* which is one of the dullest books we know, but it must be admitted that by sending Mr. Blunt to gaol he has converted a clever rhymer into an earnest and deep-thinking poet. The narrow confines of the prison cell seem to suit the 'sonnet's scanty plot of ground,' and an unjust imprisonment for a noble cause strengthens as well as deepens the nature.

In Vinculis. By Wilfrid Scawen Blunt, Author of *The Wind and the Whirlwind, The Love Sonnets of Proteus, etc. etc.* (Kegan Paul.)

THE GOSPEL ACCORDING TO WALT WHITMAN

(*Pall Mall Gazette*, January 25, 1889.)

'No one will get at my verses who insists upon viewing them as a literary performance . . . or as aiming mainly toward art and æstheticism.' '*Leaves of Grass* . . . has mainly been the outcropping of my own emotional and other personal nature—an attempt, from first to last, to put *a Person*, a human being (myself, in the latter half of the Nineteenth Century in America,) freely, fully and truly on record. I could not find any similar personal record in current literature that satisfied me.' In these words Walt Whitman gives us the true attitude we should adopt towards his work, having, indeed, a much saner view of the value and meaning of that work than either his eloquent admirers or noisy detractors can boast of possessing. His last book, *November Boughs*, as he calls it, published in the winter of the old man's life, reveals to us, not indeed a soul's tragedy, for its last note is one of joy and hope, and noble and unshaken faith in all that is fine and worthy of such faith, but certainly the drama of a human soul, and puts on record with a simplicity that has in it both sweetness and strength the record of his spiritual development, and of the aim and motive both of the manner and the matter of his work. His strange mode of expression is shown in these pages to have been the result of deliberate and self-conscious choice. The 'barbaric yawp' which he sent over 'the roofs of the world' so many years ago, and which wrung from Mr. Swinburne's lip such lofty panegyric in song and such loud clamorous censure in prose, appears here in what will be to many an entirely new light. For in his very rejection of art Walt Whitman is an artist. He tried to produce a certain effect by certain means and he succeeded. There is much method in what many have termed his madness, too much method, indeed, some may be tempted to fancy.

In the story of his life, as he tells it to us, we find him at the age of sixteen beginning a definite and philosophical study of literature:

Summers and falls, I used to go off, sometimes for a week at a stretch, down in the country, or to Long Island's seashores—there, in the presence of outdoor influences, I went over thoroughly the Old and New Testaments, and absorb'd (probably to better advantage for me than in any library or indoor room—it makes such difference where you read) Shakspere, Ossian, the best translated versions I could get of Homer, Eschylus, Sophocles, the old German Nibelungen, the ancient Hindoo poems, and one or two other masterpieces, Dante's among them. As it happened, I read the latter mostly in an old wood. The Iliad . . . I read first thoroughly on the peninsula of Orient, northeast end of Long Island, in a sheltered hollow of rock and sand, with the sea on each side. (I have wonder'd since why I was not overwhelmed by those mighty masters. Likely because I read them, as described, in the full presence of Nature, under the sun, with the far-spreading landscape and vistas, or the sea rolling in.)

Edgar Allan Poe's amusing bit of dogmatism that, for our occasions and our day, 'there can be no such thing as a long poem,' fascinated him. 'The same thought had been haunting my mind before,' he said, 'but Poe's argument . . . work'd the sum out, and proved it to me,' and the English translation of the Bible seems to have suggested to him the possibility of a poetic form which, while retaining the spirit of poetry, would still be free from the trammels of rhyme and of a definite metrical system. Having thus, to a certain degree, settled upon what one might call the 'technique' of Whitmanism, he began to brood upon the nature of that spirit which was to give life to the strange form. The central point of the poetry of the future seemed to him to be necessarily 'an identical body and soul, a personality,' in fact, which personality, he tells us frankly, 'after many considerations and ponderings I deliberately settled should be myself.' However, for the true creation and revealing of this personality, at first only dimly felt, a new stimulus was needed. This came from the Civil War. After describing the many dreams and passions of his boyhood and early manhood, he goes on to say:

These, however, and much more might have gone on and come to naught (almost positively would have come to naught,) if a sudden, vast, terrible, direct and indirect stimulus for new and national declamatory expression had not been given to me. It is certain, I say, that although I had made a start before, only from the occurrence of the Secession War, and what it show'd me as by flashes of lightning, with the emotional depths it sounded and arous'd (of course, I don't mean in my own heart only, I saw it just as plainly in others, in millions)—that only from the strong flare and provocation of that war's sights and scenes the final reasons-for-being of an autochthonic and passionate song definitely came forth.

I went down to the war fields of Virginia . . . lived thenceforward in camp—saw great battles and the days and nights afterward—partook of all the fluctuations, gloom, despair, hopes again arous'd, courage evoked—death readily risk'd—the cause, too—along and filling those agonistic and lurid following years . . . the real parturition years . . . of this henceforth homogeneous Union. Without those three or four years and the experiences they gave, Leaves of Grass would not now be existing.

Having thus obtained the necessary stimulus for the quickening and awakening of the personal self, some day to be endowed with universality, he sought to find new notes of song, and, passing beyond the mere passion for expression, he aimed at 'Suggestiveness' first.

I round and finish little, if anything; and could not, consistently with my scheme. The reader will have his or her part to do, just as much as I have had mine. I seek less to state or display any theme or thought, and more to bring you, reader, into the atmosphere of the theme or thought—there to pursue your own flight.

Another 'impetus-word' is Comradeship, and other 'word-signs' are Good Cheer, Content and Hope. Individuality, especially, he sought for:

I have allowed the stress of my poems from beginning to end to bear upon American individuality and assist it—not only because that is a great lesson in Nature, amid all her generalising laws, but as counterpoise to the leveling tendencies of Democracy—and for other reasons. Defiant of ostensible literary and other conventions, I avowedly chant 'the great pride of man in himself,' and permit it to be more or less a motif of nearly all my verse. I think this pride indispensable to an American. I think it not inconsistent with obedience, humility, deference, and self-questioning.

A new theme also was to be found in the relation of the sexes, conceived in a natural, simple and healthy form, and he protests against poor Mr. William Rossetti's attempt to Bowdlerise and expurgate his song.

From another point of view Leaves of Grass is avowedly the song of Sex and Amativeness, and even Animality—though meanings that do not usually go along with these words are behind all, and will duly emerge; and all are sought to be lifted into a different light and atmosphere. Of this feature, intentionally palpable in a few lines, I shall only say the espousing principle of those lines so gives breath to my whole scheme that the bulk of the pieces might as well have been left unwritten were those lines omitted. . . .

Universal as are certain facts and symptoms of communities . . . there is nothing so rare in modern conventions and poetry as their normal recognizance. Literature is always calling in the doctor for consultation and confession, and always giving evasions and swathing suppressions in place of that 'heroic nudity,' on which only a genuine diagnosis . . . can be built. And in respect to editions of Leaves of Grass in time to come (if there should be such) I take occasion now to confirm those lines with the settled convictions and deliberate renewals of thirty years, and to hereby prohibit, as far as word of mine can do so, any elision of them.

But beyond all these notes and moods and motives is the lofty spirit of a grand and free acceptance of all things that are worthy of existence. He desired, he says, 'to formulate a poem whose every thought or fact should directly or indirectly be or connive at an implicit belief in the wisdom, health, mystery, beauty of every process, every concrete object, every human or other existence, not only consider'd from the point of view of all, but of each.' His two final utterances are that 'really great poetry is always . . . the result of a national spirit, and not the privilege of a polish'd and select few'; and that 'the strongest and sweetest songs yet remain to be sung.'

Such are the views contained in the opening essay *A Backward Glance O'er Travel'd Roads*, as he calls it; but there are many other essays in this fascinating volume, some on poets such as Burns and Lord Tennyson, for whom Walt Whitman has a profound admiration; some on old actors and singers, the elder Booth, Forrest, Alboni and Mario being his special favourites; others on the native Indians, on the Spanish element in American nationality, on Western slang, on the poetry of the Bible, and on Abraham Lincoln. But Walt Whitman is at his best when he is analysing his own work and making schemes for the poetry of the future. Literature, to him, has a distinctly social aim. He seeks to build up the masses by 'building up grand individuals.' And yet literature itself must be preceded by noble forms of life. 'The best literature is always the result of something far greater than itself—not the hero but the portrait of the hero. Before there can be recorded history or poem there must be the transaction.' Certainly, in Walt Whitman's views there is a largeness of vision, a healthy sanity and a fine ethical purpose. He is not to be placed with the professional littérateurs of his country, Boston novelists, New York poets and the like. He stands apart, and the chief value of his work is in its prophecy, not in its performance. He has begun a prelude to larger themes. He is the herald to a new era. As a man he is the precursor of a fresh type. He is a factor in the heroic and spiritual evolution of the human being. If Poetry has passed him by, Philosophy will take note of him.

November Boughs. By Walt Whitman. (Alexander Gardner.)

THE NEW PRESIDENT

(*Pall Mall Gazette*, January 26, 1889.)

In a little book that he calls *The Enchanted Island* Mr. Wyke Bayliss, the new President of the Royal Society of British Artists, has given his gospel of art to the world. His predecessor in office had also a gospel of art but it usually took the form of an autobiography. Mr. Whistler always spelt art, and we believe still spells it, with a capital 'I.' However, he was never dull. His brilliant wit, his caustic satire, and his amusing epigrams, or, perhaps, we should say epitaphs, on his contemporaries, made his views on art as delightful as they were misleading and as fascinating as they were unsound. Besides, he introduced American humour into art criticism, and for this, if for no other reason, he deserves to be affectionately remembered. Mr. Wyke Bayliss, upon the other hand, is rather tedious. The last President never said much that was true, but the present President never says anything that is new; and, if art be a fairy-haunted wood or an enchanted island, we must say that we prefer the old Puck to the fresh Prospero. Water is an admirable thing—at least, the Greeks said it was—and Mr. Ruskin is an admirable writer; but a combination of both is a little depressing.

Still, it is only right to add that Mr. Wyke Bayliss, at his best, writes very good English. Mr. Whistler, for some reason or other, always adopted the phraseology of the minor prophets. Possibly it was in order to emphasise his well-known claims to verbal inspiration, or perhaps he thought with Voltaire that *Habakkuk était capable de tout*, and wished to shelter himself under the shield of a definitely irresponsible writer none of whose prophecies, according to the French philosopher, has ever been fulfilled. The idea was clever enough at the beginning, but ultimately the manner became monotonous. The spirit of the Hebrews is excellent but their mode of writing is not to be imitated, and no amount of American jokes will give it that modernity which is essential to a good literary style. Admirable as are Mr. Whistler's fireworks on canvas, his fireworks in prose are abrupt, violent and exaggerated. However, oracles, since the days of the Pythia, have never been remarkable for style, and the modest Mr. Wyke Bayliss is as much Mr. Whistler's superior as a writer as he is his inferior as a painter and an artist. Indeed, some of the passages in this book are so charmingly written and with such felicity of phrase that we cannot help feeling that the President of the British Artists, like a still more famous President of our day, can express himself far better through the medium of literature than he can through the medium of line and colour. This, however, applies only to Mr. Wyke Bayliss's prose. His poetry is very bad, and the sonnets at the end of the book are almost as mediocre as the drawings that accompany them. As we read them we cannot but regret that, in this point at any rate, Mr. Bayliss has not imitated the wise example of his predecessor who, with all his faults, was never guilty of writing a line of poetry, and is, indeed, quite incapable of doing anything of the kind.

As for the matter of Mr. Bayliss's discourses, his views on art must be admitted to be very commonplace and old-fashioned. What is the use of telling artists that they should try and paint Nature as she really is? What Nature really is, is a question for metaphysics not for art. Art deals with appearances, and the eye of the man who looks at Nature, the vision, in fact, of the artist, is far more important to us than what he looks at. There is more truth in Corot's aphorism that a landscape is simply 'the mood of a man's mind' than there is in all Mr. Bayliss's laborious disquisitions on naturalism. Again, why does Mr. Bayliss waste a whole chapter in pointing out real or supposed resemblances between a book of his published twelve years ago and an article by Mr. Palgrave which appeared recently in the *Nineteenth Century*? Neither the book nor the article contains anything of real interest, and as for the hundred or more parallel passages which Mr. Wyke Bayliss solemnly prints side by side, most of them are like parallel lines and never meet. The only original proposal that Mr. Bayliss has to offer us is that the House of Commons should, every year, select some important event from national and contemporary history and hand it over to the artists who are to choose from among themselves a man to make a picture of it. In this way Mr. Bayliss believes that we could have the historic art, and suggests as examples of what he means a picture of Florence Nightingale in the hospital at Scutari, a picture of the opening of the first London Board-school, and a picture of the Senate House at Cambridge with the girl graduate receiving a degree 'that shall acknowledge her to be as wise as Merlin himself and leave her still as beautiful as Vivien.' This proposal is, of course, very well meant, but, to say nothing of the danger of leaving historic art at the mercy of a majority in the House of Commons, who would naturally vote for its own view of things, Mr. Bayliss does not seem to realise that a great event is not necessarily a pictorial event. 'The decisive events of the world,' as has been well said, 'take place in the intellect,' and as for Board-schools, academic ceremonies, hospital wards and the like, they may well be left to the artists of the illustrated papers, who do them admirably and quite as well as they need be done. Indeed, the pictures of contemporary events, Royal marriages, naval reviews and things of this kind that appear in the Academy every year, are always extremely bad; while the very same subjects treated in black and white in the *Graphic* or the *London News* are excellent. Besides, if we want to understand the history of a nation through the medium of art, it is to the imaginative and ideal arts that we have to go and not to the arts that are definitely imitative. The visible aspect of life no longer contains for us the secret of life's spirit. Probably it never did contain it. And, if Mr. Barker's *Waterloo Banquet* and Mr. Frith's *Marriage of the Prince of Wales* are examples of healthy historic art, the less we have of such art the better. However, Mr. Bayliss is full of the most ardent faith and speaks quite gravely of genuine portraits of St. John, St. Peter and St. Paul dating from the first century, and of the establishment by the Israelites of a school of art in the wilderness under the now little appreciated Bezaleel. He is a pleasant, picturesque writer, but he should not speak about art. Art is a sealed book to him.

The Enchanted Island. By Wyke Bayliss, F.S.A., President of the Royal Society of British Artists. (Allen and Co.)

SOME LITERARY NOTES—II

(*Woman's World*, February 1889.)

'The various collectors of Irish folk-lore,' says Mr. W. B. Yeats in his charming little book *Fairy and Folk Tales of the Irish Peasantry*, 'have, from our point of view, one great merit, and from the point of view of others, one great fault.'

They have made their work literature rather than science, and told us of the Irish peasantry rather than of the primitive religion of mankind, or whatever else the folk-lorists are on the gad after. To be considered scientists they should have tabulated all their tales in forms like grocers' bills—item the fairy king, item the queen. Instead of this they have caught the very voice of the people, the very pulse of life, each giving what was most noticed in his day. Croker and Lover, full of the ideas of harum-scarum Irish gentility, saw everything humorised. The impulse of the Irish literature of their time came from a class that did not—mainly for political reasons—take the populace seriously, and imagined the country as a humorist's Arcadia; its passion, its gloom, its tragedy, they knew nothing of. What they did was not wholly false; they merely magnified an irresponsible type, found oftenest among boatmen, carmen, and gentlemen's servants, into the type of a whole nation, and created the stage Irishman. The writers of 'Forty-eight, and the famine combined, burst their bubble. Their work had the dash as well as the shallowness of an ascendant and idle class, and in Croker is touched everywhere with beauty—a gentle Arcadian beauty. Carleton, a peasant born, has in many of his stories, . . . more especially in his ghost stories, a much more serious way with him, for all his humour. Kennedy, an old bookseller in Dublin, who seems to have had a something of genuine belief in the fairies, comes next in time. He has far less literary faculty, but is wonderfully accurate, giving often the very words the stories were told in. But the best book since Croker is Lady Wilde's Ancient Legends. The humour has all given way to pathos and tenderness. We have here the innermost heart of the Celt in the moments he has grown to love through years of persecution, when, cushioning himself about with dreams, and hearing fairy-songs in the twilight, he ponders on the soul and on the dead. Here is the Celt, only it is the Celt dreaming.

Into a volume of very moderate dimensions, and of extremely moderate price, Mr. Yeats has collected together the most characteristic of our Irish folklore stories, grouping them together according to subject. First come *The Trooping Fairies*. The peasants say that these are 'fallen angels who were not good enough to be saved, nor bad enough to be lost'; but the Irish antiquarians see in them 'the gods of pagan Ireland,' who, 'when no longer worshipped and fed with offerings, dwindled away in the popular imagination, and now are only a few spans high.' Their chief occupations are feasting, fighting, making love, and playing the most beautiful music. 'They have only one industrious person amongst them, the *lepra-caun*—the shoemaker.' It is his duty to repair their shoes when they wear them out with dancing. Mr. Yeats tells us that 'near the village of Ballisodare is a little woman who lived amongst them seven years. When she came home she had no toes—she had danced them off.' On May Eve, every seventh year, they fight for the harvest, for the best ears of grain belong to them. An old man informed Mr. Yeats that he saw them fight once, and that they tore the thatch off a house. 'Had any one else been near they would merely have seen a great wind whirling everything into the air as it passed.' When the wind drives the leaves and straws before it, 'that is the fairies, and the peasants take off their hats and say "God bless them."' When they are gay, they sing. Many of the most beautiful tunes of Ireland 'are only their music, caught up by eavesdroppers.' No prudent peasant would hum *The Pretty Girl Milking the Cow* near a fairy rath, 'for they are jealous, and do not like to hear their songs on clumsy mortal lips.' Blake once saw a fairy's funeral. But this, as Mr. Yeats points out, must have been an English fairy, for the Irish fairies never die; they are immortal.

Then come *The Solitary Fairies*, amongst whom we find the little *Lepracaun* mentioned above. He has grown very rich, as he possesses all the treasure-crocks buried in war-time. In the early part of this century, according to Croker, they used to show in Tipperary a little shoe forgotten by the fairy shoemaker. Then there are two rather disreputable little fairies—the *Cluricaun*, who gets intoxicated in gentlemen's cellars, and the Red Man, who plays unkind practical jokes. 'The *Fear-Gorta* (Man of Hunger) is an emaciated phantom that goes through the land in famine time, begging an alms and bringing good luck to the giver.' The *Water-sheerie* is 'own brother to the English Jack-o'-Lantern.' 'The *Leanhaun Shee* (fairy mistress) seeks the love of mortals. If they refuse, she must be their slave; if they consent, they are hers, and can only escape by finding another to take their place. The fairy lives on their life, and they waste away. Death is no escape from her. She is the Gaelic muse, for she gives inspiration to those she persecutes. The Gaelic poets die young, for she is restless, and will not let them remain long on earth.' The *Pooka* is essentially an animal spirit, and some have considered him the forefather of Shakespeare's 'Puck.' He lives on solitary mountains, and among old ruins 'grown monstrous with much solitude,' and 'is of the race of the nightmare.' 'He has many shapes—is now a horse, . . . now a goat, now an eagle. Like all spirits, he is only half in the world of form.' The *banshee* does not care much for our democratic levelling tendencies; she loves only old families, and despises the *parvenu* or the *nouveau riche*. When more than one banshee is present, and they wail and sing in chorus, it is for the death of some holy or great one. An omen that sometimes accompanies the banshee is '. . . an immense black coach, mounted by a coffin, and drawn by headless horses driven by a *Dullahan*.' A *Dullahan* is the most terrible thing in the world. In 1807 two of the sentries stationed outside St. James's Park saw one climbing the railings, and died of fright. Mr. Yeats suggests that they are possibly 'descended from that Irish giant who swam across the Channel with his head in his teeth.'

Then come the stories of ghosts, of saints and priests, and of giants. The ghosts live in a state intermediary between this world and the next. They are held there by some earthly longing or affection, or some duty unfulfilled, or anger against the living; they are those who are too good for hell, and too bad for heaven. Sometimes they 'take the forms of insects, especially of butterflies.' The author of the *Parochial Survey of Ireland* 'heard a woman say to a child who was chasing a butterfly, "How do you know it is not the soul of your grandfather?" On November eve they are abroad, and dance with the fairies.' As for the saints and priests, 'there are no martyrs in the stories.' That ancient chronicler Giraldus Cambrensis 'taunted the Archbishop of Cashel, because no one in Ireland had received the crown of martyrdom. "Our people may be barbarous," the prelate answered, "but they have never lifted their hands against God's saints; but now that a people have come amongst us who know how to make them (it was just after the English invasion), we shall have martyrs plentifully."' The giants were the old pagan heroes of Ireland, who grew bigger and bigger, just as the gods grew smaller and smaller. The fact is they did not wait for offerings; they took them *vi et armis*.

Some of the prettiest stories are those that cluster round *Tír-na-n-Og*. This is the Country of the Young, 'for age and death have not found it; neither tears nor loud laughter have gone near it.' 'One man has gone there and returned. The bard, Oisen, who wandered away on a white horse, moving on the surface of the foam with his fairy Niamh lived there three hundred years, and then returned looking for his comrades. The moment his foot touched the earth his three hundred years fell on him, and he was bowed double, and his beard swept the ground. He described his sojourn in the Land of Youth to Patrick before he died.' Since then, according to Mr. Yeats, 'many have seen it in many places; some in the depths of lakes, and have heard rising therefrom a vague sound of bells; more have seen it far off on the horizon, as they peered out from the western cliffs. Not three years ago a fisherman imagined that he saw it.'

Mr. Yeats has certainly done his work very well. He has shown great critical capacity in his selection of the stories, and his little introductions are charmingly written. It is delightful to come across a collection of purely imaginative work, and Mr. Yeats has a very quick instinct in finding out the best and the most beautiful things in Irish folklore. I am also glad to see that he has not confined himself entirely to prose, but has included Allingham's lovely poem on *The Fairies*:

Up the airy mountain,
  Down the rushy glen,
We daren't go a-hunting
  For fear of little men;
Wee folk, good folk,
  Trooping all together;
Green jacket, red cap,
  And white owl's feather!

  Down along the rocky shore
  Some make their home,
They live on crispy pancakes
  Of yellow tide-foam;
Some in the reeds
  Of the black mountain lake,
With frogs for their watch-dogs
  All night awake.

  High on the hill-top
  The old King sits;
He is now so old and gray
  He's nigh lost his wits.
With a bridge of white mist
  Columbkill he crosses,
On his stately journeys
  From Slieveleague to Rosses;
Or going up with music,

On cold starry nights,
To sup with the Queen
Of the gay Northern Lights.

All lovers of fairy tales and folklore should get this little book. *The Horned Women*, *The Priest's Soul*, {411} and *Teig O'Kane*, are really marvellous in their way; and, indeed, there is hardly a single story that is not worth reading and thinking over.

The wittiest writer in France at present is a woman. That clever, that *spirituelle grande dame*, who has adopted the pseudonym of 'Gyp,' has in her own country no rival. Her wit, her delicate and delightful *esprit*, her fascinating modernity, and her light, happy touch, give her a unique position in that literary movement which has taken for its object the reproduction of contemporary life. Such books as *Autour du Mariage*, *Autour du Divorce*, and *Le Petit Bob*, are, in their way, little playful masterpieces, and the only work in England that we could compare with them is Violet Fane's *Edwin and Angelina Papers*. To the same brilliant pen which gave us these wise and witty studies of modern life we owe now a more serious, more elaborate production. *Helen Davenant* is as earnestly wrought out as it is cleverly conceived. If it has a fault, it is that it is too full of matter. Out of the same material a more economical writer would have made two novels and half a dozen psychological studies for publication in American magazines. Thackeray once met Bishop Wilberforce at dinner at Dean Stanley's, and, after listening to the eloquent prelate's extraordinary flow and fund of stories, remarked to his neighbour, 'I could not afford to spend at that rate.' Violet Fane is certainly lavishly extravagant of incident, plot, and character. But we must not quarrel with richness of subject-matter at a time when tenuity of purpose and meagreness of motive seem to be becoming the dominant notes of contemporary fiction. The side-issues of the story are so complex that it is difficult, almost impossible, to describe the plot in any adequate manner. The interest centres round a young girl, Helen Davenant by name, who contracts a private and clandestine marriage with one of those mysterious and fascinating foreign noblemen who are becoming so invaluable to writers of fiction, either in narrative or dramatic form. Shortly after the marriage her husband is arrested for a terrible murder committed some years before in Russia, under the evil influence of occult magic and mesmerism. The crime was done in a hypnotic state, and, as described by Violet Fane, seems much more probable than the actual hypnotic experiments recorded in scientific publications. This is the supreme advantage that fiction possesses over fact. It can make things artistically probable; can call for imaginative and realistic credence; can, by force of mere style, compel us to believe. The ordinary novelists, by keeping close to the ordinary incidents of commonplace life, seem to me to abdicate half their power. Romance, at any rate, welcomes what is wonderful; the temper of wonder is part of her own secret; she loves what is strange and curious. But besides the marvels of occultism and hypnotism, there are many other things in *Helen Davenant* that are worthy of study. Violet Fane writes an admirable style. The opening chapter of the book, with its terrible poignant tragedy, is most powerfully written, and I cannot help wondering that the clever authoress cared to abandon, even for a moment, the superb psychological opportunity that this chapter affords. The touches of nature, the vivid sketches of high life, the subtle renderings of the phases and fancies of society, are also admirably done. *Helen Davenant* is certainly clever, and shows that Violet Fane can write prose that is as good as her verse, and can look at life not merely from the point of view of the poet, but also from the standpoint of the philosopher, the keen observer, the fine social critic. To be a fine social critic is no small thing, and to be able to incorporate in a work of fiction the results of such careful observation is to achieve what is out of the reach of many. The difficulty under which the novelists of our day labour seems to me to be this: if they do not go into society, their books are unreadable; and if they do go into society, they have no time left for writing. However, Violet Fane has solved the problem.

The chronicles which I am about to present to the reader are not the result of any conscious effort of the imagination. They are, as the title-page indicates, records of dreams occurring at intervals during the last ten years, and transcribed, pretty nearly in the order of their occurrence, from my diary. Written down as soon as possible after awaking from the slumber during which they presented themselves, these narratives, necessarily unstudied in style, and wanting in elegance of diction, have at least the merit of fresh and vivid colour; for they were committed to paper at a moment when the effect and impress of each successive vision were strong and forceful on the mind. . . .

The most remarkable features of the experiences I am about to record are the methodical consecutiveness of their sequences, and the intelligent purpose disclosed alike in the events witnessed and in the words heard or read. . . . I know of no parallel to this phenomenon, unless in the pages of Bulwer Lytton's romance entitled The Pilgrims of the Rhine, in which is related the story of a German student endowed with so marvellous a faculty of dreaming, that for him the normal conditions of sleeping and waking became reversed; his true life was that which he lived in his slumbers, and his hours of wakefulness appeared to him as so many uneventful and inactive intervals of arrest, occurring in an existence of intense and vivid interest which was wholly passed in the hypnotic state. . . .

During the whole period covered by these dreams I have been busily and almost continuously engrossed with scientific and literary pursuits, demanding accurate judgment and complete self-possession and rectitude of mind. At the time when many of the most vivid and remarkable visions occurred I was following my course as a student at the Paris Faculty of Medicine, preparing for examinations, daily visiting hospital wards as dresser, and attending lectures. Later, when I had taken my degree, I was engaged in the duties of my profession and in writing for the Press on scientific subjects. Neither had I ever taken opium, haschish, or other dream-producing agent. A cup of tea or coffee represents the extent of my indulgences in this direction. I mention these details in order to guard against inferences which might otherwise be drawn as to the genesis of my faculty.

It may, perhaps, be worthy of notice that by far the larger number of the dreams set down in this volume occurred towards dawn; sometimes even, after sunrise, during a 'second sleep.' A condition of fasting, united possibly with some subtle magnetic or other atmospheric state, seems, therefore, to be that most open to impressions of the kind.

This is the account given by the late Dr. Anna Kingsford of the genesis of her remarkable volume, *Dreams and Dream-Stories*; and certainly some of the stories, especially those entitled *Steepside*, *Beyond the Sunset*, and *The Village of Seers*, are well worth reading, though not intrinsically finer, either in motive or idea, than the general run of magazine stories. No one who had the privilege of knowing Mrs. Kingsford, who was one of the brilliant women of our day, can doubt for a single moment that these tales came to her in the way she describes; but to me the result is just a little disappointing. Perhaps, however, I expect too much. There is no reason whatsoever why the imagination should be finer in hours of dreaming than in its hours of waking. Mrs. Kingsford quotes a letter written by Jamblichus to Agathocles, in which he says: 'The soul has a twofold life, a lower and a higher. In sleep the soul is liberated from the constraint of the body, and enters, as an emancipated being, on its divine life of intelligence. The nobler part of the mind is thus united by abstraction to higher natures, and becomes a participant in the wisdom and foreknowledge of the gods. . . . The night-time of the body is the day-time of the soul.' But the great masterpieces of literature and the great secrets of wisdom have not been communicated in this way; and even in Coleridge's case, though *Kubla Khan* is wonderful, it is not more wonderful, while it is certainly less complete, than the *Ancient Mariner.*

As for the dreams themselves, which occupy the first portion of the book, their value, of course, depends chiefly on the value of the truths or predictions which they are supposed to impart. I must confess that most modern mysticism seems to me to be simply a method of imparting useless knowledge in a form that no one can understand. Allegory, parable, and vision have their high artistic uses, but their philosophical and scientific uses are very small. However, here is one of Mrs. Kingsford's dreams. It has a pleasant quaintness about it:

THE WONDERFUL SPECTACLES

I was walking alone on the sea-shore. The day was singularly clear and sunny. Inland lay the most beautiful landscape ever seen; and far off were ranges of tall hills, the highest peaks of which were white with glittering snows. Along the sands by the sea came towards me a man accoutred as a postman. He gave me a letter. It was from you. It ran thus:

'I have got hold of the earliest and most precious book extant. It was written before the world began. The text is easy enough to read; but the notes, which are very copious and numerous, are in such minute and obscure characters that I cannot make them out. I want you to get for me the spectacles which Swedenborg used to wear; not the smaller pair—those he gave to Hans Christian Andersen—but the large pair, and these seem to have got mislaid. I think they are Spinoza's make. You know, he was an optical-glass maker by profession, and the best we ever had. See if you can get them for me.'

When I looked up after reading this letter I saw the postman hastening away across the sands, and I cried out to him, 'Stop! how am I to send the answer? Will you not wait for it?'

He looked round, stopped, and came back to me.

'I have the answer here,' he said, tapping his letter-bag, 'and I shall deliver it immediately.'

'How can you have the answer before I have written it?' I asked. 'You are making a mistake.'

'No,' he said. 'In the city from which I come the replies are all written at the office, and sent out with the letters themselves. Your reply is in my bag.'

'Let me see it,' I said. He took another letter from his wallet, and gave it to me. I opened it, and read, in my own handwriting, this answer, addressed to you:

'The spectacles you want can be bought in London; but you will not be able to use them at once, for they have not been worn for many years, and they sadly want cleaning. This you will not be able to do yourself in London, because it is too dark there to see well, and because your fingers are not small enough to clean them properly. Bring them here to me, and I will do it for you.'

I gave this letter back to the postman. He smiled and nodded at me; and then I perceived, to my astonishment, that he wore a camel's-hair tunic round his waist. I had been on the point of addressing him—I know not why—as Hermes. But I now saw that he must be John the Baptist; and in my fright at having spoken to so great a Saint I awoke.

Mr. Maitland, who edits the present volume, and who was joint-author with Mrs. Kingsford of that curious book *The Perfect Way*, states in a footnote that in the present instance the dreamer knew nothing of Spinoza at the time, and was quite unaware that he was an optician; and the interpretation of the dream, as given by him, is that the spectacles in question were intended to represent Mrs. Kingsford's remarkable faculty of intuitional and interpretative perception. For a spiritual message fraught with such meaning, the mere form of this dream seems to me somewhat ignoble, and I cannot say that I like the blending of the postman with St. John the Baptist. However, from a psychological point of view, these dreams are interesting, and Mrs. Kingsford's book is undoubtedly a valuable addition to the literature of the mysticism of the nineteenth century.

* * * * *

The Romance of a Shop, by Miss Amy Levy, is a more mundane book, and deals with the adventures of some young ladies who open a photographic studio in Baker Street to the horror of some of their fashionable relatives. It is so brightly and pleasantly written that the sudden introduction of a tragedy into it seems violent and unnecessary. It lacks the true tragic temper, and without this temper in literature all misfortunes and miseries seem somewhat mean and ordinary. With this exception the book is admirably done, and the style is clever and full of quick observation. Observation is perhaps the most valuable faculty for a writer of fiction. When novelists reflect and moralise, they are, as a rule, dull. But to observe life with keen vision and quick intellect, to catch its many modes of expression, to seize upon the subtlety, or satire, or dramatic quality of its situations, and to render life for us with some spirit of distinction and fine selection—this, I fancy, should be the aim of the modern realistic novelist. It would be, perhaps, too much to say that Miss Levy has distinction; this is the rarest quality in modern literature, though not a few of its masters are modern; but she has many other qualities which are admirable.

* * * * *

Faithful and Unfaithful is a powerful but not very pleasing novel. However, the object of most modern fiction is not to give pleasure to the artistic instinct, but rather to portray life vividly for us, to draw attention to social anomalies, and social forms of injustice. Many of our novelists are really pamphleteers, reformers masquerading as story-tellers, earnest sociologists seeking to mend as well as to mirror life. The heroine, or rather martyr, of Miss Margaret Lee's story is a very noble and graciously Puritanic American girl, who is married at the age of eighteen to a man whom she insists on regarding as a hero. Her husband cannot live in the high rarefied atmosphere of idealism with which she surrounds him; her firm and fearless faith in him becomes a factor in his degradation. 'You are too good for me,' he says to her in a finely conceived scene at the end of the book; 'we have not an idea, an inclination, or a passion in common. I'm sick and tired of seeming to live up to a standard that is entirely beyond my reach and my desire. We make each other miserable! I can't pull you down, and for ten years you have been exhausting yourself in vain efforts to raise me to your level. The thing must end!' He asks her to divorce him, but she refuses. He then abandons her, and availing himself of those curious facilities for breaking the marriage-tie that prevail in the United States, succeeds in divorcing her without her consent, and without her knowledge. The book is certainly characteristic of an age so practical and so literary as ours, an age in which all social reforms have been preceded and have been largely influenced by fiction. *Faithful and Unfaithful* seems to point to some coming change in the marriage-laws of America.

(1) *Fairy and Folk Tales of the Irish Peasantry*. Edited and Selected by W. B. Yeats. (Walter Scott.)

(2) *Helen Davenant*. By Violet Fane. (Chapman and Hall.)

(3) *Dreams and Dream-Stories*. By Dr. Anna Kingsford. (Redway.)

(4) *The Romance of a Shop*. By Amy Levy. (Fisher Unwin.)

(5) *Faithful and Unfaithful*. By Margaret Lee. (Macmillan and Co.)

ONE OF THE BIBLES OF THE WORLD

(Pall Mall Gazette, February 12, 1889.)

The Kalevala is one of those poems that Mr. William Morris once described as 'The Bibles of the World.' It takes its place as a national epic beside the Homeric poems, the Niebelunge, the Shahnameth and the Mahabharata, and the admirable translation just published by Mr. John Martin Crawford is sure to be welcomed by all scholars and lovers of primitive poetry. In his very interesting preface Mr. Crawford claims for the Finns that they began earlier than any other European nation to collect and preserve their ancient folklore. In the seventeenth century we meet men of literary tastes like Palmsköld who tried to collect and interpret the various national songs of the fen-dwellers of the North. But the *Kalevala* proper was collected by two great Finnish scholars of our own century, Zacharias Topelius and Elias Lönnrot. Both were practising physicians, and in this capacity came into frequent contact with the people of Finland. Topelius, who collected eighty epical fragments of the *Kalevala*, spent the last eleven years of his life in bed, afflicted with a fatal disease. This misfortune, however, did not damp his enthusiasm. Mr. Crawford tells us that he used to invite the wandering Finnish merchants to his bedside and induce them to sing their heroic poems which he copied down as soon as they were uttered, and that whenever he heard of a renowned Finnish minstrel he did all in his power to bring the song-man to his house in order that he might gather new fragments of the national epic. Lönnrot travelled over the whole country, on horseback, in reindeer sledges and in canoes, collecting the old poems and songs from the hunters, the fishermen and the shepherds. The people gave him every assistance, and he had the good fortune to come across an old peasant, one of the oldest of the *runolainen* in the Russian province of Wuokinlem, who was by far the most renowned song-man of the country, and from him he got many of the most splendid runes of the poem. And certainly the *Kalevala*, as it stands, is one of the world's great poems. It is perhaps hardly accurate to describe it as an epic. It lacks the central unity of a true epic in our sense of the word. It has many heroes beside Wainomoinen and is, properly speaking, a collection of folk-songs and ballads. Of its antiquity there is no doubt. It is thoroughly pagan from beginning to end, and even the legend of the Virgin Mariatta to whom the Sun tells where 'her golden babe lies hidden'—

Yonder is thy golden infant,
There thy holy babe lies sleeping
Hidden to his belt in water,
Hidden in the reeds and rushes—

is, according to all scholars, essentially pre-Christian in origin. The gods are chiefly gods of air and water and forest. The highest is the sky-god Ukks who is 'The Father of the Breezes,' 'The Shepherd of the Lamb-Clouds'; the lightning is his sword, the rainbow is his bow; his skirt sparkles with fire, his stockings are blue and his shoes crimson-coloured. The daughters of the Sun and Moon sit on the scarlet rims of the clouds and weave the rays of light into a gleaming web. Untar presides over fogs and mists, and passes them through a silver sieve before sending them to the earth. Ahto, the wave-god, lives with 'his cold and cruel-hearted spouse,' Wellamo, at the bottom of the sea in the chasm of the Salmon-Rocks, and possesses the priceless treasure of the Sampo, the talisman of success. When the branches of the primitive oak-trees shut out the light of the sun from the Northland, Pikku-Mies (the Pygmy) emerged from the sea in a suit of copper, with a copper hatchet in his belt, and having grown to a giant's stature felled the huge oak with the third stroke of his axe. Wirokannas is 'The Green-robed Priest of the Forest,' and Tapio, who has a coat of tree-moss and a high-crowned hat of fir-leaves, is 'The Gracious God of the Woodlands.' Otso, the bear, is the 'Honey-Paw of the Mountains,' the 'Fur-robed Forest Friend.' In everything, visible and invisible, there is God, a divine presence. There are three worlds, and they are all peopled with divinities.

As regards the poem itself, it is written in trochaic eight-syllabled lines with alliteration and the part-line echo, the metre which Longfellow adopted for *Hiawatha*. One of its distinguishing characteristics is its wonderful passion for nature and for the beauty of natural objects. Lemenkainen says to Tapio:

Sable-bearded God of forests,
In thy hat and coat of ermine,
Robe thy trees in finest fibres,
Deck thy groves in richest fabrics,
Give the fir-trees shining silver,
Deck with gold the slender balsams,
Give the spruces copper-belting,
And the pine-trees silver girdles,
Give the birches golden flowers,
Deck their stems with silver fretwork,
This their garb in former ages
When the days and nights were brighter,

When the fir-trees shone like sunlight,
And the birches like the moonbeams;
Honey breathe throughout the forest,
Settled in the glens and highlands,
Spices in the meadow-borders,
Oil outpouring from the lowlands.

All handicrafts and art-work are, as in Homer, elaborately described:

Then the smiter Ilmarinen
The eternal artist-forgeman,
In the furnace forged an eagle
From the fire of ancient wisdom,
For this giant bird of magic
Forged he talons out of iron,
And his beak of steel and copper;
Seats himself upon the eagle,
On his back between the wing-bones
Thus addresses he his creature,
Gives the bird of fire this order.
Mighty eagle, bird of beauty,
Fly thou whither I direct thee,
To Tuoni's coal-black river,
To the blue-depths of the Death-stream,
Seize the mighty fish of Mana,
Catch for me this water-monster.

And Wainamoinen's boat-building is one of the great incidents of the poem:

Wainamoinen old and skilful,
The eternal wonder-worker,
Builds his vessel with enchantment,
Builds his boat by art and magic,
From the timber of the oak-tree,
Forms its posts and planks and flooring.
Sings a song and joins the framework;
Sings a second, sets the siding;
Sings a third time, sets the rowlocks;
Fashions oars, and ribs, and rudder,
Joins the sides and ribs together.

. . . . .

Now he decks his magic vessel,
Paints the boat in blue and scarlet,
Trims in gold the ship's forecastle,
Decks the prow in molten silver;
Sings his magic ship down gliding,
On the cylinders of fir-tree;
Now erects the masts of pine-wood,
On each mast the sails of linen,
Sails of blue, and white, and scarlet,
Woven into finest fabric.

All the characteristics of a splendid antique civilisation are mirrored in this marvellous poem, and Mr. Crawford's admirable translation should make the wonderful heroes of Suomi song as familiar if not as dear to our people as the heroes of the great Ionian epic.

The Kalevala, the Epic Poem of Finland. Translated into English by John Martin Crawford. (G. P. Putnam's Sons.)

POETICAL SOCIALISTS

(*Pall Mall Gazette*, February 15, 1889.)

Mr. Stopford Brooke said some time ago that Socialism and the socialistic spirit would give our poets nobler and loftier themes for song, would widen their sympathies and enlarge the horizon of their vision and would touch, with the fire and fervour of a new faith, lips that had else been silent, hearts that but for this fresh gospel had been cold. What Art gains from contemporary events is always a fascinating problem and a problem that is not easy to solve. It is, however, certain that Socialism starts well equipped. She has her poets and her painters, her art lecturers and her cunning designers, her powerful orators and her clever writers. If she fails it will not be for lack of expression. If she succeeds her triumph will not be a triumph of mere brute force. The first thing that strikes one, as one looks over the list of contributors to Mr. Edward Carpenter's *Chants of Labour*, is the curious variety of their several occupations, the wide differences of social position that exist between them, and the strange medley of men whom a common passion has for the moment united. The editor is a 'Science lecturer'; he is followed by a draper and a porter; then we have two late Eton masters and then two bootmakers; and these are, in their turn, succeeded by an ex-Lord Mayor of Dublin, a bookbinder, a photographer, a steel-worker and an authoress. On one page we have a journalist, a draughtsman and a music teacher; and on another a Civil servant, a machine fitter, a medical student, a cabinet-maker and a minister of the Church of Scotland. Certainly, it is no ordinary movement that can bind together in close brotherhood men of such dissimilar pursuits, and when we mention that Mr. William Morris is one of the singers, and that Mr. Walter Crane has designed the cover and frontispiece of the book, we cannot but feel that, as we pointed out before, Socialism starts well equipped.

As for the songs themselves, some of them, to quote from the editor's preface, are 'purely revolutionary, others are Christian in tone; there are some that might be called merely material in their tendency, while many are of a highly ideal and visionary character.' This is, on the whole, very promising. It shows that Socialism is not going to allow herself to be trammelled by any hard and fast creed or to be stereotyped into an iron formula. She welcomes many and multiform natures. She rejects none and has room for all. She has the attraction of a wonderful personality and touches the heart of one and the brain of another, and draws this man by his hatred of injustice, and his neighbour by his faith in the future, and a third, it may be, by his love of art or by his wild worship of a lost and buried past. And all of this is well. For, to make men Socialists is nothing, but to make Socialism human is a great thing.

They are not of any very high literary value, these poems that have been so dexterously set to music. They are meant to be sung, not to be read. They are rough, direct and vigorous, and the tunes are stirring and familiar. Indeed, almost any mob could warble them with ease. The transpositions that have been made are rather amusing. *'Twas in Trafalgar Square* is set to the tune of *'Twas in Trafalgar's Bay*; *Up, Ye People!* a very revolutionary song by Mr. John Gregory, boot-maker, with a refrain of

Up, ye People! or down into your graves!
Cowards ever will be slaves!

is to be sung to the tune of *Rule, Britannia!* the old melody of *The Vicar of Bray* is to accompany the new *Ballade of Law and Order*— which, however, is not a ballade at all—and to the air of *Here's to the Maiden of Bashful Fifteen* the democracy of the future is to thunder forth one of Mr. T. D. Sullivan's most powerful and pathetic lyrics. It is clear that the Socialists intend to carry on the musical education of the people simultaneously with their education in political science and, here as elsewhere, they seem to be entirely free from any narrow bias or formal prejudice. Mendelssohn is followed by Moody and Sankey; the *Wacht am Rhein* stands side by side with the *Marseillaise*; *Lillibulero*, a chorus from *Norma*, *John Brown* and an air from Beethoven's *Ninth Symphony* are all equally delightful to them. They sing the National Anthem in Shelley's version and chant William Morris's *Voice of Toil* to the flowing numbers of *Ye Banks and Braes of Bonny Doon*. Victor Hugo talks somewhere of the terrible cry of 'Le Tigre Populaire,' but it is evident from Mr. Carpenter's book that should the Revolution ever break out in England we shall have no inarticulate roar but, rather, pleasant glees and graceful part-songs. The change is certainly for the better. Nero fiddled while Rome was burning—at least, inaccurate historians say he did; but it is for the building up of an eternal city that the Socialists of our day are making music, and they have complete confidence in the art instincts of the people.

They say that the people are brutal—
That their instincts of beauty are dead—
Were it so, shame on those who condemn them
To the desperate struggle for bread.
But they lie in their throats when they say it,
For the people are tender at heart,
And a wellspring of beauty lies hidden
Beneath their life's fever and smart,

is a stanza from one of the poems in this volume, and the feeling expressed in these words is paramount everywhere. The Reformation gained much from the use of popular hymn-tunes, and the Socialists seem determined to gain by similar means a similar hold upon the people. However, they must not be too sanguine about the result. The walls of Thebes rose up to the sound of music, and Thebes was a very dull city indeed.

Chants of Labour: *A Song-Book of the People*. With Music. Edited by Edward Carpenter. With Designs by Walter Crane. (Swan Sonnenschein and Co.)

MR. BRANDER MATTHEWS' ESSAYS

(*Pall Mall Gazette*, February 27, 1889.)

'If you to have your book criticized favorably, give yourself a good notice in the Preface!' is the golden rule laid down for the guidance of authors by Mr. Brander Matthews in an amusing essay on the art of preface-writing and, true to his own theory, he announces his volume as 'the most interesting, the most entertaining, and the most instructive book of the decade.' Entertaining it certainly is in parts. The essay on Poker, for instance, is very brightly and pleasantly written. Mr. Proctor objected to Poker on the somewhat trivial ground that it was a form of lying, and on the more serious ground that it afforded special opportunities for cheating; and, indeed, he regarded the mere existence of the game outside gambling dens as 'one of the most portentous phenomena of American civilisation.' Mr. Brander Matthews points out, in answer to these grave charges, that Bluffing is merely a *suppressio veri* and that it requires a great deal of physical courage on the part of the player. As for the cheating, he claims that Poker affords no more opportunities for the exercise of this art than either Whist or Ecarté, though he admits that the proper attitude towards an opponent whose good luck is unduly persistent is that of the German-American who, finding four aces in his hand, was naturally about to bet heavily, when a sudden thought struck him and he inquired, 'Who dole dem carts?' 'Jakey Einstein' was the answer. 'Jakey Einstein?' he repeated, laying down his hand; 'den I pass out.'

The history of the game will be found very interesting by all card-lovers. Like most of the distinctly national products of America, it seems to have been imported from abroad and can be traced back to an Italian game in the fifteenth century. Euchre was probably acclimatised on the Mississippi by the Canadian *voyageurs*, being a form of the French game of *Triomphe*. It was a Kentucky citizen who, desiring to give his sons a few words of solemn advice for their future guidance in life, had them summoned to his deathbed and said to them, 'Boys, when you go down the river to Orleens jest you beware of a game called Yucker where the jack takes the ace;—it's unchristian!'—after which warning he lay back and died in peace. And 'it was Euchre which the two gentlemen were playing in a boat on the Missouri River when a bystander, shocked by the frequency with which one of the players turned up the jack, took the liberty of warning the other player that the winner was dealing from the bottom, to which the loser, secure in his power of self-protection, answered gruffly, "Well, suppose he is—it's his deal, isn't it?"'

The chapter *On the Antiquity of Jests*, with its suggestion of an International Exhibition of Jokes, is capital. Such an exhibition, Mr. Matthews remarks, would at least dispel any lingering belief in the old saying that there are only thirty-eight good stories in existence and that thirty-seven of these cannot be told before ladies; and the Retrospective Section would certainly be the constant resort of any true folklorist. For most of the good stories of our time are really folklore, myth survivals, echoes of the past. The two well-known American proverbs, 'We have had a hell of a time' and 'Let the other man walk' are both traced back by Mr. Matthews: the first to Walpole's letters, and the other to a story Poggio tells of an inhabitant of Perugia who walked in melancholy because he could not pay his debts. 'Vah, stulte,' was the advice given to him, 'leave anxiety to your creditors!' and even Mr. William M. Evart's brilliant repartee when he was told that Washington once threw a dollar across the Natural Bridge in Virginia, 'In those days a dollar went so much farther than it does now!' seems to be the direct descendant of a witty remark of Foote's, though we must say that in this case we prefer the child to the father. The essay *On the French Spoken by Those who do not Speak French* is also cleverly written and, indeed, on every subject, except literature, Mr. Matthews is well worth reading.

On literature and literary subjects he is certainly 'sadly to seek.' The essay on *The Ethics of Plagiarism*, with its laborious attempt to rehabilitate Mr. Rider Haggard and its foolish remarks on Poe's admirable paper *Mr. Longfellow and Other Plagiarists*, is extremely dull and commonplace and, in the elaborate comparison that he draws between Mr. Frederick Locker and Mr. Austin Dobson, the author of *Pen and Ink* shows that he is quite devoid of any real critical faculty or of any fine sense of the difference between ordinary society verse and the exquisite work of a very perfect artist in poetry. We have no objection to Mr. Matthews likening Mr. Locker to Mr. du Maurier, and Mr. Dobson to Randolph Caldecott and Mr. Edwin Abbey. Comparisons of this kind, though extremely silly, do not do much harm. In fact, they mean nothing and are probably not intended to mean anything. Upon the other hand, we really must protest against Mr. Matthews' efforts to confuse the poetry of Piccadilly with the poetry of Parnassus. To tell us, for instance, that Mr. Austin Dobson's verse 'has not the condensed clearness nor the incisive vigor of Mr. Locker's' is really too bad even for Transatlantic criticism. Nobody who lays claim to the slightest knowledge of literature and the forms of literature should ever bring the two names into conjunction. Mr. Locker has written some pleasant *vers de société*, some tuneful trifles in rhyme admirably suited for ladies' albums and for magazines. But to mention Herrick and Suckling and Mr. Austin Dobson in connection with him is absurd. He is not a poet. Mr. Dobson, upon the other hand, has produced work that is absolutely classical in its exquisite beauty of form. Nothing more artistically perfect in its way than the *Lines to a Greek Girl* has been written in our time. This little poem will be remembered in literature as long as *Thyrsis* is remembered, and *Thyrsis* will never be forgotten. Both have that note of distinction that is so rare in these days of violence, exaggeration and rhetoric. Of course, to suggest, as Mr. Matthews does, that Mr. Dobson's poems belong to 'the literature of power' is ridiculous. Power is not their aim, nor is it their effect. They have other qualities, and in their own delicately limited sphere they have no contemporary rivals; they have none even second to them. However, Mr. Matthews is quite undaunted and tries to drag poor Mr. Locker out of Piccadilly, where he was really quite in his element, and to set him on Parnassus where he has no right to be and where he would not claim to be. He praises his work with the recklessness of an eloquent auctioneer. These very commonplace and slightly vulgar lines on *A Human Skull*:

It may have held (to shoot some random shots)
  Thy brains, Eliza Fry! or Baron Byron's;
The wits of Nelly Gwynne or Doctor Watts—
  Two quoted bards. Two philanthropic sirens

But this, I trust, is clearly understood,
  If man or woman, if adored or hated—
Whoever own'd this Skull was not so good
  Nor quite so bad as many may have stated;

are considered by him to be 'sportive and brightsome' and full of 'playful humor,' and 'two things especially are to be noted in them—individuality and directness of expression.' Individuality and directness of expression! We wonder what Mr. Matthews thinks these words mean.

Unfortunate Mr. Locker with his uncouth American admirer! How he must blush to read these heavy panegyrics! Indeed, Mr. Matthews himself has at least one fit of remorse for his attempt to class Mr. Locker's work with the work of Mr. Austin Dobson, but like most fits of remorse it leads to nothing. On the very next page we have the complaint that Mr. Dobson's verse has not 'the condensed clearness' and the 'incisive vigor' of Mr. Locker's. Mr. Matthews should confine himself to his clever journalistic articles on Euchre, Poker, bad French and old jokes. On these subjects he can, to use an expression of his own, 'write funny.' He 'writes funny,' too, upon literature, but the fun is not quite so amusing.

Pen and Ink: *Papers on Subjects of More or Less Importance*. By Brander Matthews. (Longmans, Green and Co.)

SOME LITERARY NOTES—III

(*Woman's World*, March 1889.)

Miss Nesbit has already made herself a name as a writer of graceful and charming verse, and though her last volume, *Leaves of Life*, does not show any distinct advance on her former work, it still fully maintains the high standard already achieved, and justifies the reputation of the author. There are some wonderfully pretty poems in it, poems full of quick touches of fancy, and of pleasant ripples of rhyme; and here and there a poignant note of passion flashes across the song, as a scarlet thread flashes through the shuttlerace of a loom, giving a new value to the delicate tints, and bringing the scheme of colour to a higher and more perfect key. In Miss Nesbit's earlier volume, the *Lays and Legends*, as it was called, there was an attempt to give poetic form to humanitarian dreams and socialistic aspirations; but the poems that dealt with these subjects were, on the whole, the least successful of the collection; and with the quick, critical instinct of an artist, Miss Nesbit seems to have recognised this. In the present volume, at any rate, such poems are rare, and these few felicitous verses give us the poet's defence:

> A singer sings of rights and wrongs,
>   Of world's ideals vast and bright,
> And feels the impotence of songs
>   To scourge the wrong or help the right;
> And only writhes to feel how vain
>   Are songs as weapons for his fight;
> And so he turns to love again,
>   And sings of love for heart's delight.
>
> For heart's delight the singers bind
>   The wreath of roses round the head,
> And will not loose it lest they find
>   Time victor, and the roses dead.
> 'Man can but sing of what he knows—
>   I saw the roses fresh and red!'
> And so they sing the deathless rose,
>   With withered roses garlanded.
>
> And some within their bosom hide
>   Their rose of love still fresh and fair,
> And walk in silence, satisfied
>   To keep its folded fragrance rare.
> And some—who bear a flag unfurled—
>   Wreathe with their rose the flag they bear,
> And sing their banner for the world,
>   And for their heart the roses there.
>
> Yet thus much choice in singing is;
>   We sing the good, the true, the just,
> Passionate duty turned to bliss,
>   And honour growing out of trust.
> Freedom we sing, and would not lose
>   Her lightest footprint in life's dust.
> We sing of her because we choose,
>   We sing of love because we must.

Certainly Miss Nesbit is at her best when she sings of love and nature. Here she is close to her subject, and her temperament gives colour and form to the various dramatic moods that are either suggested by Nature herself or brought to Nature for interpretation. This, for instance, is very sweet and graceful:

> When all the skies with snow were grey,
>   And all the earth with snow was white,
> I wandered down a still wood way,
>   And there I met my heart's delight
> Slow moving through the silent wood,
> The spirit of its solitude:
>   The brown birds and the lichened tree
>   Seemed less a part of it than she.
>
> Where pheasants' feet and rabbits' feet
>   Had marked the snow with traces small,
> I saw the footprints of my sweet—
>   The sweetest woodland thing of all.
> With Christmas roses in her hand,
> One heart-beat's space I saw her stand;
>   And then I let her pass, and stood
>   Lone in an empty world of wood.

And though by that same path I've passed
Down that same woodland every day,
That meeting was the first and last,
And she is hopelessly away.
I wonder was she really there—
Her hands, and eyes, and lips, and hair?
Or was it but my dreaming sent
Her image down the way I went?

Empty the woods are where we met—
They will be empty in the spring;
The cowslip and the violet
Will die without her gathering.
But dare I dream one radiant day
Red rose-wreathed she will pass this way
Across the glad and honoured grass;
And then—I will not let her pass.

And this Dedication, with its tender silver-grey notes of colour, is charming:

In any meadow where your feet may tread,
In any garland that your love may wear,
May be the flower whose hidden fragrance shed
Wakes some old hope or numbs some old despair,
And makes life's grief not quite so hard to bear,
And makes life's joy more poignant and more dear
Because of some delight dead many a year.

Or in some cottage garden there may be
The flower whose scent is memory for you;
The sturdy southern-wood, the frail sweet-pea,
Bring back the swallow's cheep, the pigeon's coo,
And youth, and hope, and all the dreams they knew,
The evening star, the hedges grey with mist,
The silent porch where Love's first kiss was kissed.

So in my garden may you chance to find
Or royal rose or quiet meadow flower,
Whose scent may be with some dear dream entwined,
And give you back the ghost of some sweet hour,
As lilies fragrant from an August shower,
Or airs of June that over bean-fields blow,
Bring back the sweetness of my long ago.

All through the volume we find the same dexterous refining of old themes, which is indeed the best thing that our lesser singers can give us, and a thing always delightful. There is no garden so well tilled but it can bear another blossom, and though the subject-matter of Miss Nesbit's book is as the subject-matter of almost all books of poetry, she can certainly lend a new grace and a subtle sweetness to almost everything on which she writes.

The Wanderings of Oisin and Other Poems is from the clever pen of Mr. W. B. Yeats, whose charming anthology of Irish fairy-tales I had occasion to notice in a recent number of the *Woman's World*. {437} It is, I believe, the first volume of poems that Mr. Yeats has published, and it is certainly full of promise. It must be admitted that many of the poems are too fragmentary, too incomplete. They read like stray scenes out of unfinished plays, like things only half remembered, or, at best, but dimly seen. But the architectonic power of construction, the power to build up and make perfect a harmonious whole, is nearly always the latest, as it certainly is the highest, development of the artistic temperament. It is somewhat unfair to expect it in early work. One quality Mr. Yeats has in a marked degree, a quality that is not common in the work of our minor poets, and is therefore all the more welcome to us—I mean the romantic temper. He is essentially Celtic, and his verse, at its best, is Celtic also. Strongly influenced by Keats, he seems to study how to 'load every rift with ore,' yet is more fascinated by the beauty of words than by the beauty of metrical music. The spirit that dominates the whole book is perhaps more valuable than any individual poem or particular passage, but this from *The Wanderings of Oisin* is worth quoting. It describes the ride to the Island of Forgetfulness:

And the ears of the horse went sinking away in the hollow light,
For, as drift from a sailor slow drowning the gleams of the world and the sun,
Ceased on our hands and faces, on hazel and oak leaf, the light,
And the stars were blotted above us, and the whole of the world was one;

Till the horse gave a whinny; for cumbrous with stems of the hazel and oak,
Of hollies, and hazels, and oak-trees, a valley was sloping away
From his hoofs in the heavy grasses, with monstrous slumbering folk,
Their mighty and naked and gleaming bodies heaped loose where they lay.

123

More comely than man may make them, inlaid with silver and gold,
  Were arrow and shield and war-axe, arrow and spear and blade,
And dew-blanched horns, in whose hollows a child of three years old
  Could sleep on a couch of rushes, round and about them laid.

And this, which deals with the old legend of the city lying under the waters of a lake, is strange and interesting:

The maker of the stars and worlds
  Sat underneath the market cross,
And the old men were walking, walking,
  And little boys played pitch-and-toss.

'The props,' said He, 'of stars and worlds
  Are prayers of patient men and good.'
The boys, the women, and old men,
  Listening, upon their shadows stood.

A grey professor passing cried,
  'How few the mind's intemperance rule!
What shallow thoughts about deep things!
  The world grows old and plays the fool.'

The mayor came, leaning his left ear—
  There were some talking of the poor—
And to himself cried, 'Communist!'
  And hurried to the guardhouse door.

The bishop came with open book,
  Whispering along the sunny path;
There was some talking of man's God,
  His God of stupor and of wrath.

The bishop murmured, 'Atheist!
  How sinfully the wicked scoff!'
And sent the old men on their way,
  And drove the boys and women off.

The place was empty now of people;
  A cock came by upon his toes;
An old horse looked across the fence,
  And rubbed along the rail his nose.

The maker of the stars and worlds
  To His own house did Him betake,
And on that city dropped a tear,
  And now that city is a lake.

Mr. Yeats has a great deal of invention, and some of the poems in his book, such as *Mosada*, *Jealousy*, and *The Island of Statues*, are very finely conceived. It is impossible to doubt, after reading his present volume, that he will some day give us work of high import. Up to this he has been merely trying the strings of his instrument, running over the keys.

* * * * *

Lady Munster's *Dorinda* is an exceedingly clever novel. The heroine is a sort of well-born Becky Sharp, only much more beautiful than Becky, or at least than Thackeray's portraits of her, which, however, have always seemed to me rather ill-natured. I feel sure that Mrs. Rawdon Crawley was extremely pretty, and I have never understood how it was that Thackeray could caricature with his pencil so fascinating a creation of his pen. In the first chapter of Lady Munster's novel we find Dorinda at a fashionable school, and the sketches of the three old ladies who preside over the select seminary are very amusing. Dorinda is not very popular, and grave suspicions rest upon her of having stolen a cheque. This is a startling *début* for a heroine, and I was a little afraid at first that Dorinda, after undergoing endless humiliations, would be proved innocent in the last chapter. It was quite a relief to find that Dorinda was guilty. In fact, Dorinda is a kleptomaniac; that is to say, she is a member of the upper classes who spends her time in collecting works of art that do not belong to her. This, however, is only one of her accomplishments, and it does not occupy any important place in the story till the last volume is reached. Here we find Dorinda married to a Styrian Prince, and living in the luxury for which she had always longed. Unfortunately, while staying in the house of a friend she is detected stealing some rare enamels. Her punishment, as described by Lady Munster, is extremely severe; and when she finally commits suicide, maddened by the imprisonment to which her husband had subjected her, it is difficult not to feel a good deal of pity for her. Lady Munster writes a very clever, bright style, and has a wonderful faculty of drawing in a few sentences the most lifelike portraits of social types and social exceptions. Sir Jasper Broke and his sister, the Duke and Duchess of Cheviotdale, Lord and Lady Glenalmond, and Lord Baltimore, are all admirably drawn. The 'novel of high life,' as it used to be called, has of late years fallen into disrepute. Instead of duchesses in Mayfair, we have philanthropic young ladies in Whitechapel; and the fashionable and brilliant young dandies, in whom Disraeli and Bulwer Lytton took such delight, have been entirely wiped out as heroes of fiction by hardworking curates in the East End. The aim of most of our modern novelists seems to be, not to write good novels, but to write novels that will do good; and I am afraid that they are under the impression that fashionable life is not an edifying subject. They wish to reform the morals, rather than to portray the manners of their age. They have made the novel the mode of propaganda. It is possible, however, that *Dorinda* points to some coming change, and certainly it would be a pity if the Muse of Fiction confined her attention entirely to the East End.

* * * * *

The four remarkable women whom Mrs. Walford has chosen as the subjects of her *Four Biographies from 'Blackwood'* are Jane Taylor, Elizabeth Fry, Hannah More, and Mary Somerville. Perhaps it is too much to say that Jane Taylor is remarkable. In her day she was said to have been 'known to four continents,' and Sir Walter Scott described her as 'among the first women of her time'; but no one now cares to read *Essays in Rhyme*, or *Display*, though the latter is really a very clever novel and full of capital things. Elizabeth Fry is, of course, one of the great personalities of this century, at any rate in the particular sphere to which she devoted herself, and ranks with the many uncanonised saints whom the world has loved, and whose memory is sweet. Mrs. Walford gives a most interesting account of her. We see her first a gay, laughing, flaxen-haired girl, 'mightily addicted to fun,' pleased to be finely dressed and sent to the opera to see the 'Prince,' and be seen by him; pleased to exhibit her pretty figure in a becoming scarlet riding-habit, and to be looked at with obvious homage by the young officers quartered hard by, as she rode along the Norfolk lanes; 'dissipated' by simply hearing their band play in the square, and made giddy by the veriest trifle: 'an idle, flirting, worldly girl,' to use her own words. Then came the eventful day when 'in purple boots laced with scarlet' she went to hear William Savery preach at the Meeting House. This was the turning-point of her life, her psychological moment, as the phrase goes. After it came the era of 'thees' and 'thous,' of the drab gown and the beaver hat, of the visits to Newgate and the convict ships, of the work of rescuing the outcast and seeking the lost. Mrs. Walford quotes the following interesting account of the famous interview with Queen Charlotte at the Mansion-House:

Inside the Egyptian Hall there was a subject for Hayter—the diminutive stature of the Queen, covered with diamonds, and her countenance lighted up with the kindest benevolence; Mrs. Fry, her simple Quaker's dress adding to the height of her figure—though a little flushed—preserving her wonted calmness of look and manner; several of the bishops standing near; the platform crowded with waving feathers, jewels, and orders; the hall lined with spectators, gaily and nobly clad, and the centre filled with hundreds of children, brought there from their different schools to be examined. A murmur of applause ran through the assemblage as the Queen took Mrs. Fry by the hand. The murmur was followed by a clap and a shout, which was taken up by the multitudes without till it died away in the distance.

Those who regard Hannah More as a prim maiden lady of the conventional type, with a pious and literary turn of mind, will be obliged to change their views should they read Mrs. Walford's admirable sketch of the authoress of *Percy*. Hannah More was a brilliant wit, a *femme d'esprit*, passionately fond of society, and loved by society in return. When the serious-minded little country girl, who at the age of eight had covered a whole quire of paper with letters seeking to reform imaginary depraved characters, and with return epistles full of contrition and promises of amendment, paid her first visit to London, she became at once the intimate friend of Johnson, Burke, Sir Joshua Reynolds, Garrick, and most of the distinguished people of the day, delighting them by her charm, and grace, and wit. 'I dined at the Adelphi yesterday,' she writes in one of her letters. 'Garrick was the very soul of the company, and I never saw Johnson in more perfect good-humour. After all had risen to go we stood round them for above an hour, laughing, in defiance of every rule of decorum and Chesterfield. I believe we should never have thought of sitting down, nor of parting, had not an impertinent watchman been saucily vociferating. Johnson outstaid them all, and sat with me for half an hour.' The following is from her sister's pen:

On Tuesday evening we drank tea at Sir Joshua's with Dr. Johnson. Hannah is certainly a great favourite. She was placed next him, and they had the entire conversation to themselves. They were both in remarkably high spirits, and it was certainly her lucky night; I never heard her say so many good things. The old genius was as jocular as the young one was pleasant. You would have imagined we were at some comedy had you heard our peals of laughter. They certainly tried which could 'pepper the highest,' and it is not clear to me that the lexicographer was really the highest seasoner.

Hannah More was certainly, as Mrs. Walford says, 'the fêted and caressed idol of society.' The theatre at Bristol vaunted, 'Boast we not a More?' and the learned cits at Oxford inscribed their acknowledgment of her authority. Horace Walpole sat on the doorstep—or threatened to do so—till she promised to go down to Strawberry Hill; Foster quoted her; Mrs. Thrale twined her arms about her; Wilberforce consulted her and employed her. When *The Estimate of the Religion of the Fashionable World* was published anonymously, 'Aut Morus, aut Angelus,' exclaimed the Bishop of London, before he had read six pages. Of her village stories and ballads two million copies were sold during the first year. *Cœlebs in Search of a Wife* ran into thirty editions. Mrs. Barbauld writes to tell her about 'a good and sensible woman' of her acquaintance, who, on being asked how she contrived to divert herself in the country, replied, 'I have my spinning-wheel and my Hannah More. When I have spun one pound of flax I put on another, and when I have finished my book I begin it again. *I want no other amusement.*' How incredible it all sounds! No wonder that Mrs. Walford exclaims, 'No other amusement! Good heavens! Breathes there a man, woman, or child with soul so quiescent nowadays as to be satisfied with reels of flax and yards of Hannah More? Give us Hannah's company, but not—not her writings!' It is only fair to say that Mrs. Walford has thoroughly carried out the views she expresses in this passage, for she gives us nothing of Hannah More's grandiloquent literary productions, and yet succeeds in making us know her thoroughly. The whole book is well written, but the biography of Hannah More is a wonderfully brilliant sketch, and deserves great praise.

* * * * *

Miss Mabel Wotton has invented a new form of picture-gallery. Feeling that the visible aspect of men and women can be expressed in literature no less than through the medium of line and colour, she has collected together a series of *Word Portraits of Famous Writers* extending from Geoffrey Chaucer to Mrs. Henry Wood. It is a far cry from the author of the *Canterbury Tales* to the authoress of *East Lynne*; but as a beauty, at any rate, Mrs. Wood deserved to be described, and we hear of the pure oval of her face, of her perfect mouth, her 'dazzling' complexion, and the extraordinary youth by which 'she kept to the last the . . . freshness of a young girl.' Many of the 'famous writers' seem to have been very ugly. Thomson, the poet, was of a dull countenance, and a gross, unanimated, uninviting appearance; Richardson looked 'like a plump white mouse in a wig.' Pope is described in the *Guardian*, in 1713, as 'a lively little creature, with long arms and legs: a spider is no ill emblem of him. He has been taken at a distance for a small windmill.' Charles Kingsley appears as 'rather tall, very angular, surprisingly awkward, with thin staggering legs, a hatchet face adorned with scraggy gray whiskers, a faculty for falling into the most ungainly attitudes, and making the most hideous contortions of visage and frame; with a rough provincial accent and an uncouth way of speaking which would be set down for absurd caricature on the boards of a comic theatre.' Lamb is described by Carlyle

125

as 'the leanest of mankind; tiny black breeches buttoned to the knee-cap and no further, surmounting spindle legs also in black, face and head fineish, black, bony, lean, and of a Jew type rather'; and Talfourd says that the best portrait of him is his own description of Braham— 'a compound of the Jew, the gentleman, and the angel.' William Godwin was 'short and stout, his clothes loosely and carelessly put on, and usually old and worn; his hands were generally in his pockets; he had a remarkably large, bald head, and a weak voice; seeming generally half asleep when he walked, and even when he talked.' Lord Charlemont spoke of David Hume as more like a 'turtle-eating alderman' than 'a refined philosopher.' Mary Russell Mitford was ill-naturedly described by L.E.L. as 'Sancho Panza in petticoats!'; and as for poor Rogers, who was somewhat cadaverous, the descriptions given of him are quite dreadful. Lord Dudley once asked him 'why, now that he could afford it, he did not set up his hearse,' and it is said that Sydney Smith gave him mortal offence by recommending him 'when he sat for his portrait to be drawn saying his prayers, with his face hidden in his hands,' christened him the 'Death dandy,' and wrote underneath a picture of him, 'Painted in his lifetime.' We must console ourselves—if not with Mr. Hardy's statement that 'ideal physical beauty is incompatible with mental development, and a full recognition of the evil of things'—at least with the pictures of those who had some comeliness, and grace, and charm. Dr. Grosart says of a miniature of Edmund Spenser, 'It is an exquisitely beautiful face. The brow is ample, the lips thin but mobile, the eyes a grayish-blue, the hair and beard a golden red (as of "red monie" of the ballads) or goldenly chestnut, the nose with semi-transparent nostril and keen, the chin firm-poised, the expression refined and delicate. Altogether just such "presentment" of the Poet of Beauty *par excellence*, as one would have imagined.' Antony Wood describes Sir Richard Lovelace as being, at the age of sixteen, 'the most amiable and beautiful person that ever eye beheld.' Nor need we wonder at this when we remember the portrait of Lovelace that hangs at Dulwich College. Barry Cornwall, described himself by S. C. Hall as 'a decidedly rather pretty little fellow,' said of Keats: 'His countenance lives in my mind as one of singular beauty and brightness,—it had an expression as if he had been looking on some glorious sight.' Chatterton and Byron were splendidly handsome, and beauty of a high spiritual order may be claimed both for Milton and Shelley, though an industrious gentleman lately wrote a book in two volumes apparently for the purpose of proving that the latter of these two poets had a snub nose. Hazlitt once said that 'A man's life may be a lie to himself and others, and yet a picture painted of him by a great artist would probably stamp his character.' Few of the word-portraits in Miss Wotton's book can be said to have been drawn by a great artist, but they are all interesting, and Miss Wotton has certainly shown a wonderful amount of industry in collecting her references and in grouping them. It is not a book to be read through from beginning to end, but it is a delightful book to glance at, and by its means one can raise the ghosts of the dead, at least as well as the Psychical Society can.

(1) *Leaves of Life*. By E. Nesbit. (Longmans, Green and Co.)

(2) *The Wanderings of Oisin and Other Poems*. By W. B. Yeats. (Kegan Paul.)

(3) *Dorinda*. By Lady Munster. (Hurst and Blackett.)

(4) *Four Biographies from 'Blackwood.'* By Mrs. Walford. (Blackwood and Sons.)

(5) *Word Portraits of Famous Writers*. Edited by Mabel Wotton. (Bentley and Son.)

MR. WILLIAM MORRIS'S LAST BOOK

(*Pall Mall Gazette*, March 2, 1889.)

Mr. Morris's last book is a piece of pure art workmanship from beginning to end, and the very remoteness of its style from the common language and ordinary interests of our day gives to the whole story a strange beauty and an unfamiliar charm. It is written in blended prose and verse, like the mediæval 'cante-fable,' and tells the tale of the House of the Wolfings in its struggles against the legionaries of Rome then advancing into Northern Germany. It is a kind of Saga, and the language in which the folk-epic, as we may call it, is set forth recalls the antique dignity and directness of our English tongue four centuries ago. From an artistic point of view it may be described as an attempt to return by a self-conscious effort to the conditions of an earlier and a fresher age. Attempts of this kind are not uncommon in the history of art. From some such feeling came the Pre-Raphaelite movement of our own day and the archaistic movement of later Greek sculpture. When the result is beautiful the method is justified, and no shrill insistence upon a supposed necessity for absolute modernity of form can prevail against the value of work that has the incomparable excellence of style. Certainly, Mr. Morris's work possesses this excellence. His fine harmonies and rich cadences create in the reader that spirit by which alone can its own spirit be interpreted, awake in him something of the temper of romance and, by taking him out of his own age, place him in a truer and more vital relation to the great masterpieces of all time. It is a bad thing for an age to be always looking in art for its own reflection. It is well that, now and then, we are given work that is nobly imaginative in its method and purely artistic in its aim. As we read Mr. Morris's story with its fine alternations of verse and prose, its decorative and descriptive beauties, its wonderful handling of romantic and adventurous themes, we cannot but feel that we are as far removed from the ignoble fiction as we are from the ignoble facts of our own day. We breathe a purer air, and have dreams of a time when life had a kind of poetical quality of its own, and was simple and stately and complete.

The tragic interest of *The House of the Wolfings* centres round the figure of Thiodolf, the great hero of the tribe. The goddess who loves him gives him, as he goes to battle against the Romans, a magical hauberk on which rests this strange fate: that he who wears it shall save his own life and destroy the life of his land. Thiodolf, finding out this secret, brings the hauberk back to the Wood-Sun, as she is called, and chooses death for himself rather than the ruin of his cause, and so the story ends.

But Mr. Morris has always preferred romance to tragedy, and set the development of action above the concentration of passion. His story is like some splendid old tapestry crowded with stately images and enriched with delicate and delightful detail. The impression it leaves on us is not of a single central figure dominating the whole, but rather of a magnificent design to which everything is subordinated, and by which everything becomes of enduring import. It is the whole presentation of the primitive life that really fascinates. What in other hands would have been mere archæology is here transformed by quick artistic instinct and made wonderful for us, and human and full of high interest. The ancient world seems to have come to life again for our pleasure.

Of a work so large and so coherent, completed with no less perfection than it is conceived, it is difficult by mere quotation to give any adequate idea. This, however, may serve as an example of its narrative power. The passage describes the visit of Thiodolf to the Wood-Sun:

The moonlight lay in a great flood on the grass without, and the dew was falling in the coldest hour of the night, and the earth smelled sweetly: the whole habitation was asleep now, and there was no sound to be known as the sound of any creature, save that from the distant meadow came the lowing of a cow that had lost her calf, and that a white owl was flitting about near the eaves of the Roof with her wild cry that sounded like the mocking of merriment now silent. Thiodolf turned toward the wood, and walked steadily through the scattered hazel-trees, and thereby into the thick of the beech-trees, whose boles grew smooth and silver-grey, high and close-set: and so on and on he went as one going by a well-known path, though there was no path, till all the moonlight was quenched under the close roof of the beech-leaves, though yet for all the darkness, no man could go there and not feel that the roof was green above him. Still he went on in despite of the darkness, till at last there was a glimmer before him, that grew greater till he came unto a small wood-lawn whereon the turf grew again, though the grass was but thin, because little sunlight got to it, so close and thick were the tall trees round about it. . . . Nought looked Thiodolf either at the heavens above, or the trees, as he strode from off the husk-strewn floor of the beech wood on to the scanty grass of the lawn, but his eyes looked straight before him at that which was amidmost of the lawn: and little wonder was that; for there on a stone chair sat a woman exceeding fair, clad in glittering raiment, her hair lying as pale in the moonlight on the grey stone as the barley acres in the August night before the reaping-hook goes in amongst them. She sat there as though she were awaiting some one, and he made no stop nor stay, but went straight up to her, and took her in his arms, and kissed her mouth and her eyes, and she him again; and then he sat himself down beside her.

As an example of the beauty of the verse we would take this from the song of the Wood-Sun. It at least shows how perfectly the poetry harmonises with the prose, and how natural the transition is from the one to the other:

In many a stead Doom dwelleth, nor sleepeth day nor night:
The rim of the bowl she kisseth, and beareth the chambering light
When the kings of men wend happy to the bride-bed from the board.
It is little to say that she wendeth the edge of the grinded sword,
When about the house half builded she hangeth many a day;
The ship from the strand she shoveth, and on his wonted way
By the mountain hunter fareth where his foot ne'er failed before:
She is where the high bank crumbles at last on the river's shore:
The mower's scythe she whetteth; and lulleth the shepherd to sleep
Where the deadly ling-worm wakeneth in the desert of the sheep.
Now we that come of the God-kin of her redes for ourselves we wot,
But her will with the lives of men-folk and their ending know we not.
So therefore I bid thee not fear for thyself of Doom and her deed,
But for me: and I bid thee hearken to the helping of my need.
Or else—Art thou happy in life, or lusteth thou to die
In the flower of thy days, when thy glory and thy longing bloom on high?

The last chapter of the book in which we are told of the great feast made for the dead is so finely written that we cannot refrain from quoting this passage:

Now was the glooming falling upon the earth; but the Hall was bright within even as the Hall-Sun had promised. Therein was set forth the Treasure of the Wolfings; fair cloths were hung on the walls, goodly broidered garments on the pillars: goodly brazen cauldrons and fair-carven chests were set down in nooks where men could see them well, and vessels of gold and silver were set all up and down the tables of the feast. The pillars also were wreathed with flowers, and flowers hung garlanded from the walls over the precious hangings; sweet gums and spices were burning in fair-wrought censers of brass, and so many candles were alight under the Roof, that scarce had it looked more ablaze when the Romans had litten the faggots therein for its burning amidst the hurry of the Morning Battle.

There then they fell to feasting, hallowing in the high-tide of their return with victory in their hands: and the dead corpses of Thiodolf and Otter, clad in precious glittering raiment, looked down on them from the High-seat, and the kindreds worshipped them and were glad; and they drank the Cup to them before any others, were they Gods or men.

In days of uncouth realism and unimaginative imitation, it is a high pleasure to welcome work of this kind. It is a work in which all lovers of literature cannot fail to delight.

A Tale of the House of the Wolfings and all the Kindreds of the Mark. Written in Prose and in Verse by William Morris. (Reeves and Turner.)

ADAM LINDSAY GORDON

(*Pall Mall Gazette*, March 25, 1889.)

A critic recently remarked of Adam Lindsay Gordon that through him Australia had found her first fine utterance in song. {452} This, however, is an amiable error. There is very little of Australia in Gordon's poetry. His heart and mind and fancy were always preoccupied with memories and dreams of England and such culture as England gave him. He owed nothing to the land of his adoption. Had he stayed at home he would have done much better work. In a few poems such as *The Sick Stockrider*, *From the Wreck*, and *Wolf and Hound* there are notes of Australian influences, and these Swinburnian stanzas from the dedication to the *Bush Ballads* deserve to be quoted, though the promise they hold out was never fulfilled:

> They are rhymes rudely strung with intent less
>   Of sound than of words,
> In lands where bright blossoms are scentless,
>   And songless bright birds;
> Where, with fire and fierce drought on her tresses,
> Insatiable summer oppresses
> Sere woodlands and sad wildernesses,
>   And faint flocks and herds.
>
>   Whence gather'd?—The locust's grand chirrup
>   May furnish a stave;
> The ring of a rowel and stirrup,
>   The wash of a wave.
> The chaunt of the marsh frog in rushes,
> That chimes through the pauses and hushes
>   Of nightfall, the torrent that gushes,
> The tempests that rave.
>
>   In the gathering of night gloom o'erhead, in
> The still silent change,
>   All fire-flushed when forest trees redden
> On slopes of the range.
> When the gnarl'd, knotted trunks Eucalyptian
> Seem carved, like weird columns Egyptian,
> With curious device—quaint inscription,
>   And hieroglyph strange;
>
>   In the Spring, when the wattle gold trembles
>   'Twixt shadow and shine,
> When each dew-laden air draught resembles
>   A long draught of wine;
> When the sky-line's blue burnish'd resistance
>   Makes deeper the dreamiest distance,
> Some song in all hearts hath existence,—
>   Such songs have been mine.

As a rule, however, Gordon is distinctly English, and the landscapes he describes are always the landscapes of our own country. He writes about mediæval lords and ladies in his *Rhyme of Joyous Garde*, about Cavaliers and Roundheads in *The Romance of Britomarte*, and *Ashtaroth*, his longest and most ambitious poem, deals with the adventures of the Norman barons and Danish knights of ancient days. Steeped in Swinburne and bewildered with Browning, he set himself to reproduce the marvellous melody of the one and the dramatic vigour and harsh strength of the other. *From the Wreck* is a sort of Australian edition of the *Ride to Ghent*. These are the first three stanzas of one of the so-called *Bush Ballads*:

> On skies still and starlit
>   White lustres take hold,
> And grey flashes scarlet,
>   And red flashes gold.
> And sun-glories cover
> The rose, shed above her,
> Like lover and lover
>   They flame and unfold.
>
> . . . . .
>
>   Still bloom in the garden
>   Green grass-plot, fresh lawn,
> Though pasture lands harden
>   And drought fissures yawn.
> While leaves, not a few fall,
> Let rose-leaves for you fall,
> Leaves pearl-strung with dewfall,
>   And gold shot with dawn.
>
>   Does the grass-plot remember
>   The fall of your feet
> In Autumn's red ember
>   When drought leagues with heat,
> When the last of the roses

Despairingly closes
In the lull that reposes
  Ere storm winds wax fleet?

And the following verses show that the Norman Baron of *Ashtaroth* had read *Dolores* just once too often:

Dead priests of Osiris, and Isis,
  And Apis! that mystical lore,
Like a nightmare, conceived in a crisis
  Of fever, is studied no more;
Dead Magian! yon star-troop that spangles
  The arch of yon firmament vast
Looks calm, like a host of white angels
  On dry dust of votaries past.

On seas unexplored can the ship shun
  Sunk rocks? Can man fathom life's links,
Past or future, unsolved by Egyptian
  Or Theban, unspoken by Sphynx?
The riddle remains yet, unravell'd
  By students consuming night oil.
O earth! we have toil'd, we have travailed:
  How long shall we travail and toil?

By the classics Gordon was always very much fascinated. He loved what he calls 'the scroll that is godlike and Greek,' though he is rather uncertain about his quantities, rhyming 'Polyxena' to 'Athena' and 'Aphrodite' to 'light,' and occasionally makes very rash statements, as when he represents Leonidas exclaiming to the three hundred at Thermopylae:

'Ho! comrades let us gaily dine—
This night with Plato we shall sup,'

if this be not, as we hope it is, a printer's error. What the Australians liked best were his spirited, if somewhat rough, horse-racing and hunting poems. Indeed, it was not till he found that *How We Beat the Favourite* was on everybody's lips that he consented to forego his anonymity and appear in the unsuspected character of a verse-writer, having up to that time produced his poems shyly, scribbled them on scraps of paper, and sent them unsigned to the local magazines. The fact is that the social atmosphere of Melbourne was not favourable to poets, and the worthy colonials seem to have shared Audrey's doubts as to whether poetry was a true and honest thing. It was not till Gordon won the Cup Steeplechase for Major Baker in 1868 that he became really popular, and probably there were many who felt that to steer Babbler to the winning-post was a finer achievement than 'to babble o'er green fields.'

On the whole, it is impossible not to regret that Gordon ever emigrated. His literary power cannot be denied, but it was stunted in uncongenial surroundings and marred by the rude life he was forced to lead. Australia has converted many of our failures into prosperous and admirable mediocrities, but she certainly spoiled one of our poets for us. Ovid at Tomi is not more tragic than Gordon driving cattle or farming an unprofitable sheep-ranch.

That Australia, however, will some day make amends by producing a poet of her own we cannot doubt, and for him there will be new notes to sound and new wonders to tell of. The description, given by Mr. Marcus Clarke in the preface to this volume, of the aspect and spirit of Nature in Australia is most curious and suggestive. The Australian forests, he tells us, are funereal and stern, and 'seem to stifle, in their black gorges, a story of sullen despair.' No leaves fall from the trees, but 'from the melancholy gum strips of white bark hang and rustle. Great grey kangaroos hop noiselessly over the coarse grass. Flights of cockatoos stream out, shrieking like evil souls. The sun suddenly sinks and the mopokes burst out into horrible peals of semi-human laughter.' The aborigines aver that, when night comes, from the bottomless depth of some lagoon a misshapen monster rises, dragging his loathsome length along the ooze. From a corner of the silent forest rises a dismal chant, and around a fire dance natives painted like skeletons. All is fear-inspiring and gloomy. No bright fancies are linked with the memories of the mountains. Hopeless explorers have named them out of their sufferings—Mount Misery, Mount Dreadful, Mount Despair.

In Australia alone (says Mr. Clarke) is to be found the Grotesque, the Weird, the strange scribblings of nature learning how to write. But the dweller in the wilderness acknowledges the subtle charm of the fantastic land of monstrosities. He becomes familiar with the beauty of loneliness. Whispered to by the myriad tongues of the wilderness, he learns the language of the barren and the uncouth, and can read the hieroglyphs of haggard gum-trees, blown into odd shapes, distorted with fierce hot winds, or cramped with cold nights, when the Southern Cross freezes in a cloudless sky of icy blue. The phantasmagoria of that wild dream-land termed the Bush interprets itself, and the Poet of our desolation begins to comprehend why free Esau loved his heritage of desert sand better than all the bountiful richness of Egypt.

Here, certainly, is new material for the poet, here is a land that is waiting for its singer. Such a singer Gordon was not. He remained thoroughly English, and the best that we can say of him is that he wrote imperfectly in Australia those poems that in England he might have made perfect.

Poems. By Adam Lindsay Gordon. (Samuel Mullen.)

THE POETS' CORNER—IX

(*Pall Mall Gazette*, March 30, 1889.)

Judges, like the criminal classes, have their lighter moments, and it was probably in one of his happiest and, certainly, in one of his most careless moods that Mr. Justice Denman conceived the idea of putting the early history of Rome into doggerel verse for the benefit of a little boy of the name of Jack. Poor Jack! He is still, we learn from the preface, under six years of age, and it is sad to think of the future career of a boy who is being brought up on bad history and worse poetry. Here is a passage from the learned judge's account of Romulus:

Poor Tatius by some unknown hand
　Was soon assassinated,
Some said by Romulus' command;
　I know not—but 'twas fated.

　Sole King again, this Romulus
　Play'd some fantastic tricks,
Lictors he had, who hatchets bore
　Bound up with rods of sticks.

　He treated all who thwarted him
　No better than a dog,
Sometimes 'twas 'Heads off, Lictors, there!'
　Sometimes 'Ho! Lictors, flog!'

　Then he created Senators,
　And gave them rings of gold;
Old soldiers all; their name deriv'd
　From 'Senex' which means 'old.'

　Knights, too, he made, good horsemen all,
　Who always were at hand
To execute immediately
　Whate'er he might command.

　But these were of Patrician rank,
　Plebeians all the rest;
Remember this distinction, Jack!
　For 'tis a useful test.

The reign of Tullius Hostilius opens with a very wicked rhyme:

As Numa, dying, only left
　A daughter, named Pompilia,
The Senate had to choose a King.
　They choose one sadly sillier.

If Jack goes to the bad, Mr. Justice Denman will have much to answer for.

After such a terrible example from the Bench, it is pleasant to turn to the seats reserved for Queen's Counsel. Mr. Cooper Willis's *Tales and Legends*, if somewhat boisterous in manner, is still very spirited and clever. *The Prison of the Danes* is not at all a bad poem, and there is a great deal of eloquent, strong writing in the passage beginning:

The dying star-song of the night sinks in the dawning day,
And the dark-blue sheen is changed to green, and the green fades into grey,
And the sleepers are roused from their slumbers, and at last the Danesmen know
How few of all their numbers are left them by the foe.

Not much can be said of a poet who exclaims:

Oh, for the power of Byron or of Moore,
To glow with one, and with the latter soar.

And yet Mr. Moodie is one of the best of those South African poets whose works have been collected and arranged by Mr. Wilmot. Pringle, the 'father of South African verse,' comes first, of course, and his best poem is, undoubtedly, *Afar in the Desert*:

Afar in the desert I love to ride,
With the silent Bush-boy alone by my side:
Away, away, from the dwelling of men
By the wild-deer's haunt, by the buffalo's glen:
By valleys remote where the oribi plays,
Where the gnu, the gazelle and the hartebeest graze,
And the kúdú and eland unhunted recline
By the skirts of grey forests o'erhung with wild vine,
Where the elephant browses at peace in his wood,
And the river-horse gambols unscared in the flood,
And the mighty rhinoceros wallows at will
In the fen where the wild ass is drinking his fill.

It is not, however, a very remarkable production.

The Smouse, by Fannin, has the modern merit of incomprehensibility. It reads like something out of *The Hunting of the Snark*:

I'm a Smouse, I'm a Smouse in the wilderness wide,
The veld is my home, and the wagon's my pride:
The crack of my 'voerslag' shall sound o'er the lea,
I'm a Smouse, I'm a Smouse, and the trader is free!
I heed not the Governor, I fear not his law,
I care not for civilisation one straw,
And ne'er to 'Ompanda'—'Umgazis' I'll throw
While my arm carries fist, or my foot bears a toe!
'Trek,' 'trek,' ply the whip—touch the fore oxen's skin,
I'll warrant we'll 'go it' through thick and through thin—
Loop! loop ye oud skellums! ot Vikmaan trek jy;
I'm a Smouse, I'm a Smouse, and the trader is free!

The South African poets, as a class, are rather behind the age. They seem to think that 'Aurora' is a very novel and delightful epithet for the dawn. On the whole they depress us.

Chess, by Mr. Louis Tylor, is a sort of Christmas masque in which the *dramatis personæ* consist of some unmusical carollers, a priggish young man called Eric, and the chessmen off the board. The White Queen's Knight begins a ballad and the Black King's Bishop completes it. The Pawns sing in chorus and the Castles converse with each other. The silliness of the form makes it an absolutely unreadable book.

Mr. Williamson's *Poems of Nature and Life* are as orthodox in spirit as they are commonplace in form. A few harmless heresies of art and thought would do this poet no harm. Nearly everything that he says has been said before and said better. The only original thing in the volume is the description of Mr. Robert Buchanan's 'grandeur of mind.' This is decidedly new.

Dr. Cockle tells us that Müllner's *Guilt* and *The Ancestress* of Grillparzer are the masterpieces of German fate-tragedy. His translation of the first of these two masterpieces does not make us long for any further acquaintance with the school. Here is a specimen from the fourth act of the fate-tragedy.

SCENE VIII.

ELVIRA. HUGO.

ELVIRA (after long silence, leaving the harp, steps to Hugo, and seeks his gaze).

HUGO (softly). Though I made sacrifice of thy sweet life. The Father has forgiven. Can the wife—Forgive?

ELVIRA (on his breast). She can!

HUGO (with all the warmth of love). Dear wife!

ELVIRA (after a pause, in deep sorrow). Must it be so, beloved one?

HUGO (sorry to have betrayed himself). What?

In his preface to *The Circle of Seasons*, a series of hymns and verses for the seasons of the Church, the Rev. T. B. Dover expresses a hope that this well-meaning if somewhat tedious book 'may be of value to those many earnest people to whom the subjective aspect of truth is helpful.' The poem beginning

Lord, in the inn of my poor worthless heart
Guests come and go; but there is room for Thee,

has some merit and might be converted into a good sonnet. The majority of the poems, however, are quite worthless. There seems to be some curious connection between piety and poor rhymes.

Lord Henry Somerset's verse is not so good as his music. Most of the *Songs of Adieu* are marred by their excessive sentimentality of feeling and by the commonplace character of their weak and lax form. There is nothing that is new and little that is true in verse of this kind:

The golden leaves are falling,
  Falling one by one,
Their tender 'Adieux' calling
  To the cold autumnal sun.
The trees in the keen and frosty air
  Stand out against the sky,
'Twould seem they stretch their branches bare
  To Heaven in agony.

It can be produced in any quantity. Lord Henry Somerset has too much heart and too little art to make a good poet, and such art as he does possess is devoid of almost every intellectual quality and entirely lacking in any intellectual strength. He has nothing to say and says it.

Mrs. Cora M. Davis is eloquent about the splendours of what the authoress of *The Circle of Seasons* calls 'this earthly ball.'

Let's sing the beauties of this grand old earth,

she cries, and proceeds to tell how

Imagination paints old Egypt's former glory,
Of mighty temples reaching heavenward,
Of grim, colossal statues, whose barbaric story
The caustic pens of erudition still record,

131

Whose ancient cities of glittering minarets
Reflect the gold of Afric's gorgeous sunsets.

'The caustic pens of erudition' is quite delightful and will be appreciated by all Egyptologists. There is also a charming passage in the same poem on the pictures of the Old Masters:

the mellow richness of whose tints impart,
By contrast, greater delicacy still to modern art.

This seems to us the highest form of optimism we have ever come across in art criticism. It is American in origin, Mrs. Davis, as her biographer tells us, having been born in Alabama, Genesee co., N.Y.

(1) *The Story of the Kings of Rome in Verse*. By the Hon. G. Denman, Judge of the High Court of Justice. (Trübner and Co.)

(2) *Tales and Legends in Verse*. By E. Cooper Willis, Q.C. (Kegan Paul.)

(3) *The Poetry of South Africa*. Collected and arranged by A. Wilmot. (Sampson Low and Co.)

(4) *Chess*. A Christmas Masque. By Louis Tylor. (Fisher Unwin.)

(5) *Poems of Nature and Life*. By David R. Williamson. (Blackwood.)

(6) *Guilt*. Translated from the German by J. Cockle, M.D. (Williams and Norgate.)

(7) *The Circle of Seasons*. By K. E. V. (Elliot Stock.)

(8) *Songs of Adieu*. By Lord Henry Somerset. (Chatto and Windus.)

(9) *Immortelles*. By Cora M. Davis. (G. P. Putnam's Sons.)

SOME LITERARY NOTES—IV

(*Woman's World*, April 1889.)

'In modern life,' said Matthew Arnold once, 'you I cannot well enter a monastery; but you can enter the Wordsworth Society.' I fear that this will sound to many a somewhat uninviting description of this admirable and useful body, whose papers and productions have been recently published by Professor Knight, under the title of *Wordsworthiana*. 'Plain living and high thinking' are not popular ideals. Most people prefer to live in luxury, and to think with the majority. However, there is really nothing in the essays and addresses of the Wordsworth Society that need cause the public any unnecessary alarm; and it is gratifying to note that, although the society is still in the first blush of enthusiasm, it has not yet insisted upon our admiring Wordsworth's inferior work. It praises what is worthy of praise, reverences what should be reverenced, and explains what does not require explanation. One paper is quite delightful; it is from the pen of Mr. Rawnsley, and deals with such reminiscences of Wordsworth as still linger among the peasantry of Westmoreland. Mr. Rawnsley grew up, he tells us, in the immediate vicinity of the present Poet-Laureate's old home in Lincolnshire, and had been struck with the swiftness with which,

As year by year the labourer tills
His wonted glebe, or lops the glades,

the memories of the poet of the Somersby Wold had 'faded from off the circle of the hills'—had, indeed, been astonished to note how little real interest was taken in him or his fame, and how seldom his works were met with in the houses of the rich or poor in the very neighbourhood. Accordingly, when he came to reside in the Lake Country, he endeavoured to find out what of Wordsworth's memory among the men of the Dales still lingered on—how far he was still a moving presence among them—how far his works had made their way into the cottages and farmhouses of the valleys. He also tried to discover how far the race of Westmoreland and Cumberland farm-folk—the 'Matthews' and the 'Michaels' of the poet, as described by him—were real or fancy pictures, or how far the characters of the Dalesmen had been altered in any remarkable manner by tourist influences during the thirty-two years that have passed since the Lake poet was laid to rest.

With regard to the latter point, it will be remembered that Mr. Ruskin, writing in 1876, said that 'the Border peasantry, painted with absolute fidelity by Scott and Wordsworth,' are, as hitherto, a scarcely injured race; that in his fields at Coniston he had men who might have fought with Henry V. at Agincourt without being distinguished from any of his knights; that he could take his tradesmen's word for a thousand pounds, and need never latch his garden gate; and that he did not fear molestation, in wood or on moor, for his girl guests. Mr. Rawnsley, however, found that a certain beauty had vanished which the simple retirement of old valley days fifty years ago gave to the men among whom Wordsworth lived. 'The strangers,' he says, 'with their gifts of gold, their vulgarity, and their requirements, have much to answer for.' As for their impressions of Wordsworth, to understand them one must understand the vernacular of the Lake District. 'What was Mr. Wordsworth like in personal appearance?' said Mr. Rawnsley once to an old retainer, who still lives not far from Rydal Mount. 'He was a ugly-faäced man, and a meän liver,' was the answer; but all that was really meant was that he was a man of marked features, and led a very simple life in matters of food and raiment. Another old man, who believed that Wordsworth 'got most of his poetry out of Hartley,' spoke of the poet's wife as 'a very onpleasant woman, very onpleasant indeed. A close-fisted woman, that's what she was.' This, however, seems to have been merely a tribute to Mrs. Wordsworth's admirable housekeeping qualities.

The first person interviewed by Mr. Rawnsley was an old lady who had been once in service at Rydal Mount, and was, in 1870, a lodging-house keeper at Grasmere. She was not a very imaginative person, as may be gathered from the following anecdote:—Mr. Rawnsley's sister came in from a late evening walk, and said, 'O Mrs. D---, have you seen the wonderful sunset?' The good lady turned sharply round and, drawing herself to her full height, as if mortally offended, answered: 'No, miss; I'm a tidy cook, I know, and "they say" a decentish body for a landlady, but I don't knaw nothing about sunsets or them sort of things, they've never been in my line.' Her reminiscence of Wordsworth was as worthy of tradition as it was explanatory, from her point of view, of the method in which Wordsworth composed, and was helped in his labours by his enthusiastic sister. 'Well, you know,' she said, 'Mr. Wordsworth went humming and booing about, and she, Miss Dorothy, kept close behint him, and she picked up the bits as he let 'em fall, and tak' 'em down, and put 'em together on paper for him. And you may be very well sure as how she didn't understand nor make sense out of 'em, and I doubt that he didn't know much about them either himself, but, howivver, there's a great many folk as do, I dare say.' Of Wordsworth's habit of talking to himself, and composing aloud, we hear a great deal. 'Was Mr. Wordsworth a sociable man?' asked Mr. Rawnsley of a Rydal farmer. 'Wudsworth, for a' he had noa pride nor nowt,' was the answer, 'was a man who was quite one to hissel, ye kna. He was not a man as folks could crack wi', nor not a man as could crack wi' folks. But there was another thing as kep' folk off, he had a ter'ble girt deep voice, and ye might see his faace agaan for long enuff. I've knoan folks, village lads and lasses, coming over by old road above, which runs from Grasmere to Rydal, flayt a'most to death there by Wishing Gaate to hear the girt voice a groanin' and mutterin' and thunderin' of a still evening. And he had a way of standin' quite still by the rock there in t' path under Rydal, and folks could hear sounds like a wild beast coming from the rocks, and childer were scared fit to be deäd a'most.'

Wordsworth's description of himself constantly recurs to one:

And who is he with modest looks,
    And clad in sober russet gown?
He murmurs by the running brooks,
    A music sweeter than their own;
He is retired as noontide dew,
Or fountain in a noonday grove.

But the corroboration comes in strange guise. Mr. Rawnsley asked one of the Dalesmen about Wordsworth's dress and habits. This was the reply: 'Wudsworth wore a Jem Crow, never seed him in a boxer in my life,—a Jem Crow and an old blue cloak was his rig, and *as for his habits, he had noan*; niver knew him with a pot i' his hand, or a pipe i' his mouth. But he was a greät skater, for a' that—noan better in these parts—why, he could cut his own naäme upo' the ice, could Mr. Wudsworth.' Skating seems to have been Wordsworth's one form of amusement. He was 'over feckless i' his hands'—could not drive or ride—'not a bit of fish in him,' and 'nowt of a mountaineer.' But he could skate. The rapture of the time when, as a boy, on Esthwaite's frozen lake, he had

                    wheeled about,
Proud and exulting like an untired horse
That cares not for his home, and, shod with steel,
Had hissed along the polished ice,

was continued, Mr. Rawnsley tells us, into manhood's later day; and Mr. Rawnsley found many proofs that the skill the poet had gained, when

    Not seldom from the uproar he retired,
Into a silent bay, or sportively
Glanced sideway, leaving the tumultuous throng
To cut across the reflex of a star,

was of such a kind as to astonish the natives among whom he dwelt. The recollection of a fall he once had, when his skate caught on a stone, still lingers in the district. A boy had been sent to sweep the snow from the White Moss Tarn for him. 'Did Mr. Wudsworth gie ye owt?' he was asked, when he returned from his labour. 'Na, but I seed him tumlle, though!' was the answer. 'He was a ter'ble girt skater, was Wudsworth now,' says one of Mr. Rawnsley's informants; 'he would put one hand i' his breast (he wore a frill shirt i' them days), and t'other hand i' his waistband, same as shepherds does to keep their hands warm, and he would stand up straight and sway and swing away grandly.'

Of his poetry they did not think much, and whatever was good in it they ascribed to his wife, his sister, and Hartley Coleridge. He wrote poetry, they said, 'because he couldn't help it—because it was his hobby'—for sheer love, and not for money. They could not understand his doing work 'for nowt,' and held his occupation in somewhat light esteem because it did not bring in 'a deal o' brass to the pocket.' 'Did you ever read his poetry, or see any books about in the farmhouses?' asked Mr. Rawnsley. The answer was curious: 'Ay, ay, time or two. But ya're weel aware there's potry and potry. There's potry wi' a li'le bit pleasant in it, and potry sic as a man can laugh at or the childer understand, and some as takes a deal of mastery to make out what's said, and a deal of Wudsworth's was this sort, ye kna. You could tell fra the man's faace his potry would niver have no laugh in it. His potry was quite different work from li'le Hartley. Hartley 'ud goa running along beside o' the brooks and mak his, and goa in the first oppen door and write what he had got upo' paper. But Wudsworth's potry was real hard stuff, and bided a deal of makking, and he'd keep it in his head for long enough. Eh, but it's queer, mon, different ways folks hes of making potry now . . . Not but what Mr. Wudsworth didn't stand very high, and was a well-spoken man enough.' The best criticism on Wordsworth that Mr. Rawnsley heard was this: 'He was an open-air man, and a great critic of trees.'

There are many useful and well-written essays in Professor Knight's volume, but Mr. Rawnsley's is far the most interesting of all. It gives us a graphic picture of the poet as he appeared in outward semblance and manner to those about whom he wrote.

* * * * *

Mary Myles is Mrs. Edmonds's first attempt at writing fiction. Mrs. Edmonds is well known as an authority on modern Greek literature, and her style has often a very pleasant literary flavour, though in her dialogues she has not as yet quite grasped the difference between *la langue parleé* and *la langue écrite*. Her heroine is a sort of Nausicaa from Girton, who develops into the Pallas Athena of a provincial school. She has her love-romance, like her Homeric prototype, and her Odysseus returns to her at the close of the book. It is a nice story.

* * * * *

Lady Dilke's *Art in the Modern State* is a book that cannot fail to interest deeply every one who cares either for art or for history. The 'modern State' which gives its title to the book is that political and social organisation of our day that comes to us from the France of

Richelieu and Colbert, and is the direct outcome of the 'Grand Siècle,' the true greatness of which century, as Lady Dilke points out, consists not in its vain wars, and formal stage and stilted eloquence, and pompous palaces, but in the formation and working out of the political and social system of which these things were the first-fruits. To the question that naturally rises on one's lips, 'How can one dwell on the art of the seventeenth century?—it has no charm,' Lady Dilke answers that this art presents in its organisation, from the point of view of social polity, problems of the highest intellectual interest. Throughout all its phases—to quote her own words—'the life of France wears, during the seventeenth century, a political aspect. The explanation of all changes in the social system, in letters, in the arts, in fashions even, has to be sought in the necessities of the political position; and the seeming caprices of taste take their rise from the same causes which went to determine the making of a treaty or the promulgation of an edict. This seems all the stranger because, in times preceding, letters and the arts, at least, appeared to flourish in conditions as far removed from the action of statecraft as if they had been a growth of fairyland. In the Middle Ages they were devoted to a virgin image of Virtue; they framed, in the shade of the sanctuary, an ideal shining with the beauty born of self-renunciation, of resignation to self-enforced conditions of moral and physical suffering. By the queenly Venus of the Renaissance they were consecrated to the joys of life, and the world saw that through their perfect use men might renew their strength, and behold virtue and beauty with clear eyes. It was, however, reserved for the rulers of France in the seventeenth century fully to realise the political function of letters and the arts in the modern State, and their immense importance in connection with the prosperity of a commercial nation.'

The whole subject is certainly extremely fascinating. The Renaissance had for its object the development of great personalities. The perfect freedom of the temperament in matters of art, the perfect freedom of the intellect in intellectual matters, the full development of the individual, were the things it aimed at. As we study its history we find it full of great anarchies. It solved no political or social problems; it did not seek to solve them. The ideal of the 'Grand Siècle,' and of Richelieu, in whom the forces of that great age were incarnate, was different. The ideas of citizenship, of the building up of a great nation, of the centralisation of forces, of collective action, of ethnic unity of purpose, came before the world. It was inevitable that they should have done so, and Lady Dilke, with her keen historic sense and her wonderful power of grouping facts, has told us the story of their struggle and their victory. Her book is, from every point of view, a most remarkable work. Her style is almost French in its clearness, its sobriety, its fine and, at times, ascetic simplicity. The whole ground-plan and intellectual-conception is admirable.

It is, of course, easy to see how much Art lost by having a new mission forced upon her. The creation of a formal tradition upon classical lines is never without its danger, and it is sad to find the provincial towns of France, once so varied and individual in artistic expression, writing to Paris for designs and advice. And yet, through Colbert's great centralising scheme of State supervision and State aid, France was the one country in Europe, and has remained the one country in Europe, where the arts are not divorced from industry. The Academy of Painting and Sculpture and the School of Architecture were not, to quote Lady Dilke's words, called into being in order that royal palaces should be raised surpassing all others in magnificence:

Bièvrebache and the Savonnerie were not established only that such palaces should be furnished more sumptuously than those of an Eastern fairy-tale. Colbert did not care chiefly to inquire, when organising art administration, what were the institutions best fitted to foster the proper interests of art; he asked, in the first place, what would most contribute to swell the national importance. Even so, in surrounding the King with the treasures of luxury, his object was twofold—their possession should, indeed, illustrate the Crown, but should also be a unique source of advantage to the people. Glass-workers were brought from Venice, and lace-makers from Flanders, that they might yield to France the secrets of their skill. Palaces and public buildings were to afford commissions for French artists, and a means of technical and artistic education for all those employed upon them. The royal collections were but a further instrument in educating the taste and increasing the knowledge of the working classes. The costly factories of the Savonnerie and the Gobelins were practical schools, in which every detail of every branch of all those industries which contribute to the furnishing and decoration of houses were brought to perfection; whilst a band of chosen apprentices were trained in the adjoining schools. To Colbert is due the honour of having foreseen, not only that the interests of the modern State were inseparably bound up with those of industry, but also that the interests of industry could not, without prejudice, be divorced from art.

Mr. Bret Harte has never written anything finer than *Cressy*. It is one of his most brilliant and masterly productions, and will take rank with the best of his Californian stories. Hawthorne re-created for us the America of the past with the incomparable grace of a very perfect artist, but Mr. Bret Harte's emphasised modernity has, in its own sphere, won equal, or almost equal, triumphs. Wit, pathos, humour, realism, exaggeration, and romance are in this marvellous story all blended together, and out of the very clash and chaos of these things comes life itself. And what a curious life it is, half civilised and half barbarous, naïve and corrupt, chivalrous and commonplace, real and improbable! Cressy herself is the most tantalising of heroines. She is always eluding one's grasp. It is difficult to say whether she sacrifices herself on the altar of romance, or is merely a girl with an extraordinary sense of humour. She is intangible, and the more we know of her, the more incomprehensible she becomes. It is pleasant to come across a heroine who is not identified with any great cause, and represents no important principle, but is simply a wonderful nymph from American backwoods, who has in her something of Artemis, and not a little of Aphrodite.

* * * * *

It is always a pleasure to come across an American poet who is not national, and who tries to give expression to the literature that he loves rather than to the land in which he lives. The Muses care so little for geography! Mr. Richard Day's *Poems* have nothing distinctively American about them. Here and there in his verse one comes across a flower that does not bloom in our meadows, a bird to which our woodlands have never listened. But the spirit that animates the verse is simple and human, and there is hardly a poem in the volume that English lips might not have uttered. *Sounds of the Temple* has much in it that is interesting in metre as well as in matter:—

Then sighed a poet from his soul:
'The clouds are blown across the stars,
And chill have grown my lattice bars;
I cannot keep my vigil whole
By the lone candle of my soul.

'This reed had once devoutest tongue,
And sang as if to its small throat
God listened for a perfect note;
As charily this lyre was strung:
God's praise is slow and has no tongue.'

But the best poem is undoubtedly the *Hymn to the Mountain*:—

Within the hollow of thy hand—
This wooded dell half up the height,
Where streams take breath midway in flight—
Here let me stand.

Here warbles not a lowland bird,
Here are no babbling tongues of men;
Thy rivers rustling through the glen
Alone are heard.

Above no pinion cleaves its way,
Save when the eagle's wing, as now,
With sweep imperial shades thy brow
Beetling and grey.

What thoughts are thine, majestic peak?
And moods that were not born to chime
With poets' ineffectual rhyme
And numbers weak?

The green earth spreads thy gaze before,
And the unfailing skies are brought
Within the level of thy thought.
There is no more.

The stars salute thy rugged crown
With syllables of twinkling fire;
Like choral burst from distant choir,
Their psalm rolls down.

And I within this temple niche,
Like statue set where prophets talk,
Catch strains they murmur as they walk,
And I am rich.

Miss Ella Curtis's *A Game of Chance* is certainly the best novel that this clever young writer has as yet produced. If it has a fault, it is that it is crowded with too much incident, and often surrenders the study of character to the development of plot. Indeed, it has many plots, each of which, in more economical hands, would have served as the basis of a complete story. We have as the central incident the career of a clever lady's-maid who personifies her mistress, and is welcomed by Sir John Erskine, an English country gentleman, as the widow of his dead son. The real husband of the adventuress tracks his wife to England, and claims her. She pretends that he is insane, and has him removed. Then he tries to murder her, and when she recovers, she finds her beauty gone and her secret discovered. There is quite enough sensation here to interest even the jaded City man, who is said to have grown quite critical of late on the subject of what is really a thrilling plot. But Miss Curtis is not satisfied. The lady's-maid has an extremely handsome brother, who is a wonderful musician, and has a divine tenor voice. With him the stately Lady Judith falls wildly in love, and this part of the story is treated with a great deal of subtlety and clever analysis. However, Lady Judith does not marry her rustic Orpheus, so the social *convenances* are undisturbed. The romance of the Rector of the Parish, who falls in love with a charming school-teacher, is a good deal overshadowed by Lady Judith's story, but it is pleasantly told. A more important episode is the marriage between the daughter of the Tory squire and the Radical candidate for the borough. They separate on their wedding-day, and are not reconciled till the third volume. No one could say that Miss Curtis's book is dull. In fact, her style is very bright and amusing. It is impossible, perhaps, not to be a little bewildered by the amount of characters, and by the crowded incidents; but, on the whole, the scheme of the construction is clear, and certainly the decoration is admirable.

(1) *Wordsworthiana*: *A Selection from Papers read to the Wordsworth Society*. Edited by William Knight. (Macmillan and Co.)

(2) *Mary Myles*. By E. M. Edmonds. (Remington and Co.)

(3) *Art in the Modern State*. By Lady Dilke. (Chapman and Hall.)

(4) *Cressy*. By Bret Harte. (Macmillan and Co.)

(5) *Poems*. By Richard Day. (New York: Cassell and Co.)

(6) *A Game of Chance*. By Ella Curtis. (Hurst and Blackett.)

MR. FROUDE'S BLUE-BOOK

(*Pall Mall Gazette*, April 13, 1889.)

Blue-books are generally dull reading, but Blue-books on Ireland have always been interesting. They form the record of one of the great tragedies of modern Europe. In them England has written down her indictment against herself and has given to the world the history of her shame. If in the last century she tried to govern Ireland with an insolence that was intensified by race hatred and religious prejudice, she has sought to rule her in this century with a stupidity that is aggravated by good intentions. The last of these Blue-books, Mr. Froude's heavy novel, has appeared, however, somewhat too late. The society that he describes has long since passed away. An entirely new factor has appeared in the social development of the country, and this factor is the Irish-American and his influence. To mature its powers, to concentrate its actions, to learn the secret of its own strength and of England's weakness, the Celtic intellect has had to cross the Atlantic. At home it had but learned the pathetic weakness of nationality; in a strange land it realised what indomitable forces nationality possesses. What captivity was to the Jews, exile has been to the Irish. America and American influence has educated them. Their first practical leader is an Irish-American.

But while Mr. Froude's book has no practical relation to modern Irish politics, and does not offer any solution of the present question, it has a certain historical value. It is a vivid picture of Ireland in the latter half of the eighteenth century, a picture often false in its lights and exaggerated in its shadows, but a picture none the less. Mr. Froude admits the martyrdom of Ireland but regrets that the martyrdom was not more completely carried out. His ground of complaint against the Executioner is not his trade but his bungling. It is the bluntness not the cruelty of the sword that he objects to. Resolute government, that shallow shibboleth of those who do not understand how complex a thing the art of government is, is his posthumous panacea for past evils. His hero, Colonel Goring, has the words Law and Order ever on his lips, meaning by the one the enforcement of unjust legislation, and implying by the other the suppression of every fine national aspiration. That the government should enforce iniquity and the governed submit to it, seems to Mr. Froude, as it certainly is to many others, the true ideal of political science. Like most penmen he overrates the power of the sword. Where England has had to struggle she has been wise. Where physical strength has been on her side, as in Ireland, she has been made unwieldy by that strength. Her own strong hands have blinded her. She has had force but no direction.

There is, of course, a story in Mr. Froude's novel. It is not simply a political disquisition. The interest of the tale, such as it is, centres round two men, Colonel Goring and Morty Sullivan, the Cromwellian and the Celt. These men are enemies by race and creed and feeling. The first represents Mr. Froude's cure for Ireland. He is a resolute 'Englishman, with strong Nonconformist tendencies,' who plants an industrial colony on the coast of Kerry, and has deep-rooted objections to that illicit trade with France which in the last century was the sole method by which the Irish people were enabled to pay their rents to their absentee landlords. Colonel Goring bitterly regrets that the Penal Laws against the Catholics are not rigorously carried out. He is a '*Police* at any price' man.

'And this,' said Goring scornfully, 'is what you call governing Ireland, hanging up your law like a scarecrow in the garden till every sparrow has learnt to make a jest of it. Your Popery Acts! Well, you borrowed them from France. The French Catholics did not choose to keep the Hugonots among them, and recalled the Edict of Nantes. As they treated the Hugonots, so you said to all the world that you would treat the Papists. You borrowed from the French the very language of your Statute, but they are not afraid to stand by their law, and you are afraid to stand by yours. You let the people laugh at it, and in teaching them to despise one law, you teach them to despise all laws—God's and man's alike. I cannot say how it will end; but I can tell you this, that you are training up a race with the education which you are giving them that will astonish mankind by and bye.'

Mr. Froude's resume of the history of Ireland is not without power though it is far from being really accurate. 'The Irish,' he tells us, 'had disowned the facts of life, and the facts of life had proved the strongest.' The English, unable to tolerate anarchy so near their shores, 'consulted the Pope. The Pope gave them leave to interfere, and the Pope had the best of the bargain. For the English brought him in, and the Irish . . . kept him there.' England's first settlers were Norman nobles. They became more Irish than the Irish, and England found herself in this difficulty: 'To abandon Ireland would be discreditable, to rule it as a province would be contrary to English traditions.' She then 'tried to rule by dividing,' and failed. The Pope was too strong for her. At last she made her great political discovery. What Ireland wanted was evidently an entirely new population 'of the same race and the same religion as her own.' The new policy was partly carried out:

Elizabeth first and then James and then Cromwell replanted the Island, introducing English, Scots, Hugonots, Flemings, Dutch, tens of thousands of families of vigorous and earnest Protestants, who brought their industries along with them. Twice the Irish . . . tried . . . to drive out this new element . . . They failed. . . . [But] England . . . had no sooner accomplished her long task than she set herself to work to spoil it again. She destroyed the industries of her colonists by her trade laws. She set the Bishops to rob them of their religion. . . . [As for the gentry,] The purpose for which they had been introduced into Ireland was unfulfilled. They were but alien intruders, who did nothing, who were allowed to do nothing. The time would come when an exasperated population would demand that the land should be given back to them, and England would then, perhaps, throw the gentry to the wolves, in the hope of a momentary peace. But her own turn would follow. She would be face to face with the old problem, either to make a new conquest or to retire with disgrace.

Political disquisitions of this kind, and prophecies after the event, are found all through Mr. Froude's book, and on almost every second page we come across aphorisms on the Irish character, on the teachings of Irish history and on the nature of England's mode of government. Some of them represent Mr. Froude's own views, others are entirely dramatic and introduced for the purpose of characterisation. We append some specimens. As epigrams they are not very felicitous, but they are interesting from some points of view.

Irish Society grew up in happy recklessness. Insecurity added zest to enjoyment.

We Irish must either laugh or cry, and if we went in for crying, we should all hang ourselves.

Too close a union with the Irish had produced degeneracy both of character and creed in all the settlements of English.

We age quickly in Ireland with the whiskey and the broken heads.

The Irish leaders cannot fight. They can make the country ungovernable, and keep an English army occupied in watching them.

No nation can ever achieve a liberty that will not be a curse to them, except by arms in the field.

[The Irish] are taught from their cradles that English rule is the cause of all their miseries. They were as ill off under their own chiefs; but they would bear from their natural leaders what they will not bear from us, and if we have not made their lot more wretched we have not made it any better.

'Patriotism? Yes! Patriotism of the Hibernian order. The country has been badly treated, and is poor and miserable. This is the patriot's stock in trade. Does he want it mended? Not he. His own occupation would be gone.'

Irish corruption is the twin-brother of Irish eloquence.

England will not let us break the heads of our scoundrels; she will not break them herself; we are a free country, and must take the consequences.

The functions of the Anglo-Irish Government were to do what ought not to be done, and to leave undone what ought to be done.

The Irish race have always been noisy, useless and ineffectual. They have produced nothing, they have done nothing, which it is possible to admire. What they are, that they have always been, and the only hope for them is that their ridiculous Irish nationality should be buried and forgotten.

The Irish are the best actors in the world.

Order is an exotic in Ireland. It has been imported from England, but it will not grow. It suits neither soil, nor climate. If the English wanted order in Ireland, they should have left none of us alive.

When ruling powers are unjust, nature reasserts her rights.

Even anarchy has its advantages.

Nature keeps an accurate account. . . . The longer a bill is left unpaid, the heavier the accumulation of interest.

You cannot live in Ireland without breaking laws on one side or another. Pecca fortiter, therefore, as . . . Luther said.

The animal spirits of the Irish remained when all else was gone, and if there was no purpose in their lives, they could at least enjoy themselves.

The Irish peasants can make the country hot for the Protestant gentleman, but that is all they are fit for.

As we said before, if Mr. Froude intended his book to help the Tory Government to solve the Irish question he has entirely missed his aim. The Ireland of which he writes has disappeared. As a record, however, of the incapacity of a Teutonic to rule a Celtic people against their own wish, his book is not without value. It is dull, but dull books are very popular at present; and as people have grown a little tired of talking about *Robert Elsmere*, they will probably take to discussing *The Two Chiefs of Dunboy*. There are some who will welcome with delight the idea of solving the Irish question by doing away with the Irish people. There are others who will remember that Ireland has extended her boundaries, and that we have now to reckon with her not merely in the Old World but in the New.

The Two Chiefs of Dunboy: or An Irish Romance of the Last Century. By J. A. Froude. (Longmans, Green and Co.)

SOME LITERARY NOTES—V

(*Woman's World*, May 1889.)

Miss Caroline Fitz Gerald's volume of poems, *Venetia Victrix*, is dedicated to Mr. Robert Browning, and in the poem that gives its title to the book it is not difficult to see traces of Mr. Browning's influence. *Venetia Victrix* is a powerful psychological study of a man's soul, a vivid presentation of a terrible, fiery-coloured moment in a marred and incomplete life. It is sometimes complex and intricate in expression, but then the subject itself is intricate and complex. Plastic simplicity of outline may render for us the visible aspect of life; it is different when we come to deal with those secrets which self-consciousness alone contains, and which self-consciousness itself can but half reveal. Action takes place in the sunlight, but the soul works in the dark.

There is something curiously interesting in the marked tendency of modern poetry to become obscure. Many critics, writing with their eyes fixed on the masterpieces of past literature, have ascribed this tendency to wilfulness and to affectation. Its origin is rather to be found in the complexity of the new problems, and in the fact that self-consciousness is not yet adequate to explain the contents of the Ego. In Mr. Browning's poems, as in life itself which has suggested, or rather necessitated, the new method, thought seems to proceed not on logical lines, but on lines of passion. The unity of the individual is being expressed through its inconsistencies and its contradictions. In a strange twilight man is seeking for himself, and when he has found his own image, he cannot understand it. Objective forms of art, such as sculpture and the drama, sufficed one for the perfect presentation of life; they can no longer so suffice.

The central motive of Miss Caroline Fitz Gerald's psychological poem is the study of a man who to do a noble action wrecks his own soul, sells it to evil, and to the spirit of evil. Many martyrs have for a great cause sacrificed their physical life; the sacrifice of the spiritual life has a more poignant and a more tragic note. The story is supposed to be told by a French doctor, sitting at his window in Paris one evening:

How far off Venice seems to-night! How dim
The still-remembered sunsets, with the rim
Of gold round the stone haloes, where they stand,
Those carven saints, and look towards the land,
Right Westward, perched on high, with palm in hand,
Completing the peaked church-front. Oh how clear
And dark against the evening splendour! Steer
Between the graveyard island and the quay,
Where North-winds dash the spray on Venice;—see

The rosy light behind dark dome and tower,
Or gaunt smoke-laden chimney;—mark the power
Of Nature's gentleness, in rise or fall
Of interlinkèd beauty, to recall
Earth's majesty in desecration's place,
Lending yon grimy pile that dream-like face
Of evening beauty;—note yon rugged cloud,
Red-rimmed and heavy, drooping like a shroud
Over Murano in the dying day.
I see it now as then—so far away!

The face of a boy in the street catches his eye. He seems to see in it some likeness to a dead friend. He begins to think, and at last remembers a hospital ward in Venice:

'Twas an April day,
The year Napoleon's troops took Venice—say
The twenty-fifth of April. All alone
Walking the ward, I heard a sick man moan,
In tones so piteous, as his heart would break:
'Lost, lost, and lost again—for Venice' sake!'
I turned. There lay a man no longer young,
Wasted with fever. I had marked, none hung
About his bed, as friends, with tenderness,
And, when the priest went by, he spared to bless,
Glancing perplexed—perhaps mere sullenness.
I stopped and questioned: 'What is lost, my friend?'
'My soul is lost, and now draws near the end.
My soul is surely lost. Send me no priest!
They sing and solemnise the marriage feast
Of man's salvation in the house of love,
And I in Hell, and God in Heaven above,
And Venice safe and fair on earth between—
No love of mine—mere service—for my Queen.'

He was a seaman, and the tale he tells the doctor before he dies is strange and not a little terrible. Wild rage against a foster-brother who had bitterly wronged him, and who was one of the ten rulers over Venice, drives him to make a mad oath that on the day when he does anything for his country's good he will give his soul to Satan. That night he sails for Dalmatia, and as he is keeping the watch, he sees a phantom boat with seven fiends sailing to Venice:

I heard the fiends' shrill cry: 'For Venice' good!
Rival thine ancient foe in gratitude,
Then come and make thy home with us in Hell!'
I knew it must be so. I knew the spell
Of Satan on my soul. I felt the power
Granted by God to serve Him one last hour,
Then fall for ever as the curse had wrought.
I climbed aloft. My brain had grown one thought,
One hope, one purpose. And I heard the hiss
Of raging disappointment, loth to miss
Its prey—I heard the lapping of the flame,
That through the blanchèd figures went and came,
Darting in frenzy to the devils' yell.
I set that cross on high, and cried: 'To Hell
My soul for ever, and my deed to God!
Once Venice guarded safe, let this vile clod
Drift where fate will.'
    And then (the hideous laugh
Of fiends in full possession, keen to quaff
The wine of one new soul not weak with tears,
Pealing like ruinous thunder in mine ears)
I fell, and heard no more. The pale day broke
Through lazar-windows, when once more I woke,
Remembering I might no more dare to pray.

The idea of the story is extremely powerful, and *Venetia Victrix* is certainly the best poem in the volume—better than *Ophelion*, which is vague, and than *A Friar's Story*, which is pretty but ordinary. It shows that we have in Miss Fitz Gerald a new singer of considerable ability and vigour of mind, and it serves to remind us of the splendid dramatic possibilities extant in life, which are ready for poetry, and unsuitable for the stage. What is really dramatic is not necessarily that which is fitting for presentation in a theatre. The theatre is an accident of the dramatic form. It is not essential to it. We have been deluded by the name of action. To think is to act.

Of the shorter poems collected here, this *Hymn to Persephone* is, perhaps, the best:

Oh, fill my cup, Persephone,
With dim red wine of Spring,
    And drop therein a faded leaf
    Plucked from the Autumn's bearded sheaf,
Whence, dread one, I may quaff to thee,
    While all the woodlands ring.

Oh, fill my heart, Persephone,
With thine immortal pain,
    That lingers round the willow bowers
    In memories of old happy hours,
When thou didst wander fair and free
    O'er Enna's blooming plain.

Oh, fill my soul, Persephone,
With music all thine own!
    Teach me some song thy childhood knew,
    Lisped in the meadow's morning dew,
Or chant on this high windy lea,
    Thy godhead's ceaseless moan.

But this *Venetian Song* also has a good deal of charm:

Leaning between carved stone and stone,
As glossy birds peer from a nest
Scooped in the crumbling trunk where rest
Their freckled eggs, I pause alone
    And linger in the light awhile,
        Waiting for joy to come to me—
    Only the dawn beyond yon isle,
        Only the sunlight on the sea.

I gaze—then turn and ply my loom,
Or broider blossoms close beside;
The morning world lies warm and wide,
But here is dim, cool silent gloom,
    Gold crust and crimson velvet pile,
        And not one face to smile on me—
    Only the dawn beyond yon isle,
        Only the sunlight on the sea.

Over the world the splendours break
Of morning light and noontide glow,
And when the broad red sun sinks low,
And in the wave long shadows shake,
    Youths, maidens, glad with song and wile,
        Glide and are gone, and leave with me
    Only the dawn beyond yon isle,
        Only the sunlight on the sea.

Darwinism and Politics, by Mr. David Ritchie, of Jesus College, Oxford, contains some very interesting speculations on the position and the future of women in the modern State. The one objection to the equality of the sexes that he considers deserves serious attention is that made by Sir James Stephen in his clever attack on John Stuart Mill. Sir James Stephen points out in *Liberty, Equality, Fraternity*, that women may suffer more than they have done, if plunged into a nominally equal but really unequal contest in the already overcrowded labour market. Mr. Ritchie answers that, while the conclusion usually drawn from this argument is a sentimental reaction in favour of the old family ideal, as, for instance, in Mr. Besant's books, there is another alternative, and that is the resettling of the labour question. 'The elevation of the status of women and the regulation of the conditions of labour are ultimately,' he says, 'inseparable questions. On the basis of individualism, I cannot see how it is possible to answer the objections of Sir James Stephen.' Mr. Herbert Spencer, in his *Sociology*, expresses his fear that women, if admitted now to political life, might do mischief by introducing the ethics of the family into the State. 'Under the ethics of the family the greatest benefits must be given where the merits are smallest; under the ethics of the State the benefits must be proportioned to the merits.' In answer to this, Mr. Ritchie asks whether in any society we have ever seen people so get benefits in proportion to their merits, and protests against Mr. Spencer's separation of the ethics of the family from those of the State. If something is right in a family, it is difficult to see why it is therefore, without any further reason, wrong in the State. If the participation of women in politics means that as a good family educates all its members, so must a good State, what better issue could there be? The family ideal of the State may be difficult of attainment, but as an ideal it is better than the policeman theory. It would mean the moralisation of politics. The cultivation of separate sorts of virtues and separate ideals of duty in men and women has led to the whole social fabric being

139

weaker and unhealthier than it need be. As for the objection that in countries where it is considered necessary to have compulsory military service for all men, it would be unjust and inexpedient that women should have a voice in political matters, Mr. Ritchie meets it, or tries to meet it, by proposing that all women physically fitted for such purpose should be compelled to undergo training as nurses, and should be liable to be called upon to serve as nurses in time of war. This training, he remarks, 'would be more useful to them and to the community in time of peace than his military training is to the peasant or artisan.' Mr. Ritchie's little book is extremely suggestive, and full of valuable ideas for the philosophic student of sociology.

* * * * *

Mr. Alan Cole's lecture on Irish lace, delivered recently before the Society of Arts, contains some extremely useful suggestions as to the best method of securing an immediate connection between the art schools of a country and the country's ordinary manufactures. In 1883, Mr. Cole was deputed by the Department of Science and Art to lecture at Cork and at Limerick on the subject of lace-making, and to give a history of its rise and development in other countries, as well as a review of the many kinds of ornamental patterns used from the sixteenth century to modern times. In order to make these lectures of practical value, Mr. Cole placed typical specimens of Irish laces beside Italian, Flemish, and French laces, which seem to be the prototypes of the lace of Ireland. The public interest was immediately aroused. Some of the newspapers stoutly maintained that the ornament and patterns of Irish lace were of such a national character that it was wrong to asperse them on that score. Others took a different view, and came to the conclusion that Irish lace could be vastly improved in all respects, if some systematic action could be taken to induce the lace-makers to work from more intelligently composed patterns than those in general use. There was a consensus of opinion that the workmanship of Irish laces was good, and that it could be applied to better materials than those ordinarily used, and that its methods were suited to render a greater variety of patterns than those usually attempted.

These and other circumstances seem to have prompted the promoters of the Cork Exhibition to further efforts in the cause of lace-making. Towards the close of the year 1883 they made fresh representations to Government, and inquired what forms of State assistance could be given. A number of convents in the neighbourhood of Cork was engaged in giving instruction to children under their care in lace and crochet making. At some, rooms were allotted for the use of grown-up workers who made laces under the supervision of the nuns. These convents obviously were centres where experiments in reform could be tried. The convents, however, lacked instruction in the designing of patterns for laces. An excellent School of Art was at work at Cork, but the students there had not been instructed in specially designing for lace. If the convents with their workrooms could be brought into relation with this School of Art, it seemed possible that something of a serious character might be done to benefit lace-makers, and also to open up a new field in ornamental design for the students at the School of Art. The rules of the Department of Science and Art were found to be adapted to aid in meeting such wants as those sketched out by the promoters at Cork. As the nuns in the different lace-making convents had not been able to attend in Cork to hear Mr. Cole's lectures, they asked that he should visit them and repeat them at the convents. This Mr. Cole did early in 1884, the masters of the local Schools of Art accompanying him on his visits. Negotiations were forthwith opened for connecting the convents with the art schools. By the end of 1885 some six or seven different lace-making convents had placed themselves in connection with Schools of Art at Cork and Waterford. These convents were attended not only by the nuns but by outside pupils also; and, at the request of the convents, Mr. Cole has visited them twice a year, lecturing and giving advice upon designs for lace. The composition of new patterns for lace was attempted, and old patterns which had degenerated were revised and redrawn for the use of the workers connected with the convents. There are now twelve convents, Mr. Cole tells us, where instruction in drawing and in the composition of patterns is given, and some of the students have won some of the higher prizes offered by the Department of Science and Art for designing lace-patterns.

The Cork School of Art then acquired a collection of finely-patterned old laces, selections from which are freely circulated through the different convents connected with that school. They have also the privilege of borrowing similar specimens of old lace from the South Kensington Museum. So successful has been the system of education pursued by Mr. Brennan, the head-master of the Cork School of Art, that two female students of his school last year gained the gold and silver medals for their designs for laces and crochets at the national competition which annually takes place in London between all the Schools of Art in the United Kingdom. As for the many lace-makers who were not connected either with the convents or with the art schools, in order to assist them, a committee of ladies and gentlemen interested in Irish lace-making raised subscriptions, and offered prizes to be competed for by designers generally. The best designs were then placed out with lace-makers, and carried into execution. It is, of course, often said that the proper person to make the design is the lace-maker. Mr. Cole, however, points out that from the sixteenth century forward the patterns for ornamental laces have always been designed by decorative artists having knowledge of the composition of ornament, and of the materials for which they were called upon to design. Lace pattern books were published in considerable quantity in Italy, France and Germany during the sixteenth and seventeenth centuries, and from these the lace-makers worked. Many lace-makers would, no doubt, derive benefit from practice in drawing, in discriminating between well and badly shaped forms. But the skill they are primarily required to show and to develop is one of fine fingers in reproducing beautiful forms in threads. The conception, arrangement, and drawing of beautiful forms for a design, have to be undertaken by decorative artists acquainted with the limitations of those materials and methods which the ultimate expression of the design involves.

This lovely Irish art of lace-making is very much indebted to Mr. Cole, who has really re-created it, given it new life, and shown it the true artistic lines on which to progress. Hardly £20,000 a year is spent by England upon Irish laces, and almost all of this goes upon the cheaper and commoner kinds. And yet, as Mr. Cole points out, it is possible to produce Irish laces of as high artistic quality as almost any foreign laces. The Queen, Lady Londonderry, Lady Dorothy Nevill, Mrs. Alfred Morrison, and others, have done much to encourage the Irish workers, and it rests largely with the ladies of England whether this beautiful art lives or dies. The real good of a piece of lace, says Mr. Ruskin, is 'that it should show, first, that the designer of it had a pretty fancy; next, that the maker of it had fine fingers; lastly, that the wearer of it has worthiness or dignity enough to obtain what is difficult to obtain, and common-sense enough not to wear it on all occasions.'

* * * * *

The High-Caste Hindu Woman is an interesting book. It is from the pen of the Pundita Ramabai Sarasvati, and the introduction is written by Miss Rachel Bodley, M.D., the Dean of the Woman's Medical College of Pennsylvania. The story of the parentage of this learned lady is very curious. A certain Hindu, being on a religious pilgrimage with his family, which consisted of his wife and two daughters, one nine and the other seven years of age, stopped in a town to rest for a day or two. One morning the Hindu was bathing in the sacred river Godavari, near the town, when he saw a fine-looking man coming there to bathe also. After the ablution and the morning prayers were over, the father inquired of the stranger who he was and whence he came. On learning his caste, and clan, and dwelling-place, and also that he was a widower, he offered him his little daughter of nine in marriage. All things were settled in an hour or so; next day the marriage was concluded, and the little girl placed in the possession of the stranger, who took her nearly nine hundred miles away from her home, and gave her into the charge of his mother. The stranger was the learned Ananta Shastri, a Brahman pundit, who had very advanced views on the subject of woman's education, and he determined that he would teach his girl-wife Sanskrit, and give her the intellectual culture that had been always denied to women in India. Their daughter was the Pundita Ramabai, who, after the death of her parents, travelled all over India advocating the cause of female education, and to whom seems to be due the first suggestion for the establishment of the profession of women doctors. In 1866, Miss Mary Carpenter made a short tour in India for the purpose of finding out some way by which women's condition in that country might be improved. She at once discovered that the chief means by which the desired end could be accomplished was by furnishing women teachers for the Hindu Zenanas. She suggested that the British Government should establish normal schools for training women teachers, and that scholarships should be awarded to girls in order to prolong their school-going period, and to assist indigent women who would otherwise be unable to pursue their studies.

In response to Miss Carpenter's appeal, upon her return to England, the English Government founded several schools for women in India, and a few 'Mary Carpenter Scholarships' were endowed by benevolent persons. These schools were open to women of every caste; but while they have undoubtedly been of use, they have not realised the hopes of their founders, chiefly through the impossibility of keeping caste rules in them. Ramabai, in a very eloquent chapter, proposes to solve the problem in a different way. Her suggestion is that houses should be opened for the young and high-caste child-widows, where they can take shelter without the fear of losing their caste, or of being disturbed in their religious belief, and where they may have entire freedom of action as regards caste rules. The whole account given by the Pundita of the life of the high-caste Hindu lady is full of suggestion for the social reformer and the student of progress, and her book, which is wonderfully well written, is likely to produce a radical change in the educational schemes that at present prevail in India.

(1) *Venetia Victrix*. By Caroline Fitz Gerald. (Macmillan and Co.)

(2) *Darwinism and Politics*. By David Ritchie, Jesus College, Oxford. (Swan Sonnenschein and Co.)

(3) *The High-Caste Hindu Woman*. By the Pandita Ramabai Sarasvati. (Bell and Sons.)

OUIDA'S NEW NOVEL

(*Pall Mall Gazette*, May 17, 1889.)

Ouida is the last of the romantics. She belongs to the school of Bulwer Lytton and George Sand, though she may lack the learning of the one and the sincerity of the other. She tries to make passion, imagination, and poetry part of fiction. She still believes in heroes and in heroines. She is florid and fervent and fanciful. Yet even she, the high priestess of the impossible, is affected by her age. Her last book, *Guilderoy* as she calls it, is an elaborate psychological study of modern temperaments. For her, it is realistic, and she has certainly caught much of the tone and temper of the society of our day. Her people move with ease and grace and indolence. The book may be described as a study of the peerage from a poetical point of view. Those who are tired of mediocre young curates who have doubts, of serious young ladies who have missions, and of the ordinary figureheads of most of the English fiction of our time, might turn with pleasure, if not with profit, to this amazing romance. It is a resplendent picture of our aristocracy. No expense has been spared in gilding. For the comparatively small sum of £1, 11s. 6d. one is introduced to the best society. The central figures are exaggerated, but the background is admirable. In spite of everything, it gives one a sense of something like life.

What is the story? Well, we must admit that we have a faint suspicion that Ouida has told it to us before. Lord Guilderoy, 'whose name was as old as the days of Knut,' falls madly in love, or fancies that he falls madly in love, with a rustic Perdita, a provincial Artemis who has 'a Gainsborough face, with wide-opened questioning eyes and tumbled auburn hair.' She is poor but well-born, being the only child of Mr. Vernon of Llanarth, a curious recluse, who is half a pedant and half Don Quixote. Guilderoy marries her and, tiring of her shyness, her lack of power to express herself, her want of knowledge of fashionable life, returns to an old passion for a wonderful creature called the Duchess of Soriá. Lady Guilderoy becomes ice; the Duchess becomes fire; at the end of the book Guilderoy is a pitiable object. He has to submit to be forgiven by one woman, and to endure to be forgotten by the other. He is thoroughly weak, thoroughly worthless, and the most fascinating person in the whole story. Then there is his sister Lady Sunbury, who is very anxious for Guilderoy to marry, and is quite determined to hate his wife. She is really a capital sketch. Ouida describes her as 'one of those admirably virtuous women who are more likely to turn men away from the paths of virtue than the wickedest of sirens.' She irritates herself, alienates her children, and infuriates her husband:

'You are perfectly right; I know you are always right; I admit you are; but it is just that which makes you so damnably odious!' said Lord Sunbury once, in a burst of rage, in his town house, speaking in such stentorian tones that the people passing up Grosvenor Street looked up at his open windows, and a crossing-sweeper said to a match-seller, 'My eye! ain't he giving it to the old gal like blazes.'

The noblest character in the book is Lord Aubrey. As he is not a genius he, naturally, behaves admirably on every occasion. He begins by pitying the neglected Lady Guilderoy, and ends by loving her, but he makes the great renunciation with considerable effect, and, having induced Lady Guilderoy to receive back her husband, he accepts 'a distant and arduous Viceroyalty.' He is Ouida's ideal of the true politician, for Ouida has apparently taken to the study of English politics. A great deal of her book is devoted to political disquisitions. She believes that the proper rulers of a country like ours are the aristocrats. Oligarchy has great fascinations for her. She thinks meanly of the people and adores the House of Lords and Lord Salisbury. Here are some of her views. We will not call them ideas:

The House of Lords wants nothing of the nation, and therefore it is the only candid and disinterested guardian of the people's needs and resources. It has never withstood the real desire of the country: it has only stood between the country and its impetuous and evanescent follies.

A democracy cannot understand honour; how should it? The Caucus is chiefly made up of men who sand their sugar, put alum in their bread, forge bayonets and girders which bend like willow-wands, send bad calico to India, and insure vessels at Lloyd's which they know will go to the bottom before they have been ten days at sea.

Lord Salisbury has often been accused of arrogance; people have never seen that what they mistook for arrogance was the natural, candid consciousness of a great noble that he is more capable of leading the country than most men composing it would be.

Democracy, after having made everything supremely hideous and uncomfortable for everybody, always ends by clinging to the coat tails of some successful general.

The prosperous politician may be honest, but his honesty is at best a questionable quality. The moment that a thing is a métier, it is wholly absurd to talk about any disinterestedness in the pursuit of it. To the professional politician national affairs are a manufacture into which he puts his audacity and his time, and out of which he expects to make so much percentage for his lifetime.

There is too great a tendency to govern the world by noise.

Ouida's aphorisms on women, love, and modern society are somewhat more characteristic:

Women speak as though the heart were to be treated at will like a stone, or a bath.

Half the passions of men die early, because they are expected to be eternal.

It is the folly of life that lends charm to it.

What is the cause of half the misery of women? That their love is so much more tenacious than the man's: it grows stronger as his grows weaker.

To endure the country in England for long, one must have the rusticity of Wordsworth's mind, and boots and stockings as homely.

It is because men feel the necessity to explain that they drop into the habit of saying what is not true. Wise is the woman who never insists on an explanation.

Love can make its own world in a solitude à deux, but marriage cannot.

Nominally monogamous, all cultured society is polygamous; often even polyandrous.

Moralists say that a soul should resist passion. They might as well say that a house should resist an earthquake.

The whole world is just now on its knees before the poorer classes: all the cardinal virtues are taken for granted in them, and it is only property of any kind which is the sinner.

Men are not merciful to women's tears as a rule; and when it is a woman belonging to them who weeps, they only go out, and slam the door behind them.

Men always consider women unjust to them, when they fail to deify their weaknesses.

No passion, once broken, will ever bear renewal.

Feeling loses its force and its delicacy if we put it under the microscope too often.

Anything which is not flattery seems injustice to a woman.

When society is aware that you think it a flock of geese, it revenges itself by hissing loudly behind your back.

Of descriptions of scenery and art we have, of course, a large number, and it is impossible not to recognise the touch of the real Ouida manner in the following:

It was an old palace: lofty, spacious, magnificent, and dull. Busts of dusky yellow marble, weird bronzes stretching out gaunt arms into the darkness, ivories brown with age, worn brocades with gold threads gleaming in them, and tapestries with strange and pallid figures of dead gods, were all half revealed and half obscured in the twilight. As he moved through them, a figure which looked almost as pale as the Adonis of the tapestry and was erect and motionless like the statue of the wounded Love, came before his sight out of the darkness. It was that of Gladys.

It is a manner full of exaggeration and overemphasis, but with some remarkable rhetorical qualities and a good deal of colour. Ouida is fond of airing a smattering of culture, but she has a certain intrinsic insight into things and, though she is rarely true, she is never dull. *Guilderoy*, with all its faults, which are great, and its absurdities, which are greater, is a book to be read.

Guilderoy. By Ouida. (Chatto and Windus.)

SOME LITERARY NOTES—VI

(*Woman's World*, June 1889.)

A writer in the *Quarterly Review* for January 1874 says:

No literary event since the war has excited anything like such a sensation in Paris as the publication of the Lettres à une Inconnue. Even politics became a secondary consideration for the hour, and academicians or deputies of opposite parties might be seen eagerly accosting each other in the Chamber or the street to inquire who this fascinating and perplexing 'unknown' could be. The statement in the Revue des Deux Mondes that she was an Englishwoman, moving in brilliant society, was not supported by evidence; and M. Blanchard, the painter, from whom the publisher received the manuscripts, died most provokingly at the very commencement of the inquiry, and made no sign. Some intimate friends of Mérimée, rendered incredulous by wounded self-love at not having been admitted to his confidence, insisted that there was no secret to tell; their hypothesis being that the Inconnue was a myth, and the letters a romance, with which some petty details of actual life had been interwoven to keep up the mystification.

But an artist like Mérimée would not have left his work in so unformed a state, so defaced by repetitions, or with such a want of proportion between the parts. The *Inconnue* was undoubtedly a real person, and her letters in answer to those of Mérimée have just been published by Messrs. Macmillan under the title of *An Author's Love.*

Her letters? Well, they are such letters as she might have written. 'By the tideless sea at Cannes on a summer day,' says their anonymous author, 'I had fallen asleep, and the plashing of the waves upon the shore had doubtless made me dream. When I awoke the yellow paper-covered volumes of Prosper Mérimée's *Lettres à une Inconnue* lay beside me; I had been reading the book before I fell asleep, but the answers—had they ever been written, or had I only dreamed?' The invention of the love-letters of a curious and unknown personality, the heroine of one of the great literary flirtations of our age, was a clever idea, and certainly the author has carried out his scheme with wonderful success; with such success indeed that it is said that one of our statesmen, whose name occurs more than once in the volume, was for a moment completely taken in by what is really a *jeu-d'esprit*, the first serious joke perpetrated by Messrs. Macmillan in their publishing capacity. Perhaps it is too much to call it a joke. It is a fine, delicate piece of fiction, an imaginative attempt to complete a real romance. As we had the letters of the academic Romeo, it was obviously right that we should pretend we had the answers of the clever and somewhat *mondaine* Juliet. Or is it Juliet herself, in her little Paris boudoir, looking over these two volumes with a sad, cynical smile? Well, to be put into fiction is always a tribute to one's reality.

As for extracts from these fascinating forgeries, the letters should be read in conjunction with those of Mérimée himself. It is difficult to judge of them by samples. We find the *Inconnue* first in London, probably in 1840.

Little (she writes) can you imagine the storm of indignation you aroused in me by your remark that your feelings for me were those suitable for a fourteen-year-old niece. Merci. Anything less like a respectable uncle than yourself I cannot well imagine. The rôle would never suit you, believe me, so do not try it.

Now in return for your story of the phlegmatic musical animal who called forth such stormy devotion in a female breast, and who, himself cold and indifferent, was loved to the extent of a watery grave being sought by his inamorata as solace for his indifference, let me ask the question why the women who torment men with their uncertain tempers, drive them wild with jealousy, laugh contemptuously at their humble entreaties, and fling their money to the winds, have twice the hold upon their affections that the patient, long-suffering, domestic, frugal Griseldas have, whose existences are one long penance of unsuccessful efforts to please? Answer this comprehensively, and you will have solved a riddle which has puzzled women since Eve asked questions in Paradise.

Later on she writes:

Why should all natures be alike? It would make the old saws useless if they were, and deprive us of one of the truest of them all, 'Variety is the spice of life.' How terribly monotonous it would be if all the flowers were roses, every woman a queen, and each man a philosopher. My private opinion is that it takes at least six men such as one meets every day to make one really valuable one. I like so many men for one particular quality which they possess, and so few men for all. Comprenez-vous?

In another place:

Is it not a trifle dangerous, this experiment we are trying of a friendship in pen and ink and paper? A letter. What thing on earth more dangerous to confide in? Written at blood heat, it may reach its destination when the recipient's mental thermometer counts zero, and the burning words and thrilling sentences may turn to ice and be congealed as they are read. . . . A letter; the most uncertain thing in a world of uncertainties, the best or the worst thing devised by mortals.

Again:

Surely it was for you, mon cher, that the description given of a friend of mine was originally intended. He is a trifle cynical, this friend, and decidedly pessimistic, and of him it was reported that he never believed in anything until he saw it, and then he was convinced that it was an optical illusion. The accuracy of the description struck me.

They seem to have loved each other best when they were parted.

I think I cannot bear it much longer, this incessant quarrelling when we meet, and your unkindness during the short time that you are with me. Why not let it all end? it would be better for both of us. I do not love you less when I write these words; if you could know the sadness which they echo in my heart you would believe this. No, I think I love you more, but I cannot understand you. As you have often said, our natures must be very different, entirely different; if so, what is this curious bond between them? To me you seem possessed with some strange restlessness and morbid melancholy which utterly spoils your life, and in return you never see me without overwhelming me with reproaches, if not for one thing, for another. I tell you I cannot, will not, bear it longer. If you love me, then in God's name cease tormenting me as well as yourself with these wretched doubts and questionings and complaints. I have been ill, seriously ill, and there is nothing to account for my illness save the misery of this apparently hopeless state of things existing between us. You have made me weep bitter tears of alternate self-reproach and indignation, and finally of complete miserable bewilderment as to this unhappy condition of affairs. Believe me, tears like these are not good to mingle with love, they are too bitter, too scorching, they blister love's wings and fall too heavily on love's heart. I feel worn out with a dreary sort of hopelessness; if you know a cure for pain like this send it to me quickly.

Yet, in the very next letter, she says to him:

Although I said good-bye to you less than an hour ago, I cannot refrain from writing to tell you that a happy calm which seems to penetrate my whole being seems also to have wiped out all remembrance of the misery and unhappiness which has overwhelmed me lately. Why cannot it always be so, or would life perhaps be then too blessed, too wholly happy for it to be life? I know that you are free to-night, will you not write to me, that the first words my eyes fall upon to-morrow shall prove that to-day has not been a dream? Yes, write to me.

The letter that immediately follows is one of six words only:

Let me dream—Let me dream.

In the following there are interesting touches of actuality:

Did you ever try a cup of tea (the national beverage, by the way) at an English railway station? If you have not, I would advise you, as a friend, to continue to abstain! The names of the American drinks are rather against them, the straws are, I think, about the best part of them. You do not tell me what you think of Mr. Disraeli. I once met him at a ball at the Duke of Sutherland's in the long picture gallery of Stafford House. I was walking with Lord Shrewsbury, and without a word of warning he stopped and introduced him, mentioning with reckless mendacity that I had read every book he had written and admired them all, then he coolly walked off and left me standing face to face with the great statesman. He talked to me for some time, and I studied him carefully. I should say he was a man with one steady aim: endless patience, untiring perseverance, iron concentration; marking out one straight line before him so unbending that despite themselves men stand aside as it is drawn straightly and steadily on. A man who believes that determination brings strength, strength brings endurance, and endurance brings success. You know how often in his novels he speaks of the influence of women, socially, morally, and politically, yet his manner was the least interested or deferential in talking that I have ever met with in a man of his class. He certainly thought this particular woman of singularly small account, or else the brusque and tactless allusion to his books may perhaps have annoyed him as it did me; but whatever the cause, when he promptly left me at the first approach of a mutual acquaintance, I felt distinctly snubbed. Of the two men, Mr. Gladstone was infinitely more agreeable in his manner, he left one with the pleasant feeling of measuring a little higher in cubic inches than one did before, than which I know no more delightful sensation. A Paris, bientôt.

Elsewhere, we find cleverly-written descriptions of life in Italy, in Algiers, at Hombourg, at French boarding-houses; stories about Napoleon III., Guizot, Prince Gortschakoff, Montalembert, and others; political speculations, literary criticisms, and witty social scandal; and everywhere a keen sense of humour, a wonderful power of observation. As reconstructed in these letters, the *Inconnue* seems to have been not unlike Mérimée himself. She had the same restless, unyielding, independent character. Each desired to analyse the other. Each, being a critic, was better fitted for friendship than for love. 'We are so different,' said Mérimée once to her, 'that we can hardly understand each other.' But it was because they were so alike that each remained a mystery to the other. Yet they ultimately attained to a high altitude of loyal and faithful friendship, and from a purely literary point of view these fictitious letters give the finishing touch to the strange romance that so stirred Paris fifteen years ago. Perhaps the real letters will be published some day. When they are, how interesting to compare them!

The Bird-Bride, by Graham R. Tomson, is a collection of romantic ballads, delicate sonnets, and metrical studies in foreign fanciful forms. The poem that gives its title to the book is the lament of an Eskimo hunter over the loss of his wife and children.

Years agone, on the flat white strand,
　I won my sweet sea-girl:
Wrapped in my coat of the snow-white fur,
I watched the wild birds settle and stir,
　The grey gulls gather and whirl.

One, the greatest of all the flock,
　Perched on an ice-floe bare,
Called and cried as her heart were broke,
And straight they were changed, that fleet bird-folk,
　To women young and fair.

Swift I sprang from my hiding-place
　And held the fairest fast;
I held her fast, the sweet, strange thing:
Her comrades skirled, but they all took wing,
　And smote me as they passed.

I bore her safe to my warm snow house;
　Full sweetly there she smiled;
And yet, whenever the shrill winds blew,
She would beat her long white arms anew,
　And her eyes glanced quick and wild.

But I took her to wife, and clothed her warm
　With skins of the gleaming seal;
Her wandering glances sank to rest
When she held a babe to her fair, warm breast,
　And she loved me dear and leal.

Together we tracked the fox and the seal,
　And at her behest I swore
That bird and beast my bow might slay
For meat and for raiment, day by day,
　But never a grey gull more.

Famine comes upon the land, and the hunter, forgetting his oath, slays four sea-gulls for food. The bird-wife 'shrilled out in a woful cry,' and taking the plumage of the dead birds, she makes wings for her children and for herself, and flies away with them.

'Babes of mine, of the wild wind's kin,
　Feather ye quick, nor stay.
Oh, oho! but the wild winds blow!
Babes of mine, it is time to go:
　Up, dear hearts, and away!'

And lo! the grey plumes covered them all,
  Shoulder and breast and brow.
I felt the wind of their whirling flight:
Was it sea or sky? was it day or night?
  It is always night-time now.

  Dear, will you never relent, come back?
  I loved you long and true.
O winged white wife, and our children three,
Of the wild wind's kin though you surely be,
  Are ye not of my kin too?

  Ay, ye once were mine, and, till I forget,
  Ye are mine forever and aye,
Mine, wherever your wild wings go,
While shrill winds whistle across the snow
  And the skies are blear and grey.

Some powerful and strong ballads follow, many of which, such as *The Cruel Priest*, *Deid Folks' Ferry*, and *Märchen*, are in that curious combination of Scotch and Border dialect so much affected now by our modern poets. Certainly dialect is dramatic. It is a vivid method of re-creating a past that never existed. It is something between 'A Return to Nature' and 'A Return to the Glossary.' It is so artificial that it is really naïve. From the point of view of mere music, much may be said for it. Wonderful diminutives lend new notes of tenderness to the song. There are possibilities of fresh rhymes, and in search for a fresh rhyme poets may be excused if they wander from the broad highroad of classical utterance into devious byways and less-trodden paths. Sometimes one is tempted to look on dialect as expressing simply the pathos of provincialisms, but there is more in it than mere mispronunciations. With the revival of an antique form, often comes the revival of an antique spirit. Through limitations that are sometimes uncouth, and always narrow, comes Tragedy herself; and though she may stammer in her utterance, and deck herself in cast-off weeds and trammelling raiment, still we must hold ourselves in readiness to accept her, so rare are her visits to us now, so rare her presence in an age that demands a happy ending from every play, and that sees in the theatre merely a source of amusement. The form, too, of the ballad—how perfect it is in its dramatic unity! It is so perfect that we must forgive it its dialect, if it happens to speak in that strange tongue.

  Then by cam' the bride's company
    Wi' torches burning bright.
'Tak' up, tak' up your bonny bride
    A' in the mirk midnight!'

  Oh, wan, wan was the bridegroom's face
    And wan, wan was the bride,
But clay-cauld was the young mess-priest
    That stood them twa beside!

  Says, 'Rax me out your hand, Sir Knight,
    And wed her wi' this ring';
And the deid bride's hand it was as cauld
    As ony earthly thing.

  The priest he touched that lady's hand,
    And never a word he said;
The priest he touched that lady's hand,
    And his ain was wet and red.

  The priest he lifted his ain right hand,
    And the red blood dripped and fell.
Says, 'I loved ye, lady, and ye loved me;
    Sae I took your life mysel'.'

  . . . . .

  Oh! red, red was the dawn o' day,
    And tall was the gallows-tree:
The Southland lord to his ain has fled
    And the mess-priest's hangit hie!

Of the sonnets, this *To Herodotus* is worth quoting:

  Far-travelled coaster of the midland seas,
    What marvels did those curious eyes behold!
    Winged snakes, and carven labyrinths of old;
The emerald column raised to Heracles;
King Perseus' shrine upon the Chemmian leas;
    Four-footed fishes, decked with gems and gold:
    But thou didst leave some secrets yet untold,
And veiled the dread Osirian mysteries.

And now the golden asphodels among
Thy footsteps fare, and to the lordly dead
Thou tellest all the stories left unsaid
Of secret rites and runes forgotten long,
Of that dark folk who ate the Lotus-bread
And sang the melancholy Linus-song.

Mrs. Tomson has certainly a very refined sense of form. Her verse, especially in the series entitled *New Words to Old Tunes*, has grace and distinction. Some of the shorter poems are, to use a phrase made classical by Mr. Pater, 'little carved ivories of speech.' She is one of our most artistic workers in poetry, and treats language as a fine material.

(1) *An Author's Love*: Being the Unpublished Letters of Prosper Mérimée's 'Inconnue.' (Macmillan and Co.)

(2) *The Bird-Bride*: A Volume of Ballads and Sonnets. By Graham R. Tomson. (Longmans, Green and Co.)

A THOUGHT-READER'S NOVEL

(*Pall Mall Gazette*, June 5, 1889.)

There is a great deal to be said in favour of reading a novel backwards. The last page is, as a rule, the most interesting, and when one begins with the catastrophe or the *dénoûment* one feels on pleasant terms of equality with the author. It is like going behind the scenes of a theatre. One is no longer taken in, and the hairbreadth escapes of the hero and the wild agonies of the heroine leave one absolutely unmoved. One knows the jealously-guarded secret, and one can afford to smile at the quite unnecessary anxiety that the puppets of fiction always consider it their duty to display. In the case of Mr. Stuart Cumberland's novel, *The Vasty Deep*, as he calls it, the last page is certainly thrilling and makes us curious to know more about 'Brown, the medium.'

Scene, a padded room in a mad-house in the United States.

A gibbering lunatic discovered dashing wildly about the chamber as if in the act of chasing invisible forms.

'This is our worst case,' says a doctor opening the cell to one of the visitors in lunacy. 'He was a spirit medium and he is hourly haunted by the creations of his fancy. We have to carefully watch him, for he has developed suicidal tendencies.'

The lunatic makes a dash at the retreating form of his visitors, and, as the door closes upon him, sinks with a yell upon the floor.

A week later the lifeless body of Brown, the medium, is found suspended from the gas bracket in his cell.

How clearly one sees it all! How forcible and direct the style is! And what a thrilling touch of actuality the simple mention of the 'gas bracket' gives us! Certainly *The Vasty Deep* is a book to be read.

And we have read it; read it with great care. Though it is largely autobiographical, it is none the less a work of fiction and, though some of us may think that there is very little use in exposing what is already exposed and revealing the secrets of Polichinelle, no doubt there are many who will be interested to hear of the tricks and deceptions of crafty mediums, of their gauze masks, telescopic rods and invisible silk threads, and of the marvellous raps they can produce simply by displacing the *peroneus longus* muscle! The book opens with a description of the scene by the death-bed of Alderman Parkinson. Dr. Josiah Brown, the eminent medium, is in attendance and tries to comfort the honest merchant by producing noises on the bedpost. Mr. Parkinson, however, being extremely anxious to revisit Mrs. Parkinson, in a materialised form after death, will not be satisfied till he has received from his wife a solemn promise that she will not marry again, such a marriage being, in his eyes, nothing more nor less than bigamy. Having received an assurance to this effect from her, Mr. Parkinson dies, his soul, according to the medium, being escorted to the spheres by 'a band of white-robed spirits.' This is the prologue. The next chapter is entitled 'Five Years After.' Violet Parkinson, the Alderman's only child, is in love with Jack Alston, who is 'poor, but clever.' Mrs. Parkinson, however, will not hear of any marriage till the deceased Alderman has materialised himself and given his formal consent. A seance is held at which Jack Alston unmasks the medium and shows Dr. Josiah Brown to be an impostor—a foolish act, on his part, as he is at once ordered to leave the house by the infuriated Mrs. Parkinson, whose faith in the Doctor is not in the least shaken by the unfortunate exposure.

The lovers are consequently parted. Jack sails for Newfoundland, is shipwrecked and carefully, somewhat too carefully, tended by 'La-ki-wa, or the Star that shines,' a lovely Indian maiden who belongs to the tribe of the Micmacs. She is a fascinating creature who wears 'a necklace composed of thirteen nuggets of pure gold,' a blanket of English manufacture and trousers of tanned leather. In fact, as Mr. Stuart Cumberland observes, she looks 'the embodiment of fresh dewy morn.' When Jack, on recovering his senses, sees her, he naturally inquires who she is. She answers, in the simple utterance endeared to us by Fenimore Cooper, 'I am La-ki-wa. I am the only child of my father, Tall Pine, chief of the Dildoos.' She talks, Mr. Cumberland informs us, very good English. Jack at once entrusts her with the following telegram which he writes on the back of a five-pound note:—

Miss Violet Parkinson, Hotel Kronprinz, Franzensbad, Austria.—Safe. JACK.

But La-ki-wa, we regret to say, says to herself, 'He belongs to Tall Pine, to the Dildoos, and to me,' and never sends the telegram. Subsequently, La-ki-wa proposes to Jack who promptly rejects her and, with the usual callousness of men, offers her a brother's love. La-ki-wa, naturally, regrets the premature disclosure of her passion and weeps. 'My brother,' she remarks, 'will think that I have the timid heart of a deer with the crying voice of a papoose. I, the daughter of Tall Pine—I a Micmac, to show the grief that is in my heart. O, my brother, I am ashamed.' Jack comforts her with the hollow sophistries of a civilised being and gives her his photograph. As he is on his way to the steamer he receives from Big Deer a soiled piece of a biscuit bag. On it is written La-ki-wa's confession of her disgraceful behaviour about the telegram. 'His thoughts,' Mr. Cumberland tells us, 'were bitter towards La-ki-wa, but they gradually softened when he remembered what he owed her.'

146

Everything ends happily. Jack arrives in England just in time to prevent Dr. Josiah Brown from mesmerising Violet whom the cunning doctor is anxious to marry, and he hurls his rival out of the window. The victim is discovered 'bruised and bleeding among the broken flower-pots' by a comic policeman. Mrs. Parkinson still believes in spiritualism, but refuses to have anything to do with Brown as she discovers that the deceased Alderman's 'materialised beard' was made only of 'horrid, coarse horsehair.' Jack and Violet are married at last and Jack is horrid enough to send to 'La-ki-wa' another photograph. The end of Dr. Brown is chronicled above. Had we not known what was in store for him we should hardly have got through the book. There is a great deal too much padding in it about Dr. Slade and Dr. Bartram and other mediums, and the disquisitions on the commercial future of Newfoundland seem endless and are intolerable. However, there are many publics, and Mr. Stuart Cumberland is always sure of an audience. His chief fault is a tendency to low comedy; but some people like low comedy in fiction.

The Vasty Deep: *A Strange Story of To-day*. By Stuart Cumberland. (Sampson Low and Co.)

THE POETS' CORNER—X

(*Pall Mall Gazette*, June 24, 1889.)

Is Mr. Alfred Austin among the Socialists? Has somebody converted the respectable editor of the respectable *National Review*? Has even dulness become revolutionary? From a poem in Mr. Austin's last volume this would seem to be the case. It is perhaps unfair to take our rhymers too seriously. Between the casual fancies of a poet and the callous facts of prose there is, or at least there should be, a wide difference. But since the poem in question, *Two Visions*, as Mr. Austin calls it, was begun in 1863 and revised in 1889 we may regard it as fully representative of Mr. Austin's mature views. He gives us, at any rate, in its somewhat lumbering and pedestrian verses, his conception of the perfect state:

Fearless, unveiled, and unattended
  Strolled maidens to and fro:
Youths looked respect, but never bended
  Obsequiously low.

  And each with other, sans condition,
  Held parley brief or long,
Without provoking coarse suspicion
  Of marriage, or of wrong.

  All were well clad, and none were better,
  And gems beheld I none,
Save where there hung a jewelled fetter,
  Symbolic, in the sun.

  I saw a noble-looking maiden
  Close Dante's solemn book,
And go, with crate of linen laden
  And wash it in the brook.

  Anon, a broad-browed poet, dragging
  A load of logs along,
To warm his hearth, withal not flagging
  In current of his song.

  Each one some handicraft attempted
  Or helped to till the soil:
None but the aged were exempted
  From communistic toil.

Such an expression as 'coarse suspicion of marriage' is not very fortunate; the log-rolling poet of the fifth stanza is an ideal that we have already realised and one in which we had but little comfort, and the fourth stanza leaves us in doubt whether Mr. Austin means that washerwomen are to take to reading Dante, or that students of Italian literature are to wash their own clothes. But, on the whole, though Mr. Austin's vision of the *citta divina* of the future is not very inspiriting, it is certainly extremely interesting as a sign of the times, and it is evident from the two concluding lines of the following stanzas that there will be no danger of the intellect being overworked:

  Age lorded not, nor rose the hectic
  Up to the cheek of youth;
But reigned throughout their dialectic
  Sobriety of truth.

  And if a long-held contest tended
  To ill-defined result,
It was by calm consent suspended
  As over-difficult.

Mr. Austin, however, has other moods, and, perhaps, he is at his best when he is writing about flowers. Occasionally he wearies the reader by tedious enumerations of plants, lacking indeed reticence and tact and selection in many of his descriptions, but, as a rule, he is very pleasant when he is babbling of green fields. How pretty these stanzas from the dedication are!

147

When vines, just newly burgeoned, link
Their hands to join the dance of Spring,
Green lizards glisten from cleft and chink,
And almond blossoms rosy pink
Cluster and perch, ere taking wing;

Where over strips of emerald wheat
Glimmer red peach and snowy pear,
And nightingales all day long repeat
Their love-song, not less glad than sweet
They chant in sorrow and gloom elsewhere;

Where purple iris-banners scale
Defending walls and crumbling ledge,
And virgin windflowers, lithe and frail,
Now mantling red, now trembling pale,
Peep out from furrow and hide in hedge.

Some of the sonnets also (notably, one entitled *When Acorns Fall*) are very charming, and though, as a whole, *Love's Widowhood* is tedious and prolix, still it contains some very felicitous touches. We wish, however, that Mr. Austin would not write such lines as

Pippins of every sort, and codlins manifold.

'Codlins manifold' is a monstrous expression.

Mr. W. J. Linton's fame as a wood-engraver has somewhat obscured the merits of his poetry. His *Claribel and Other Poems*, published in 1865, is now a scarce book, and far more scarce is the collection of lyrics which he printed in 1887 at his own press and brought out under the title of *Love-Lore*. The large and handsome volume that now lies before us contains nearly all these later poems as well as a selection from *Claribel* and many renderings, in the original metre, of French poems ranging from the thirteenth century to our own day. A portrait of Mr. Linton is prefixed, and the book is dedicated 'To William Bell Scott, my friend for nearly fifty years.' As a poet Mr. Linton is always fanciful with a studied fancifulness, and often felicitous with a chance felicity. He is fascinated by our seventeenth-century singers, and has, here and there, succeeded in catching something of their quaintness and not a little of their charm. There is a pleasant flavour about his verse. It is entirely free from violence and from vagueness, those two besetting sins of so much modern poetry. It is clear in outline and restrained in form, and, at its best, has much that is light and lovely about it. How graceful, for instance, this is!

BARE FEET

O fair white feet! O dawn-white feet
Of Her my hope may claim!
Bare-footed through the dew she came
Her Love to meet.

Star-glancing feet, the windflowers sweet
Might envy, without shame,
As through the grass they lightly came,
Her Love to meet.

O Maiden sweet, with flower-kiss'd feet!
My heart your footstool name!
Bare-footed through the dew she came,
Her Love to meet.

'Vindicate Gemma!' was Longfellow's advice to Miss Héloïse Durant when she proposed to write a play about Dante. Longfellow, it may be remarked, was always on the side of domesticity. It was the secret of his popularity. We cannot say, however, that Miss Durant has made us like Gemma better. She is not exactly the Xantippe whom Boccaccio describes, but she is very boring, for all that:

GEMMA. The more thou meditat'st, more mad art thou.
Clowns, with their love, can cheer poor wives' hearts more
O'er black bread and goat's cheese than thou canst mine
O'er red Vernaccia, spite of all thy learning!
Care I how tortured spirits feel in hell?
DANTE. Thou tortur'st mine.
GEMMA. Or how souls sing in heaven?
DANTE. Would I were there.
GEMMA. All folly, naught but folly.
DANTE. Thou canst not understand the mandates given
To poets by their goddess Poesy. . . .
GEMMA. Canst ne'er speak prose? Why daily clothe thy thoughts
In strangest garb, as if thy wits played fool
At masquerade, where no man knows a maid
From matron? Fie on poets' mutterings!
DANTE (to himself). If, then, the soul absorbed at last to whole—
GEMMA. Fie! fie! I say. Art thou bewitched?
DANTE. O! peace.

GEMMA. Dost thou deem me deaf and dumb?
DANTE. O! that thou wert.

Dante is certainly rude, but Gemma is dreadful. The play is well meant but it is lumbering and heavy, and the blank verse has absolutely no merit.

Father O'Flynn and Other Irish Lyrics, by Mr. A. P. Graves, is a collection of poems in the style of Lover. Most of them are written in dialect, and, for the benefit of English readers, notes are appended in which the uninitiated are informed that 'brogue' means a boot, that 'mavourneen' means my dear, and that 'astore' is a term of affection. Here is a specimen of Mr. Graves's work:

'Have you e'er a new song,
  My Limerick Poet,
To help us along
  Wid this terrible boat,
Away over to Tork?'
  'Arrah I understand;
For all of your work,
  'Twill tighten you, boys,
To cargo that sand
To the overside strand,
  Wid the current so strong
  Unless you've a song—
A song to lighten and brighten you, boys. . . . '

It is a very dreary production and does not 'lighten and brighten' us a bit. The whole volume should be called *The Lucubrations of a Stage Irishman.*

The anonymous author of *The Judgment of the City* is a sort of bad Blake. So at least his prelude seems to suggest:

Time, the old viol-player,
  For ever thrills his ancient strings
With the flying bow of Fate, and thence
Much discord, but some music, brings.

  His ancient strings are truth,
  Love, hate, hope, fear;
  And his choicest melody
  Is the song of the faithful seer.

As he progresses, however, he develops into a kind of inferior Clough and writes heavy hexameters upon modern subjects:

Here for a moment stands in the light at the door of a playhouse,
One who is dignified, masterly, hard in the pride of his station;
Here too, the stateliest of matrons, sour in the pride of her station;
With them their daughter, sad-faced and listless, half-crushed to their likeness.

He has every form of sincerity except the sincerity of the artist, a defect that he shares with most of our popular writers.

(1) *Love's Widowhood and Other Poems*. By Alfred Austin. (Macmillan and Co.)

(2) *Poems and Translations*. By W. J. Linton. (Nimmo.)

(3) *Dante*: *a Dramatic Poem*. By Héloïse Durant. (Kegan Paul.)

(4) *Father O'Flynn and Other Irish Lyrics*. By A. P. Graves. (Swan Sonnenschein and Co.)

(5) *The Judgment of the City and Other Poems*. (Swan Sonnenschein and Co.)

MR. SWINBURNE'S LAST VOLUME

(*Pall Mall Gazette*, June 27, 1889.)

Mr. Swinburne once set his age on fire by a volume of very perfect and very poisonous poetry. Then he became revolutionary and pantheistic, and cried out against those that sit in high places both in heaven and on earth. Then he invented Marie Stuart and laid upon us the heavy burden of *Bothwell*. Then he retired to the nursery and wrote poems about children of a somewhat over-subtle character. He is now extremely patriotic, and manages to combine with his patriotism a strong affection for the Tory party. He has always been a great poet. But he has his limitations, the chief of which is, curiously enough, the entire lack of any sense of limit. His song is nearly always too loud for his subject. His magnificent rhetoric, nowhere more magnificent than in the volume that now lies before us, conceals rather than reveals. It has been said of him, and with truth, that he is a master of language, but with still greater truth it may be said that Language is his master. Words seem to dominate him. Alliteration tyrannises over him. Mere sound often becomes his lord. He is so eloquent that whatever he touches becomes unreal.

Let us turn to the poem on the Armada:

The wings of the south-west wind are widened; the breath of his fervent lips,
More keen than a sword's edge, fiercer than fire, falls full on the plunging ships.
The pilot is he of the northward flight, their stay and their steersman he;

A helmsman clothed with the tempest, and girdled with strength to constrain the sea.
And the host of them trembles and quails, caught fast in his hand as a bird in the toils;
For the wrath and the joy that fulfil him are mightier than man's, whom he slays and spoils.
And vainly, with heart divided in sunder, and labour of wavering will,
The lord of their host takes counsel with hope if haply their star shine still.

Somehow we seem to have heard all this before. Does it come from the fact that of all the poets who ever lived Mr. Swinburne is the one who is the most limited in imagery? It must be admitted that he is so. He has wearied us with his monotony. 'Fire' and the 'Sea' are the two words ever on his lips. We must confess also that this shrill singing—marvellous as it is—leaves us out of breath. Here is a passage from a poem called *A Word with the Wind*:

Be the sunshine bared or veiled, the sky superb or shrouded,
  Still the waters, lax and languid, chafed and foiled,
Keen and thwarted, pale and patient, clothed with fire or clouded,
  Vex their heart in vain, or sleep like serpents coiled.
Thee they look for, blind and baffled, wan with wrath and weary,
  Blown for ever back by winds that rock the bird:
Winds that seamews breast subdue the sea, and bid the dreary
  Waves be weak as hearts made sick with hope deferred.
Let the clarion sound from westward, let the south bear token
  How the glories of thy godhead sound and shine:
Bid the land rejoice to see the land-wind's broad wings broken,
  Bid the sea take comfort, bid the world be thine.

Verse of this kind may be justly praised for the sustained strength and vigour of its metrical scheme. Its purely technical excellence is extraordinary. But is it more than an oratorical *tour de force*? Does it really convey much? Does it charm? Could we return to it again and again with renewed pleasure? We think not. It seems to us empty.

Of course, we must not look to these poems for any revelation of human life. To be at one with the elements seems to be Mr. Swinburne's aim. He seeks to speak with the breath of wind and wave. The roar of the fire is ever in his ears. He puts his clarion to the lips of Spring and bids her blow, and the Earth wakes from her dreams and tells him her secret. He is the first lyric poet who has tried to make an absolute surrender of his own personality, and he has succeeded. We hear the song, but we never know the singer. We never even get near to him. Out of the thunder and splendour of words he himself says nothing. We have often had man's interpretation of Nature; now we have Nature's interpretation of man, and she has curiously little to say. Force and Freedom form her vague message. She deafens us with her clangours.

But Mr. Swinburne is not always riding the whirlwind and calling out of the depths of the sea. Romantic ballads in Border dialect have not lost their fascination for him, and this last volume contains some very splendid examples of this curious artificial kind of poetry. The amount of pleasure one gets out of dialect is a matter entirely of temperament. To say 'mither' instead of 'mother' seems to many the acme of romance. There are others who are not quite so ready to believe in the pathos of provincialisms. There is, however, no doubt of Mr. Swinburne's mastery over the form, whether the form be quite legitimate or not. *The Weary Wedding* has the concentration and colour of a great drama, and the quaintness of its style lends it something of the power of a grotesque. The ballad of *The Witch-Mother*, a mediæval Medea who slays her children because her lord is faithless, is worth reading on account of its horrible simplicity. *The Bride's Tragedy*, with its strange refrain of

In, in, out and in,
Blaws the wind and whirls the whin:

The *Jacobite's Exile*—

O lordly flow the Loire and Seine,
  And loud the dark Durance:
But bonnier shine the braes of Tyne
  Than a' the fields of France;
And the waves of Till that speak sae still
Gleam goodlier where they glance:

The Tyneside Widow and *A Reiver's Neck-verse* are all poems of fine imaginative power, and some of them are terrible in their fierce intensity of passion. There is no danger of English poetry narrowing itself to a form so limited as the romantic ballad in dialect. It is of too vital a growth for that. So we may welcome Mr. Swinburne's masterly experiments with the hope that things which are inimitable will not be imitated. The collection is completed by a few poems on children, some sonnets, a threnody on John William Inchbold, and a lovely lyric entitled *The Interpreters*.

In human thought have all things habitation;
  Our days
Laugh, lower, and lighten past, and find no station
  That stays.
But thought and faith are mightier things than time
  Can wrong,
Made splendid once by speech, or made sublime
  By song.
Remembrance, though the tide of change that rolls

Wax hoary,
Gives earth and heaven, for song's sake and the soul's,
  Their glory.

Certainly, 'for song's sake' we should love Mr. Swinburne's work, cannot, indeed, help loving it, so marvellous a music-maker is he. But what of the soul? For the soul we must go elsewhere.

Poems and Ballads. Third Series. By Algernon Charles Swinburne. (Chatto and Windus.)

THREE NEW POETS

(*Pall Mall Gazette*, July 12, 1889.)

Books of poetry by young writers are usually promissory notes that are never met. Now and then, however, one comes across a volume that is so far above the average that one can hardly resist the fascinating temptation of recklessly prophesying a fine future for its author. Such a book Mr. Yeats's *Wanderings of Oisin* certainly is. Here we find nobility of treatment and nobility of subject-matter, delicacy of poetic instinct and richness of imaginative resource. Unequal and uneven much of the work must be admitted to be. Mr. Yeats does not try to 'out-baby' Wordsworth, we are glad to say; but he occasionally succeeds in 'out-glittering' Keats, and, here and there, in his book we come across strange crudities and irritating conceits. But when he is at his best he is very good. If he has not the grand simplicity of epic treatment, he has at least something of the largeness of vision that belongs to the epical temper. He does not rob of their stature the great heroes of Celtic mythology. He is very naïve and very primitive and speaks of his giants with the air of a child. Here is a characteristic passage from the account of Oisin's return from the Island of Forgetfulness:

And I rode by the plains of the sea's edge, where all is barren and grey,
Grey sands on the green of the grasses and over the dripping trees,
Dripping and doubling landward, as though they would hasten away
Like an army of old men longing for rest from the moan of the seas.

Long fled the foam-flakes around me, the winds fled out of the vast,
Snatching the bird in secret, nor knew I, embosomed apart,
When they froze the cloth on my body like armour riveted fast,
For Remembrance, lifting her leanness, keened in the gates of my heart.

Till fattening the winds of the morning, an odour of new-mown hay
Came, and my forehead fell low, and my tears like berries fell down;
Later a sound came, half lost in the sound of a shore far away,
From the great grass-barnacle calling, and later the shore-winds brown.

If I were as I once was, the gold hooves crushing the sand and the shells,
Coming forth from the sea like the morning with red lips murmuring a song,
Not coughing, my head on my knees, and praying, and wroth with the bells,
I would leave no Saint's head on his body, though spacious his lands were and strong.

Making way from the kindling surges, I rode on a bridle-path,
Much wondering to see upon all hands, of wattle and woodwork made,
Thy bell-mounted churches, and guardless the sacred cairn and the earth,
And a small and feeble populace stooping with mattock and spade.

In one or two places the music is faulty, the construction is sometimes too involved, and the word 'populace' in the last line is rather infelicitous; but, when all is said, it is impossible not to feel in these stanzas the presence of the true poetic spirit.

A young lady who seeks for a 'song surpassing sense,' and tries to reproduce Mr. Browning's mode of verse for our edification, may seem to be in a somewhat parlous state. But Miss Caroline Fitz Gerald's work is better than her aim. *Venetia Victrix* is in many respects a fine poem. It shows vigour, intellectual strength, and courage. The story is a strange one. A certain Venetian, hating one of the Ten who had wronged him and identifying his enemy with Venice herself, abandons his native city and makes a vow that, rather than lift a hand for her good, he will give his soul to Hell. As he is sailing down the Adriatic at night, his ship is suddenly becalmed and he sees a huge galley

        where sate
Like counsellors on high, exempt, elate,
The fiends triumphant in their fiery state,

on their way to Venice. He has to choose between his own ruin and the ruin of his city. After a struggle, he determines to sacrifice himself to his rash oath.

I climbed aloft. My brain had grown one thought,
One hope, one purpose. And I heard the hiss
Of raging disappointment, loth to miss
Its prey—I heard the lapping of the flame,
That through the blenchèd figures went and came,
Darting in frenzy to the devils' yell.
I set that cross on high, and cried: 'To hell
My soul for ever, and my deed to God!
Once Venice guarded safe, let this vile clod

Drift where fate will!'
    And then (the hideous laugh
Of fiends in full possession, keen to quaff
The wine of one new soul not weak with tears,
Pealing like ruinous thunder in mine ears)
I fell, and heard no more. The pale day broke
Through lazar-windows, when once more I woke,
Remembering I might no more dare to pray.

Venetia Victrix is followed by *Ophelion*, a curious lyrical play whose *dramatis personæ* consist of Night, Death, Dawn and a Scholar. It is intricate rather than musical, but some of the songs are graceful—notably one beginning

    Lady of heaven most pure and holy,
    Artemis, fleet as the flying deer,
Glide through the dusk like a silver shadow,
    Mirror thy brow in the lonely mere.

Miss Fitz Gerald's volume is certainly worth reading.

Mr. Richard Le Gallienne's little book, *Volumes in Folio* as he quaintly calls it, is full of dainty verse and delicate fancy. Lines such as

And lo! the white face of the dawn
    Yearned like a ghost's against the pane,
    A sobbing ghost amid the rain;
Or like a chill and pallid rose
Slowly upclimbing from the lawn,

strike, with their fantastic choice of metaphors, a pleasing note. At present Mr. Le Gallienne's muse seems to devote herself entirely to the worship of books, and Mr. Le Gallienne himself is steeped in literary traditions, making Keats his model and seeking to reproduce something of Keats's richness and affluence of imagery. He is keenly conscious how derivative his inspiration is:

    Verse of my own! why ask so poor a thing,
    When I might gather from the garden-ways
Of sunny memory fragrant offering
    Of deathless blooms and white unwithering sprays?

    Shakspeare had given me an English rose,
    And honeysuckle Spenser sweet as dew,
Or I had brought you from that dreamy close
    Keats' passion-blossom, or the mystic blue

    Star-flower of Shelley's song, or shaken gold
    From lilies of the Blessed Damosel,
Or stolen fire from out the scarlet fold
    Of Swinburne's poppies. . . .

Yet now that he has played his prelude with so sensitive and so graceful a touch, we have no doubt that he will pass to larger themes and nobler subject-matter, and fulfil the hope he expresses in this sextet:

    For if perchance some music should be mine,
    I would fling forth its notes like a fierce sea,
To wash away the piles of tyranny,
    To make love free and faith unbound of creed.
O for some power to fill my shrunken line,
    And make a trumpet of my oaten reed.

(1) *The Wanderings of Oisin and Other Poems*. By W. B. Yeats. (Kegan Paul.)

(2) *Venetia Victrix*. By Caroline Fitz Gerald. (Macmillan and Co.)

(3) *Volumes in Folio*. By Richard Le Gallienne. (Elkin Mathews.)

A CHINESE SAGE

(*Speaker*, February 8, 1890.)

A eminent Oxford theologian once remarked that his only objection to modern progress was that it progressed forward instead of backward—a view that so fascinated a certain artistic undergraduate that he promptly wrote an essay upon some unnoticed analogies between the development of ideas and the movements of the common sea-crab. I feel sure the *Speaker* will not be suspected even by its most enthusiastic friends of holding this dangerous heresy of retrogression. But I must candidly admit that I have come to the conclusion that the most caustic criticism of modern life I have met with for some time is that contained in the writings of the learned Chuang Tzŭ, recently translated into the vulgar tongue by Mr. Herbert Giles, Her Majesty's Consul at Tamsui.

The spread of popular education has no doubt made the name of this great thinker quite familiar to the general public, but, for the sake of the few and the over-cultured, I feel it my duty to state definitely who he was, and to give a brief outline of the character of his philosophy.

Chuang Tzŭ, whose name must carefully be pronounced as it is not written, was born in the fourth century before Christ, by the banks of the Yellow River, in the Flowery Land; and portraits of the wonderful sage seated on the flying dragon of contemplation may still be found on the simple tea-trays and pleasing screens of many of our most respectable suburban households. The honest ratepayer and his healthy family have no doubt often mocked at the dome-like forehead of the philosopher, and laughed over the strange perspective of the landscape that lies beneath him. If they really knew who he was, they would tremble. For Chuang Tzŭ spent his life in preaching the great creed of Inaction, and in pointing out the uselessness of all useful things. 'Do nothing, and everything will be done,' was the doctrine which he inherited from his great master Lao Tzŭ. To resolve action into thought, and thought into abstraction, was his wicked transcendental aim. Like the obscure philosopher of early Greek speculation, he believed in the identity of contraries; like Plato, he was an idealist, and had all the idealist's contempt for utilitarian systems; he was a mystic like Dionysius, and Scotus Erigena, and Jacob Böhme, and held, with them and with Philo, that the object of life was to get rid of self-consciousness, and to become the unconscious vehicle of a higher illumination. In fact, Chuang Tzŭ may be said to have summed up in himself almost every mood of European metaphysical or mystical thought, from Heraclitus down to Hegel. There was something in him of the Quietist also; and in his worship of Nothing he may be said to have in some measure anticipated those strange dreamers of mediæval days who, like Tauler and Master Eckhart, adored the *purum nihil* and the Abyss. The great middle classes of this country, to whom, as we all know, our prosperity, if not our civilisation, is entirely due, may shrug their shoulders over all this and ask, with a certain amount of reason, what is the identity of contraries to them, and why they should get rid of that self-consciousness which is their chief characteristic. But Chuang Tzŭ was something more than a metaphysician and an illuminist. He sought to destroy society, as we know it, as the middle classes know it; and the sad thing is that he combines with the passionate eloquence of a Rousseau the scientific reasoning of a Herbert Spencer. There is nothing of the sentimentalist in him. He pities the rich more than the poor, if he ever pities at all, and prosperity seems to him as tragic a thing as suffering. He has nothing of the modern sympathy with failures, nor does he propose that the prizes should always be given on moral grounds to those who come in last in the race. It is the race itself that he objects to; and as for active sympathy, which has become the profession of so many worthy people in our own day, he thinks that trying to make others good is as silly an occupation as 'beating a drum in a forest in order to find a fugitive.' It is a mere waste of energy. That is all. While, as for a thoroughly sympathetic man, he is, in the eyes of Chuang Tzŭ, simply a man who is always trying to be somebody else, and so misses the only possible excuse for his own existence.

Yes; incredible as it may seem, this curious thinker looked back with a sigh of regret to a certain Golden Age when there were no competitive examinations, no wearisome educational systems, no missionaries, no penny dinners for the people, no Established Churches, no Humanitarian Societies, no dull lectures about one's duty to one's neighbour, and no tedious sermons about any subject at all. In those ideal days, he tells us, people loved each other without being conscious of charity, or writing to the newspapers about it. They were upright, and yet they never published books upon Altruism. As every man kept his knowledge to himself, the world escaped the curse of scepticism; and as every man kept his virtues to himself, nobody meddled in other people's business. They lived simple and peaceful lives, and were contented with such food and raiment as they could get. Neighbouring districts were in sight, and 'the cocks and dogs of one could be heard in the other,' yet the people grew old and died without ever interchanging visits. There was no chattering about clever men, and no laudation of good men. The intolerable sense of obligation was unknown. The deeds of humanity left no trace, and their affairs were not made a burden for posterity by foolish historians.

In an evil moment the Philanthropist made his appearance, and brought with him the mischievous idea of Government. 'There is such a thing,' says Chuang Tzŭ, 'as leaving mankind alone: there has never been such a thing as governing mankind.' All modes of government are wrong. They are unscientific, because they seek to alter the natural environment of man; they are immoral because, by interfering with the individual, they produce the most aggressive forms of egotism; they are ignorant, because they try to spread education; they are self-destructive, because they engender anarchy. 'Of old,' he tells us, 'the Yellow Emperor first caused charity and duty to one's neighbour to interfere with the natural goodness of the heart of man. In consequence of this, Yao and Shun wore the hair off their legs in endeavouring to feed their people. They disturbed their internal economy in order to find room for artificial virtues. They exhausted their energies in framing laws, and they were failures.' Man's heart, our philosopher goes on to say, may be 'forced down or stirred up,' and in either case the issue is fatal. Yao made the people too happy, so they were not satisfied. Chieh made them too wretched, so they grew discontented. Then every one began to argue about the best way of tinkering up society. 'It is quite clear that something must be done,' they said to each other, and there was a general rush for knowledge. The results were so dreadful that the Government of the day had to bring in Coercion, and as a consequence of this 'virtuous men sought refuge in mountain caves, while rulers of state sat trembling in ancestral halls.' Then, when everything was in a state of perfect chaos, the Social Reformers got up on platforms, and preached salvation from the ills that they and their system had caused. The poor Social Reformers! 'They know not shame, nor what it is to blush,' is the verdict of Chuang Tzŭ upon them.

The economic question, also, is discussed by this almond-eyed sage at great length, and he writes about the curse of capital as eloquently as Mr. Hyndman. The accumulation of wealth is to him the origin of evil. It makes the strong violent, and the weak dishonest. It creates the petty thief, and puts him in a bamboo cage. It creates the big thief, and sets him on a throne of white jade. It is the father of competition, and competition is the waste, as well as the destruction, of energy. The order of nature is rest, repetition, and peace. Weariness and war are the results of an artificial society based upon capital; and the richer this society gets, the more thoroughly bankrupt it really is, for it has neither sufficient rewards for the good nor sufficient punishments for the wicked. There is also this to be remembered—that the prizes of the world degrade a man as much as the world's punishments. The age is rotten with its worship of success. As for education, true wisdom can neither be learnt nor taught. It is a spiritual state, to which he who lives in harmony with nature attains. Knowledge is shallow if we compare it with the extent of the unknown, and only the unknowable is of value. Society produces rogues, and education makes one rogue cleverer than another. That is the only result of School Boards. Besides, of what possible philosophic importance can education be, when it serves simply to make each man differ from his neighbour? We arrive ultimately at a chaos of opinions, doubt everything, and fall into the vulgar habit of arguing; and it is only the intellectually lost who ever argue. Look at Hui Tzu. 'He was a man of many ideas. His works would fill five carts. But his doctrines were paradoxical.' He said that there were feathers in an egg, because there were feathers on a chicken; that a dog could be a sheep, because all names were arbitrary; that there was a moment when a swiftly-flying arrow was neither moving nor at rest; that if you took a stick a foot long, and cut it in half every day, you would never come to the end of it; and that a bay horse and a dun cow were three, because taken separately they were two, and taken together they were one, and one and two made up three. 'He was like a man running a race with his own shadow, and making a noise in order to drown the echo. He was a clever gadfly, that was all. What was the use of him?'

Morality is, of course, a different thing. It went out of fashion, says Chuang Tzǔ, when people began to moralise. Men ceased then to be spontaneous and to act on intuition. They became priggish and artificial, and were so blind as to have a definite purpose in life. Then came Governments and Philanthropists, those two pests of the age. The former tried to coerce people into being good, and so destroyed the natural goodness of man. The latter were a set of aggressive busybodies who caused confusion wherever they went. They were stupid enough to have principles, and unfortunate enough to act up to them. They all came to bad ends, and showed that universal altruism is as bad in its results as universal egotism. They 'tripped people up over charity, and fettered them with duties to their neighbours.' They gushed over music, and fussed over ceremonies. As a consequence of all this, the world lost its equilibrium, and has been staggering ever since.

Who, then, according to Chuang Tzǔ, is the perfect man? And what is his manner of life? The perfect man does nothing beyond gazing at the universe. He adopts no absolute position. 'In motion, he is like water. At rest, he is like a mirror. And, like Echo, he answers only when he is called upon.' He lets externals take care of themselves. Nothing material injures him; nothing spiritual punishes him. His mental equilibrium gives him the empire of the world. He is never the slave of objective existences. He knows that, 'just as the best language is that which is never spoken, so the best action is that which is never done.' He is passive, and accepts the laws of life. He rests in inactivity, and sees the world become virtuous of itself. He does not try to 'bring about his own good deeds.' He never wastes himself on effort. He is not troubled about moral distinctions. He knows that things are what they are, and that their consequences will be what they will be. His mind is the 'speculum of creation,' and he is ever at peace.

All this is of course excessively dangerous, but we must remember that Chuang Tzǔ lived more than two thousand years ago, and never had the opportunity of seeing our unrivalled civilisation. And yet it is possible that, were he to come back to earth and visit us, he might have something to say to Mr. Balfour about his coercion and active misgovernment in Ireland; he might smile at some of our philanthropic ardours, and shake his head over many of our organised charities; the School Board might not impress him, nor our race for wealth stir his admiration; he might wonder at our ideals, and grow sad over what we have realised. Perhaps it is well that Chuang Tzǔ cannot return.

Meanwhile, thanks to Mr. Giles and Mr. Quaritch, we have his book to console us, and certainly it is a most fascinating and delightful volume. Chuang Tzǔ is one of the Darwinians before Darwin. He traces man from the germ, and sees his unity with nature. As an anthropologist he is excessively interesting, and he describes our primitive arboreal ancestor living in trees through his terror of animals stronger than himself, and knowing only one parent, the mother, with all the accuracy of a lecturer at the Royal Society. Like Plato, he adopts the dialogue as his mode of expression, 'putting words into other people's mouths,' he tells us, 'in order to gain breadth of view.' As a story-teller he is charming. The account of the visit of the respectable Confucius to the great Robber Chê is most vivid and brilliant, and it is impossible not to laugh over the ultimate discomfiture of the sage, the barrenness of whose moral platitudes is ruthlessly exposed by the successful brigand. Even in his metaphysics, Chuang Tzǔ is intensely humorous. He personifies his abstractions, and makes them act plays before us. The Spirit of the Clouds, when passing eastward through the expanse of air, happened to fall in with the Vital Principle. The latter was slapping his ribs and hopping about: whereupon the Spirit of the Clouds said, 'Who are you, old man, and what are you doing?' 'Strolling!' replied the Vital Principle, without stopping, for all activities are ceaseless. 'I want to *know* something,' continued the Spirit of the Clouds. 'Ah!' cried the Vital Principle, in a tone of disapprobation, and a marvellous conversation follows, that is not unlike the dialogue between the Sphinx and the Chimera in Flaubert's curious drama. Talking animals, also, have their place in Chuang Tzǔ's parables and stories, and through myth and poetry and fancy his strange philosophy finds musical utterance.

Of course it is sad to be told that it is immoral to be consciously good, and that doing anything is the worst form of idleness. Thousands of excellent and really earnest philanthropists would be absolutely thrown upon the rates if we adopted the view that nobody should be allowed to meddle in what does not concern him. The doctrine of the uselessness of all useful things would not merely endanger our commercial supremacy as a nation, but might bring discredit upon many prosperous and serious-minded members of the shop-keeping classes. What would become of our popular preachers, our Exeter Hall orators, our drawing-room evangelists, if we said to them, in the words of Chuang Tzǔ, 'Mosquitoes will keep a man awake all night with their biting, and just in the same way this talk of charity and duty to one's neighbour drives us nearly crazy. Sirs, strive to keep the world to its own original simplicity, and, as the wind bloweth where it listeth, so let Virtue establish itself. Wherefore this undue energy?' And what would be the fate of governments and professional politicians if we came to the conclusion that there is no such thing as governing mankind at all? It is clear that Chuang Tzǔ is a very dangerous writer, and the publication of his book in English, two thousand years after his death, is obviously premature, and may cause a great deal of pain to many thoroughly respectable and industrious persons. It may be true that the ideal of self-culture and self-development, which is the aim of his scheme of life, and the basis of his scheme of philosophy, is an ideal somewhat needed by an age like ours, in which most people are so anxious to educate their neighbours that they have actually no time left in which to educate themselves. But would it be wise to say so? It seems to me that if we once admitted the force of any one of Chuang Tzǔ's destructive criticisms we should have to put some check on our national habit of self-glorification; and the only thing that ever consoles man for the stupid things he does is the praise he always gives himself for doing them. There may, however, be a few who have grown wearied of that strange modern tendency that sets enthusiasm to do the work of the intellect. To these, and such as these, Chuang Tzǔ will be welcome. But let them only read him. Let them not talk about him. He would be disturbing at dinner-parties, and impossible at afternoon teas, and his whole life was a protest against platform speaking. 'The perfect man ignores self; the divine man ignores action; the true sage ignores reputation.' These are the principles of Chuang Tzǔ.

Chuang Tzǔ: Mystic, Moralist, and Social Reformer. Translated from the Chinese by Herbert A. Giles, H.B.M.'s Consul at Tamsui. (Bernard Quaritch.)

MR. PATER'S LAST VOLUME

(*Speaker*, March 22, 1890.)

When I first had the privilege—and I count it a very high one—of meeting Mr. Walter Pater, he said to me, smiling, 'Why do you always write poetry? Why do you not write prose? Prose is so much more difficult.'

It was during my undergraduate days at Oxford; days of lyrical ardour and of studious sonnet-writing; days when one loved the exquisite intricacy and musical repetitions of the ballade, and the villanelle with its linked long-drawn echoes and its curious completeness; days when one solemnly sought to discover the proper temper in which a triolet should be written; delightful days, in which, I am glad to say, there was far more rhyme than reason.

I may frankly confess now that at the time I did not quite comprehend what Mr. Pater really meant; and it was not till I had carefully studied his beautiful and suggestive essays on the Renaissance that I fully realised what a wonderful self-conscious art the art of English prose-writing really is, or may be made to be. Carlyle's stormy rhetoric, Ruskin's winged and passionate eloquence, had seemed to me to spring from enthusiasm rather than from art. I do not think I knew then that even prophets correct their proofs. As for Jacobean prose, I thought it too exuberant; and Queen Anne prose appeared to me terribly bald, and irritatingly rational. But Mr. Pater's essays became to me 'the golden book of spirit and sense, the holy writ of beauty.' They are still this to me. It is possible, of course, that I may exaggerate about them. I certainly hope that I do; for where there is no exaggeration there is no love, and where there is no love there is no understanding. It is only about things that do not interest one, that one can give a really unbiassed opinion; and this is no doubt the reason why an unbiassed opinion is always valueless.

But I must not allow this brief notice of Mr. Pater's new volume to degenerate into an autobiography. I remember being told in America that whenever Margaret Fuller wrote an essay upon Emerson the printers had always to send out to borrow some additional capital 'I's,' and I feel it right to accept this transatlantic warning.

Appreciations, in the fine Latin sense of the word, is the title given by Mr. Pater to his book, which is an exquisite collection of exquisite essays, of delicately wrought works of art—some of them being almost Greek in their purity of outline and perfection of form, others mediæval in their strangeness of colour and passionate suggestion, and all of them absolutely modern, in the true meaning of the term modernity. For he to whom the present is the only thing that is present, knows nothing of the age in which he lives. To realise the nineteenth century one must realise every century that has preceded it, and that has contributed to its making. To know anything about oneself, one must know all about others. There must be no mood with which one cannot sympathise, no dead mode of life that one cannot make alive. The legacies of heredity may make us alter our views of moral responsibility, but they cannot but intensify our sense of the value of Criticism; for the true critic is he who bears within himself the dreams and ideas and feelings of myriad generations, and to whom no form of thought is alien, no emotional impulse obscure.

Perhaps the most interesting, and certainly the least successful, of the essays contained in the present volume is that on *Style*. It is the most interesting because it is the work of one who speaks with the high authority that comes from the noble realisation of things nobly conceived. It is the least successful, because the subject is too abstract. A true artist like Mr. Pater is most felicitous when he deals with the concrete, whose very limitations give him finer freedom, while they necessitate more intense vision. And yet what a high ideal is contained in these few pages! How good it is for us, in these days of popular education and facile journalism, to be reminded of the real scholarship that is essential to the perfect writer, who, 'being a true lover of words for their own sake, a minute and constant observer of their physiognomy,' will avoid what is mere rhetoric, or ostentatious ornament, or negligent misuse of terms, or ineffective surplusage, and will be known by his tact of omission, by his skilful economy of means, by his selection and self-restraint, and perhaps above all by that conscious artistic structure which is the expression of mind in style. I think I have been wrong in saying that the subject is too abstract. In Mr. Pater's hands it becomes very real to us indeed, and he shows us how, behind the perfection of a man's style, must lie the passion of a man's soul.

As one passes to the rest of the volume, one finds essays on Wordsworth and on Coleridge, on Charles Lamb and on Sir Thomas Browne, on some of Shakespeare's plays and on the English kings that Shakespeare fashioned, on Dante Rossetti, and on William Morris. As that on Wordsworth seems to be Mr. Pater's last work, so that on the singer of the *Defence of Guenevere* is certainly his earliest, or almost his earliest, and it is interesting to mark the change that has taken place in his style. This change is, perhaps, at first sight not very apparent. In 1868 we find Mr. Pater writing with the same exquisite care for words, with the same studied music, with the same temper, and something of the same mode of treatment. But, as he goes on, the architecture of the style becomes richer and more complex, the epithet more precise and intellectual. Occasionally one may be inclined to think that there is, here and there, a sentence which is somewhat long, and possibly, if one may venture to say so, a little heavy and cumbersome in movement. But if this be so, it comes from those side-issues suddenly suggested by the idea in its progress, and really revealing the idea more perfectly; or from those felicitous after-thoughts that give a fuller completeness to the central scheme, and yet convey something of the charm of chance; or from a desire to suggest the secondary shades of meaning with all their accumulating effect, and to avoid, it may be, the violence and harshness of too definite and exclusive an opinion. For in matters of art, at any rate, thought is inevitably coloured by emotion, and so is fluid rather than fixed, and, recognising its dependence upon moods and upon the passion of fine moments, will not accept the rigidity of a scientific formula or a theological dogma. The critical pleasure, too, that we receive from tracing, through what may seem the intricacies of a sentence, the working of the constructive intelligence, must not be overlooked. As soon as we have realised the design, everything appears clear and simple. After a time, these long sentences of Mr. Pater's come to have the charm of an elaborate piece of music, and the unity of such music also.

I have suggested that the essay on Wordsworth is probably the most recent bit of work contained in this volume. If one might choose between so much that is good, I should be inclined to say it is the finest also. The essay on Lamb is curiously suggestive; suggestive, indeed, of a somewhat more tragic, more sombre figure, than men have been wont to think of in connection with the author of the *Essays of Elia*. It is an interesting aspect under which to regard Lamb, but perhaps he himself would have had some difficulty in recognising the

155

portrait given of him. He had, undoubtedly, great sorrows, or motives for sorrow, but he could console himself at a moment's notice for the real tragedies of life by reading any one of the Elizabethan tragedies, provided it was in a folio edition. The essay on Sir Thomas Browne is delightful, and has the strange, personal, fanciful charm of the author of the *Religio Medici*, Mr. Pater often catching the colour and accent and tone of whatever artist, or work of art, he deals with. That on Coleridge, with its insistence on the necessity of the cultivation of the relative, as opposed to the absolute spirit in philosophy and in ethics, and its high appreciation of the poet's true position in our literature, is in style and substance a very blameless work. Grace of expression and delicate subtlety of thought and phrase, characterise the essays on Shakespeare. But the essay on Wordsworth has a spiritual beauty of its own. It appeals, not to the ordinary Wordsworthian with his uncritical temper, and his gross confusion of ethical and æsthetical problems, but rather to those who desire to separate the gold from the dross, and to reach at the true Wordsworth through the mass of tedious and prosaic work that bears his name, and that serves often to conceal him from us. The presence of an alien element in Wordsworth's art is, of course, recognised by Mr. Pater, but he touches on it merely from the psychological point of view, pointing out how this quality of higher and lower moods gives the effect in his poetry 'of a power not altogether his own, or under his control'; a power which comes and goes when it wills, 'so that the old fancy which made the poet's art an enthusiasm, a form of divine possession, seems almost true of him.' Mr. Pater's earlier essays had their *purpurei panni*, so eminently suitable for quotation, such as the famous passage on *Mona Lisa*, and that other in which Botticelli's strange conception of the Virgin is so strangely set forth. From the present volume it is difficult to select any one passage in preference to another as specially characteristic of Mr. Pater's treatment. This, however, is worth quoting at length. It contains a truth eminently suitable for our age:

That the end of life is not action but contemplation—being as distinct from doing—a certain disposition of the mind: is, in some shape or other, the principle of all the higher morality. In poetry, in art, if you enter into their true spirit at all, you touch this principle in a measure; these, by their sterility, are a type of beholding for the mere joy of beholding. To treat life in the spirit of art is to make life a thing in which means and ends are identified: to encourage such treatment, the true moral significance of art and poetry. Wordsworth, and other poets who have been like him in ancient or more recent times, are the masters, the experts, in this art of impassioned contemplation. Their work is not to teach lessons, or enforce rules, or even to stimulate us to noble ends, but to withdraw the thoughts for a while from the mere machinery of life, to fix them, with appropriate emotions, on the spectacle of those great facts in man's existence which no machinery affects, 'on the great and universal passions of men, the most general and interesting of their occupations, and the entire world of nature'—on 'the operations of the elements and the appearances of the visible universe, on storm and sunshine, on the revolutions of the seasons, on cold and heat, on loss of friends and kindred, on injuries and resentments, on gratitude and hope, on fear and sorrow.' To witness this spectacle with appropriate emotions is the aim of all culture; and of these emotions poetry like Wordsworth's is a great nourisher and stimulant. He sees nature full of sentiment and excitement; he sees men and women as parts of nature, passionate, excited, in strange grouping and connection with the grandeur and beauty of the natural world:—images, in his own words, 'of men suffering, amid awful forms and powers.'

Certainly the real secret of Wordsworth has never been better expressed. After having read and reread Mr. Pater's essay—for it requires re-reading—one returns to the poet's work with a new sense of joy and wonder, and with something of eager and impassioned expectation. And perhaps this might be roughly taken as the test or touchstone of the finest criticism.

Finally, one cannot help noticing the delicate instinct that has gone to fashion the brief epilogue that ends this delightful volume. The difference between the classical and romantic spirits in art has often, and with much over-emphasis, been discussed. But with what a light sure touch does Mr. Pater write of it! How subtle and certain are his distinctions! If imaginative prose be really the special art of this century, Mr. Pater must rank amongst our century's most characteristic artists. In certain things he stands almost alone. The age has produced wonderful prose styles, turbid with individualism, and violent with excess of rhetoric. But in Mr. Pater, as in Cardinal Newman, we find the union of personality with perfection. He has no rival in his own sphere, and he has escaped disciples. And this, not because he has not been imitated, but because in art so fine as his there is something that, in its essence, is inimitable.

Appreciations, with an Essay on Style. By Walter Pater, Fellow of Brasenose College. (Macmillan and Co.)

PRIMAVERA

(*Pall Mall Gazette*, May 24, 1890.)

In the summer term Oxford teaches the exquisite art of idleness, one of the most important things that any University can teach, and possibly as the first-fruits of the dreaming in grey cloister and silent garden, which either makes or mars a man, there has just appeared in that lovely city a dainty and delightful volume of poems by four friends. These new young singers are Mr. Laurence Binyon, who has just gained the Newdigate; Mr. Manmohan Ghose, a young Indian of brilliant scholarship and high literary attainments who gives some culture to Christ Church; Mr. Stephen Phillips, whose recent performance of the Ghost in *Hamlet* at the Globe Theatre was so admirable in its dignity and elocution; and Mr. Arthur Cripps, of Trinity. Particular interest attaches naturally to Mr. Ghose's work. Born in India, of purely Indian parentage, he has been brought up entirely in England, and was educated at St. Paul's School, and his verses show us how quick and subtle are the intellectual sympathies of the Oriental mind, and suggest how close is the bond of union that may some day bind India to us by other methods than those of commerce and military strength.

There is something charming in finding a young Indian using our language with such care for music and words as Mr. Ghose does. Here is one of his songs:

Over thy head, in joyful wanderings
Through heaven's wide spaces, free,
Birds fly with music in their wings;
And from the blue, rough sea

The fishes flash and leap;
There is a life of loveliest things
   O'er thee, so fast asleep.

  In the deep West the heavens grow heavenlier,
   Eve after eve; and still
The glorious stars remember to appear;
   The roses on the hill
   Are fragrant as before:
Only thy face, of all that's dear,
   I shall see nevermore!

It has its faults. It has a great many faults. But the lines we have set in italics are lovely. The temper of Keats, the moods of Matthew Arnold, have influenced Mr. Ghose, and what better influence could a beginner have? Here are some stanzas from another of Mr. Ghose's poems:

Deep-shaded will I lie, and deeper yet
  In night, where not a leaf its neighbour knows;
Forget the shining of the stars, forget
  The vernal visitation of the rose;
And, far from all delights, prepare my heart's repose.

 'O crave not silence thou! too soon, too sure,
  Shall Autumn come, and through these branches weep:
Some birds shall cease, and flowers no more endure;
  And thou beneath the mould unwilling creep,
And silent soon shalt be in that eternal sleep.

 'Green still it is, where that fair goddess strays;
  Then follow, till around thee all be sere.
Lose not a vision of her passing face;
  Nor miss the sound of her soft robes, that here
Sweep over the wet leaves of the fast-falling year.'

The second line is very beautiful, and the whole shows culture and taste and feeling. Mr. Ghose ought some day to make a name in our literature.

Mr. Stephen Phillips has a more solemn classical Muse. His best work is his *Orestes*:

Me in far lands did Justice call, cold queen
Among the dead, who, after heat and haste
At length have leisure for her steadfast voice,
That gathers peace from the great deeps of hell.
She call'd me, saying: I heard a cry by night!
Go thou, and question not; within thy halls
My will awaits fulfilment.

   . . . . . .

   And she lies there,
My mother! ay, my mother now; O hair
That once I play'd with in these halls! O eyes
That for a moment knew me as I came,
And lighten'd up, and trembled into love;
The next were darkened by my hand! Ah me!
Ye will not look upon me in that world.
Yet thou, perchance, art happier, if thou go'st
Into some land of wind and drifting leaves,
To sleep without a star; but as for me,
Hell hungers, and the restless Furies wait.

Milton, and the method of Greek tragedy are Mr. Phillips's influences, and again we may say, what better influences could a young singer have? His verse is dignified, and has distinction.

* * * * *

Mr. Cripps is melodious at times, and Mr. Binyon, Oxford's latest Laureate, shows us in his lyrical ode on *Youth* that he can handle a difficult metre dexterously, and in this sonnet that he can catch the sweet echoes that sleep in the sonnets of Shakespeare:

I cannot raise my eyelids up from sleep,
But I am visited with thoughts of you;
Slumber has no refreshment half so deep
As the sweet morn, that wakes my heart anew.

I cannot put away life's trivial care,
But you straightway steal on me with delight:

157

My purest moments are your mirror fair;
My deepest thought finds you the truth most bright

    You are the lovely regent of my mind,
The constant sky to the unresting sea;
Yet, since 'tis you that rule me, I but find
A finer freedom in such tyranny.

    Were the world's anxious kingdoms govern'd so,
Lost were their wrongs, and vanish'd half their woe!

    On the whole *Primavera* is a pleasant little book, and we are glad to welcome it. It is charmingly 'got up,' and undergraduates might read it with advantage during lecture hours.

    Primavera: *Poems*. By Four Authors. (Oxford: B. H. Blackwell.)

Made in the USA
Las Vegas, NV
10 March 2025

19317700R00090